IF NO ONE KNOWS THEY WERE THERE THEN IT DIDN'T HAPPEN

FLED TO MEXICO

STEPHEN M. RINGLER

STRATTON
—PRESS—
Publishing Life

Fled To Mexico
Copyright © 2020 **Stephen M. Ringler**

Stratton Press Publishing
831 N Tatnall Street Suite M #188,
Wilmington, DE 19801
www.stratton-press.com
1-888-323-7009

ISBN (Paperback): 978-1-64895-195-4
ISBN (Ebook): 978-1-64895-196-1

Printed in the United States of America

CONTENTS

ACKNOWLEDGMENTS

To Detective Tim Roberts, Santa Barbara Police Department, my gratitude for your generous contribution and insight into the real *fled to Mexico (FTM)* cases that became front page headline news in Santa Barbara and relentlessly pursued by you and the tireless efforts of the SBPD.

My gratitude to the US Department of Justice, Office of International Affairs, Criminal Division, Washington, DC, for providing the relevant data to help support the premise of the story's plot.

To the command and crew of the Santa Barbara–based Coast Guard cutter *Blackfin*, Marine Protector Class, for providing the proper background information on all things maritime along the Mexico and US Pacific Coast.

To the Santa Barbara Harbor Patrol officers for their added perspective to the water and dockside activities of their vigilant daily watch.

To Stan Eisele for his editorial eagle eye and tireless dedication to the quality assurance process. But above all, for his friendship.

High praise and appreciation go to designer extraordinaire Damien Castaneda for his talented collaboration with me on the book covers and map and masterful finished work.

A heartfelt thank you to all of our US Border Patrol and law enforcement officers and support personnel who remain dedicated and at the ready to protect their fellow citizens and bring to justice all who dare bring harm to them.

1

PROFESSIONAL CHUTZPAH

Santa Barbara, California

The pretty, young woman stepped inside Kings Liquor on South Central Avenue in the Nuestro Barrio area of South Phoenix with her boyfriend two strides behind her. Their entry surprised Pedro Luis Sanchez, whose attention was on the two store clerks behind the checkout counter three aisles away. He saw the moment of opportunity to exit with a free carton of canned beer when the young couple had entered. He continued for the door when the girl bravely questioned him about shoplifting. A black pistol suddenly appeared from behind the beer held waist high. As the boyfriend leaped in front of the girl with his back to Pedro, a .45 caliber bullet penetrated his body and hit his heart with mortal impact. He dropped to the floor, pulling the girl down with him, her survivor, him a victim and new Phoenix homicide statistic. The surveillance camera would clock the elapsed time of the tragic incident as seven seconds.

Unencumbered without the six cans of beer, Pedro made it safely to his parent's apartment on the run in under a minute. Taking his father's 2004 Dodge pickup, he entered the Maricopa Freeway eastbound in a minute, thirty seconds, to the southbound Interstate-10 in four minutes, arriving in Tucson on Interstate-19 in two hours, where he continued to its southern terminus, Nogales in one hour and fifteen minutes. Arizona's largest border town, Nogales, was known for its ease of crossing the border. Pedro Luis Sanchez certainly thought so six minutes later as he stepped into his native Mexico a free man, untouchable from the reach of United States laws and neutered enforcers. He had fled to Mexico in a total elapsed time from Kings Liquor to the border in an easy three hours, twenty-seven minutes, and thirty seconds. Pedro looked skyward to thank God and the Mexican government for protecting him from US justice.

* * *

Across the northern US border with Canada, a private Citation-X jet touched down at the Vancouver International Airport with the tower's permission to proceed directly to the private aircraft hangar. The pilot's flight plan requested a stopover only for refueling and crew change following a 6,500-mile flight from Hong Kong. No passengers were scheduled to depart the plane, *scheduled* being the operative word.

One special Chinese passenger on the flight was, however, scheduled fourteen hours earlier to be picked up by a private limo from the Peninsula Hong Kong Hotel following a deluxe Cantonese meal in the Shanghainese Spring Moon five-star dining room. His dining guest was his travel planner, a tall, young, beautiful American brunette lady responsible for Li Deng's timely departure and, above all, his safe delivery to his special unknown hosts. He thought his destination to be Las Vegas, USA; she knew it to be Vancouver, Canada.

Accompanying Mr. Li Deng was a fellow deep pocket gambler at the Macau casinos, known as the Monte Carlo of the Orient, neighboring Hong Kong. He was a midforties American who employed the pretty brunette and flight crew and was known to all only as Taylor. His large athletic physique was casually wrapped in a high-end custom-tailored, all white linen suit and a high-roller gold Swiss watch. Li had been invited to Las Vegas by Taylor for the high stakes gaming and purported business opportunity to become a partner with one of the biggest American gaming companies with operations in Macau and Nevada. Li had made his sizable fortune in Canadian real estate neglecting to pay millions in commercial debt, partner shares, and Canadian taxes before fleeing to his native Hong Kong.

The last onboard beverage served to Li by the accommodating young lady caused him to slumber well after touchdown in Vancouver, spoiling his much anticipated night time aerial view of the spectacular Vegas Strip, so the planner had promised. He was instead awoken to an intense flashlight beam shining on his face. The hangar lights were off and the ground crew gone for the night. The plane had been refueled and the new crew now in the cabin readying their bird for flight. Taylor and his travel assistant delivered their special passenger to three agents of the Canadian Security Intelligence Service on the ground. One of them pressed a key on his laptop producing a beeping sound on Taylor's smart phone indicating the successful transfer of funds to his Bahamian account. He and the pretty brunette boarded the Citation-X for a fast flight south to sunny Santa Barbara, California. This destination would be for real, to prepare their most elaborate travel plan ever.

Taylor was the last of seven to board the *Conch II*, a luxury yacht moored in the Santa Barbara harbor. The face-to-face meeting was a make or break contract concession his new six coemployers had given into. It was a condition of employment he called freedom insurance, a *"get out of jail free"* card. He would accept the risks of arrest, imprisonment, heavy fines, and possible death, but he would not accept the possibility of being hung out to dry or double-crossed by his employers. Their shared risk was his knowing their identities as his financial backers. The days of rich people hiring surrogates to do their dirty work at the risk of death and not being responsible for their own deal gone wrong was long gone. No one in his line of business would do otherwise, and they knew it. It's their mission, their money, their responsibility. If not, *"Do it yourself,"* was now the reply to those asking for absolute anonymity. Taylor's contract Delta team would be no one's fool or fall guy.

The military-style black rubber-banded watch he wore went with the cut of the man—ramrod straight posture, Popeye forearms, black hair cropped in a West Point crew cut, sculpted jaw, and linear nose with a small scar across the bridge. A wireless radio fob was inserted in his right ear. Beneath his navy-blue shirt, a radio/cell phone was holstered on a brown canvas belt. At six feet, four inches tall, zero body fat on a pro athlete's physique, the forty-four-year-old Taylor had already convinced his employers that they were getting the real deal in paramilitary personnel.

He referred to the six Champagne-status employers as the Six-Pack. They had originally insisted on remaining anonymous, operating in the shadows for their own protection or bad publicity at best. The Delta team's insurance was in knowing exactly who every participant was. Beyond Taylor's core group knowing, he had promised the backers absolute confidentiality. It would be counterproductive anyway for him to divulge the backers' identities. Yet the backers would not know any of Taylor's team members or covert contacts. This was to be a highly classified foreign operation conducted by professional covert operatives trained in stealth. The military communication policy and procedure of "on a need to know basis" was applied.

They were known in the back-channel search and seizure business as a private Delta Force for hire. All were ex-military Special Forces plus one former CIA agent. During their former active military duty, they were the ones sent behind enemy lines to bring out a downed pilot, POW, or MIA. Some referred to them as the Lost and Found Department. They simply thought of it as a game of *hide-and-go-seek*, except most often they had to do the hiding and seeking simultaneously. Strategically they operated the same in peacetime where the declared war was against some really bad guys who had killed before and would kill again, possibly them.

With a wide, enthusiastic grin, Taylor reached for the black canvas bag he had brought on board. Placing the bag gently on a deck table, he spoke with the confidence of a school kid who knew the answer to the teacher's question before it was asked. His posture was erect and proud as he zipped open the bag. Taylor knew that his six financial backers already enjoyed high local and national stature as supersuccessful businessmen. The Forbes 400 list of the wealthiest Americans noted four of the six as billionaires and two as megamillionaires. They all had their own charitable foundations funded with millions of dollars in blue chip assets. In a couple of words, money was not an *obstacle*, nor was it an *objective*.

Taylor reached into the long bag and handed each Six-Pack member a flat, one-inch thick, nine by twelve–inch brown paper package.

"I came prepared with the answer to the question you've been asking yourselves from the moment Mr. McKinney contacted our team for hire. Are they really capable of entering a foreign country and extracting six nationals wanted in the US for capital felony killings and no one knowing about it from beginning to end? A preview answer to that question you now have in your hands. Please open your personalized packages now so that you will be satisfied," Taylor tactfully ordered.

On command, all six men tore away the paper wrappers with their respective names on them. The responses came all at once in a symphony of gasps, profanity, bewildered groans, and astonishment. "What the hell, how in the hell, holy shit, where in the hell," echoed from their mouths with equally amazed looks of disbelief on their wide-eyed faces. Like surprised kids on Christmas morning staring at that unexpected gift not on their Santa wish list, they each held a nicely framed photo, each approximately eight inches by eleven inches.

They instantly recognized their individually posed photographs with their respective wife, which hours earlier were exhibited in their respective home.

Taylor broke their stunned trance with, "Gentlemen, as to whether or not my six field operatives are capable of accomplishing your mission, you have before you a dramatic indicator. I gave each ops leader twelve hours to conduct the necessary reconnaissance on one assigned home per leader among your six secured, fenced Santa Barbara estates. The additional and final twelve hours were allowed for planning and executing their individual undetected entry, seizure of the targeted framed photo, and safe, undetected exit. The operatives had to have their framed photos of you with your wife in my hands by 0500 this morning," he said very matter-of-factly.

"You mean to tell us that all six of these photos were stolen from our secured homes last night while we slept?" Mr. Boyer asked incredulously.

"Borrowed, Mr. Boyer, not stolen. When you return home today, you can count your silverware. It's all there. My team members aren't cat burglars. And yes, they all conducted the six seizures last night in under fifteen minutes each," he reported proudly.

Mr. Hilman showed signs of anger and disappointment when he declared, "I'll have you know that I just invested thousands of dollars in what I was told was a state-of-the-art security system that in reality is worthless crap. I even pay the bastards a monthly responder fee. Well they can pull it out and stuff it!" he protested.

"Mr. Hilman, not to brag, but America's best burglar doesn't know what we know. Besides, the ops leader who entered your home was indeed impressed with the security system. But for Mr. Rincon, please tell your cook to quit feeding your Rottweilers Mexican leftovers. They've become flaccid, fat, and complacent. Last night they became complicit after the ops leader treated them to one burrito each."

The group laughed as Mr. Rincon swore, "I'll feed the cook to the damn dogs since they like Mexican food so much. This is embarrassing. I was burglarized by the burrito bandito for Christ's sake."

Mr. Carpenter offered, "Good Lord, your men could have walked out of our homes with our wives."

"I can only hope," Heiman commented with mock lament. "If your man can return tonight, I'll leave the alarm off," he added with levity. The group was laughing in part because they were definitely unnerved by the impressive but brazen intrusion of their homes. "Professional chutzpah," Mr. Laisum called it.

McKinney broke in saying, "Gentlemen, although this is indeed embarrassing for all of us, it also is proof positive that we are working with high-caliber professionals."

The only enemies Taylor had signed on for were six FTM contract targets in Mexico. It came with a guarantee of success in capturing the six felony fugitives from US justice, six Mexican nationals who had murdered six innocent citizens in Santa Barbara then fled to Mexico with impunity, a safe haven from extradition. Taylor's contract would commit his Delta team to returning the six FTM fugitives to Santa Barbara to face the law of the land—US Federal law. In return, he was guaranteed that the Delta team would not be left to rot in a Mexican prison if the local authorities caught any of them in the commission of transborder abductions. His field team was mindful of what happened to a group of *hotdog haphazard bounty hunters* in the highly publicized Allen Larsen case. They were arrested in Mexico for kidnapping the US fugitive Larsen and were sentenced to four years in jail plus fat six figure fines. The Delta team members were not soldiers of fortune, although they charged one.

For that moment, only seven individuals knew about the totality of their extraction mission, and they were all aboard the *Conch II* yacht. The Santa Barbara law enforcement authorities, district attorney (DA), and court investigators weren't aware of what was to take place. Most understandable, the families of the six murder victims would not know until after the mission was completed. Absolute secrecy was essential to the ultimate success of their mission. Taylor was given assurances that even after the mission's completion, not a single word from the Six-Pack would ever be uttered regarding their role in the plan. During the Iranian hostage crisis thirty years earlier, the nation had lauded Texas businessman Ross Perot. He had financed the rescue of his two American employees from an Iranian prison by an elite, private, clandestine paramilitary team. He was elevated to national hero status because of it. In 2011, the active Special Forces black ops team gave the personal walking stick of slain Osama bin Laden to Ross Perot. For the secret six sponsors, mere success in the mission would be sufficient private tribute.

Taylor's employers had a different mission and motivation. They wanted justice on their side, American style. Ironically it was the US Feds they were concerned about. They would want them to play by their diplomatic State Department rules, which meant burying the cases under the ineffectual international bureaucracy of the American-Mexican Extradition Treaty. Taylor fully understood law enforcement's frustration with the controversial matter of treaty protection knowing that in reality, its legal language expressly provides that extradition of nationals was a matter of discretion. The treaty doesn't explicitly prohibit it, allowing state law enforcement and local prosecutors to request it, albeit historically a prolonged exercise in futility.

The six mission patrons were greatly revered for their generous philanthropy and social activism in the Santa Barbara community, known for its charity to all citizens in need, including the ongoing illegal alien population. Taylor knew that the anger these six good men shared was not about revenge. This was about suffering insult to injury from a so-called good neighbor, Mexico, by them telling Americans the laws of their land were meaningless to the Mexican citizens and government.

The yacht's owner and captain, Michael McKinney, told Taylor he would make the formal introductions once they were out of the harbor and underway. "Help yourself to a Bloody Mary or otherwise," McKinney offered, gesturing toward the top deck wet bar.

His 2012 special edition yacht wasn't the largest—sixty-eight feet from stem to stern, or most luxurious boat in the harbor—but it was by far the most high-tech. It had more antennae sticking up than a Coast Guard cutter. Taylor recognized Mr. McKinney from his telephone voice, southern-smooth and gentile yet authoritative and sharp. Age seventy-five and looking considerably younger from his many hours on the tennis court and yacht, McKinney was one of the early innovators and entrepreneurs in the booming cell phone and radiophone industry. The *Conch II* was outfitted with every leading-edge electronic device designed to receive, send, scramble, or block transmitted messages. It was "wired," as they say. He had agreed to supply Taylor's team with his latest field telecommunication equipment that would keep the members connected as well as protected from detection. Taylor noted his enthusiasm to have them tested under covert, adverse field conditions. There would be no bragging rights to follow, only pride in "inventorship."

As the leader of the pack, McKinney's aggressive, can-do attitude made Taylor think he had invented 911 as well. He exuded a high sense of urgency, not from impatience, but rather for economy of time and energy expended. This he liked. It would make for a compatible, efficient working relationship. Wasted time in the field of covert operations could be a silent enemy. The Delta team must create opportunities of engagement, never depending on Lady Luck to provide them. Extracting only one target would be a relatively quick in-and-out operation. But finding, capturing, and extracting six completely different targets from different locations was a Herculean odyssey with the clock working exponentially against them. Their mission plan must function like a fine Swiss watch if they were to succeed, *like synchronized swimming without the water or the babes,* Taylor thought.

The agenda for the day's short ocean outing on a cloudless Saturday morning was strictly 411. Everyone onboard had a need to know the mission, the risks, and the Delta team's capability to succeed. The purpose of the sponsor's mission was clear to all: to send a simple yet forceful message to Mexico and to Mexican nationals in Santa Barbara, "You break the law in our land, you will be tried and do time in our land, including a life or death sentence." This Taylor would hear repeatedly from the Six-Pack, each in their own way, each with different levels of angst, all with the same solid conviction that, "Justice must be served, and served on our side."

He had noticed the uniform casual wear worn by the Six-Pack, some more nautical than others, explaining why McKinney had asked him to sport the same fashion for common effect in case there were any outside wondering eyes. They were, to the passing eye, a bunch of rich, old white guys out to watch the whales, although he was twenty-five years or more their junior.

Taylor's first impression when he boarded was that he was looking at the geriatric male movie cast of *Cocoon.* He sensed they had already seen most of the world's tourist highlights from a touring car with the high-end binoculars strapped around their necks. McKinney had been told that no cameras were to be on board while Taylor was there.

The only radical departure from the uniform dress of the day was Taylor's white, low-cut, athletic topsiders. The others sported the *de rigueur* yacht-wear blue topsiders. But since white men can't jump anyway, *why should they care about athletic footwear?* he told himself. This group paid others to jump for them.

Filling a tall glass with ice, he began to concoct the Taylor classic Bloody Mary, a slight variation of the original recipe he had discovered in its country of origin, *Bora Bora.* Two shots of Reyka vodka, four shots of Sacramento tomato juice, four dashes of Tabasco sauce and Worcestershire sauce, the juice of half a lemon, three hard shakes of pepper, and celery salt, stirred well with a celery stalk. *Leave the horseshit horseradish for the metro males at Harry's Bar,* Taylor would say. Completing his celery swizzle, he glanced up to see that a pack member wearing a blue-banded Panama hat had been scrutinizing his Bloody Mary mixology. The man joined McKinney on the captain's deck as the yacht began moving out of its slip. Taylor observed McKinney at the helm with his guest. He suspected they were ex-navy with a seaman's fifth sensibility about them.

The yacht cleared the No Wake Zone and harbor's 500-yard breakwater with its two dozen or more white flag poles. The light southerly breeze wasn't enough to help identify the multicolored flags, which he assumed had some community symbolism. Bearing northwest, they entered the Santa Barbara Channel full throttle gliding over the small chop with ease and comfort. They took a common route for whale watchers that time of the year, particularly for sighting the humpbacks and the gigantic blue whales feeding on krill and plankton north of the small chain of five Channel Islands. The local commercial fishermen would not be in their restrictive fishing zones diving for abalone and squid on a Saturday morning. The local pleasure boaters and regatta racers wouldn't appear until the breezy afternoon. The *Conch II* had the day's 0800 long sea to herself, *some wise planning by McKinney,* Taylor thought, bringing little attention to the master plotters.

Forty-five minutes out into the dark-blue 25-mile-wide channel, the solid white yacht began to slow down. The northeastern verdure tip of uninhabited Santa Cruz Island was ten minutes off the port side. Taylor had kept to himself on the open deck, adding another layer of tan to his already bronze face and arms. Taylor had made his second Bloody Mary earlier while the same man as before observed his every move. Next to him sat a smaller, portly pack member who held a piece of paper and pen, marking something down every few seconds during Taylor's Mary-making. The yacht stopped as Taylor finished his last full drink. The portly gentleman handed the first man the paper and a ten-dollar bill accompanied with light comments and laughter.

2

JUSTICE ON OUR SIDE

Channel Islands Pacific Channel

With the push of two buttons, McKinney dropped two anchors then joined the others on the deck. With a tall glass of orange juice on the rocks, a screwdriver Taylor speculated, McKinney gestured to their special guest, saying officially, "Gentleman, you've met Taylor. Whether it is his first or last name, we will never know. We only need to know that he and his company are fully vetted and highly regarded for their successes, integrity, and belief in the American criminal justice system, which we all share equally. And the latter is precisely why we are here, to see that justice is properly served. As a peace-loving community, we do not want to live with the fear that an increasing number of our southern neighbors will enter our country illegally, kill our family members, friends, and fellow citizens, thumb their noses at our laws, then disappear to their protective homeland, free men. In just four short years, the number of such Fled to Mexico felony murders in Santa Barbara has gone from one to six." McKinney counted off for dramatic affect.

He intentionally ignored the egregious and violent FTM cases of child molestation, forcible rape, kidnapping, robbery, and aggravated assault numbering in the thousands. In Los Angeles alone, 85 percent of the felony warrants were for illegal immigrants. Six Santa Barbara homicides were more than enough for now, McKinney had concluded.

The significance of that number had profoundly impacted the Six-Pack, causing them to form their secret six-member action group months earlier. It had now become a quasi-vigilante posse operating through a professional proxy named Taylor. The Six-Pack had conducted a careful, arm's length search and selection for a clandestine group of international operatives experienced in extracting expatriates from hostile situations in foreign lands. "It's something you don't find in the Yellow Pages," McKinney would say. Taylor's company, out of Las Vegas and the Bahamas, was chosen because of their perfect track record and absolute discretion. They were extremely expensive because their work was guaranteed. "If your subject is not returned to the US, your money is," was the guarantee.

Once again, McKinney gestured with his glass in the air, saying, "My friends, we have convened on many an occasion to pool resources for humanitarian purposes, writing charitable checks for worthy causes ranging from education to cancer research, flood and fire disaster relief, to the 911 victims fund. This time it is personal. This time it's too close to home with the potential to get worse if something isn't done soon." Pausing for effect, he punctuated the air with his glass while the group listened intently. "We all previously forfeited our final opportunity to walk away from this mission with no questions asked, no answers offered. We are all willing volunteers pooling our resources equally. We are all dedicated to the same cause of justice for our community and country and protection for our families. The rule of law of our land must be respected and feared by not only US citizens but also foreigners alike. When it was not, we suffered six murders in Santa Barbara where the crime wouldn't have paid if the killer had stayed. In Southern States, there are hundreds of FTM homicide cases. It's not just a border states problem. No telling how many hundreds of Fled to Mexico cases there are nationwide, including a recent one up in Connecticut. But the six FTMs here can quickly grow to seven, eight, and beyond if we don't take action soon. And yesterday is soon enough. No more! A firm stand and a strong public statement must be made before we become another Milwaukee!" he exclaimed vehemently.

Taylor had read the *Milwaukee Journal Sentinel* article sent by McKinney reporting that in 2005, of the city's twenty-three homicides, twenty were committed by illegal immigrants who then fled to Mexico and Central America.

It was apparent why McKinney was the leader of the pack, impassioned, articulate, and full of conviction. Taylor would admit that he had taken on some past missions with tepid enthusiasm. It was the character of the men with the money that always influenced his decisions. Assignments were turned down for lack of a moral connection with the client's mission. Acceptance of a mission made the two parties partners, albeit silent partners with the emphasis on *silent*.

Santa Barbara wasn't Taylor's community, but it was in his country, which meant his own backyard. "And we Americans don't like shit happening in our own backyards," he declared vigorously.

McKinney's first introduction interrupted Taylor's thoughts. "Taylor, the gentleman to your far left is Henry Helman, formerly of the Wall Street investment bank of Wiseman, Helman, and Winslow. Henry, please," he said, inviting him to speak.

Leaning forward in his blue canvas deck chair, the distinguished-looking, salt-and-pepper hair man spoke with an Eastern educated air and New York edge. He got right to the point, saying, "Taylor, we are here because each of us knows someone who was murdered by a killer who knew in advance that he could get away with murder by getting away to Mexico," sounding like a sarcastic travel poster.

Taylor had reviewed the FTM cases in advance and noted the SBPD's speculation that the six killers would not have killed if they had no expedient escape plan and safe refuge. They knew there were no hiding places within the US justice system on the matter of first-degree murder. But there was a gigantic hole in the wall at the Mexican border, not just coming into the US, but going back out as fugitives from American justice. Taylor had always known the DOJ's persistent complaint of the 24-7 welcome mat called the Mexican constitution, which had no provision for capital punishment except in the military. That served as *carte blanche* for Mexican nationals to kill in the United States with a free conscience according to many legal scholars. Most national FTM case report summaries had implied that the felony Mexican national fugitives had contemplated the commission of the crimes in the US, knowing they could easily hit and run to a safe base, Mexico, as though they had virtual diplomatic immunity.

Taylor had always put the pro and con arguments on capital punishment into perspective, knowing that fifty-eight nations actively practiced it. He realized that for these six citizens, the question wasn't one of pro or con, but rather to have a consequential law of the land that would serve as a real and present deterrent to murder with dire consequences. But if noncitizens enjoyed foreign-born immunity, Taylor believed, then it's as though the Mexican nationals are all privileged foreign ambassadors, behaving at will with no accountability.

"Some argue that the guarantee of a free pass in Mexico from extradition might even be the definitive incentive that motivates them to kill. Why? Because if they know they can get away with murder, why not?" Helman exclaimed pointedly.

Taylor was nodding in silent agreement hearing Henry discuss his personal FTM case. Taylor had the case file opened, reading about Helman's sister-in-law, widowed five years earlier. Helman's brother had left her with a sizable coastal estate at Hope Ranch. In her late sixties, she required help to manage her expansive property. Her two Mexican gardeners had been with her for over four years and were beneficiaries of her constant generosity, which included higher than average wages, holiday bonuses, and occasional loans without conditions or questions. But that wasn't enough for Juan Diego Leon. The felony case evidence showed how Leon repaid her by taking her ATM card then beating her until she divulged her PIN access code. The CSI photos told the rest of the murder story with a brutally savaged corpse stabbed repeatedly to silence her forever. The homicide report was followed with a grand theft auto report of Mrs. Helman's car and $3,800 in electronic ATM withdrawals from her checking account. Video tape records show that Leon crossed the border in Tijuana four hours following the ATM withdrawals, as though on an AAA traveler's schedule.

"The FTM file says that he's from Tijuana. That's all I need to know for now," Taylor stated with confidence.

Henry Helman continued with a slight breaking of his firm voice. "I promised my dying brother that I would look after his wife after he passed. Leon made a liar out of me. I want the murderous coward taken care of!" he growled bitterly.

Taylor quickly interjected, "I understand your sentiments, Mr. Heiman, and I'm sure that you mean here to face our judicial process. I know all of you have been told that we are not hired guns. We'd only use firearms to defend ourselves. We are methodical, cunning, and careful. We never roll the dice. Our intelligence gathering is actionable, our moves are premeditated and tactical every step of the way. That way we avoid any reenactment of the O. K. Corral," he said evenly.

McKinney interjected that Taylor save any operational explanations for the Q&A at the end of the introductions. He then pointed to a lanky, tan man with thinning gray hair in his midsixties. A thick layer of white sunscreen covered his entire thick nose. He was introduced as Stan Laisum, originally from Chicago, transplanted to Texas where he created a retail petroleum products empire. He had since retired, luxuriating in one of Santa Barbara's largest estates.

Laisum's aging voice was raspy and strained. "In an attempted burglary of our house, a Miguel Bravo attacked our forty-eight-year-old cook, Rocio, who'd been with us for seventeen years. We were her family, and she in turn was dedicated to us to her death. She had returned alone to the house with groceries where this Bravo bastard was hiding outside the back service entrance. Although he had breached our back fence, he was unable to break into the house because of our state-of-the-art security system throughout our home. Bravo then stabbed her to death because she refused to give him the electronic keypad code to unlock the doors. The entire hideous incident was captured by our surveillance video camera." He paused for an emotional breath.

"Now Rocio's dead and Bravo's alive, free in Mexico. I can just see him laughing, waving the extradition treaty at us, yelling, 'Can't touch me, Gringos!' Well, guess what? I'm going to pay what it takes to reach out over his paper border and not only touch the motherfucker, but bring his sorry ass back to face a US judge and jury," Laisum concluded with a trembling voice.

McKinney handed Laisum a glass of ice water in one hand and patted his back sympathetically with the other. He then leaned to his left to tap the broad shoulder of a balding, white hair man with a round face and reddish complexion. "Taylor, this is Karl Boyer, retired media mogul and moviemaker extraordinaire. If you ever saw *Planet California*, you'd know why this man is a genius."

Taylor interjected, "You won several awards for that film if I recall."

Boyer spoke with a hardened resolve, saying, "Taylor, I'll give you and your crew all of my awards if you can bring to US justice this wife killer, orphan maker, Jose Taboada. Carmen was her name. My wife and I knew her as one of the ten local recipients of college scholarships sponsored by our foundation. Carmen had just completed the two-year program at Santa Barbara City College and was accepted to enter Westmont College in the fall. Jose Taboada was a perpetual underachiever, unemployed parasite who lived off of twenty-eight-year-old Carmen's full-time job income. He didn't want her in school on her free time and was so jealous of her advancements in life that he eventually took hers. Fearful for her life, she moved out of their house and filed for a divorce two days before Juan slit her throat in the Sears parking lot. It happened in the La Cumbre shopping center where Carmen worked. She made a dying declaration of the killer's positive ID while bleeding to death as he fled the scene and soon after to Mexico. He left a two-year-old daughter and a four-year-old son without a mother or father."

Taylor sighed before asking, "What's become of the children?"

"The monies allocated from my foundation for Carmen's college scholarship was matched dollar for dollar by each of my fine friends here. Those monies are now transferred into a newly created trust fund for the two kids, Margarita and Enrique, who now live with the maternal grandparents in Ventura."

With a deep frown forming on his forehead, McKinney stated, "As disgusting as these first three murder cases are, Taylor, the final three are even more despicable as you are aware from your set of FTM files."

The six sponsors had done a thorough job gathering what he would find to be reliable background information on the aging murder cases while still not calling any attention to themselves and their mission. He was now learning that these six highly principled gentlemen had invested as much emotion in the FTM cases as money.

McKinney stood directly behind the seated *Latino*-looking gentleman who could have passed as Ricardo Montalbán's double. He had dimpled cheeks and chin with a facial shadow, crowned with a head of wavy black hair and white sideburns. McKinney introduced him as Robert Rincon, one of the largest apartment complex developers on the southwest California coast. Although he was born in the states, he spoke lovingly of his Mexican heritage and the Mexican people with one harsh exception.

"Taylor, there is not one person among us who doesn't know how proud I am of my Latin lineage and Catholic upbringing. But I have also made clear the shame I harbor for the shameful sense of justice the Mexican people have for protecting murderers, all in the name of their compassionate Catholic church and constitutional jingoism. The church's historical hypocrisy is ignored. They stood by in the fifteenth and sixteenth centuries and allowed the Indians in Mexico to be systematically exterminated while preaching a new brotherhood to those willing to convert and serve the church. The priests in the conquered *Nueva España* had orders to rid the land of all pagan religions. They destroyed temples of Indian worship. They used the salvaged stone as building material to construct the first Catholic churches upon those temple ruins. The next couple of centuries saw evolved social constitutional reforms in Mexico, which separated the overbearing church from the government. Today, the Vatican's weight upon the government is far more subtle and nuanced, yet still present," Rincon said derisively.

The other group members were listening intently as though it was the first time they had heard Rincon speak so profoundly about the origin and evolution of Mexico's judicial philosophy. Taylor was impressed with his historical perspective and passion on the matter.

Rincon continued with increased fervor, like a courtroom prosecutor in his closing arguments. "If you want more evidence to support the argument of church supremacy, then look no further than the symbolism of the Mexican flag. Unlike the separation of church and state in the US and most democratic countries, the Mexican flag has white as the 'Purity of the Catholic Church' as its central symbolic color. It is no accident that the white symbolism serves as the foundation for the official government seal. So it is no surprise to find official church doctrine at the very foundation of the paradoxical Mexican constitution, counterbalanced with anticlerical articles to socially restrict the church's reach. But the church is still present, just as is the white on the flag," Rincon affirmed.

Rincon was not saying a government shouldn't weave compassion into the fabric of its constitution and criminal laws. But do not do it at the expense of fairness and equal protection and justice for the crime victims. The US consensus has been that the Mexican government had no judicial or moral authority to impose their sense and form of justice on people of other nations when it came to the application of the extradition treaties. Mr. Boyer quoted the moral leader Martin Luther King Jr. saying, "Injustice anywhere is injustice everywhere."

Rincon reinforced his argument, saying, "In the US, we promote the absolute certainty that you will suffer the punishment of life in prison or death for a corporal crime. Now that makes you think twice about that inevitability. That absolute deters you. Serious laws regarding serious crimes must have serious consequences for those who chose to disobey them. That's the way it is with the law of our land. So when you murder here, you suffer the consequences here. It's not negated by fleeing to a safe haven country. You do the crime here, you do the time here, even if it's an eternity," Rincon concluded with a demanding voice.

Taylor realized that these men had months of pent up emotions they needed to vent. They had kept all their angst to themselves since they dared not go public. They were also trying to rationalize their mission to him not knowing that they're preaching to the choir. He believed every word he'd heard so far and then some. His views on the matter were more simplistic and cynical. Mexico has been the poor southern cousin to the US for centuries. They had a popular saying there: "Poor Mexico. Too far from God and too close the United

States." So now with their no-extradition protectionist laws, it was their opportunity to exert some semblance of control over their powerful neighbor to the north. The more Americans screamed about it, the more powerful Mexicans felt.

"Do you have connections with the victim?" Taylor asked Rincon.

"I can't claim to have known Antonio Navaro personally, but professionally he was a member of a three-man hardwood floor installation crew. He was a nationalized American citizen, hardworking, good-humored young man who worked for two weeks at our home. He told us that half of his income went to Mexico to support his aging parents.

The crew completed their work on a Friday, and Antonio and another worker returned on Saturday to put the furniture back in place. My wife was so pleased with their work, she paid them extra, insisting that they do something special for themselves that evening," Rincon stated proudly.

His voiced hardened when he expressed the horrible shock when he opened the local Sunday paper the next morning to see Antonio Navaro's name on the front page. He had become a random victim of a downtown shooting Saturday evening by a gangbanger from LA who was in the US illegally. The known shooter's name was Olivel Morales. He entered Santa Barbara to earn his entrance into *La Eme*, better known as the Mexican Mafia. Young recruits became full-fledged members by killing someone, anyone. That earned them their badge of honor, a tattoo of a black hand on their back, according to the news article. Taylor knew of it "as a sick symbol for a pat on the back for a job well done by the hand of death."

"It's the singular most common tattoo of any throughout the California prison population, the Mexican Mafia's black badge of ultimate machismo courage. And it also sends a message to all non-members: 'Don't fuck with me or you fuck with every *La Eme* member,'" Taylor shared with his attentive audience.

He further explained that every member of the Mexican Mafia had killed someone, and if a *La Eme* member tried to leave the gang, he would be killed, a gang rule of "Blood in, blood out." The newspaper reported that *La Eme* historically relied on murder and intimidation to organize drug trafficking among hundreds of Latino street gangs in Southern California. They listed the Latin Kings, Domino's, Latin Leones, and *Los Solidos* as some of the most aggressive. The article noted that incarcerated Mexican Mafia leaders throughout the California penal system controlled every prison yard as well as the estimated 17,000-member 18th Street gang, the largest and most deadly in Southern California.

"So if you touch one member, you touch them all, is that what you're saying?" Hilman asked with a concerned voice.

"Pretty much," Taylor casually replied.

"Well aren't you concerned that by capturing this Olivel Morales character, you'll be poking the beehive?" Carpenter asked.

"When a bee is killed on the windshield of a car, I don't see a swarm of bees attacking the car," Taylor responded. "Besides, they won't know Olivel's fate until he lands behind bars in Santa Barbara. That's when his real death sentence begins because *La Eme* will think that he had deserted the gang by fleeing to Mexico," he continued.

"But we don't know that he did," Laisum questioned.

"He will if he wants to survive. Now any cell he ends up in here or there becomes his death row from day 1," Taylor added. "That's just the harsh reality of his world, not ours," he concluded.

"Taylor, I'm sure you see the concern here, that there might be retribution by *La Eme*," McKinney contributed.

"Retribution against whom? Not our Delta Force. We don't exist. Not against anyone here because they'll know nothing about your involvement, right?"

The Six-Pack looked at one another for shared agreement and assurance, finding it among the collective nervous nods of their heads.

"Now you can appreciate the value of absolute discretion at all costs," Taylor underscored. The group head nodding became more demonstrative.

"We all understand and agree, Taylor. At the risk of sounding like a boat full of sissies, I believe the question here seems to be but just, what if?" Carpenter insisted.

"Fair question. If we foresee or suddenly encounter such a risk, we would eliminate it," Taylor exclaimed harshly.

"What do you mean by eliminate it?" Hillman asked naively.

"You don't want to know, Mr. Hilman," was Taylor's blunt response, causing the Six-Pack to sit up erect in their seats.

McKinney subtly moderated the topic with assurances that Taylor's answer was as clear as it needed to be and they needed to know nothing more. He said, "Let's move on to a similar case involving a drug deal that went bad one night on Milpas Street two years ago. It resulted in the drug dealer Lionel Mario Madrid shooting at his would-be buyer and missing. The errant bullets hit and killed a nineteen-year-old Julio Torrents, who was walking his girlfriend home at the time. I don't subscribe to the media's notion that poor Julio was just in the wrong place at the wrong time. That's BS! He was in the right place, his place, at the time of his life. It was Madrid who was in the wrong place doing the wrong thing. Now he must pay his time," he stressed.

"None of us has any direct connection with the victim. Santa Barbara is called both a small city and a large town. I prefer the latter because regardless of size, we are all one people here. We especially don't like it when an outside drug dealer trying to ply his poison on our streets and guns down one of our neighbors. Every street belongs to every one of us. We all interconnect to form a community." McKinney took a drink of water and a deep breath before continuing.

"Lionel Mario Madrid has to be brought back from Mexico for more than just killing a US citizen. He must return to stand trial as an example to other drug dealers who think that they can enter Santa Barbara with guns blazing, deal drugs, and walk away unscathed. They must know that the consequences for dealing in our town will be just as deadly for them. They cannot be allowed to think that they're untouchable here. If so, the assault problem will compound itself," McKinney concluded.

Taylor didn't want to frighten or burden the Six-Pack with the reality that the Madrid felony murder case might take them to place were they won't want to be. Drug-related cases always had a plurality about them where you discover the snake you're after is a ten-headed one. Get the head you want only to have nine separate sets of fangs coming at you later. The illegal drug business was a family affair called a cartel, networking out to several Latin American countries and the United States. It was not *ajuste de cuentas* (retribution) they'd be concerned about. Mario Leon Madrid was just a *pelone* (pawn) in the big scheme of things. What the drug lords would be concerned about were any secrets about their underworld operations reaching the DEA or other law enforcement offices. If they now distrusted Leon, Taylor knew that there would be an attempted *levantado* to silence him.

McKinney had finally turned to the last member to speak, Charles Carpenter. The members referred to him as CC, a carryover from his former corporate calling card. Now retired as founder and chairman of the nation's largest pharmacy chain, CC was now a full-time philanthropist. They had deliberately delayed his presentation for last for reasons Taylor was about to learn.

Mike McKinney had expressed-mailed all six FTM case files to Taylor for his review prior to his signing on. They all lacked necessary information for tracking the six fugitives within Mexico, containing only anecdotal information that was in the public domain. Had they gone around playing *Inspector Clouseau,* these high-profile gentlemen would have blown their covert cover. Through his own private contact, Taylor had obtained the basic police felony homicide reports with photos of the victims except for the FTM case CC was now presenting.

"Taylor, usually the best is saved for last in presentations. Unfortunately, you are about to see the worst in terms of victimization. Not only is it the worst among these six homicide cases, according to the DOJ, it ranks as one of the worst nationwide," CC said emphatically.

CC handed Taylor his case file with the comment, "The three photos here were obtained only two days ago. Obviously we are even more revolted now than before and naturally with more resolve than ever to bring fugitive Pedro Barajas back from Mexico." CC paused with a deep groan. Taylor starred in repulsed shock at the three photos of the two burn victims. Instant flashbacks of battle scenes struck his field veteran mind. His face grimaced when he saw the completely burned corpse of Barajas's wife, Pilar. When he came to the photo of Barajas's seven-year-old son, Miguel, with a burned body that resembled a toasted marshmallow, his imagination was transported for a morose moment to the war zone. He heard CC say Miguel had survived just as he flipped to the third picture. It was of Miguel today at age ten, after three years of skin grafting and reconstructive surgery. The boy's hairless head was solid scar tissue, minus lips, ears, and a partial nose. He spun around to grip the boat's outer grab rail as though in combat mode. He closed the file in a fury. It ramped up to rage when McKinney put a fourth photo in front of him. Taylor saw a picture of a normal, handsome, smiling seven-year-old Miguel one month before he and his mother were torched alive.

Taylor continued to face the ocean starboard side when CC described the murder case from the FTM file. It started with a police record of domestic problems and spousal abuse. Barajas had violated his current restraining order by returning one night to his home drunk. This time though, he carried a can of gasoline and a lighter. While the mother and son were asleep in her bedroom, Barajas poured the gas over the floor, closed the door, and secured it with electrical wire strung over to another doorknob. He then struck his lighter beneath the bedroom door. Pilar and Miguel couldn't escape out the window because of the flaming linens and curtains. The fire investigators suspect the mother pushed Miguel into the closet, which ultimately saved his life, the report surmised.

"Miguel has endured countless acute burn and restorative operations. He has permanent lung damage and the loss of one eye. There are some whom believe he'd be better off dead. But Miguel doesn't, and that's all that matters. He's one hell of a fighter but admits that he's still frightened that his dad might return to try and kill him again. This poor child still asks the question, 'Why?'" CC reported with disgust.

Taylor involuntarily began to block out CC's presentation telling how the collective foundations of these generous Samaritans had established a special trust to care for Miguel's every need, medical, home care, and schooling. It was Rincon who first noticed the bulging veins on Taylor's neck. Taylor turned to face them with a crimson complexion and engorged muscles and veins networking down the neck. Boyer had seen that look before among the combat marines in Korea. He was in fight mode. Taylor had witnessed his share of wartime atrocities. But to your own innocent son was unthinkable, but not unspeakable, as Taylor let loose with a verbal barrage.

"That's enough, Mr. Carpenter! I've heard enough and seen enough! There's not a hell hot enough for that sick fuck! His seizure won't be easy. But I will promise Miguel personally that his psycho dad will never harm him or anyone again. And one more thing for the record, my portion of the payment for Barajas's return to the US courts, it's to go to Miguel. Add it to his trust, buy him something, spoil him, anything. Is that clear, Mr. McKinney?" Taylor demanded like a drill sergeant barking at his troops.

"That's very generous, Taylor, but the trust has more than ample funds to cover his needs," McKinney said with added assurance.

"My modest amount for this single capture will be there then for whatever he wants, not needs. It's like 'Make a Wish' play money. Now are we clear, sir?" Taylor asked, knowing the answer.

Glancing at his five colleagues, all with warm smiles, he responded with the expected, "Yes, sir. Consider it done."

The Six-Pack just caught a rare personal picture of this man, raising their esteem yet even higher. He lifted a glass of ice water while the others took a muted pause. The yacht swayed lazily in the calm waters, soothing the piqued nerves of all on board. A Heermann's gull made a soft hovercraft-like landing on the bow of the boat.

Finishing his ice water, Taylor faced the Six-Pack again, now feeling more relaxed. "Gentlemen, I'm aware of your growing curiosity of how such a challenging mission can be accomplished in total secrecy when one of your ultimate objectives is to make a public statement with its very accomplishment. Simply said, the operation in its entirety will be covert. That's what a Delta Force is, a strictly clandestine military operations unit. Because our private missions for hire are not military, we can actually operate more effectively on the QT than if they were. CNN will never know. Otherwise they'd have a camera crew at every seizure site with the lights on the subject before we arrived," Taylor exclaimed with a bemused expression.

The men nodded with chuckles of agreement.

"But until our six targets are behind Santa Barbara bars, we don't breathe a word to the media. At that time, we will initiate an organized media blitz to broadcast your 'Don't tread on me' message throughout California, the US, and Mexico. It will be done surreptitiously through reliable, friendly news dissemination organizations. We want the same six fugitives' photos on the front page again of the local news press, this time all dressed in orange and accessorized in chains."

The Six-Pack grinned widely in unison.

Rincon asked, "Back to your comments on your secret operations. Can you share with us how your nonmilitary approach can operate without performing as a military unit? It appears to be a paradox on the surface, a contradiction in terms."

"It's a perfectly logical question to what seems to be an illogical operation in the conventional, and historical, military sense. The answer is we are not at war, nor do we want to initiate one. However, warlike stratagem, tactics, and dispositions should be employed when you have targets that will treat you like the enemy and will fight back when engaged. Every war college teaches the 2,300-year-old military wisdom of the Chinese *general Sun Tzu*. His popular book, *The Art of War*, is still used today by the US military as an officer's training manual. In it, he states, 'Supreme excellence consists in breaking the enemy's resistance without fighting.' You know that we could take out these six murderers in six seconds with six shots. But that's not the mission. We can extract them without firing a shot. At least that's the plan," Taylor said with confidence.

Laisum asked, "Are there any other pages of this Sun general's book you could apply to our mission?"

"There are several. The one which your group is already aware of, in Sun Tzu's words is, 'He will win who has military capacity and is not interfered with by the sovereign.'"

"The sovereign meaning us, of course?" Laisum asked rhetorically. Taylor confirmed his answer with a positive nod.

"But to understand our Delta Force's *modus operandi,* you must understand the modern US military concept, 'the OODA loop.' No, it's not Chinese," he said, noting the puzzled looks on the faces of his audience.

"The intellectual leader of our contemporary Delta Forces' art of modern warfare was the late air force colonel John Boyd. His cardinal tenet was the OODA loop—'Success is observing, orienting, deciding, and acting faster than your enemy.' Over the years, all branches of the Pentagon have worked diligently to create new technologies and systems that will provide us with the capability to convert that concept into an effective reality. That's to say with field equipment that is the fastest, most accurate, most reliable, and most practical."

"What about most affordable?" Rincon asked.

Hilman interjected, "Most affordable? The Pentagon? When did they ever stay under budget?"

"Well, Mr. Hilman is right in terms of the Pentagon spending top dollar. But it's always with the objective of assuring that their fighting forces are always victorious in the field of battle as well as safe. And that same field, attitude carries over to my ops team. I've never lost a man or woman, and I don't plan on it with this mission," Taylor stated flatly.

"When can you get started?" Laisum asked bluntly.

"As soon as I step off this yacht, we have begun," Taylor replied with the answer they all had been waiting for.

Hearing those definitive words, McKinney leaped up to his captain's chair on the bridge and leaned over his laptop that appeared to be already online. A few key strokes sent his message to the Bahamas. In less than a minute, he rejoined the others on deck. Helman was speaking to Taylor for the entire group when he said, "The decision to go forth with this special mission did not come easy for us, Taylor. Its short-term purpose is to see justice served. The long-term objective is a strong message to all Mexican nationals contemplating a hit-and-run murder in the US. Don't do it because in time, justice will be served on our side."

"We've been careful not to be perceived as an arbitrary court, a secretive Star Chamber serving our self-interests. There exists today more than sufficient *prima facie* evidence to bring these six defendants to trial in an American court where they will enjoy our fair, due process of the law," Carpenter proclaimed.

"That's more than their victims received," Laisum snapped.

Hilman continued, saying, "We do not enjoy having to go to these extremes. Nor do we enjoy spending good money on bad people. But in the final analysis, given our personal resources, we have an opportunity to make something so terribly wrong, in some moral measure, right. We are the victims' advocates for their lost rights for criminal justice."

At that moment, all heads turned upward toward a faint beeping sound coming from the captain's bridge. It became increasingly louder, causing McKinney to climb up to the bridge for a look. The intermittent siren-like sound was coming from an early warning radar system signaling an approaching vessel in their direct path. He watched the radar monitor to locate the position of the inbound boat advancing toward his anchored craft. He looked in all directions and saw nothing. Then as he turned around in a slow circular sweep of the ocean's horizon, he saw it, a hundred feet off starboard, a large adult humpback whale breaching the calm sea surface. It was moving away from the *Conch II* in its own water world. Placing his binoculars to his eyes, he studied the horizon and saw nothing. He remembered the technician who installed it saying that large whales or pods of orcas or dolphins could set it off. These were their feeding grounds, he reminded himself, as he reset the alarm. He then rejoined the others who had waited on his return.

Taylor felt that he should respond to assure the group that he sincerely believed they were doing the right thing and that he was truly onboard for the mission, not just the paycheck. "Gentlemen, I fully understand and appreciate what you've gone through to arrive at your conclusion and ultimate decision. My ops team will not take lightly your mission and our obligation to fulfill it. You have my word and commitment. We will not fail you," he exclaimed fervently.

Boyer rose to his feet. "Taylor, I believe I speak for everyone here in saying that what we've heard from you and seen in you thus far fits the bill. You are what we've bargained for, although not exactly what I'd call a bargain." The other pack members exhibited guarded grins with Boyer's remark until the sight of Taylor's big smile gave them tacit permission to laugh out loud.

It was Boyer who had closely observed Taylor's Bloody Mary–mixing method both times when he confessed, "I must admit, sir, that

I was as confident as I was curious about your precision drink-making being the exact same both times."

"What do you mean the same," Taylor asked.

"I made a mental note of your Bloody Mary recipe. When you started to make a second one later, I remarked to Carpenter here, with a friendly wager, that I was confident you'd concoct it precisely the same with no variance in your ingredient portions. I wrote them down and Carpenter checked them off. I won. You were consistent with your precision, which shows me that it's in your character. I commend you," Boyer said sincerely.

Taylor was amused, saying, "I'm glad I've provided an early return on Mr. Boyer's investment here. As for Mr. Carpenter, my advice for the future is never bet against the Delta Force. I'm guessing Mr. Boyer's military experience taught him that being precise is only praiseworthy if done consistently."

Surprised, Boyer asked, "How did you know I was ex-military?"

"Because you still wear it well, sir. Navy officer, right?" Taylor offered with admiration.

"Yes. Right again. Thanks for noticing," Boyer said with a grin.

"We had all guessed, army grunt," Laisum chuckled along with his colleagues.

Returning to the topic of the mission, Rincon suggested that "entry, seizure, and exit" operations on the streets of Mexico with the "six dirt bag fugitives" should be a "cakewalk" compared to the high wall, gated, alarmed estates of Santa Barbara.

Taylor rejected that assumption, stating, "On the surface one might think so, except for one critical element. Our six targeted subjects are filled with suspicion, fear of detection, capture by rogue bounty hunters, or retribution by family members. They are always looking over their shoulders and around corners. They are constantly on the defensive, on the move, one eye always open when they sleep at night. Their guilty conscience is different than ours. With ours, we feel remorse and regret. Their guilty conscious is a generator for their innate radar, an early warning system helping them stay one step ahead of their pursuers. All of that amounts to having their personal innate security system. Moreover, their inner security system can be a formidable force. It can and will fight back," Taylor concluded.

"So how do your ops leaders deal with that element?" Rincon asked.

"We are trained to deal with the individual's psyche, especially the criminal mind and the fugitive's fear. It's like mental judo. You don't resist the opposite force. You go with their energy flow, but always in your favor. If he is a runner, get him to run to you, not away. You're then in control. The rest, gentlemen, are trade secrets I'm afraid," he said, receiving nods of acknowledgment from the Six-Pack.

3

FIGMENT OF YOUR IMAGINATION

Channel Islands Channel

McKinney suggested that if there were no more questions, they would conclude the meeting. "I know where some big beautiful blues are. Taylor is now a social guest only, unless he has anything else of ours to return," he said jokingly.

"Out of curiosity, I do have a serious question for Mr. McKinney," Taylor said with his professional face still on.

"Shoot," McKinney casually invited.

"Your yacht's name, *Conch II*, what is its origin, its significance?"

"Easy enough," McKinney said. "The conch (konk), as you know, is a sea mollusk, a sea snail that grows its own protective home in the form of either a large right-handed or left-handed swirled shell. That's to say that absent the conch, the host animal, the shell's natural curled design either curls to the left or to the right, spiraling inward, allowing them to be held naturally by the appropriate hand. But only the correct hand can hold them. When held to the mouth properly and blown into heartedly, a unique bass horn–like sound emits that can be heard for miles. In ancient times, islanders would call on the conch shell to others on nearby islands with coded messages. Early mariners aboard sailing ships used them to call out in heavy fog or moonless nights. They were in fact the very first wireless cell phones, not from Ma Bell but from Ma Nature. So in deference to the very first cell phone on earth, I named my boat Conch the Second."

"I'm sincerely impressed." Taylor slowly saluted McKinney.

"And McKinney was there when the first one was created too," Carpenter laughingly threw out there to everyone's amusement.

"Well some of you have probably never heard the conch shell sound before. So for your listening enjoyment, I'll take my two shells out of the display case below deck and give a little demonstration," he said with enthusiasm.

McKinney turned to go below deck when Taylor quickly asked, "Sir, would these two conch shells do?" From his black bag, he hoisted one shell in each hand high above his head. The pack members were once again mesmerized by the surprise appearance of objects before believed to be unknown to Taylor, not to mention out of his reach. The pinkish, beige shells sparkled with their polished shine drawing everyone's attention away from McKinney's dumbstruck face. Boyer and Rincon immediately testified that Taylor had never been below deck from the moment he came aboard.

McKinney, still staring in disbelief, stuttered, "Those, those are my conch shells!"

Taylor apologetically exclaimed, "Mr. McKinney, I never ask my ops leaders to take a test challenge for a client without my doing the same."

McKinney, still stunned, said, "But our docks are gated at night with four harbor security guards on the water and three on land. Are you a former Navy SEAL too?"

"No. They aren't the only Special Forces who can hold their breath underwater for more than four minutes. A SEAL's only specialty is balancing a beach ball on its nose. My team is trained in water, on land, and in the air. I felt it only fair and fitting that I satisfy your curiosity firsthand as did the others," he said with restrained modesty.

The other pack members applauded with an undercurrent of laughter at McKinney's expense. Meanwhile, Taylor was reminding himself of his other private reasons for wanting to covertly board McKinney's yacht last night in the harbor. He wanted to sweep the boat for any hidden listening devices or cameras before the meeting, which came up negative. He was curious to see the buffet of high-tech communications equipment McKinney had installed on the *Conch II*. Lastly, Taylor felt it necessary to attach a hidden GPS tracking device to the *Conch II* for reasons he hadn't determined yet but felt compelled to do so, *just for the hell of it*, he told himself. Secretly he also wanted bragging rights with his teammates. Keeping his Special Forces skills "field-tested" sharp was a point of pride for Taylor. He didn't have the benefit of military war games anymore, so client games craftily came into play at every opportunity he could create one. After all, "creating opportunities" was his tactical mantra.

Handing the two conch shells over to McKinney, Taylor politely commented, "I'm ready for that sound demonstration now, sir, if you are still willing."

"Most definitely. Lend me your ear," he said with a smirk as he jokingly leaned toward Taylor's head. He then pulled back with a laugh, curled his right hand around the shell's inner curvature, placed his lips to the apex of the shell's tight tip blow hole, and blew with the power of Dizzy Gillespie. A deep, billowy bass sound spiraled around inside before launching itself into the air and ears of everyone onboard, bringing impressed smiles to their amazed faces.

As though Neptune himself had used the conch shell to summon his sea chariot, there appeared alongside the yacht the sleekest racing boat McKinney and his comrades had ever seen. No one saw or heard it coming, no alarm or flashing yellow light. The entire Six-Pack were on their feet along the starboard rail starring in awe at the aerodynamically sleek, 46-foot long, all-black cigarette-style, high-performance racing boat with an unusually thin tapered hull. The coast guard had nicknamed them Go Fasts, popular among the drug runners in the Caribbean. But this one was definitely a newer generation, McKinney observed, possibly a concept model, he opined.

In the boat's cockpit stood a tall, attractive, young brunette woman dressed in an all-black, loose-fitting nylon, waterproof windbreaker and pants. Her black cap was on backward, allowing full view of her tan, athletic face. The black wraparound sunglasses hid her aquamarine eyes. A phone headset extended from one ear around to the narrow black microphone bar in front of her mouth, calling attention to her full sensual lips. She stood behind the pilot's wheel in a pose befitting a professional photoshoot while the muted rumbling of its 2x Mercury Racing 1,075-SCI engines idled.

The Six-Pack were silent, seemingly stupefied by the sight before them, their eyes alternating between the mystery woman in black and the mysterious black boat, which were merged as a single secret package. They were mesmerized by what appeared to be a mirage, an image of a boat that was difficult to delineate in the sparkling water. Boyer sensed something strange about this boat, admitting though that maybe it was the Bloody Marys and the reflective sea sunshine affecting his vision. Every square inch of the boat was painted flat black, no chrome, no glass, and no reflectors. All of the exposed accessories were black, the cleats flush with the body. He found it difficult to discern the sea's surface next to the boat, both a blended sparkling blue gray.

Then it struck him. Boyer had habitually kept up with the US Naval Institute (USNI) *Proceedings* magazine regarding new technology and innovative equipment. The navy was always looking for a stealth paint application for their fleet of ships. He had recently read about a nanotechnology additive to the paints used by the navy that they called chameleon camouflage. It acted as a nonglare, smoked glass mirror. When applied in the form of millions of minuscule pixel grains in the flat black paint, it captured the ever-changing water tones over the mass of the boat. Wherever it moved to, it would adopt the natural color tones thrown off by its immediate surroundings, a mirror image of its physical environment. It became one with nature, virtually invisible from a distance. Boyer never dreamed that he would ever see it to believe it, albeit, barely.

He was excited to tell his friends that they, too, were witnesses to the greatest advancement in naval stealth in maritime history. Its virtual invisibility had been tested in sun, moon, pyrotechnics, and search lights. He assumed it to be mixed with the already successful state-of-the-art radar-scattering paint used on all of our stealth planes since the Blackbird SR-71 in 1964, the F-117 Nighthawk in the '70s, Tacit Blue in the '80s, B-2 Batwing in the '90s, and F-22 Raptor for the new millennium. The high-precision attachment of the radar-resistant skin had a very fine tolerance of 0.009 inches, giving its mass a low radar signature. And it was low enough in the water that its silhouette on the horizon was negligible. The boat's low agitation propeller, ceramic exhaust, and closed cooling systems eliminated 94 percent of its normal wake and 85 percent of its high-speed wake. Its custom-molded, high tensile strength, wave-piercing hull was of the latest composite technology using lightweight carbon and Kevlar, low detection properties for low-probability-of-intercept radar. If that were not enough, it had a passive radar receiver in order not to provide a transmission signature. In a full throttle dash, it could reach an incredible 130-mph and carve a hard turn at 100-mph. The noise abatement technology used on commercial jets was also applied to this powerful machine, contributing to its overall stealth.

Taylor and the pilot were the only team members with the need to know knowledge that this high-tech toy was a beta test loaner from the highest US Naval command via their black ops intelligence back channels. They wanted it field tested with no military markings in noncombat waters by trusted civilians with top classified clearance. What better civilians to test it than the pilot, a former Navy Intelligence officer, and its passenger, a former Special Forces officer.

McKinney began to connect some dots in his mind as to the black boat's sudden and timely appearance, starting with no yellow, flashing dot. How did this mysterious female pilot know where and exactly when to show up? The craft had not appeared on his radar, not a single bleep. Yet mere minutes after he had made the money transfer to Taylor's Bahamian account, the boat came alongside precisely when they had concluded their meeting. The only one onboard not surprised by its timely arrival was Taylor. But how, he pondered. How did she know to pace her speed to arrive on the second they had concluded the meeting? McKinney was wondering what other high-tech tricks they had hidden away. If this was an example of how he was going to conduct the mission, then why should he concern himself about the what, and how. More power to him, he concluded. He just wished he could witness the whole mission unfold into an action adventure movie for his viewing.

40

Rincon broke the silence, asking Taylor, "Did you borrow Batman's boat?"

Taylor laughed as he threw his black bag over to the pilot. "The idea is to make others feel as blind as a bat, Mr. Rincon."

He then stood up on the rail, balanced himself before making a standing five-foot leap to the black boat, landing on the passenger's seat.

Carpenter asked Taylor, "I don't see a name, what is she called?"

"Figment."

"Of your imagination?" Carpenter responded.

"No. Of yours," Taylor corrected.

McKinney called out to Taylor, "Right-handed or left-handed?"

"Left," came the reply.

McKinney tossed the left-handed conch shell with ease to Taylor. He caught it with a thankful smile and then placed it to his lips. He blew hard on the tip opening, producing a deep bellow bass sound as though sending a signal to the pilot to push on. Aligned along the rail, the Six-Pack applauded approvingly on cue. With Taylor and the pilot now seated, the black boat launched forward like an arrow from a bow, morphing into the ocean's blue-gray surface as one, a whisper in the soft wind of the channel.

4

THE MEXICAN EYE OF GOD

Mexico City, Mexico

In an unprecedented move by Mexico's attorney general, 737 agents of the Federal Judicial Police (PJF) and the National Institute to Combat Drugs (INDC) were fired to shake up its own agency. In addition, two-thirds of the INDC's regional offices were closed across the republic. The PJF was abolished and a new force, the *Policia Federal de Investigación y Apoyo Judicial* (PFIAJ / Federal Police of Investigation and Judicial Support), was created. The PFIAJ was now in charge of fighting drug trafficking, corruption, and other federal crimes.

The massive termination of federal law enforcement officers and investigative agents in Mexico followed United States congressional hearings where incriminating evidence was presented citing that US DEA funds were being misused in Mexico to protect the very drug cartels they were supposed to be fighting. Although corruption was endemic in Mexico, it was shown to be rampant and out of control at all levels of the federal police and judicial departments.

A survivor of the firings was the department's top-ranking female, Maria Teresa Colima. The female element, she claimed, helped to save her from the "guilt by association" with the all-male, inner circle, criminal element of the investigative department. The

Mexican macho culture would never have allowed her in, not that she wanted in with her high ethical standards. She proudly boasted that her uncompromising core values were never in question, in contrast with members of the "brotherhood," with the emphasis on *hood*, as she referred to them. Maria Teresa credited her father with instilling those personal and professional sound principles in her by example. He would remind her, "*El que con lobos anda, a aullar se ensena* (He who keeps company with wolves, learns to howl)." The memory of such a shining example had become bittersweet since her father, Marc Antonio Colima, had not survived to become part of the new, sanitized PFIAJ. This was not as a result of the attorney general's purge but rather by an unknown assassin's bullets sent successfully to silence him two days after the agency firings.

Sr. Colima was an honest, senior-level official in the federal justice department who knew something about someone, worthy of murder, so it seemed. Mattie, her father's nickname of endearment for Maria Teresa, had received a phone call at work from her father five hours before the fatal shooting. They were to have dinner together and share professional off-the-record notes, conspiracy theories, and crime buster stories as they always did when they met. For the last several months, he had been saying, "The corrupt federal police and judicial agency was a cancer in the nation. They could no longer ignore or deny it was there. It must be cut out."

Mattie had followed her father's professional footsteps on a career path that began with local, routine police investigative work. She quickly moved on to the Federal District Judicial Police Department and soon after with the Federal Judicial Police, where she transitioned over to the all-new PFIAJ.

Mattie's unblemished career record and solid work ethic had been rewarded with the new, nonpolitical, high-ranking title of Deputy Director, second in command in the Office of Investigative and Judicial Liaison within the PFIAJ. What the position lacked in hierarchic operational power, compared to the headquarters' command positions, it made up for with its administrative control over the gathering and dissemination of all criminal records. This included ongoing investigative cases, prosecutorial files, and a vast national computer network and archive of known criminal profiles. Albeit classified, she had a direct line of communication with the General Directorate of Intelligence and National Security (DISEN / *Direction de Information de Seguridad Nacional).*

Now Mattie stood in the polished mahogany-framed doorway of the PFIAJ director's vacant office. It was hard to believe that her Deputy Director promotion had taken place just four years earlier. She would now occupy the vacated director's office, effective immediately. Her boss's retirement, because of failing health, came sooner than expected. Mattie felt she had been ready for the promotion for some time, eager to instill her own ideas for more proactive communications in national crimefighting. "We must tag and track every known criminal from the very first conviction to the grave and beyond," she would exaggerate for effect.

She was pleased with the positive turnaround of the PFIAJ that her predecessor had affected, virtually free of the corruption that had caused the demise of the PJF administration. It was a daunting task, and she gave the deserved credit to her now retired boss. Hers was to be a different task—one that was self-imposed. It would challenge every moral fiber of her being and take her on a journey of justice and revenge that she had been waiting to travel for four patient years. Mattie had been persistent and meticulous in searching for the truth about her father's assassination. Every free moment and discreet opportunity to investigate her father's murder case, she did. She rigorously pursued every lead and theory conceived of by herself and others on the case. Two years ago, the justice department had declared the murder case "Cold," then a year later officially "Closed." With the formal acceptance of the directorship position, in control of the powerful, omnipresent PFIAJ's intelligence liaison sector, she secretly vowed in her father's memory and honor to covertly open the case and pursue that dark path, to make it "Hot" again—very hot!

Three office workers excused themselves as they moved past her in the office entranceway. They were carrying boxes from her old office to unpack in her new headquarters, a plush, burnished wood-paneled room with a large, rectangular oriental rug covering three quarters of the blonde hardwood floor. The requisite, large, black framed photograph of Mexico's president dominated the wall behind the credenza with the Mexican flag on its wood and brass staff to the left.

One box in particular she instructed to leave alone on top of the credenza. She wanted to unpack it with care. While the workers quickly placed her books and manuals on shelves and files in the cabinets, she remained in the doorway at the office edge assessing the enormity of the new position. She had always been told that, "Knowledge is power." And here she found herself at the very fountain of knowledge, the mother's milk of national intelligence gathering, archiving, and dissemination. She was now the keeper and controller of all the officially gathered data on the country's violators of the law, both national and international as they related to Mexico. Mattie knew that she not only had unobstructed access to every criminal's *dossier* but also how and to whom they would be distributed. She knew now she could avenge her father's murder.

With her new office now ready to occupy, she symbolically and purposefully took the first step of her new journey as she set her foot forward into the director's domain, the nation's memory bank of the lawless. She would soon make her first withdrawals.

Before Mattie took her place in the director's dark-red leather, high back chair, she reached into the one box left on the credenza. She tenderly began to place framed photos atop the long, polished, dark wood credenza behind her desk. The first four pictures showed Mattie, her parents, and younger brother, Angelino, from different celebratory moments in her youth. The fifth framed photo was a wide angle shot of Mattie alongside her father and six other well-dressed, high-ranking government officials taken less than a year before his assassination. Professionally, Marc Antonio Colima had known them all intimately throughout his entire career. Maybe too intimately.

The sixth and final framed photo she placed on the left side of her desk, and she then sat down in the oversized director's chair. This photo showed a bright sky blue background with two tall, beautiful, dark aquamarine-eyed, brunette, female college students dressed in graduation gowns and mortarboards. They were smiling happily, displaying their diploma in one hand, with their other arm around one another in a close embrace, causing the illusion of seeing identical twins.

Turning away from the photo of her former college roommate and long-time best friend, Mattie placed her maiden cell phone call from her new office. An energetic female voice answered on the third ring, "Lori Sandberg."

"*Como estas tu, mi amigita gringita? Habla Mattie* (How are you my dear American friend? This is Mattie)."

"Mattie! I can't believe it. I was going to call you this afternoon. We still have that ESP thing going after all these years. How are you and your sweet *mamacita*?"

"We are all just fine. Mama is well and remains active teaching at the university."

"You are both strong women, Mattie. And you could write a book on survival skills. When do I hear about your next exciting installment?"

"We must definitely still have our ESP linkup going. Because here is the title of my next chapter, 'Maria Teresa Colima, Director of the Federal Investigative and Judicial Liaison Office,' the memory bank of the investigative brain trust, crime bust agency, at your service."

"Director Mattie! I am so proud of you. Congratulations! And I know your *papi* would be so very proud. You've always been the agency's 'go-to gal.' And mine too. This is great news. My plan to call you is even timelier now than before. But I need to talk to you in person, Mattie, soon."

"That's why I really called as well. The news of my promotion is secondary to what I need to discuss privately with you, Lori. Now that I have more control and latitude to operate within the agency, you are my 'go-to gal,' for a personal and professional matter all wrapped into one."

"Thanks, babe. But what about your 'go-to guy' brother of yours?"

"Still in Rome. He's my secret weapon when needed, which I'll explain later. What about you? How can I help?" Mattie offered sincerely.

"My matter is urgent for resource and logistical reasons. How soon can we meet?" Lori asked with a needy undertone in her voice.

"First of all, where are you? It's hard to tell with cell phones nowadays," Mattie asked.

"In Las Vegas. And my phone is a secured line in case you were wondering. How about you?"

"Same here. With your work, I assumed as much," she said, aware of Lori's clandestine logistical and recon work for US government security and intelligence agencies.

Over the years, the two had cooperated with one another at various levels of transborder intelligence sharing in seeking and capturing the bad guys from both countries. For now, neither one realized that their individual agendas would soon become a symbiotic alliance at the highest level of cooperation, codependency, and shared survival skills.

"I have to be in Washington, DC, in a few days for formal introductions and briefings with your federal alphabet soup," she said, referring to the US DEA, FBI, INS, and CIA. "I can be in Vegas tomorrow, late afternoon. We both have a lot of ground to cover, *amigita*, so I'll stay for as long as we both need."

Lori took those words literally, realizing that the "ground to cover" could well be the entire Republic of Mexico. But she would save her commentary on that broad subject for Mattie's arrival. "You are awesome, Mattie. Mexico's new Wonder Woman," she said, recalling their college days when they would watch the television reruns of the comic book character that actress Linda Carter made famous. They would jokingly fantasize about one day being action adventure heroines, bringing the evildoers to justice with their golden "truth rope."

"Do you think Wonder Woman wears a Wonder Bra?" Lori asked laughingly.

"Well I'm sure we can find a couple of Wonder Woman outfits in Vegas," Mattie speculated jovially.

"Yes. But here in Vegas, they would be topless with dollar bills stuffed around the rim of the satin blue bottoms," Lori snickered aloud.

They recalled their college dormitory days, practicing the Wonder Woman costume spin in their bra and underpants, then wrestling their athletic yet voluptuous bodies on the bed to see who really had the superstrength to rule the "Wonder World," laughing louder with every remembrance.

"Please stop. You're killing me," Lori pleaded, as though out of breath.

"I agree. We'll have time to reminisce later. For now, expect me to call you from the Las Vegas airport. We'll need to be as discreet as possible, so don't pick me up. Just tell me the hotel when I call. Does that work for you?"

"Sounds perfect, babe. We'll discuss other security measures when you're here. And, Mattie, please don't forget to bring our bottle of Agave Suave," Lori implored her.

"I would never forget Big Blue. My *Reserva de Casa* is your *Reserva de Casa*," Mattie offered openly.

Hanging up the phone, Mattie's finger moved adroitly over the keypad. She knew *Mi Tio's* bar wouldn't be open until 11:00 a.m., but Tio Chuey was always in his bar office by nine every weekday morning. Chuey Cuellar was an old family friend from the Federal Police force where he retired two years before the old department was abolished. Being an honest field investigator, the corrupt inner circle of hoods had pushed him out. He would not tolerate the senior officials' self-serving interpretation of the laws for their own personal gain and power. Chuey had openly recited the traditional "Four Ps" of the Mexican government: pedigree, position, power, and pesos as being "the corruptive forces that have raped and pillaged our country throughout our history." Marc Antonio would sadly remind his friend, "*Alla van leyes, donde quieren reyes* (Laws go wherever kings want them to go)."

Now, at the age of sixty-one, Chuey Cuellar was the owner and operator of the well-renowned *Mi Tio's* tequila saloon, boasting the largest offering of tequila brands on the planet, over 364 labels at last tally. Patrons, from tourists to the hardcore regulars, could choose from the low cost Silver (Blanco) tequila shots or upgrade to the "young gold, aged gold, and old gold" (*Joven, Reposado*, and *Anejo*). But Tio Chuey kept the *Reserva de Casa* (house reserve, extra *anejo*, ultrapremium) brands locked behind a shatter-proof, glass door showcase. They were made available to the most discriminating connoisseurs of 100 percent Weber blue agave, three distillations, and three to five years aged, golden tequila. His smoothest sipping, ultrapremium tequilas were *Cuervo Presidential, Don Julio, Porfidio, Patron, Jose Cuervo Reserva de la Familia,* and *Agave Suave.* The latter he described as rich liquid silk. "When I come back to earth reincarnated, I want to be a highly evolved maguey worm living in a bottle of *Agave Suave* (smooth agave)," Chuey would confess to Mattie.

Mi Tio's was one block north of the city's main center, Constitution Plaza, better known as the *Zócalo.* It was on the other side of Guatemala Street on the corner of *Avenida 5 de Febrero,* directly behind the Metropolitan Cathedral. "That's God's way of closing his eyes while the priests enjoy a shot or two," Tio Chuey would whisper, as though in the confessional. Chuey had suggested to the cathedral priests that instead of cheap grape juice and a dry wafer for mass, they should serve a wedge of lime, a pinch of salt, and a shot of Jose Cuervo to bring more parishioners into the flock. The priests' only response was whether Jose Cuervo was a Catholic or not? "He's a saint to many," Chuey respond.

Tio Chuey greeted Mattie warmly as always, asking how he could be of service to his best friend's daughter and contemporary co-conspirator.

"*Mi cardio Tio* (My dear uncle), is it possible to have a liter of *Agave Suave* sent over to my office this afternoon?" she asked pleadingly.

"For you my *concentida* (my favorite), anything you desire. And this *Reserva de Casa* is on the *casa* to congratulate you for your much anticipated and deserved promotion to director," he said with great pride. "Your beloved father must be beaming with happiness for his Mattie."

"Thank you so much, Tio. You're so sweet. But we both know what it will take to really put a smile on his face," she said, having to say no more to the man who had partnered with her profound motivation for revenge and justice. "How did you know about the promotion, Tio? There hasn't been a press release yet," she asked rhetorically. She knew he would be way ahead of the media on any given day. She had been aware of Chuey's unofficial, covert role as an informant for her father, and for years providing her with the gossip openly and inadvertently whispered at his bar. *Mi Tio's* had become a local watering hole for government officials and bureau-crats alike from the nearby federal buildings. "Drunken tongues are talking tongues," Chuey would say to her. He did not discourage it, but rather carefully and skillfully encouraged it. He was old enough to remember the Second World War US defense slogan, "Loose Lips Sink Ships."' The loose lips at *Mi Tio's* were serving him well in his shared mission with Mattie. But their sights were set on "ships of state," the corrupt oligarchs at the helm.

Mattie hung up and turned her executive chair toward the framed photos on the credenza. She then took the only item left out of the box. It was a *Huichol* Indian–crafted, multicolored weaving of yarn, referred to as the Eye of God, the *Ojo de Dios*. It was the size of a large hand forming eight concentric-like squares, each a different bright color of the rainbow. The one square inch center was a soft yellow yarn, bordered by red yarn, followed by purple, orange, green, blue, yellow, and red for the outer square.

Two 10-inch long, crossed thin sticks created the simple back support frame for the eight tightly stretched colored squared designs called rhomboids of woven yarn. The outer tips of the eight rhom-boids sported small yellow pompoms, giving the handcrafted piece a festive look. But the intended look was indeed to be the *Ojo de Dios*.

Mattie held the thirty-eight-year-old Eye of God with fondness. Borrowed from the traditional Mexican *Huichol* Indian folklore, her father had placed it by her crib when a newborn baby, praying that God would keep an eye on her. She never parted with it, even during her college days. As an adult, it had remained in her office, now with a strong sense of irony, wishing that it had been nearer to her father.

Mattie placed the weaving to the edge of the wide framed photo of the six posed senior government associates of her fathers. Focusing sternly on one man in particular wearing a red silk tie, she placed her finger on the yellow center square of the Eye of God. Speaking aloud, she solemnly vowed, "*Cosas a Dios dejadas, son bien vengadas* (Things left to God are well avenged)." She then pressed her finger over the same man in the group photo, paraphrasing in an angry whisper, "*Cosas a Mattie dejadas, son bien vengadas!*"

Chuey Cuellar reached into his private glass cabinet and carefully removed a tall blue bottle of *Agave Suave*, ultrapremium tequila. He placed it reverently in a long, rectangular wooden box lined with a cushion of crumpled newspaper pages. He folded a handwritten card of congratulations and placed it alongside the reposed bottle before securing the wooden top. Chuey knew the box would be X-rayed by her agency's security guards in the Federal Police building lobby, but not opened. It didn't matter either way, he thought. Only Mattie would understand his congratulatory message, which read, "The good news of your promotion was not in today's paper, although the future was foretold in the past. Here is a one-liter toast, wishing you much success. Your loyal friend and servant, fondly, Tio Chuey."

He handed the sealed wooden box to a bicycle messenger along with a 100-peso note. The young man would ride one block past the south end of the *Zócalo* to Mattie's office building. It would be one of many cumshaw bottles that arrived daily at the PFIAJ.

5

VATICAN CITY SPOOK

Rome, Italy

Vatican City, Rome, Italy, described by British writer Byron as "the city of the soul." It had been the working residence for the young Mexican priest for over five years. Compared to the elder papal hierarchy, his thirty-seven years of age made him a youngster within *La Santa Sede*, the Holy See of Rome. Father Angelino was there at the service of Cardinal Montenegro of Mexico, laboring six days a week at the Vatican's complex of offices that administered church affairs at the highest level. His greatly admired intellect and multilingual skills provided him with the opportunities to research and help write doctrinal policies, speeches, and official letters for a number of the twelve different pontifical councils.

In his youth, Angelino Colima had been an honor student at the best private schools in Mexico City, for the most part, because he had been homeschooled during his free time by his professor mother. She was an academician who held a master's degree in North American history from the University of Texas and a doctorate degree in political science from Georgetown University in Washington, DC. Angelino chose his mother's alma mater in Washington for both under- and postgraduate degrees, again with honors.

While studying in Washington, he became a devotee of former US President Thomas Jefferson, admiring his wisdom on matters of secular religion and of the separation of church and state. Becoming a Catholic priest never changed his Jeffersonian view on the parting of religion and government founded on traditional English deism. Thus followed that governments were to be formed and run by the people, not as an extension of the dogma provided by the church for the people's moral guidance. Such was his church's attempted hegemony over his government and people—all in profound conflict with his own private position of separation of church and state, in particular an oligarchy.

Growing up in Mexico and serving as a young priest there, he learned of the church's long historical Catholic imperium originally imposed on government politics, official national policy, and social education. Over time, with periodical revised constitutions by Federal reformists, the government pushed the Mexican church's hierarchy back with so many restrictive articles that scholars would refer to the Mexican constitution as the Catholic constitution. The current postrevolution constitution of 1917 had so many anticlerical articles and social reforms restricting the power and reach of the Catholic church that scholars then deemed the constitution "hostile" to the issue of church and state separation. By 1992, the anticlerical articles were substantially reformed, lifting most restrictions and restoring legal status to all religious groups. Church and state in Mexico now existed with only a couple of degrees of separation—a confidential phone call, an unofficial visit.

This motivated Angelino to fervently share Jefferson's belief that the alliance of religion and government corrupted both, and that endangered the liberty of the human mind. He would not allow that to happen to himself, although his soul remained devoted to his God. Intellectually he moved in a different direction than the Roman Catholic church, away from its intended dominion of Mexico and its oppressed people. He knew that leaving the church was not the answer. He felt compelled to learn more about it at its highest level, at the Holy See in Vatican City. His religious beliefs were not an issue. At this juncture in his young life, he believed two truths as absolutes, that his God was the universe, and that as a Holy Father, he was a fraud. But his persistence to carry on came from the pursuit of a third truth, which was the cause and impetus for his rebellious spirit and dogged determination to find it.

Young Angelino learned the game of chess from his father at a young age. Before departing for Rome, he posed a very profound and foretelling question to his son, "Always ask yourself, why is there a bishop on the board among kings, queens, and knights?" While at the Holy See, he learned why the bishop moved diagonally.

The inspiration for his rebellious spirit was an eighteenth-century Mexican priest, national hero, and icon, the egalitarian Miguel Hidalgo. In his time, Father Hidalgo had read books banned by the church. He had challenged the absolute authority of the Popes in Rome. He openly denounced the Spanish rulers for their three hundred years' domination and pillage of Mexico. On September 17, 1810, this priest stood before his humble little church in the pueblo of Guanajuato and gave a shout heard throughout the nation, known as *El Grito*, "*Que Viva Mexico—Que viva la independencia*! (Long live Mexico—Long live independence!)" It became the country's enduring cry for the nation's enduring independence. Now Angelino wanted to cry out but had not yet found the words. Until then he would continue his search in Vatican City, Mexico City, or wherever the truth could be found.

During his thirteen years as a priest, Father Angelino had never harbored any desire to be a member of the clergy or pontifical academies. "Papal material I am not," he had told his family with amused admission. He wanted to be close to the *Secretaria Apostolica*, the Secretary of State, the closest assistant to the Pope, the Holy See's equivalent of a prime minister. Neither religiosity nor personal ambition motivated him. The search for the truth did. And it could only be found at the Roman Curia, the Pope's governing high court. He didn't possess the keys to the kingdom, but he did have something of greater importance for his purposes—the heavily guarded computer password to access the confidential Curia archives on matters of the most sensitive nature, not to mention political value worldwide. His interest was only Mexico.

Any student of the Roman Catholic church knew its history of espionage and counterespionage as far back as Judas. Father Angelino's knowledge of such covert practices was profound from centuries-past Papist anarchists to the benign gathering of information on the Papal States until they united as democratic Italian territories in 1870. Internal spying was commonplace between church reformers and conservatives, between European Pope supporters and non-European detractors. He recalled the underground activities of Vatican Secretariat of State Monsignor Umberto Benigi, to gag Catholic scholars of the modernist movement.

The church's most notable counterintelligence operation was the sending of ordinary priests into the old, "Godless" Soviet Union. In the early 1940s, they discovered an apostate Catholic monk working for the Nazis. And so it was within the Holy See, employing an elite cadre of spies around the globe by bishops and clergy while outside intelligence operatives spied on the Vatican to discover its secrets and to anticipate its more impactful movements and proclamations.

The Holy See's emphasis on secrecy went beyond its sensitivity to meddling from the outside. Father Angelino was acutely aware of the periodical complex bug-sweeps conducted by high-tech teams keen on foiling a spy. Both subjective and objective circumstances in Mexico had turned him into one of those spies, albeit unwillingly. As an insider of the Holy See, his trusted position and innate cunning would be his only tools of the clandestine craft. His purpose was not for political dissent or fractious activism. He simply wanted the truth and to act upon it justly. He had surreptitiously discovered more than he had cared to. He had no choice but to act, and now.

Father Angelino had visited his home in Mexico City only once during his five-year-tenure in Vatican City, sadly to attend his father's funeral. He had begun his service to the church at the Mexico City diocese at the age of twenty-four, rising quickly in the Bishopric staff hierarchy. He soon reported to the then Archbishop Montenegro, one of Mexico's four cardinals. When he ascended to the level of cardinal, Father Angelino was the first one called to serve his administrative needs on matters of general affairs for Mexico's seventy-five million Catholics. When Cardinal Montenegro became involved in

Vatican matters of foreign affairs, Father Angelino moved to Rome. Following his father's death, Angelino requested and received permission to work exclusively with the Pontifical Council for the Pastoral Care of Migrants and Itinerant People.

From this new vista of the world's populous, he had become a witness to the 175 million people currently residing in a country different from their country of origin, the United States in particular. He not only immersed himself in studying official pontifical doctrine on the matter, he also had been diligently tracking the migration data of Mexicans into the United States for three years with astonishment and had concluded one thing for certain. The five thousand Mexicans per day migration stream into the US was no incidental flow of humanity immigrating to a neighboring country. It was a deliberate insertion of one foreign society into another's with purpose, well calculated, organized, politically supported, and most definitely economically beneficial for both Mexico and the Catholic church with a more affluent flock.

Father Angelino had paid special attention to the Roman Curia's official words as well as deeds in support of the mass Mexican migration into the US. It had become more vocal and aggressive recently as the numbers of their flock from one impoverished nation into an affluent one became more beneficial for Mexico. *If the pasture is indeed greener on the other side, by all means, cross over, especially if you can send some of that green back home as well*, the church supported, he discovered.

Such official Vatican support and sympathy for Mexican and worldwide migrants came stamped with the Roman pontiff's "supreme, full, and immediate power in the universal church," his Holiness's seal of approval, *Christus Dominus 9*, "for the good of the churches and in the service of the sacred pastors."

If Father Angelino had learned one thing during his service at the Vatican, it was that the Roman Catholic church could produce and promote any cause they cared to for whatever gain, real or divine, as long as it was signed off with the imprimatur "*Christus Dominus 9*," known to all in the Holy See and universal church as *Jus Divinum*, Divine Law.

The pertinent council *Jus Divinum* documents in the form of papal doctrine, letters, and speeches on migrants were now all secretly copied and bundled into an official Vatican courier satchel and sealed by Father Angelino. Downloading onto a disc was impossible from his protected office, nor would he take the risk of electronic file transfers being traced. Fortunately, hard copy reproductions could be made given the church's penchant for paper that could be officially hand-stamped or sealed the old fashion way, the arcane Roman Curia's way. At times he thought the Vatican would prefer to go back to the age of quills and ink, rather than the computer.

This occasion called for him to be the official courier of the secreted sealed satchel aboard his afternoon Alitalia flight #318 to Mexico City. The same Vatican seal on his passport would be as good as a diplomatic pass, sending him through airport immigration and customs hassle free from Rome to Mexico City. That would be the easy part, he thought.

For now Father Angelino was confronted by the most difficult moment of his priesthood. He had to face his Lord with his antipathy through prayer regarding his self-imposed exile from the Vatican, the holiest center of the Catholic church of Christendom. This premeditated decision was finalized the day before when he received a long-awaited e-mail message from Mexico that said nothing more than, "The Eye of God has seen the truth."

His discreet, cryptic, electronic response was a full screen, black and white photograph with no text of a well-known marble sculpture in Rome by the famous seventeenth-century artist Gianlorenzo Bernini. The large, elongated statue portrayed a seated naked woman upon a long drapery that had concealed her form. In her raised right hand, she held the rays of the sun while her left foot was on a large globe. The quizzical image could only be interpreted by the recipient in Mexico. The moment it was received, their cabal would be set in motion.

The Mexican Father Angelino would not stand out among the scores of Vatican City priests with his tall, lean Italian looks, cropped black hair, Romanesque nose, and white warm smile. Up close, his blue eyes set him apart from his Mediterranean brethren. Neatly dressed in his freshly pressed black vestments, he left his apartment in the early morning. He journeyed for the final time by foot to the grand *Piazza San Pietro* to the Basilica of Saint Peter, Vatican City's most venerable landmark, the largest church in Christendom.

Standing momentarily at its entrance, he did not feel the intended inviting embrace of Bernini's vast, outstretched colonnades, which he described as a pair of "motherly arms," curving around the two sides of the grand oblong piazza, drawing all in its midst into the bosom of the basilica. Today he felt as though the inspired 284 Doric columns formed illusory massive arms that wanted to reach in and choke him. His gait quickened as he neared the imposing basilica that dominated the cityscape of Rome. Rancor shadowed every determined step forward across the 1,100-foot long piazza. There would be no turning back, today or tomorrow.

During his years in Rome, this was always his favorite walk, one he had enjoyed hundreds of times on his way to mass or to witness the Pope's ceremonial appearance from the center balcony window to bless worshipers and visitors. Beneath, the timeless Swiss Guards were standing their protocol posts dressed in the same colorful uniforms designed by Michelangelo nearly four hundred years ago. He had always wondered where Michelangelo was when the design order went out for the priests' vestments.

He understood all too well a priest's vow of poverty, although he had never possessed the religious fervor and piety of his priestly brothers. Father Angelino had always followed the rules. His loyalty and obedience to the church was without question, which is why now he had to be truthful before his God and clear his tortured conscience.

His first step toward divine reconciliation would be which door to enter the Basilica of Saint Peter by—the bronze Holy Door on the right, the original ancient basilica door in the center, or the Door of the Dead on the left? He removed his black biretta. For the first time ever, he entered on the left.

His entrance into St. Peters this day did not provide the spiritual perspective as in his past visits. The dramatic Baroque interior of stagey Catholic iconography, marble saints, winged angels, and statues that spoke to the faithful of piety, ecstasy, pain, and rage, this day communicated the latter two expressions to Father Angelino. All else felt inconsequential. His last three years of private pain and recent damning discoveries drove his rage to this unwanted moment of resolution.

He had forty-five altars to choose from for prayer. Instead, he walked with purpose around the massive church portals to the left nave of the enormous Michelangelo-designed basilica dome of golden light, the largest in the world. He continued past a magnificent array of ecclesiastical art works, memorials of marble and bronze, and stone portraits of Popes, toward his planned destination, Bernini's monument for the tomb of Pope Alexander VII. It was set into a large, 25-foot high concave niche with the statue of the Pope kneeling in hand-clasped prayer at the top of a base of multicolored marble. Bernini had surmounted it with a flowing red marble shroud that was held aside by a bronze skeleton. It was portrayed emerging from the tomb, holding up to the living an hourglass, a reminder of time's inexorable passage.

On one side of the base were allegorical figures of Prudence and Charity, which he felt defined his early years as a priest. The other side exhibited the figures of Truth, representing his recent travails at the Holy See in Rome, and Justice, foretelling the pursuit of a cause and its consequence awaiting him in Mexico. He knelt down on both knees beneath Truth and Justice with prayerful effusion and a solemn oath to his father. He stared darkly at the two statues, his hands vised tightly together, deliberately lowered with a quietus resolve, his heart aching as the day his father had died.

His invocation began as a prayer in whispered finality, "Dear Fathers in Heaven."

6

WONDER WOMEN ACTION FIGURES

Las Vegas, Nevada

C learing immigration and customs inspection with ease at the Las Vegas McClarran International Airport, Mattie headed straight to the lower terminal taxi stand. She punched in Lori's cell phone number and immediately heard her voice. "Hard Rock Hotel/Casino. How may I direct your call?"

"With reservations please."

Following a brief pause, the same-sounding woman responded, "Thank you for calling Hard Rock Hotel/Casino reservations. How may I help you?"

"Would you please quote me your best rate on a penthouse suite?" Mattie asked politely.

"Why certainly. That would be 790 dollars per night. What dates did you have in mind?"

"I'll call back in thirty minutes to let you know. Thank you," Mattie concluded while signing off quickly.

Thirty minutes later, Mattie was knocking on room door 790 at the Hard Rock Hotel off the Vegas strip. The door opened to the surprising and sexy presence of Wonder Woman, authentically costumed from her signature tiara to her well-exposed and ample bustier, down to her high red leather boots. She teasingly held up a loosely wound, gold-braided rope, threatening the new arrival jokingly. "Tonight, you will admit the truth, that I am the real Wonder Woman! Enter at your own risk!"

The morning was welcomed by Lori opening the balcony curtains and door to daylight and breezy desert air.

"The beauty of Big Blue comes through in the morning when you awaken with a clear head instead of a hangover," Mattie professed with a relaxed voice.

"And without a cleared-out stomach," Lori added in agreement. "Tell your Tio Chuey, I owe him a big wet kiss for the *Aquave Suave.*"

"Careful. Women call him *Mount Popocatépetl*, the volcano. There may be snow on top, but there's still fire down below," Mattie warned.

She had shared everything on her disquieted mind with Lori until midnight when they both had agreed, "A good day begins the night before."

Their a.m. breakfast had been delivered to the room where the two friends would remain sequestered until a one o'clock break. They both remained attired in only black bikini underpants, enjoying the fresh desert air drifting in from the balcony's opened double doors. Just as when they were college roommates doing their homework, they sat erect atop their folded legs at opposite corners on the end of the bed, leaning over to share notes between them as they studied the subject at hand.

They began their morning session with a candid exchange of assurances that their individual missions would remain classified, with information shared only as needed to protect the other party. Lori gave Mattie a secured cell phone programmed for dedicated communication only for themselves. Security codes, encryptions, and password were explained to Mattie. She was most impressed with the kill code for a timer, that when initiated would begin to meltdown the memory chip and circuit board within five seconds if ever it was at risk. "We call it our *Mission Impossible* feature," Lori said with a chuckle. "If that were ever to happen, I would receive an alert alarm followed by a text message showing the phone's last GPS location and of course, vice versa. You can also broadcast a silent signal to me telling your current GPS location with fifteen-minute automatic updates to track your movements covertly, just by pressing the keys 4-4-2. Just remember the letter code H-I-A."

"But 4-4-2 is easier I think," Mattie suggested.

"Not if you remember 'Here I Am,'" Lori simplified with a grin. "With all of the numbered codes and phone numbers to remember, that one is my fave."

Professionals in the intelligence community understood that numbers of any significance, classified or not, were never to be recorded. Lori reminded her of the uncompromising rule that, "A number written is your ass bitten."

"Yes, because it will come back to bite you in the butt," Mattie verified her English understanding of the rule. "And I'm counting on that happening to the one responsible for my father's murder," she added crisply.

"What do you mean?"

Mattie rose to draw a pad of paper from her briefcase. She placed the notepad in front of Lori displaying a clear white sheet of paper with a single line of eight random, handwritten digits.

"50807507. I'm hoping this number will not only bite but kick some ass. I need answers as to why my father wanted me to have those numbers just before he was killed," she said with a sharp edge to her voice.

"Start by telling me where you got this," Lori queried with a professional tone.

"Whoever shot father tried to find this set of numbers on him. The killer took his wallet as well. But father was too streetwise to ever put anything confidential or politically incriminating on his person. Remember, he was a federal police investigator. You don't trust your shadow."

"He trusted you, Mattie."

"Yes, babe, I know. And that's why he wanted me to have that number and the story behind it. I need more to go on than just a random series of digits. I discovered it on a small list of things he was going to talk with me about at his home. He had jotted down abbreviated notes to himself at home as a habit days before we met. But he never carried the notes with him."

"So this note never left your house?"

"Never. I found it where he left it, on top of his dresser."

"What else was on the list?"

"Only three insignificant subjects that I've looked into—nothing to them—small talk really. But this number was the fourth and last item on his list."

"Which means something?" Lori pursued with interest.

"This always meant that it was the most important thing he wanted to discuss. He always left the most pressing subject for the last—to make it an open-ended item—to discuss, 'ad nauseum,' as he would say."

"And after four years, you haven't come up with even a guess, not a clue?" Lori asked in frustration.

"Understand, Lori, that my department processes a billion bytes of data per day, a third is numbers. The first thing I did was to crosscheck this number with the number IDs of convicts countrywide. Nothing."

"So all Mexican convicts have the same eight numbers of digits?"

"Yes, the number follows you for life. You die—it goes with you. New convicts get new 'virgin numbers.' There are two prefix letters that only change when the 'con' changes his incarceration address."

"Have your investigators or code breakers taken a crack at it?"

"I couldn't risk anyone knowing that I was running a parallel investigation during the first two years the case was open, and a greater risk since the case was reclassified 'Closed.' That's why I'm asking you now, Lori, to run this by your people to see what they might make of it," Mattie solicited more as a friend than official investigator.

"Sure I can. And I will," she responded without hesitation. "But it helps if they have something contextual to put it into perspective. Like for instance, did it appear anywhere else among your father's personal effects at home or his office, a directory maybe? Had he been investigating money-laundering cases?"

"I'm sorry I don't have more than that. I was fortunate that the list was still there on his dresser. As a habit, he would review his list at home before leaving the house to meet me for dinner. He'd always look at the list then toss it in the wastebasket on the way out of the bedroom, a habit he fortunately broke that evening. Maybe subconsciously he thought the number should remain there in case his memory was permanently erased," Mattie said with a fatalistic tone.

Lori paused for a moment to process this new information before pursuing a different direction of questioning. She realized that Mattie had been going it alone for four years in her private investigation with no one to bounce ideas off of, or to play devil's advocate with. She sensed that her friend appreciated this opportunity to look at new angles with someone who was outside of the proverbial forest, with an expertise in counterintelligence to boot. What Lori also sensed was that Mattie knew that someone else was familiar with her father's weekly dining out habits with her. Somebody knew his routine, somebody close enough both professionally and personally. Lori decided not to take that path of probing at this time, preferring that Mattie be the one to raise that possibility or certitude. Back to the numbers, she decided.

"Short-term memory or not, Mattie, your father left the number at home because he had committed it to memory in order to recite it to you that evening. It had to be important enough and sensitive enough for him to make that extra effort, don't you think?" Lori gazed at her questionably.

"I've never stopped thinking that, plus the fact that 'numbers don't lie.' That number is wrapped around the killer and his sponsor—they are connected, I'm certain of that," Mattie said heatedly.

"And I'm certain you are correct, *mi amigita*. Hold that thought and take a breath while I make a phone call," Lori requested gently.

Mattie walked out onto the balcony to take that breath, delighted to inhale the fresh desert air caressing her bare skin as she leaned forward of the metal railing to see the long blue pool seven floors below. She did not listen to Lori's laconic phone conversation until her words were directed at her. "They're on it, Mattie—said they'd get right back to me."

"That's it? That quick?" Mattie questioned in awe.

"My guy is a 'super decoder' with access to a supercomputer, a 'grey research' model from the future, blinking lights and synthetic voice. They live to break codes," she said confidently.

"So you just said, 'here's an eight digit number,' and that's it?"

"No. I told him the number was from Mexico."

"Babe, it's not a Mexican number, it's a universal number, it's a number, number," Mattie responded, amused at the contextual perspective her friend had put the number in.

"That's precisely what code crackers do, determine if numbers are merely numbers. I had to give him something to play with anyway, the more foreign, the better."

"I hear you. Just like Mexican jumping beans. They sound more fun being that they're Mexican. If they were simply known as jumping beans, the novelty would be gone, lost," Mattie confessed, as they both laughed at the analogy.

Lori put her serious face back on. She stood to stretch and walk around the spacious room collecting her thoughts before continuing. Resuming her position on the corner of the bed, she asked, "Do you think the shooter was specifically after the list or something material that showed the number?"

Mattie had not forgotten the gruesome details of the violent death her father had suffered: one bullet in each eye, one inside each ear, and one in the mouth, known as the "See no evil, hear no evil, and speak no evil message," a mortal warning to potential informants.

"Absolutely, realizing father's urgency to share it with me. The killer and his sponsor made no attempts to look for it at our house or father's office. They simply wanted to silence him forever. I'm certain they knew that he had evidence of internal criminal activities at high political levels, and those numbers would eventually reveal the parties involved," Mattie deduced.

"You realize, Mattie, you would have been a target of interest if they thought you knew what your father knew. Because he never met with you has probably saved your life, or at the very least allowed you to have been promoted to your new position in the department. After all this time, they don't have a clue that you might actually have a case-breaking clue, this mystery number," Lori contributed emphatically.

"Somebody in a high position of power was afraid of my father and what he knew. When the attorney general fired over seven hundred agents of the PJF and INCD, abolishing their offices, my father was not included in the purge. That automatically made him suspect as an informant," she exclaimed glumly.

"But, Mattie, weren't there others at your father's level who also survived the mass firing?"

"Yes, and it's also true that no others were assassinated later. That's why my brother and I believe that his investigative work was headed in a different direction than drugs and money laundering," Mattie declared with an air of certitude.

"As in a higher, vertical direction?"

"Precisely. And that's the same direction we've taken over the last three years, upward and onward," Mattie stated with conviction.

"So who had him killed was close enough to know that he was close on his trail and acted out of desperate self-preservation," Lori surmised.

"Yes again. It was self-preservation both personally and politically. To kill someone, you have to have a lot at stake, in this case, a big political future. And in Mexico, no *politico* acts alone politically. They always act in pairs or packs," Mattie declared disdainfully.

"So the person who hired the shooter also had some other powerful politico's blessing?" Lori speculated.

"When they stab someone in the back, they need another someone to watch their back. The more, the better, if we remember the story of the Roman gang in togas sticking it to poor old Julius Caesar."

"*Et tu Brutus?*" Lori added with a frown.

"And father had his *Brutus*, a cowardly one who hired someone to do his dirty work. His *Brutus* was a professional friend, not personal family friend. There's a huge difference in our culture. Professional friends are of convenience, there to facilitate and expedite favors for one another. I'll scratch your back if you'll scratch mine."

"That was one back scratch your father didn't need. Do you know who his *quid pro quo* friends are?"

"I do. So I waited, observed, investigated, and with Tio Chuey's help, saw which one benefited the most from father's death. Once that was determined, we dug even deeper to first verify our theory, but also, with Angelino's help, discover the unlawful activities this person and his corrupt cronies are involved in."

"But there's a critical piece of the puzzle still missing, right? Like the significance of the number code?" Lori underscored.

"I'm hoping the mystery number will be the correct combination to unlock that black box of answers. Beyond that, Angelino will be my secret weapon," she stated with a confident grin.

"Because he knows the kept secrets of your father's enemy?" Lori conjectured quizzically.

"I'll know next week what he's learned. He wouldn't be returning home if he didn't have salient evidence of some serious subterfuge afoot. Angelino is a twenty-first-century Diogenes, always seeking the truth, the honest man. While members of his cloth live in the realm of 'blind faith,' my brother is of a different cut. Angelino is of the belief that truth foments faith, a faith that need not be in doubt because its creation is true. He is his father's son first, and a priest second," Mattie proudly punctuated her characterization of her beloved brother.

The ring from Lori's cell phone interrupted her thought. She first read the caller's number on her phone display, and then spoke. "Why so long?" she answered in jest. She listened briefly and then asked Mattie, "Do you have a handheld calculator with you?"

"Yes. Hold on." She pulled it out of the interior pocket of her brief case and turned it on. It was the same dimension as Lori's outstretched hand. The display brightened with a series of green, linear zeros, then changed to 50807507 as Lori keyed in the number. She then looked at the display of eight digits upside down, chuckled, and thanked her caller profusely with the promise of a "big wet kiss" when she saw him next. She then showed the illuminated eight digits to Mattie in the same upside-down fashion. "Are those Mexican numbers or what?" Lori questioned rhetorically.

"*A Dios Mio!* (Oh my God!) I don't believe this. *Los Lobos.* How did you know, Lori?"

"I didn't. But super decoder needed something to look for. When small calculators first came on the market, it was popular to play digital, letter read-out games, to create words with the numbers when turned upside down. Our super decoder tried it after his super computer ran all permutations and came up empty."

"*Que pendeja soy yo.* (What an idiot I am.) The words were right here all along."

"Don't be so hard on yourself, *amigita*. That's why it's called a code, Mattie. It's not discernable on a computer screen, only on the small, single line display frame of a calculator. Whoever created that numbered word code started there," Lori believed.

"And it's probably embedded in other data, buried deep in my database, or something I've simply overlooked. I'll have to redo my crosschecking search," she said with a resigned sigh.

"But even then, it's just a number until you find the significance of *Los Lobos* as it relates to your father's investigation. It wasn't only the number *per se* he wanted to discuss with you. It was about 'the Wolves,' whoever they are."

"I can start with the strong possibility that I'm looking for more than a single wolf since it's in the plural tense. And I don't mean the popular Mexican band *Los Lobos*, although their drummer looks suspect," Mattie observed with an attempt to add levity to the serious discussion.

"There's a large and dangerous street gang named *Los Lobos* in San Diego and Los Angeles that I'll check out. But they're gang activities are far removed from Mexico City," Lori offered with professional certainty.

"One thing is for certain, Lori, the wolf is ominous, intimidating by nature, a predator that stalks it prey in a very calculated way before the kill," she exclaimed warily.

"True. Its controller is sending a threatening message that *Los Lobos* has fangs and exists to kill. It exists for no other purpose," Lori stated emphatically. "I'll wager that the shooter is one of the wolf pack," she added confidently.

Suddenly Mattie's entire body shook with the shivers, visible goose bumps, appearing all over her body. She instantly rose from her seated position at the foot of the bed and wrapped her arms across her chest and shoulders, a frown of fright masked her beautiful Latin face.

"Are you okay, babe? What's up?" Lori questioned with concern as she, too, stood up.

"The thought of someone preying upon my father like a hungry animal and simply killing to kill is too much to imagine—the image is more than chilling," she declared in alarm, rubbing her own shoulders for warmth. Lori pulled her arms away and embraced her warmly with comforting words. "We have silver bullets we can give you that will eradicate *Los Lobos*. Not to worry, *amigita*, Wonder Woman can kick wolfman's ass any day, anyway!" she assured her friend and crime-fighting partner.

Lori believed Mattie's repressed fear for her own safety had finally surfaced, the harsh reality hit home, that both she and her brother could become victims of a *Los Lobos'* bullet if it smelled the threat of discovery or capture. Mattie now realized that she and Angelino could easily become the hunted as well as the hunters. Lori loosened her embrace of Mattie without letting go. She made direct eye contact while remaining close enough to get rid of Mattie's chill with her body warmth.

"Mattie, you know that when you ask for my help, you tap into all of my resources, which are considerable. The timing is perfect for you to ask because my most forceful and effective resources will be in your neighborhood and at your disposal. You will not be alone. Tell me what you need now or later and it's done," she affirmed with a firm hug. Almost instantly, she could feel Mattie's cold skin warm, not only to her touch, but with the assurance that her good and trusted friend Lori would be there for her, that she was no longer going it alone. What she did not know was that the forceful and effective resource her friend referred to would be former elite Special Forces from the United States Marines, unknown to Mexican citizens as the Delta Force. And they soon would be in her neighborhood.

Mattie sincerely thanked Lori for her support and safety net. She fixed herself a hot cup of lemon tea and joined her atop their bed meeting place with their laptops open. Mattie had asked to shift the topic of discussion to Lori's area of operation and learn how she could assist her in her upcoming mission. Lori would not eschew the confidential matters of the sensitive mission and private Delta Force company. Mattie was not told that somebody was coming into Mexico to remove six fugitives from US justice. The screen on Lori's laptop only displayed the photos of the six Fled to Mexico (FTM) felony fugitives. She would never see the same big, badass boys the fugitives would ever see.

"Just click on each fugitive photo to read their criminal case files. When you've finished, I'll fill in the blanks," Lori suggested pointedly.

"Will do," Mattie replied as she placed a notepad and pen next to the computer to jot down the questions she'd ask later. Lori went out on the balcony for the warmth of the sunshine and garden view below. She leaned over the railing with her arms outstretched, allowing the sun's rays to wash over her long, firm back. She had no tan lines, and was determined to keep it that way.

Mattie took her time studying the information provided by the Santa Barbara law enforcement authorities and what little else other California state agencies and immigration intelligence had on the FTM fugitives. What impressed her the most was that there was a "known whereabouts" of all six Mexican nationals, some precise addresses, others more approximate, such as his home *pueblo* only. She had seen that before with attempted extradition cases when the fugitive in question is confident his government will not extradite him so is not afraid to cooperate to the extent of disclosing his address. She read in some of the criminal case files that the Santa Barbara police even came to Mexico to interrogate the FTM fugitive at his local police precinct, only to tell the investigating detective to "piss off," before walking out of the police station as he entered, a free man on a free pass from justice, untouchable.

Mattie's liaison office had cooperated on a daily basis with foreign law enforcement and justice departments in providing up-to-date information on known criminals and suspects of interest in Mexico. As a legal practitioner, she was mindful of her nation's constitutional article 15, that "no treaty be entered into which restricts the guarantees and rights of its citizens which the constitution grants." Her judicial question then followed: *Why then bother having an extradition treaty with the US when both nations state that foreign law shall not be applied when it is invoked as an attempt to evade the application of their sovereign laws? Shouldn't the laws of the country that were violated trump the laws of the native country of the violator?* Mattie would challenge.

The only difference with Lori's request was that it was coming from a private, clandestine organization. But for Mattie, her friendship with Lori aside, it was all about crime fighting and winning. "The criminals don't fight fair, why should we," she would remind her partner in crime fighting.

Mattie called Lori back into the room where she first splashed cool water over her face before resuming her place at the foot of the bed.

"I'm sorry, Lori!"

"For?"

"For the chronic criminal behavior of my countrymen in your country. It's more than an embarrassment, it's humiliating. And do you know what the worst part of it is?"

"No. What?"

"That I'm not at all surprised by it. These six killers came from a lawless nation. Not that laws don't exist on the books, but that they don't exist in practice in a nation where corruption and street crime are endemic to our culture. Every citizen has been given permission 'to get away with it if they can' because their role model is the government, from the presidency on down to the street corner traffic cop. Crime in Mexico is sadly institutionalized, a fundamental part of our system, our answer to a 'free market economy.' Except that we have a more liberal interpretation of what is 'free,' as in free to take what you can get away with," she summarized gloomily.

"Hey, corruption abounds in America as well, only with bigger numbers," Lori replied bluntly.

"Unfortunately, money is the key that opens the doors of Mexican justice a little wider for some than for those with less. Citizens believe that it's futile to seek redress in court because those in power or those with money to buy unequal influence control the police and judges. And it's known that those in power, including ranking military, are above the law, exempt from prosecution, or at best, conviction in the courts that they control. So the majority of our ordinary citizens find themselves outside the law, without advocacy, or in the case of the poor, without any possibility of access to the legal system."

"Disenfranchised for lack of resources?" Lori asked rhetorically.

"Completely. For the poor, it is futile, completely hopeless. But in a country where true incorruptible justice is nonexistent, it's hopeless for the entire nation," Mattie sighed.

"You mean to tell me that there is zero pursuit of the truth in a Mexican court of law?" Lori asked incredulously.

"Consider this when trying to understand our courts' pursuit of the truth. Mexican courts do not recognize the concept of perjury because their official position is that, 'It is human nature to lie, especially when it entails saving yourself from a criminal conviction,' that it is expected that you do so, it is your right to do so. And to do so is not punishable by a court of law. Is that a true pursuit of the truth? I think not," Mattie explained heatedly.

"I understand, 'the first primordial law of man is the law of self-preservation,'" Lori rejoined. She had not seen her friend so passionately inflamed against her country, to the point of surprise and concern for her outspokenness. She knew that Mattie found comfort and candor in her presence within the United States and would never sound off this way in the company of her fellow federal workers.

"So in the real pursuit of truth and justice, you then would have no problem if six of your countrymen ended up back in the United States at the scene of the crime to stand trial under our judicial system?" Lori solicited, seeking assurance of her unconditional support.

"Let me answer it this way. If an American commits murder in Mexico, regardless of the victim's nationality, we would want justice served, and served 'a la Mexicana,' the Mexican way. We would not compare our laws with those of the criminal's homeland. They have no relevance in Mexico. His American rights end where our border begins, and vice versa," she reaffirmed sternly.

"So you'd take the legal and diplomatic action to bring the fugitive killer back to Mexico to stand trial?" Lori asked with finality.

"We have, and we will. You want these six fugitives back to stand trial? From my point of view, they're yours. What makes them so privileged that they can't be subjected to the laws of the land where they violated those laws? Just because they were born on foreign soil should not exempt them. They soiled US land, that's where it must be cleaned up. If the Mexican government ignores your legal right to extradite the fugitives, then why should I obstruct your willingness to do otherwise? What my liaison office does on a regular basis is cooperate with foreign law enforcement authorities in providing the whereabouts of criminals from international justice, not just domestic. According to these FTM case files, the Santa Barbara PD contacted the appropriate Mexican police departments regarding the location and apprehension of all six fugitives. For me to supply you with additional intelligence will merely be a matter of official follow-up protocol and routine criminal data dissemination. And yes, I'll be more than discreet, although there is no oversight to such communication when it flows from the director's desk."

"As in, Director Mattie Colima?" Lori punctuated with a big grin.

"As of yesterday," Mattie reminded herself, more than for Lori. She was feeling proud of her new authority to actually rein in six more bad guys, not caring if they met their fate in the US or Mexico, as long as they were locked up.

"Mexican law and church doctrine forbid capital punishment. California and other states are for it. Have you factored that in?" Lori questioned sincerely.

"Forbid? That's such hypocrisy on both of their parts. If it is written so on the basis of moral righteousness of 'Thou shall not kill,' then why does the Mexican government allow for the death penalty in their military for 'violent acts of insubordination, treason, and desertion during times of war.' The hypocritical message is that it's a sin to execute a citizen criminal for killing someone but not a killer clad in a Mexican military uniform. The cloths you wear determine the sin!" Mattie stated tersely.

"I missed that one in my youth Bible studies," Lori said sarcastically. She saw that Mattie was now really fired up. She had struck an exposed nerve that caused her Latin ire to soar, turning her face as red as her temperament.

"What I will not do, Mattie, is compromise your position and safety. What I'm asking has to come with the promise that you won't put yourself at risk over my mission. Can you promise me that?" Lori asked with insistence in her voice. She was not soliciting Mattie's *imprimatur*. The mission could and would proceed without her input, albeit, becoming a much greater odyssey and risk without it.

"*Te lo prometo, mi amigita* (I promise you, my friend), I'll begin covering my tracks when I'm in Washington, DC, this week with your alphabet boys and girls," she said, referring to the US Federal DEA, CIA, FBI, and DOJ.

"How so?"

"I'll randomly fold in the names of your six FTMs with my three dozen or so other criminal cases I brought to discuss with them. They'll want information from my office, I'll ask for the same from theirs. These are always 'give-and-take' meetings," Mattie stated the obvious.

"Well I do have some US-based statistics that will help put the six cases in perspective as to our concern for the apprehension and conviction of the FTMs. These six undocumented Mexicans who crossed into the United States illegally and murdered six innocent American citizens in peaceful, little Santa Barbara are but a minute microcosm of the bigger picture of what's happening throughout the United States," Lori stated with alarm. Standing, she leaned over Mattie's shoulder to click on the laptop mouse, highlighting a new screen file of "US Prison Statistics." The numbers ran into the thousands of foreign nationals incarcerated throughout the US: 28,171 in federal prisons, 34,809 in state prisons, the vast majority Mexican nationals. The southern border states held the majority of noncitizen Mexicans at a taxpayer cost of $31,000 per inmate annually. "That's a twenty-four-billion-dollar taxpayer burden per year when including the related law enforcement and Justice Department costs." Lori pointed to the highlighted statistic. Those convicted of murder that didn't make it back across the Mexican border numbered only a few hundred.

"Do you see where less than a hundred of those convicted of first-degree murder are actually on death row?" Lori said with a sigh.

"I do. Which can only mean fugitive border crossing escapes are easier than we thought, as easy as one, two, three, hit and run and home again," Mattie summarized with a sense of amazement.

"The prison population numbers are frightening, the upward trends alarming. I'll transfer all of these statistical files onto your laptop." Lori pointed to the screen.

"Keeping track of our own state and federal prison population numbers is our largest intelligence task, our number 1 priority, because it's the one database that is an absolute—criminals with a known name, face, and number. Only prison address changes are the most challenging variable we face. If they enter the US illegally, we don't hear about it until they're caught committing a crime there. So fleeing to Mexico has to be their number 1 objective. Our judicial system literally allows them to get away with murder," Mattie concluded with an audible groan.

"Don't I know! What if we leave this depressing data pool and dip into a cool wet one?" Lori suggested invitingly.

"Followed by a tall cold one with a tiny umbrella on it!" Mattie smiled enthusiastically.

The large, elliptical pool area was populated with the usual mix of Hard Rock Hotel guests. They ranged from honeymoon couples, teenagers wearing earphones attached to iPods, and the "boomer generation," there to relate with the "oldie but goodie" rock and roll era one more time in one more way. Las Vegas always lowered people's inhibitions as well as guiltless necklines and exposed booties, often inspired by the onstage beauties performing in the casino skin shows. Skimpy swimsuits were the way for many of the willing women to strut their stuff, if indeed they had the stuff to strut. The pool and patio area was the platform for such an innocent beauty pageant with single to married and teenage to middle-aged women in full bloom, "eye candy," and "head-turners."

But this day at the Hard Rock Hotel pool, more heads turned to eye the two look-alike buxom babes with the firm bodies and showgirl figures than commuters gawking at a car wreck. The honeymoon husbands broke their bridle trances of adoration to take a long lusting look at the two long-legged, sexy brunettes crossing the pool patio to place their beach towels over the low lounge chairs near the diving board. Grown men looked more like bobblehead dolls as they watched the two women bounce high off of the diving board into the glistening blue pool, each man lifting an imaginary square sign up in his mind that read a perfect 10. Swimmers stopped swimming so they could admire the synchronized strokes of the sleek, two-woman team cutting through the water effortlessly. Lorie and Mattie would continue their leisurely laps in the pool for twenty minutes before stepping out on the corner chrome pool ladder. Every adult male within a hundred feet counted the beads of water on every square inch of the two wet, curvaceous forms emerging from the pool.

A lone, middle-aged man in blue shorts and a white T-shirt was snapping photos of the sexy duo like a Japanese tourist at an Elvis sighting. Mattie and Lori rotated their near nude, tan bodies like a rotisserie to dry off in the 82-degree sunshine. After thirty minutes, they transferred to a shaded table to enjoy a cold piña colada and cool lobster salad. Mattie was the first to speak up about the paparazzi admirer still pointing his camera in their direction from a distance of fifty feet.

"I could swear, Lori, that the man across the way, in the blue shorts and white T-shirt, has been photographing us from below our table. Look how low he's aiming his lens."

"I wasn't sure, but I thought he was doing the same thing when we were lying on the lounges. He was definitely taking shots when we entered and exited the pool."

"Do you recognize him?"

"Sure don't. But he sure is starting to annoy me."

"You have to wonder, why so many shots of us, for what?"

Turning to Mattie, Lori said, "I'm going to do something here, and you tell me if he snaps a picture, okay?"

"Go for it," Mattie agreed, pretending to gaze off in the distance beyond the man. Lori casually spread her bended legs apart and held them wide open until Mattie spoke, "Bingo! We have a pervert in the audience. He aimed directly at you, a real cheap shot!"

"Cheap? I don't think so. This is not a free peep show for perverts," Lori snapped.

"I still want to know what the photos are for, and I'm going to find out," Mattie said huffily.

Lori signed the lunch check and leisurely walked with Mattie in the direction of the photographer, avoiding eye contact. He was seated in the shade of a large red and white–striped table umbrella with his camera resting on his lap. The two women walked on opposite sides of his chair. Lori caught his attention with a soft salutation of, "Good afternoon." He looked up at her with a surprised smile. In that instant, Mattie swooped down with her left hand to seize the camera from his loose grip. He began to rise from his chair in a defensive attempt to recover it when Lori's right hand grabbed hold of his shoulder and pressed him back down in his chair.

"Hey! What the hell are you doing? Give me my camera!" he demanded angrily.

"The question to be answered, sir, is what are you doing with the camera? Why all the snapshots of us—from the moment we arrived to when we were having our lunch?" Mattie asked in protest.

"I'm just a tourist taking photos of my trip—you know—hotel, pool, other tourists," he replied nervously.

Mattie passed the camera to Lori who inspected it more closely.

"This is a high-end digital camera, one used more by the pros than tourists. And since we are professional models, you've captured our images without our professional permission or commercial compensation. So we have no other choice but to recover those images for our own professional protection," Lori demanded.

"You can't do that," he countered, attempting to rise again as Mattie held him in his seat with her left hand pressing down on his other shoulder. Lori depressed a small button and removed the digital photo card from the side of the camera.

"You have no right—I want it back—now!" he demanded with a perspiring red face.

"Here is your camera back. If you want to argue further about your photo card with our images on it, then we can do it with the head of hotel security. I'm sure he'd like to hear about this," Lori threatened as she waved the card in the air. He placed his brown straw hat down tightly on his balding head and slumped low in his canvas chair, swearing under his laboring breath as the women walked innocently away.

Back in the controlled environment of their seventh-floor suite, Lori loaded the confiscated photo card into her laptop computer and clicked on her photo management program for the download. The photo gallery format edited the nearly one hundred thumbnail-size pictures onto six screen pages displaying a *mélange* of subjects too small to readily identify in detail at first glance. Lori clicked to enlarge them into four per screen page. They leaned in closer to view them, one by one, silently at first. Their surprised gasps were followed by exclamations of disgust and dismay. It wasn't the gallery of near nude women that surprised them but rather the distasteful camera angles used to capture the private body areas of the unsuspecting female subjects in and around the pool.

"Cleavage I can understand. But this pervert zoomed in on the crotch, front and back, even of all these prepubescent girls," Lori said in disgust.

"*A dios mio*! Enlarge this one, Lori," Mattie said, touching the screen on the bottom right hand corner.

The screen filled with a photo of Mattie taken from a distance at ground level shooting up to the seventh-floor balcony where she was leaning topless over the railing. "This guy has been scouting us out since this morning. Go to the next screen page to see if he caught you out there as well," she requested impatiently.

"Right there, he shot me," Lori confirmed, "catching some rays. Jesus, I don't mind someone sneaking a peek with their bare eyes of my bare breasts. But this pervert treats this place like a free flesh market."

"Of all of the striptease parlors in Vegas and he chooses this hotel," Mattie said sarcastically.

"The perv must think 'Hard Rock' means rock hard," Lori complained. "My best guess is that he intended to download these photos onto his home computer to get off on, and then put them out on the Internet."

"On some perv chat room?" Mattie said dully.

"Exactly. He'll be a hero for a night with all of the loners and losers asking the perv, 'Hey, dude, where did you score all the awesome chick skin, dude.' Pathetic sick bastards!"

"We need to make Mr. Hard Rocks here become a limp stalagmite," Mattie suggested with earnest.

"Agreed. He'll never get this digital photo card back, but he is probably shooting a newly loaded one now as we speak. We need to do something more convincing, more lasting. We need to send him packing," Lori said with determination.

"We can no longer prove that these are his photos, so hotel management won't boot him," Mattie shrugged.

"And hotel security won't do what I have in mind for this perv, but I do know who will," Lori said with a devilish grin. She picked up her cell phone and pressed speed dial, prompting the highlighted name "Bolinski Assoc."

The cell phone holstered on the left side of Mr. Bolinski's belt rang. He listened intently to Lori's situation and straightforward request.

"I'll send one of my associates over to handle it, but this is what I need for you to do." He instructed Lori on what their combined role would be in the plan to rid themselves and the hotel of the perv problem. She thanked Mr. Bolinski and gave him a grateful goodbye. She repeated the conversation to Mattie, then lifted the receiver on their portable room phone and marked "Pool." A youthful sounding voice answered, "Poolside."

"Yes. I'm a hotel guest and need to speak briefly to a friend seated on the garden side of the pool facing the diving board. He's wearing pale blue shorts, a white Hard Rock T-shirt, black shoes and socks, and possibly wearing a brown straw hat." There was a brief pause, then, "Yes ma'am, I see him under a table umbrella. Do you want me to give him a message?"

"No. It's personal—really important. Would you please just hand him your portable receiver for a quick second?" she asked pleasantly.

"Why certainly. Give me a moment to walk over there."

Still in their bikinis, Lori and Mattie stood by the balcony railing looking down to watch a college age "pool boy" approach their mark. He looked up hesitantly at the pool boy, pausing before taking the receiver.

"Who's this?" he asked, more cautiously than curiously.

"This is Tammy and Tonya calling to apologize for our rudeness earlier. Please understand that as professional models, we like to know who is shooting us. Sorry we were so defensive."

"What did you do with my pictures? They're still mine and I want them back," he insisted with a harsh voice.

"I'm sorry. What's your name?"

"Howard."

"Well, Howard, that's the other reason we're calling. We've seen your pictures on our computer up here in our suite. And quite honestly, we are really quite happy with everything we've seen. Tonya and I think you have a really good eye, know what to look for with the lens. If you're interested in taking more of the same, and then some, you can swing by at five this afternoon, and we can accommodate you," Lori (Tammy) offered sweetly.

There was a muted pause where Lori was certain she heard heavy breathing on the other end.

"Will I get my photo card back?" his tone of voice softened, yet firm.

"Of course, unconditionally. Like I said, Howard, we want to apologize for our bad manners and make it up to you if we can. It's just that you caught us off guard earlier. But now we know what you're looking for, and this is Las Vegas, if you know what I mean," she baited him teasingly.

Now Lori was positive Howard's breathing was laboring. He looked up at their room balcony to spot Tammy and Tonya in their bikinis, waving at him like beauty pageant contestants.

"Does suite 790 at five o'clock sharp work for you, Howard?"

"Well, yeah, sure, okay then. As you said, this is Las Vegas. Room 790, at five, right?"

"Right, Howard. I hope you're not a shy photographer. See you then. Bye."

The two pretenders quickly ducked back into their suite to give themselves a congratulatory high-five slap of their hands, punctuating the success of phase 1 of Mr. Bolinski's plan.

"You sounded a little too convincing there, Lori. Tell me again about this top-secret job of yours in Vegas," Mattie said, gazing at her questionably.

"You mean Tammy, don't you?"

"Right. But the Internet pervs will want more of Tonya, not Tammy." Mattie smirked peevishly, taking off her swimsuit. "So I'd better take a shower now for Howard later," she chuckled on the way to the marble bathroom. Lori chanted loudly, "Howie loves Tammy," repeatedly for Mattie to hear as she moved rhythmically in the warm shower to the surround sounds of *the Miami Sound Machine.*

It was three o'clock when Mattie and Lori turned their laptops back on, resuming their al fresco positions on the foot of the bed. It was back to the give-and-take of information that would aid Lori in her forthcoming mission.

At exactly twenty minutes before five, there was a loud knock on their door. They hurriedly put on their white sheer cotton cloth beach blouses, opened slightly in the front and loosely flowing down to the top of their bikini bottoms. Mattie went to the door and politely asked, "Yes. Who is it?" as she looked through the tiny glass peephole.

"I'm an associate of Mr. Bolinski. Is this Ms. Lori's room?"

Lori replied yes and gave a nod to Mattie to let the associate in. He formally introduced himself with a photo ID and then was taken to a table where Lori had just set her laptop. He was shown all of the pervs downloaded photos as Mattie explained the past events with their unwanted mark. He agreed that the "paparazzi" type of Peeping Tom could become more and more persistent and intrusive when there was resistance. "As you might expect, 'Sin City' does draw flies as well. If he's not stopped early and convincingly, he could become more than just a nuisance," he warned.

Both of the women were most impressed with the Bolinski associate, professional, poised, confident, and definitely big enough to handle Howard if he became aggressive. The plan of action for the five o'clock encounter was reviewed one final time. The women knew their parts in the play and waited calmly. The associate was standing behind the suite entrance door when the knock came at three minutes past the appointed hour. Lori asked cordially, "Who is it?"

"Howard. Is that you, Tammy?" came the reply with a pitch of excitement in his voice.

"Yes, I'm coming."

The associate then opened the door in a flurry. The first thing Howard saw, and the last thing he heard was *bam* as he dropped to the floor, unconscious before he hit the soft carpet. With one arm, the associate lifted the limp body up by the front pant belt and set him down inside before closing the door. Mattie picked up his fallen camera. The associate unzipped Howard's pants, and with a dry washcloth in his hand, extracted the victim's penis from his boxer shorts, then stood back. Using Howard's camera, Mattie took five photos of him from different angles, before the washcloth was placed over his front pant opening.

The associate bent over and opened Howard's left eyelid. He rose to look at Lori standing next to the room phone. "Go ahead and make your call. My work is done here. Thank you for calling Bolinski and Associates," he said officially with a warm grin. The women thanked him sincerely before the call was made. LVPD Detective John Cushman, who just happened to be in the hotel lobby, answered. She succinctly reported how she and Mattie were near victims of a forced entry into their room by an indecently exposed man carrying a camera, the same one who had been taking pictures of them earlier. He said he would be right up to handle the matter and for her to call the hotel manager. He went directly to the lobby level bank of room elevators. The first available one opened to the sight of a very large Afro American man getting off, who looked down at him to say, "Good afternoon, John. Thanks for coming."

"You're welcome, Clarence—always a pleasure," the detective replied sincerely.

Mattie let Detective Cushman into the room with a caution not to step on Howard. "Ouch. Looks like the door got him square in the face—really hard too. That had to hurt," he said in a dry monotone.

"I think the hurt will start when he wakes up," Lori amended coolly.

The manager and three hotel security officers arrived with deepest regrets and apologies for the unfortunate intrusion. Lori told their new audience the entire tale of the paparazzi perv, from their negative poolside experience to the attempted forced entry into their room, all supported by the gallery of photos taken by none other than the perv himself. Mattie and Lori smiled to themselves as the detective and hotel manager became fixated on the two photos on the laptop showing them leaning over the room balcony.

"This must be how the intruder determined which room you were in, just counted the floor level and number of balconies from the corner of the building," Detective Cushman speculated with the manager.

"Possibly. But some suites have two balconies," the manager contended, pointing to the screen photo of Lori stretched out over the railing.

"Really?" the detective wondered, looking more closely at the photo.

Lori interrupted their intimate crime investigation with the proposal that she and Mattie would not press any charges against the perv if the hotel and LVPD would agree to put him on a plane back home today.

"If Howard doesn't go along with the proposal, tell him that our complete set of photos of the exposed Howard will be exposed on the Internet," Mattie exclaimed with resolve in her tone.

She handed the detective Howard's camera. "They are all in here, if you're looking for real incriminating evidence, Detective. And please tell Howard that if he ever points a camera at us or any little girls again, we will post him on every loser chat room on the World Wide Web," Lori threatened, fingering her computer screen now displaying the recent photo of Howard, exposed. The two male investigators showed no interest in viewing that particular one.

The security staff placed the groggy Howard in a wheel chair and rolled him to the service elevator. The detective finished his report and received grateful handshakes from both victims as they said goodbye.

They shed their beach blouses and resumed their places on the corners of the bed, again focused on their Mexico missions. They would not be packing their bikinis.

7

VEGAS AND THE VIRGIN

Las Vegas

Taylor always said there was no greater escape destination in the United States than Las Vegas. Within one small patch in the desert, you could visit Paris, New York City, Rio de Janeiro, New Orleans, Egypt, Morocco, Monte Carlo, Mandalay, Tahiti, and Venice, Italy. The wide variety of venues attracted an equally diverse type of characters to its flame of fun, fantasy, and fortune-seeking. It wasn't called America's Playground for nothing. In its early days of Sinatra and the Rat Pack, it was known strictly for its "booze, betting, and broads." Sin City, city of false promises, it was labeled. It was no less that today except for those who lived and worked there could enjoy the added dimension of homogenized anonymity.

Up and down the Las Vegas Strip and throughout the Fremont district, you became everybody else, one of them, the anonymous thrill-seeking guy from Dubuque, Iowa, another every day and night tourist blending in among the masses, just another blinking light at the intersection of the underworld and upper world.

Anonymity was what the Delta team wanted, and they had it there in spades. In the streets of any other city, Hollywood included, they'd stand out like the Shriners at a convention. It wasn't like they were on anybody's Most Wanted list. Federal law enforcement and investigative organizations knew that they existed, yet they had never been questioned or shadowed by any of them. It was more suitable and safer for government agencies not to recognize them. Ignorance of their existence made it politically convenient to deny any knowledge of the contract ops team to those questioning their possible involvement in any mysterious activities in foreign lands. And until some influential politico or foreign power cried foul to our State Department, they were allowed to operate, albeit, on the fringe. Taylor would remind his team leaders that all world government agencies violated more foreign laws and treaties in the shadows daily than their private Delta Force could do in their best year. Besides, after 9/11, the US Feds had more important things to be concerned about than what the clandestine team was doing in Saudi Arabia, Russia, Lebanon, Italy, Spain, Hong Kong, Canada, and now Mexico.

Their first cardinal tenet was to never violate the 1878 US *Posse Comitatus Act*, not to employ military-like force or type activities in support of law enforcement within the United States. Their ambit of operations for this mission was strictly within Mexico. Ironically, if any of their six fugitive targets were in the US, they wouldn't touch them.

Absent any major foul-up while in Mexico, Taylor didn't expect their mission to appear on any government agency radar screen. The greater their mission's success, the larger and louder the blip would be on the mainstream media radar screen. That was the plan; that was the goal. In the meantime, the team would enter its preparedness mode. It was a professional carry over from their military days of physical conditioning, repetitive drills with field equipment and intelligence briefings. The briefings would translate, in time, into the strategical plans for entry, seizure, and extraction of their six FTM—Fled to Mexico fugitive targets. There was one major difference now compared to their US military days. They were now voluntary private citizens. They were more vulnerable now out of uniform.

Taylor's company could draw from over twenty highly trained and field-seasoned professionals for any given mission, all former SFOD-D, 1st Special Forces Operational Detachment–Delta Strike Force. He selected the very best suited for the task at hand. The others knew nothing more than they were active and away. The one absolute condition for mission selection was that if called upon, you will come. If not, you were permanently off the call list. He had yet to delete anyone.

General Sun Tzu's words reminded him that, "Those who establish a viable organization will survive even if they are small, those who do not will perish even if they are large."

Today, the chosen six team leaders would join Taylor at 1900 at the Bullpen in Las Vegas.

The first phone call Taylor makes upon arriving in Las Vegas and the last one upon leaving was to his best buddy, Bull, owner of the Bullpen. Bull Bolinski was a living Las Vegas legend. Besides being one of the most trusted individuals in the gaming industry, he was one of the most beloved. His more than twenty-five years of providing employee investigative services to the casinos and hotels had developed into a personnel reference network unmatched by any other single vetting source in the country.

Bull came to Las Vegas as a police investigator to nab a fugitive from New York justice. He not only accomplished what the local and federal law enforcement departments combined couldn't do, he caught the bad guy and uncovered a major scam that was ready to be played on the casinos, avoiding potential losses into the millions of dollars. After his man was extradited to New York, Bull was enticed to stay in Las Vegas at the lucrative behest of the casinos. For over two decades, the Bolinski and Associates Investigative Services had provided in-depth background checks on individuals wishing to work in the Nevada gaming and hospitality industries.

The Bolinski certification on a job application was equivalent to the *Good Housekeeping* Seal of approval for new hirers. Even the Nevada Gaming Commission looked for it when considering license approvals. Bull's word was as good as gold in Nevada and cost just as much.

Taylor's call went to Bull's secured number on his cell phone attached to the left side of his thick western belt. The cell phone attached to the right side of the belt, he would say, was for "those who could write a check."

Bull's cell tone ring was "*God Bless America*." The voice answered, "If you haven't got any money, press 1. If you have a lot of money, this is Bull. How my I help you?"

"This is Taylor, and I have enough money to make you my bitch!" he growled.

"You can only wish, you pervert. You're back early, Taylor. Must mean something. What's up?"

"We're only a day early, eager to get started on our new project." Taylor knew Bull would not ask questions about his projects, although he did know the line of work he was in, assisting with background checks on nonmilitary support personnel when requested. Such an urgent need prompted Taylor's call to Bull, having made a request six days earlier. "We'll be arriving at the Bullpen beginning at 2000, seven in total," he confirmed.

"Jesus, Taylor, please tell me this isn't a remake of *The Magnificent Seven*," Bull teased.

"Well, it's not *Snow White and the Seven Dwarfs* unless you want to play Snow White," Taylor offered sarcastically.

"Compared to my personal stature, I'd hardly consider your guys dwarfs," Bull countered.

Taylor smiled at the thought knowing what Bull meant, with a stature of five feet, six inches, a 19-inch neck, and a 50-inch chest. Taylor once asked Bull if his nickname came from his surname or his appearance. The answer was low and lethal, "From mounting your mama." Taylor never brought it up again. A New York associate of Bull's said the pseudonym came from his aggressive, "no bull" reputation on the city police force. Either way, Taylor mused, the man's keen business acumen had played off of the name brilliantly.

The Bullpen was a nine-year-old bar, restaurant, dance hall with a unique western niche. From Bull's job applicant investigative work, he learned the inside dynamics of the Las Vegas job market. In the entertainment field, there were always more aspiring women than job opportunities. The part-time and newly arrived chorus line dancers took temporary jobs at the flesh clubs while waiting for their turn in the casino shows. The endless supply of stage women willing to diminish their attire was so great that he created an entertainment enterprise to manage that supply and demand. He aptly named it the Bullpen, known as the "warm-up" venue where professionals could remain in stage shape and get exposure before being called up to the casinos' starlight stages.

Men knew its name for what it meant to the primal male, a casual hangout for guys to goggle bodacious babes willing to bare their assets, while they imbibed copious quantities of beer, barbecued beef ribs, dance to lively country western music, and watch film highlights of professional bull riders trying to ride very large, mean bulls. Bull would boast about how he had simplified the Hooters restaurant concept, reducing the theme to its lowest common denominator for the common male market: babes, beer, barbecue, and bull riding—the Killer Bs, he termed them. "Our women don't hide inside T-shirts. We offer only one brand of beer and one cut of beef ribs. Why offer more than what a man wants or can handle?" he insisted confidently.

"Who's working your front door this evening?" Taylor asked.

"A new guy, Clarence, nicknamed Booby Gump because he reminds us of Bubba in the *Forest Gump* film. You'll see why when you show up at eight."

"Well tell ole Booby that I have seven names for him. Are you ready?"

"Fire away," Bull said as he pulled out a pen and paper from his Wrangler, blue denim shirt pocket.

"Cam, Nep, Rap, Cope, Grav, Eizzo, and yours truly," Taylor noted the anonyms slowly for Bull to write down.

"Where's Grumpy and Sneezy?" Bull poked at his friend. He knew the appellations to be the abbreviated Delta radio handles for each of the six team leaders, used in their field operations as Camera, Neptune, Rapids, Copenhagen, Gravity, and Eizzo, respectively.

"That's your A-Team, my man. There's got to be some serious shit happening for you to bring in these big boys. Cope will be happy to see me regarding an old, friendly wager. I owe him a Benjamin," Bull confessed.

"Let me guess. You bet Cope he couldn't stay on some badass bull, right?"

"Cherry Popper, at the Cheyenne Frontier Rodeo. He threw every rider here at the National Finals. But Cope went the 'eight' on him in Cheyenne," Bull exclaimed with amazement.

"Damn, that means he'll be showing off a new tattoo on that bony ass of his," Taylor bemoaned, referring to Cope's ritual of tattooing his buttock with the names of the "Super Bulls" he had successfully ridden at rodeos in the US and Canada. The better, ranker bulls had the best marquee names to fit their rank, rough riding temperaments, like War Dance, Kryptonite, Code Red, Down-and-Dirty, Fat Chance, Ball Buster, Mudslinger, Widow Maker, Rest in Peace, Nine One One, Category Five, Thunder Rode, DEFCON-1, and Fogetaboutit.

"You know he'll want to 'trou-down' to show off his new 'Too' for the guys. You better reserve a private corner booth for us so Cope doesn't scare off your customers. They come to see the beauty, not the beast," Taylor kindly warned.

Bull agreed with laughter as he confirmed the names and hour of arrival.

The Bullpen was a routine rendezvous spot for Taylor's men before starting their mission preparation at his 2,600-acre Sun Ranch, thirty-two miles northeast of Las Vegas on the western side of the Virgin River. He always wanted his men to have one last boys night out before being sequestered at the remote ranch for weeks under near military camp conditions. Bull once exclaimed that for the Delta men "to go from Vegas to the Virgin was a poetic practical joke, reality in reverse." They all knew that tonight would be their last chance to revel and get rowdy until after their mission's completion. Taylor's military experience had taught him that good moral in the field began by letting his men "raise a little hell before giving them hell!"

Taylor knew the Mexico mission to be complex, a multifaceted challenge of transborder logistics within a *terra incognito* where the best of strategic planning and tactical preparation could fly in their face with one single foul-up. He didn't believe in bad timing, only timing that was badly planned. He realized the mission would not be a slam dunk. They would plan and train for every imaginable contingency at the ranch until their intel officer gave them the green light to roll. But for tonight, he simply wanted to reunite the team leaders as one cohesive unit. Their camaraderie came easily. They described themselves as "brothers from different mothers." But for this deep penetration mission into Mexico for an extended period, the men Taylor had selected took on another brotherhood of sorts, that of "blood brothers," all with type A blood. If a serious injury befell one member, any one of the others could transfuse their blood.

Operating militarily as a Delta Force in the past was like riding a bicycle; you never forgot. As a private Delta Force, they now brought their own special vocational skills developed from their postmilitary years between private missions. Cam was a charter fixed wing pilot and aerial photographer in Hawaii; Grav, a smoke jumper/forest firefighter based in Idaho; Cope, a professional bull rider; Rap, a Mad River Rapids boatman out west; Eizzo, a high-tower construction worker and mountain rescue team member in Alaska; and Nep, a captain and owner of a charter private yacht business based out of the Port of San Diego. Whether or not the Mexico mission would demand any of their professional skills remained to be seen.

Ten days earlier, Taylor had made his *"call of the wild"* phone calls to his team members, always promising them seven days to get their private affairs in order. The phone calls were always direct, succinct, and secure. The first call went to Cam, the one farthest away from Las Vegas. As expected, he was piloting some tourists over the Big Island of Hawaii on a photo tour. The second call was to Eizzo in Alaska who was atop a 50-foot metal, high-power tower at the base of Mt. McKinley. He caught Nep sixty-five nautical miles from San Diego aboard his inbound charter yacht. Contacting Rap, rafting on the Snake River in Wyoming, took some effort because of the many deep canyon dead spots for wireless communications. The call to Grav was patched into the twin-prop Sherpa jump ship. He and his eight smokejumper trainees were flying three thousand feet over their Idaho wilderness firefighting target. Once the trainees had jumped, he removed his static line from his parachute jump cable and returned to Boise with only the flight crew and spotters. The last call found Cope in Canada next in line to mount his rodeo bull at the Calgary Stampede. The bull's name was I Don't Think So.

The seven Delta members rendezvoused eight days later in Los Angeles and were in Santa Barbara the following day. Concluding Taylor's successful meeting there aboard the *Conch II* with the Six-Pack employers, the team drove to Las Vegas, not wanting to leave an airline paper trail to their Nevada home base. They would arrive at the Bullpen in pairs and singles beginning at eight in the evening. Their gathering inside would be casual and incidental, avoiding the appearance of an organized group.

If Las Vegas was America's Playground, then the Bullpen was the Jungle Gym. Although there were many fun clubs of greater notoriety, such as the Palomino, the Lipstick Lounge, Cheetahs, Jaguars, Can-Can Room, and the Spice House, the Bullpen had its own allure. The sexy, sassy female bartenders and servers wore tight Daisy Duke denim short-shorts and very small red and white pattern bandana cloth tops that covered less than one-third of their ample breasts. Their beautifully developed dancer legs rose exotically out of their red, white, and blue cowgirl boots. There were always forty "cowgals" on the floor including those dancing on the bar tops. The hootin and hollerin, trash-talking, beer-swilling bash went on, as Bull would say, only on days that ended with the letter *Y*. The music, food, and beverage were served with attitude. If you asked for water, you'd get sprayed.

On Paradise Road, one block off of the Vegas Strip behind the Riviera Hotel-Casino, sat the Bullpen. It was a welcomed paradox to the glamour and glitz the monster hotels and casinos brought to the nightly party. Its facade was a western barn made of smooth, blonde, shellacked lodgepole logs with large double doors in the center attached by oversized brass hinges. Above appeared The Bullpen name formed in gold scripted letters from a neon western rope. The illuminated rope continued on to form a lariat that tightly wrapped around a buxom, scantily clad, sexy-looking brunette that was formed from bright multicolored neon lights, her left blue eye blinking flirtatiously.

Taylor and Eizzo approached the Bullpen entrance dressed in western wear, knowing the club's infamous reputation for cutting off men's ties with sheep shears. Eizzo's formfitting red cowboy shirt accentuated his broad upper body, what Taylor described as an inverted pyramid. His physique explained his extraordinary rope climbing and rappelling abilities that were legendary in the Special Forces. Climbing high poles, towers, and steep cliff walls for Eizzo was child's play, strictly recreational in his mind. Alaska's Mt. McKinley was his backyard as a supreme mountaineer and leader of its "first call" rescue team. Alongside Taylor, at the same height, they were an intimidating presence.

Eclipsing one half of the double doors before them stood an equally imposing figure, the doorman/bouncer, equal to the two of them combined. Towering an athletic 6'7" tall was Clarence, a handsome, jovial black man in his early thirties. He had a professional wrestler's girth with thick, cut muscles wrapped tightly in a white knit shirt covered by a black leather western vest. Bending down from the left side of his white felt cowboy hat was an earphone and lip mic that he talked into as he greeted the waiting patrons.

"My God, Taylor. Bull didn't mention that his Booby Gump doorman was the whole damn double door. I'm guessing four hundred pounds. What do you think?" Eizzo said, turning to Taylor.

"Well I hope Booby is getting paid double because there used to be two doormen here," Taylor exclaimed.

"I know I'm going to behave tonight," Eizzo confessed. "That guy's a group photo."

"His cowboy hat I'm guessing to be a twenty gallon," Taylor added.

As they queued up behind four others waiting to enter, they could hear a lyrical Alabama-accented delivery of a carnival barker promoting to all within the sound of his voice what they would find under the tent. The customers in line already knew, or they wouldn't be there. But they enjoyed Booby Gump's pronounced promise of plenty beautiful "Tatas, Tetons, Torpedoes, Casabas, Cha-Chas, and Congas. You'll see Bassoons, Bazongas, Bazookas, Bonbons, and Boobies. Did I mention beautiful Butterballs, Cannon Balls, Cantaloupes, and Carumbas?"

"I don't know about you, but it all sounds a lot more appetizing than shrimp scampi, shrimp Creole, shrimp jambalaya, breaded shrimp, garlic shrimp, butterfly shrimp, shrimp, shrimp!" Eizzo suggested.

Two college-age boys presented their driver's licenses upon Booby Gump's demand.

After a quick read of their IDs, he glared at the two boys and declared, "You'all can't come in!" in his pronounced Southern drawl.

"What the hell! We're both twenty-one," the tallest of the two protested.

With his illiest persona, he exclaimed, "Clarence knows that. But my God, child, look at these photos, and look at you'alls right here, both butt ugly!"

The two young men drifted back a step with their mouths wide open in disbelief. "Say what?" the shorter boy shouted.

With a stern face and tone, Clarence continued his objection, "You'all gots to understand that the Bullpen is full of awesome Love Muffins, Eggplants, Ear Muffins, Gazonas, Goombas, Honkers, Hooters, Howitzers, and bodacious Pagodas. We can't have you two weeds among the flowers. Now get the hell out of Las Vegas!" he snapped.

Now even Eizzo and Taylor took a step back in amazement as the taller boy responded with, "This place should be called the Bullshit! Not the Bullpen," throwing his arms up in defeat.

That brought a big Chiclets smile and high-pitched laughter from Clarence, who apologetically said, "Clarence is just playing with you'all now. I just wanted to see if you were men enough to handle the Bullpen. Now show Clarence some love," as he wrapped his leg-size arms around the two men, pulling them into his trunk-size torso before they could react. They gasped for air as he released them with his benevolent invitation to enter, as though it was the pearly gates to paradise and he was Saint Peter.

"Now get your ugly butts on in there and tell them Clarence is buying you'alls first beer 'cause he loves ya. But don't go grabbing no Moo Moos, Mambos, Melons, Meat Loafs, or Mother Loads, or I'll call yo mamas, ya hear? I know where you live now," as he handed back their driver's licenses. With stunned expressions of gratitude, the boys nervously disappeared through the doors to paradise as Clarence now set his sights on Taylor and Eizzo.

"Clarence, I'm Taylor and this is Eizzo. Bull put us on your guest list."

He silently picked up a clipboard and ran his size 20 ring finger down the list. As it stopped midway, Taylor identified the bracelet-size ring as a 1993 Alabama Sugar Bowl Champions ring. The hand holding the clipboard displayed a four-letter tattoo, one letter each on his four thick outer fingers between the upper knuckles. When pressed into a tight fist, they spelled BAMA.

Clarence looked up with a serious face and said, "Yep. You'alls names are here with a note from Bull. He says you'll be happier at one of those leather bars, you'all know what I mean? And from the looks of you'alls *Drugstore Cowboy*, giddy-up gear, you'all should be watching the Chippendales show over at the Rio, if you'all know what I mean?"

Eizzo pushed his suede cowboy hat back off of his forehead, grinned warmly as he looked up at Clarence, declaring, "The two of us really wanted to know if you'd join us in a threesome?"

Now Clarence stepped back, paused to study his two new subjects superficially, and then broke into uproarious laughter, quaking his entire body. Taking a deep breath, he gestured with his meaty hands toward himself, saying, "Look at me. I AM a threesome: me, myself, and I. I don't need you'alls *Brokeback Mountain* bony asses. Now give Clarence some sugar, come on now, a group hug here."

Before they knew it, they were trapped in Clarence's vised arms, struggling to breathe.

"You' all were just playing with Clarence. I like that. Now you' all get your sweet pants inside. But don't go tweaking no Gongas, Guavas, Headlamps, Headsets, Jugs, Jawbreakers, Pompoms, Twin Peaks, Wahwahs, Cupcakes, Doozies, Woofers, or Zeppelins, ya hear?"

Taylor and Eizzo swiftly sidestepped their new best friend, Clarence, a.k.a. Booby Gump, and entered the Bullpen. The scene inside was country western from its sawdust floor to its high-rise log rafters. The toe-tapping country music set the mood and the rhythm of the Cowgals as they deftly worked the crowd, serving beer, beef ribs, or riding the five mechanical bulls stationed in high-visibility points around the four-hundred-people capacity room. It was designed as a livestock barn might be. The stock here were live, wild, fun-seeking people who wanted nothing more than to have a few uninhibited laughs while escaping the restrictions of their real worlds outside.

The more private, larger booths were along the three outer walls, each one divided by a five-foot high, smooth log fence, which supported a fully tooled ranch saddle on the top log. Prominently displayed on the wall above each outer booth was a 6'×6' photograph of the country's top bull riders, creating an unofficial Wall of Fame for the world's toughest sport. The old-time bull riding greats—Freckles Brown, Jessie Bail, Lyle Sankey, Larry Mahan, and Donnie Gay—were the champions displayed along the right wall, all hanging on to some high-kicking, whirlwind-spinning, whiplash-bucking monster bull. The left wall showed off the contemporary champions—Tuff Hedeman, Lane Frost, Ty Murray, Cody Hancock, and Terry Don West. The far back wall supported a narrow dance stage. Above it was a rear projection movie screen showing a continuous loop of bull riding from every rodeo venue in the US, Canada, and Australia over the last twenty years. The bar ran perpendicular to it coming straight down the center of the long room toward the entrance. The bartenders worked in the middle of the two parallel bar tops that had thirty western saddles for bar stools on both sides.

Greeting you when you entered the barn-sized room, atop the front end of the bar was one of the sexy Cowgals. She was mounted on a moving, coin-operated, miniature, mechanical horse, the kind you find in front of a drugstore. She waved with her red cowgirl hat above her blonde head, welcoming all who entered the Bullpen. Immediately recognizing Taylor, she called out with a loud, "Howdy there, cowboy. Long time, no see. Who's your cute date?" giving Eizzo the once over.

"It's his first night out since his sex change operation, so go easy on him," Taylor jested while throwing his arm over Eizzo's shoulders. Eizzo quickly pointed at his Adam's apple on his thick neck, defensively rejoining, "I'm Adam, he's Eve," pointing with his other hand at Taylor.

"Well then, welcome to the Garden of Eden, darlings. I'll be by to see ya'all later with my own apples," she said, winking at the two easy prospects. Taylor asked Eizzo to literally saddle up to the bar and look for the remaining five team members while he went to Bull's office in the back. Passing through a long, back hallway, he arrived at a black metal door with a glass peephole in the center-top. A white metal, wall-mounted security camera aimed directly at him from above the door. He knocked three times and then raised a middle finger to the camera.

Within seconds, the door opened. "I'm glad you remembered the secret clubhouse pass, Taylor," Bull chuckled as he welcomed his friend with a firm hand grasp. "Two more of your team just arrived in front." He gestured to one of the ten video monitors stacked on a wide wall console providing management with multiple views of the club. Taylor viewed the one showing Cope and Grav in the arm embrace of Booby Gump.

"Where in the hell did you find Clarence? And do you pay him by the pound?"

"You've gotta love this man's showmanship," Bull said with pride, flipping on the audio switch to Clarence's microphone to hear, "...them Chi-Chis, Tater Tots, Sugar Plums, Snuggle Puffs, Sweet Rolls, Bumper Crops, and Lulus. You'll see..."

He turned off the sound to hear Taylor chuckling, "I think Booby Gump was on the tit too long as a baby. The man's obsessed," Taylor declared.

"Wait until you see his girlfriend who could double for Olive Oyl. She usually shows up later to check on her man," Bull explained. "Speaking of checking on, I have your two lady recruits waiting to meet with you. As requested, I narrowed the field down to two finalists for 'field wardrobe.' I'll send them in here, so as always, feel at home while I go find Cope," he said with a surrendering smile.

"You're the best, Bull. I'll look for you when I finish here. Oh, and one thing more, what about Clarence?" Taylor persisted in knowing his background.

"Yes, of course. Clarence, all-American tackle for National Champions–Alabama in the early '90s, heart murmur kept him out of the pros, got a graduate degree from UNLV in criminal justice, and is now a Bolinski Investigative Associate. He 'bounces' here three nights a week because he needs to exercise his charisma and 380-pound physique. The other four nights, I have two men working the entrance."

"Just as I thought. And the BAMA knuckle tattoo—stands for 'Alabama,' right?"

"Right. But there's more to it. His teammates said that the BAMA tattoo became legendary in his Alabama games, instilling the fear of God into his opponents. They'd have to stare across the line of scrimmage at that huge BAMA fist while he was poised in his attack stance. When the ball snapped, Clarence would explode across the line with a frightful forearm shiver to the face of the poor quivering kid in front of him, shouting, 'BAMA!' upon contact. By the second half of the game, Clarence owned the slot in front of him, explaining his school record number of sacks and tackles."

"Well, his personality is as big as he is, a great addition to both your businesses, Bull," Taylor said sincerely.

"And as bright as he is big. You'd have to be, to remember that many names for knockers," Bull laughed roundly.

* * *

Concluding his twenty minutes of interviews, Taylor entered the Bullpen's main floor from the back. Twenty beautiful, vivacious Cowgals were just finishing their Rockettes style dance line routine on the long, narrow dance stage in the rear. Instead of the arms-over-shoulders line of dancers stepping and high-kicking, they used a single, hundred-foot long rodeo rope for their western high-step and stomping dance number. It became their support bar and stage prop for riding and gliding across the stage to the wild, whistling delight of the male patrons. It was called the Boots and Bootie Ballet. Bull would boast, "It's an art form that you won't see at Radio City Music Hall."

By the time Taylor had arrived at their reserved corner booth, all of his men had assembled. A shapely, five-foot, eight-inch tall Cowgal server with blonde pigtails, dark-brown eyes framed by long eyelashes was seductively leaning over the table. She had just placed a banquet size platter of barbecue beef ribs in the center. Three pitchers of beer had already been reduced to tiny suds lining the clear glass bottoms.

"Pull up a chair, Taylor. We were just swapping lies until the bones came," Rap reported, reaching into the platter with his long, callused hand. "I'm tired of trout. If I'm going to pick at bones, let it be beef."

Cope proudly pulled a folded, crisp one-hundred-dollar bill from his red western Wrangler shirt pocket and waved it boastfully at Taylor. "What have I always said, my friend?"

Taylor smiled graciously with his routine reply. "All you need in life is your horse, your rope, and bull-riden' money."

"You got it, partner. Life doesn't get any better than this when you throw in some barbecue bones and beer," he said, putting the money back into his pocket while lifting his beer glass with the other hand.

A few years earlier, Cope would have included a tin of Copenhagen chewing tobacco on his life-list of priorities, until he dated a cowgirl on the rodeo circuit who "chewed," and then realized how disgusting it was. "I don't want to die from second-hand chew," he explained as his reason for quitting. The only remnants from his old snuff habit was his nickname, Cope, from Copenhagen, and the circular, faded denim imprint from the former chewing tobacco tin kept in the right rear pocket of his old worn jeans.

Looking around the walls at the photos of his bull riding heroes, Cope declared soulfully, "I've always imagined heaven like this, because anything else will just be hell."

The others all laughed. "But don't be surprised, Cope, that when you arrive at the pearly gates, Saint Peter hands you a shovel and points to the heavenly horse stalls," Nep suggested in a joyous tone.

The camaraderie continued with its comedic chiding and friendly teasing of one another, diverting their jocular jargon to their sexy young server, Dolly, whenever she was table side with more food and beverage. Cam had offered her "a little grass shack in Hawaii and a skirt to match"; Eizzo asked her if she'd like "a shack up in the woods"; Nep invited her on "a sea cruise with a private seat at his captain's table"; and Cope asked her is she'd like to see his "Super Bull tattoos?"

Her sharp, sassy, replies were swift: if she were ever to go to Hawaii with a man, his last name would have to be Dole; that "the only shack in the woods for her would be a pump house for her Alaskan oil well"; and Nep would have to rename his yacht "Dolly's Boy Toy" and lower his rank to galley slave. She sweetly informed Cope that she wanted "a cowboy who could stay on for more than eight seconds." But if his private part had a single line tattoo that read, "Cope's Restaurant and Saloon, Albuquerque, New Mexico, Entertainment Nightly," she would marry him.

"Darlins," she summarized, "you'all must understand a Cowgal's motivation. Women have to be in the mood, men just have to be in the room."

As Cope, Rap, Eizzo, and Cam "cried in their beers," Grav and Nep enjoyed dancing with the Cowgals to their favorite Chris Ledoux songs, "One Ride in Vegas" and "Cowboys Like a Little Rock." Cope naturally requested Ledoux's "Copenhagen Angel." The partying continued with more pitchers and western dancing. Bull had come by earlier to patiently hear the men's age-old plea for him to be more cooperative by sending seven Cowgals out to the ranch with them. "Only if I can include the pastor from the Vegas Chapel of Wed'em and Bed'em so we can have a remake of *Seven Brides for Seven Brothers*," he said, receiving a choral response of moans and groans.

By eleven o'clock, Bull had returned to the corner booth to talk privately with Taylor a few feet from the table.

"Clarence has a situation developing at the entrance. I've been monitoring it from the office. He's verbally been able to keep six badass bikers from coming in. But four more just rode up. I'm certain they're the same Road Hog Harley gang we kept out of here last year."

"And now they're back with a new plan, I suppose," Taylor said.

"Exactly. If I send my floor bouncers out there, it will provoke them. I could call the LVPD, but the bikers would like that because it would get ugly. Vegas to them is the devil's playground," Bull said with a grimace on his concerned face. As a former cop, he knew trouble when he saw it. But now a civilian and business owner, he was more prudent in his eagerness to respond.

"And biker gangs love ugly," Taylor stated knowingly.

"And I don't need ugly publicity, which in part is their strategy to get into reputable clubs. 'Let us in or we'll open up a can of ugly!' Any thoughts, Taylor, on how to encourage them to leave without a confrontation?"

"Let me see them from your office monitor. I'll bring the boys back there with me—discreetly."

Bull nodded in agreement and left for his office alone. Taylor turned toward their booth to find Dolly preparing to take a new order from four of the men still seated. He wrapped his thick arm around her bare shoulders. "Darlin', each one of these guys would love to take you home to meet their mamas, if they knew who their mamas were. So you'll just have to say goodnight to our orphans now," he said politely with a gentle smile and firm hug against his rock hard body, causing her to blush fire engine red. He placed a fresh, folded one-hundred-dollar bill into her deep, buxom cleavage, kissed her forehead, turned her gently around, and sent her softly off down the sawdust aisle.

Taylor interrupted the men's protesting with a firm statement they all immediately recognized. "Gentlemen, we have a present, internal ops situation. Bull needs our help. Eizzo, you know where his back office is. Go get Nep and Grav off the dance floor and meet us there in thirty seconds. Rap, Cope, Cam, come with me," Taylor ordered, putting his men into a *quasi*-military mode.

The audio from Clarence's microphone was on high speaker volume in Bull's office. The two front entrance cameras pointed at the gang of ten bikers, one in wide angle, the second in sweeping close-up, both controlled on the office console.

"Clarence just turned around and whispered into his mic. He said he was waiting for another biker to show up for it to be a fair fight. He's used to eleven men on the other side," Bull clarified with proud laughter, confident that his indomitable doorman sincerely viewed the overwhelming odds of opponents to be doable.

Taylor studied the scene on the wide-angle shot and confirmed the count of ten bikers, all large, muscular men in their thirties and early forties. The facial hair hid their natural identities. He also counted ten motorcycles parked end-to-end along the No Parking / Loading Zone curb in front of the Bullpen.

The close-up camera showed half of the bulky men wore differing styles of sunglasses popular among bikers, flame red and pearl blue wraps, and black Badlander and Road Hog goggles. The riding gear were well-worn jeans, leather vests and chaps, denim vests, and jackets with embroidered patches making rebellious statements of Independence: "Ride Free, Brother;" "Ride Hard—Die Free;" "If You're on Anything But a Harley—You're a Homo." And Cope's favorite, "If You Don't Limp—You Ain't Shit." Others promoted a badass biker nickname like Dark Rider, Grim Rider, Hell Rider, Chopper Dog, Bad Company, Iron Horse, and Bruiser Cruiser.

The men took turns viewing the gang members, admiring Clarence's surety, poise, intimidating posture, and fortitude before such odds. Eizzo pointed out that the ten bikers showed three things in common: "heavy black, hard toe boots, prison tattoos, and facial scars."

"No visible weapons. The only chains are a couple of vest extenders," Cam reported.

"I just spoke with LVPD Detective Houser. They have an unmarked car on the corner, opposite side of the street. These bikers are a 'hang around gang,' rowdy tuffs with records, but not part of any organized, sanctioned run," Bull relayed. He was referring to what every cop knew to be the country's three largest and deadliest biker gangs, the Hell's Angels, the Banditos, and the Outlaws. "Detective Houser said they are watchful of them, and we should be too," Bull concluded.

The watchful troopers now knew what they were up against. "Observe and orientate," Taylor said out loud. "Now we decide and act."

"Rap, how long is your Harley?" Taylor asked.

"Almost eight feet."

"Bull. How long is the Cowgal's dance rope?"

"Exactly one hundred feet."

"Perfect. Bull, get back with Detective Houser and ask for his 'unmarked' to ignore a couple of cowboys near the two-wheelers. Give them the description of my pickup, then stay behind the entrance doors with your headset on. I'll remain on watch here."

Taylor sent Grav and Cam with Bull to the inside front entrance to remain "at the ready," as backup for Clarence, if needed. He sent Nep to the dance stage to bring back the 100-foot long rodeo rope. Rap and Cope exited from the back and circled around the side with the rope and Taylor's plan "Operation Hog-Tie."

Even though he was selected for his smaller size, Rap still had to lower his above-average frame down into a marine crawl in order to be completely out of sight behind the Harleys. The five-inch ground clearance of the long, low motorcycles would not reveal his presence because of the concrete curb. The biggest challenge he saw before him was his absolute, unabashed adoration of the Harley Davidson motorcycle. He had locked up his "electric cherry red" Sportster 1200-Roadster–XL in Alpine, Wyoming, before departing on his new mission. When he wasn't rafting the mountain rapids, he was riding their roads and hairpin turns.

Now Rap was looking down a curbside lineup of extreme custom, classic Harleys: a couple of Dyna Wide Glides, one a low rider; a silver Super Glide; a black Night Train; a candy cobalt Deuce, a platinum and slate gray Springer, a red Deluxe; and directly in front of him, a black Screamin' Eagle Fat Boy, the street rod of his dreams. "I can only guess how the Road Hogs paid the price of these sweet things," he muttered to himself.

He secured the anchor knot tightly to the back polished spun-aluminum wheel, then wound it twice around the shotgun exhaust, once around the heat shields of the slash down mufflers, pausing briefly to admire the Twin Cam-103 Beta engine, the chrome fuel tank panel, and leather tank panel. He sighed heavily with envy and then slipped the rope in between the fat chrome forks in front before winding it three times around the spokes of the front spun-aluminum wheel. He quickly crawled to the second bike as Cope joined him from behind. Lying prone alongside the first tied bike, he whispered to Rap, "You're supposed to rope these babies, not make love to them."

"There are ten bikes here. Do you think they'd miss one?"

"Keep rope'n, rookie," Cope laughed in a muffled voice.

Rap weaved the rope only through the wheels' spokes of the second bike, repeating the same process on the other bikes until he arrived at the tenth and last Harley. There he weaved the identical rope web as on the first bike, establishing a second, and end anchor to the chain of attached Harleys. For added assurance, Cope had followed behind Rap, letting a few pounds of air pressure out of each front tire, leaving enough to ride away, but not in full throttle hot pursuit of their pranksters.

They were so close to the gathered Harley boys, they could read the words printed on the back of one of the biker's black leather jacket, "*If You Can Read This—The Bitch on the Back Fell Off.*"

Hunched down together behind the ninth and tenth bikes, Rap flashed his small flashlight in the direction of the pickup fifty feet away. They silently crotched down in a sprinter's start position. A bright silver metallic, new model Dodge Ram SRT-10 pickup truck cruised quickly to where the two men were waiting. They leaped up from their street side hiding and into the bed of the pickup. Rap held on to the remaining nine feet of rope, assuming a secure spot in the end corner of the truck bed. Cope stood up behind the truck cab and waved his white cowboy hat high in the air. He yelled toward the gang of ten bikers by the Bull Pen entrance, "Yo! Road Hogs—over here!"

Eizzo honked the horn for ten seconds until all of the bikers were looking his way. Again, Cope waved his hat wildly above his head. "This street is for cowboys with cattle, not Harleys with road hogs!" he hollered with his best west Texas country call. That was the signal for Eizzo to pull away slowly with Rap holding the rope firmly with both hands. With the rope pulled taut, he gave it a hard tug, tipping the ten Harleys over gently onto the asphalt street. They weighed between 650 and 700 pounds each, causing the ground to quake slightly upon impact. The sound of their collective grounding of metal could not be heard over the choir of loud cries and shouts of profanity coming from their owners a few feet away. They all scrambled for their respective bike's rescue, bumping and tripping over one another, their deep screams of reprisals ranging from promises of horrific torture, to death threats, to even some unspeakable acts against the mothers of the three fleeing pranksters.

Safely one block away from the scene of the prank, designated driver Eizzo stopped the Ram pickup for Rap and Cope to join him in the cab. "I've never seen so many men so unhappy about so little," Eizzo declared with an innocent smile. "It's like their bikes had never tipped over before."

"I'm tellen' you, it hurt me more than it hurt them, fellas. Those were classic Harleys, guys. I don't know if I can ever forgive myself," Rap agonized sorrowfully to the loud laughter of his partners in crime.

Rap gasped in disbelief at Eizzo's expressed desire to have "dragged the bikes down the street to test the trucks 525 pounds of torque."

"Buckle up, my brothers, because no street rod can match this Ram at a world record 154.5 miles per hour," Eizzo forewarned them. Turning on to a less traveled road parallel to the Vegas Strip, he found an open lane, launching them from fifteen miles per hour to sixty in four seconds. Cope turned up the stereo to the preset song by Thin Lizzy, "*The Boys Are Back in Town.*"

In a flash, they had arrived at the highway entrance where Cope reached forward to the dashboard to turn on the radar detector and emergency vehicle scanner. Both appeared clear of pending police traffic.

"Five hundred horsepower from a V-10 Viper engine should put some distance between us and the Road Hogs," Eizzo exclaimed, pressing his size 13, lizard skin cowboy boot down on the accelerator. Within seconds, the speedometer needle topped the 120-mph mark. The mobile phone rang. Rap answered it with his name only. He listened intently for a minute and then hung up with only a "Copy."

"Taylor said the Road Hogs got a little tied up and not to expect them to come along for the ride. Booby Gump asked them if he should call Triple A. Chopper Dog called him a Triple A-hole. Booby Gump's girlfriend had arrived and heard Chopper Dog's comment to her Clarence and got into Chopper Dog's hog face, tore him a new Triple A-hole. In conclusion, a good time was had by all," Rap chuckled with the others. "Oh and, Eizzo, Taylor said his Ram truck-tracker alarm went off at the eighty miles per hour mark and rising, said he'd call your parents if it happens again,"

"Oops! I guess I won't get to use the pickup for the prom," Eizzo said with mock disappointment. He punched in the stereo selector to the sounds of the Dells singing "*Oh What a Night.*"

Fifteen minutes later, designated driver Taylor drove Nep, Cam, and Grav in the ranch SUV to the Virgin River, Sun Ranch. They met the three earlier arriving guests waiting for them inside the gate entrance, still at the ready should Taylor call them. The team mentality was ever present, at play or at work. Tomorrow, and for weeks to come, it would be all work. Once you passed through the Sun Ranch gate, the party was over. The Delta team's paradoxical transference from Vegas to the Virgin would soon begin. The tall, black wrought iron gate spread out beneath a large overhanging, round metal symbol of a golden sunburst. It closed electronically behind them. On the ranch side of the shiny sunburst sign, etched in small Chinese characters known only to the Delta members, were two words, *Sun Tzu.*

Taylor would always tell his men, "If you want Eastern philosophy, read Confucius, Buddha, Tao, or a fortune cookie. If you want the fundamental principles on the *Art of War*, there is only one master, *Sun Tzu.*" His ancient classic writings were the oldest military treatise in the world, considered a staple and basis for all military men's training when it came to strategies and tactics of warfare. All that was taught and practiced at the Sun Ranch emanated from those profound fifth-century BC principles. "The Sun Ranch doesn't raise cattle or crops," Taylor would admit. "It develops principled military minds capable of one thing, victory in all they pursue."

Campbell, the ranch cook, was the only one awake at the ranch house. He welcomed the men home with his routine warning not to raid the refrigerator or kitchen pantry. "If you want Oreo cookies and milk before bedtime, call your mothers. Breakfast will be served at 0800 tomorrow and at 0700 every morning after that. Be showered and fully dressed, or no mess," he ruled. They were accustomed to Campbell's house rules and ingrained military bark. They were unfazed by his stern demeanor, knowing that beneath the gruff exterior, there was a generous person who understood the common military man and the special needs of his special ranch guests.

Taylor walked in with Nep, Cam and Grav joining the still amused Eizzo, Cope, and Rap relaxing in the main living room commonly called the cowpoke quarters. Down the wooden wall hallway was the sleeping quarters with individual beds lined up like a firehouse dorm room. Taylor had given instructions earlier to the men to not enter the bunk room until they were all together. Following a brief laugh-out-loud recap the evening's events at the Bullpen, he said he had a surprise awaiting them courtesy of Bull.

"The only hint I'll give is that your bitching to Bull all these years has finally paid off. Go for it!" he said invitingly as he gestured with his open arm for them to enter the bunk room. Like little kids on Christmas morning, they hurried one behind the other into the dark sleeping quarters. Immediately Taylor flicked on the ceiling lights for all to see that Bull had indeed granted their wishes to have six bodacious babes waiting for them at the ranch. Lying completely nude atop six of the beds were six blue-eyed, anatomically correct rubber blow up dolls, two each with red hair, black hair, and of course blonde. They were five feet, two inches tall, or long depending upon your perspective or desire, and busty enough to place a couple of 10-gallon cowboy hats across their chests. Their ruby red lips were pursed in a perfect circle forming a deep cavity, sufficient in circumference and depth to hold a thick, long, unlit Dominican Robusto Opus X cigar, Bull's brand of choice. In a high-pitched cacophony of groans, moans, and laughter, each man walked to the foot of their bed to inspect the sad practical joke before them. Their collective high hopes for the real deal dashed, they began speaking of revenge on their tormentor, "Bull the bullshitter must be strapped naked on one of his mechanical bulls and cranked up to the max," Rap threatened.

Cam pointed to his red-headed blow-up doll. "Check out the big old Xs across each boob and written above them, 'Dos Equis.' A real comedian, that Bull."

"Must be her nickname. Check out the others," he observed with his waving arm. Marked above the inflated D-cup breasts of the remaining five in large black letters were Bohemia, Tecate, Modelo, Sol, and Superior.

"That's just great, Bull. Tease us with beer brands in a dry ranch. I'll have his name tattooed on my butt when I get through with his," Cope pledged.

"Just make sure you take your spurs off first, Cope, so your new cowgirl friend won't fly all over the room," Eizzo warned to the chuckles of the others.

"Well, the only person deflating these hot air babes will be Campbell, who has to pack them back up for safekeeping from you perverts. You do get to keep the cigars though. We'll light them up the night before we move out to Mexico. You can deal with Bull when we return," he placated them. "For tonight, you have only to dream of them, thirty minutes before lights out," he concluded to a chorus of boos.

8

WATCH THE BIRDIE

Virgin River, Nevada

The snow-packed mountains of southwestern Utah fed the Virgin River, one of the few western rivers not dam-controlled. The high mountain run off turned from white water rapids to a chocolate brown as it descends the steep riverbed of the desert gorges, flowing leisurely over the northwest tip of Arizona, its last thirty miles crossing the southeastern edge of Nevada to form the north arm of Lake Mead. Its final journey would be in the flow of the mighty Colorado River bound for the Mexico border. The Sun Ranch bordered the river arm allowing access to the Lake Mead reservoir, forty miles east of Las Vegas. It provided the Delta team with the perfect training terrain, diverse in topography and variety of natural environments. Taylor knew the word *training* to be a misnomer for his seasoned troops using his ranch and river corridor for the purpose of field fitness conditioning. They would continue to temporize at the ranch with the conditioning regimen until Lori concluded the necessary intel gathering for the Mexico mission.

The basic foundation for the physical and intellectual conditioning at the Sun Ranch was built upon Taoist lore: "Deep knowledge and strong action. Strong action is training the body without being burdened by the body, exercising the mind without being used by the mind, carrying out tasks without being obstructed by tasks." Such were the ways and means of the coming week's agenda.

Over the next several weeks, the men would hike the windy plateaus, shoreside meadows, sculptured gorges, climb the sheer rock walls, rappel from the narrow weeping canyon walls, raft the river and lake, and practice a new field exercise for them called bird-watching.

The field conditioning would be interspersed with mission briefings at the ranch house whenever new intelligence was gleaned on their FTM fugitives. Relevant historical and cultural information about Mexico would be provided along with Spanish language lessons. The preparatory focus would be on Mexico, their intel concentration on the six hard target fugitives. It was the latter that they waited on, the need to know exactly where to enter the fugitives' loops and where to extract them.

Lori Sandburg was their go-to gal when it came to where-to-go-to. Taylor would receive her intel communiqués two to three times weekly, permitting him to formulate their overall strategic plan for entry into Mexico for search and seizure of the six fugitives and safe exit out of the country.

To remain the formidable force it was militarily intended to be, the independent and private Delta Force was structured with different skill groups needed to fit mission requirements. Having operational (ops) field experience was a must. It was a given in order to have been preselected for the private Delta company. All of the troops on the selection roster had seen three or more military missions where they were tasked with a highly specialized responsibility critical to its planned outcome.

Between Delta's foreign military missions, Taylor's job had been to provide for the unit's ongoing exchange of tactics, equipment, and training programs with foreign counterterrorist units such as Britain's 22-SAS, France's GIGN, Germany's GSG-9, Israel's Sayeret Matkal-269, and Australia's own Special Service Regiment. A "cross-pollination" of empirical knowledge and innovative ideas was considered vital for future global antiterrorists events requiring the coordinated efforts of the different collaborating Special Forces. Taylor was "cross-trained to the max" in military parlance.

The one person the private Delta members held in the highest esteem, not surprising to Taylor, was the only woman on his covert roster, Lori Sandburg. She had grown up living around the military world as the precocious daughter of a US Naval Intelligence officer. After graduating from Georgetown University with a STIA major (Science, Technology, and International Affairs) she stayed in Washington, DC, to become a member of the US Department of Defense's Intelligence Community. Her career advances were both vertical and lateral, going from the DIA (Defense Intelligence Agency) to the NRO (National Reconnaissance Office) to her father's old job site at NI (Naval Intelligence). There she transitioned into MCIA (Marine Corps Intelligence Activity), where Lori met Taylor and some of his future private Delta troops.

At MCIA, Taylor observed Lori's deft, pragmatic skills multitasking the preparation for the operations' logistical support on quick response missions. Because Delta units did not choose when or where they would be needed, they depended upon MCIA for last-minute intel and ongoing field logistical support to make their mission safe and successful. Lori Sandburg was the name they heard the most and the one they had remembered ever since. She joined Taylor's company for the challenge, adventure, and opportunity to run her own private Intelligence Activity Unit. She brought with her a vast intelligence network of domestic and foreign contacts that were critical logistical resources for covert supply of equipment, government documents, as well as field ops facilitation, from financial to medical. Some operated in the shadows of the in-country military and law enforcement, others with free trade activities and a willingness to reach out to a fellow do-gooder like Lori Sandburg. Taylor openly characterized Lori as "the queen on the chess board in the world's chess game of counter intelligence." "High praise," she thought, "coming from the king."

Lori was tied up in Las Vegas so could not be present at the Sun Ranch for the first group breakfast and initial briefing. The men enjoyed a 0800 breakfast prepared by Cookie Campbell, a meat quiche made with Campbell's cream of mushroom soup, ranch eggs, light cream, cooked crumbled bacon, ham, chorizo, spinach, nutmeg, in an 8" piecrust per person. "Real soldiers eat meat quiche," declared Taylor proudly. The troops would not allow Campbell to use his real name of Roy Bell around a group of men with only nicknames for identification, monikers that where bestowed either by accident or with a purpose. His dining guests had baptized him Campbell for his penchant for using Campbell's soups as a principal flavoring ingredient in all of his meal entrees.

Following twenty years as a shipboard navy cook, he had sworn off military mess hall meals, promising himself a civilian cooking career based on his KISS culinary method: "Kitchen Includes Soup, Stupid." After his navy retirement, he had discovered a used copy of *Cooking with Campbell's Soup* and declared himself a "born-again cook," a man with a can and a plan. He was now for hire. Lori found him first, and he had been at Sun Ranch ever since.

Taylor was convinced he was the little Campbell kid on the soup can commercials, now fully grown, the pleasingly plump adult version. His dining guests had found it curious that the kitchen pantry was filled with cans of Campbell, but they were never served soup. His answer was always, "Stealth training begins with a healthy, stealthy meal." His recipes were classified kitchen documents. But he openly promised no "mystery meat" at the Sun Ranch, only the finest cuts of prime, select meats and farm fresh produce. Hardship in the field meant healthy, hearty meals on the table. No alcohol or smoking was permitted. Live television was permitted for the evening news only. The multimedia room included a new library of travelogues on Mexico and old, black and white Mexican movies. They were the cinema classics from the golden decade of the 1940s with Dolores del Rio, Jorge Negrete, Pedro Infante, Cantinflas, and Pedro Armendariz. Two hours every evening would be dedicated to Spanish lessons in the multimedia room, which served as the foreign language lab, complete with audio and videotapes, CD-ROMs, and dialogue practice. The men would enter the language-learning center with different levels of Spanish proficiency, a prerequisite for the Mexico mission.

Delta troopers are known to possess the most advanced weaponry and mission ready equipment available, much of their gear highly customized. What is not known to the public is the state-of-the-art reconnaissance equipment used in the special operations arsenal. They are taught that all successful field operations begin with reconnaissance, observe, and orientate. And all effective reconnaissance begins with a telescope and ends with a microscope. "View your enemy first from afar, then up close when safety permits," *Sun Tsu* would teach them.

The high technology telescopes developed for spying from outer space via satellites and from high altitude aircraft were available as well for ground level reconnaissance by the Delta team. Short- and long-range camera and spotting lenses was a recon mission's best tool to detect who, what, and where, all on the sly, often from a mile away. Taylor knew that such equipment was only as good as its operator, and practice made perfect. If they were to successfully pluck six specific fugitive fish from a sea of one hundred million fish, they better have the best fish finders available in the hands of the best fishermen. Both were to be tested on and around the Sun Ranch. But for training purposes, their practice prey would be in the air. They would be the 353 species of wild birds officially recorded in the region, from tiny hummingbirds to soaring eagles. After all, Taylor reasoned, what better way to become a "birder" than to scope them out as you would any mission target?

He formally announced to his men, "There can be no better field training exercise for our Mexico mission than to go birding. It will keep us sharp on our recon skills, put us onto a variety of topography similar to rural Mexico, and most importantly, give us the empirical knowledge to pull off a birding masquerade—our only safe and effective way to enter and travel Mexico over an extended period of time and wide area of the country. It's the perfect cover. Our guise as serious American birders photographing and recording native and migratory birds will not appear uncommon there. American and European birders, both hobbyists and retirees, go there by the hundreds to add new species to their personal 'life lists' of sighted birds in the wild. We'll take with us a serious portfolio of bird photos, sounds, and relevant avian factoids so that we can talk the talk, and walk the walk."

"And chirp the chirp?" Eizzo interrupted.

"A real, authentic, serious birder in-country will detect a poser, a phony. We cannot afford any negative exposure or suspicion," Taylor underscored slowly in a baritone voice.

"Won't we have to go a little geeky with the wardrobe then?" Cam asked.

"I have a wardrobe expert named Tina in Las Vegas working on that as we speak, including regular tourist traveling clothes."

"Please tell us she doesn't do Siegfried and Roy's wardrobes," Eizzo asked in a begging posture.

"Did you tell her briefs, not boxers for me, and thongs for Cope?" Rap submitted to everyone's amusement.

Chuckling still, Taylor added, "We will have two sets of camo wear each, for day and night. They must remain concealed in the RV, used only if the tactical operation requires them. Your current G. I. Joe–looking buzz cuts will all be grown out by the time we leave. Our in-country image will be peace-loving civilians in civvies traveling as serious bird-watching tourists," he said drolly.

"Back to the regional birds here. Will we train with a specific check list of birds we're after, or are they on the come?" Cam inquired.

"Both. I'll explain. In the short time we'll be in the area, you are to photograph a minimum of 180 different species, more than half of the recorded species here. To our benefit, we are in the northern fly zone, and the winter migratory birds are beginning to arrive. In terms of a specific list, you'll receive a representative number of species to find from the diverse field environments in the region which you'll train in."

"Such as?" Grav asked.

"Such as all of them. Mexico has them all, cliffs, canyons, chaparral, brush, groves, thickets, open fields, deserts, grasslands, aquatic, shores, beaches, flats, woodlands, and of course riparian, along the Virgin. Did I miss any?" Taylor concluded.

"Yeah. Urban, the chicks in town," Rap interjected.

"The Chicken Ranch has closed, Rap. Sorry," Taylor shot back with a grin.

The Sun Ranch's resident manager, nicknamed by him, Monster Man, entered the room as though on cue to speak. "This is a good time to warn all of you. If you get close enough to a bird to kiss it, don't. You might contract a canarial disease called 'chirpies,' and it's not 'tweetible.'"

The joke was met with a mixture of laughter and boos. Nep responded, "Monster Man, you've been in the Nevada desert too long," shaking his head with a look of amused pity.

Taylor rose to his rescue. "Timing is everything, so this is a good time to have our good friend and ranch resident bird expert have the floor. You all know Mario, a.k.a. Monster Man, who will give you a specific target bird list. It's your must-have checklist for your photo portfolio in order for the training mission to be successful," Taylor instructed.

Mario was considered by his fellow troopers as more of a war victim than mere veteran. He had overcome the horrific wounds of war to become a functioning, permanent member of Taylor's team. He wore his facial burn scars well, without embarrassment, although choosing the remote ranch life to that of the city. Sun Ranch was his to run, Taylor had declared.

The men all sat up straight, leaning forward to eagerly receive the one-page, typed handout from Mario. The men enthusiastically accepted the new challenge, excited to compete against all odds. They lived for overcoming obstacles that would test their skills and problem-solving acuity. Their "Bring it on!" attitude was infectious, all members sharing a single goal, to succeed in their mission. The competition was never against one another. Trained as a team, they would always support their brother in arms toward the common objective, never divisive, always cohesive. "Never make you the obstacle," Taylor had taught them. They were all cogs on the same wheel, all rotating at the same speed, all moving in the same direction.

"You will have the same style of digital cameras but share the different special lenses, of which there are two of each. Every day you will upload your photo shoot of the day onto a single laptop computer at camp. You'll edit the photos on a digital photo album. The album will be duplicated, and both will travel on the two RV laptops into Mexico for reference, or 'show and tell,' should you encounter a more than curious Mexican audience," he said, referring to possible hostile local authorities who might challenge their birder masquerade.

"There are some Nevada bird species to be found in Mexico. But nearly all of the categories of species will be there, such as hummingbirds, wrens, sparrows, chickadees, swallows, ducks, egrets, birds of prey, grosbeaks, doves, gulls, woodpeckers, owls, quail, and more." Mario paused, to take a breath.

He reminded the men that although he was not an ornithologist, he was an active member of the region's bird-watchers network and conservation stewardship "to keep common birds common."

"Of the fifty states, Nevada ranks eleventh in species diversity and third in rarity and risk level. That's the good news. The bad news is Nevada ranks eleventh in extinctions with a number of species in decline," he stressed.

"Because of natural habitat decline?" Eizzo questioned.

"Yes. But this list is not necessarily of threatened and endangered species. I compiled my own sightings with the Red Rock Audubon Society's list in order to challenge and educate you. You'll need to learn bird morphology—field identification of bird markings that distinguish the species, like crown, forehead, eye ring, nape, back, wing, covert, chin, throat, breast, *et cetera*. You'll each receive a local field guide. When we prepare for Mexico birding, you'll receive the *Peterson Field Guide to Mexican Birds*."

"I see five different sparrows on this list. Sparrows all look alike to me. Why not choose just one?" Rap wondered.

"Not in the sparrow kingdom, they're not. Cousins maybe, but there are marked differences between the white-crowned, Brewer, vesper, chipping, and Savannah sparrows. The flighty little things are difficult to distinguish to the casual eye. But the discerning, patient eye can with practice," Mario exclaimed with patience of his own.

Taylor stood up. "Two months from now, you'll be in a crowd of fifty male Mexicans, one of whom is your FTM fugitive target. All you have to go on is a single photo of the target and a second-hand profile. That will narrow the field down to five suspects. You'll remember the distinguishable body markings like scars and tattoos, which two of the final five candidates have. Now how do you pick your man out correctly?" he challenged.

"You shout out his name and see who runs?" Rap said in jest.

"And after fifty men answer with guns drawn?" Taylor shot back with a smirk.

"Never mind. You were saying?" Rap rejoined with a peevish smile.

"The lesson learned is, never assume that who appears to be your ID target is the correct ID. Always check and recheck against all photo types. If your target acquisition is wrong, it will be impossible to reinsert yourself into the same grid for the correct one. Beyond his physical ID, we will study habits and behavior, which will be your final distinguishing factor in the field."

"As if the sparrows weren't small enough, Mario, you had to include hummingbirds?" Cope casually protested.

"They're easy to photograph. Wait around their flower food source, and while they're sipping the nectar in stationary flight, shoot at a high f-stop and you'll also catch their eighty wing beats per second in a still shot," Mario suggested.

Eizzo raised his paper in the air. "I recognize the bald eagle, red tail hawk, red shoulder hawk, but not the loggerhead shrike. And why is it underlined?"

"Because its eating behavior is so unique and also because it is your primary target for situational photography. It won't be enough to simply spot it and shoot its portrait. You must observe it preparing and eating its meal," Mario insisted.

"Bad table manners?" Nep asked.

"Bingo! Although it's a member of the falcon family, its legs and talons are not strong enough to securely hold and tear their killed prey apart to eat. After a small bird or small mammal is caught and killed by the shrike, it will impale it on the long spine of a cactus where it will then tear at it to eat or leave it to dry out in the desert sun," Mario explained, to the amusement of his audience.

"Sort of a 'bird kabob,'" Grav offered.

"Or a 'chick on a stick,'" Cope added.

"I'm thinking 'bird jerky,'" Nep wisecracked with the others.

"I told you, Mario, that they'd jump all over that one," Taylor confirmed, shaking his head.

"Well then, gentlemen, jump on this little curveball I'm going to throw you. Look on the list for 'cactus wren.' It uses the spiny branches of the cholla cactus to protect its nest, built from desert plant stems and flower stalks."

"Sounds easy enough. See the cholla cactus, see the nest, see the cactus wren," Rap said confidently.

"But which nest? A pair of wrens will build up to ten nests. Only one will be used to raise their young. The unoccupied nests will serve to confuse and frustrate their predators, like brother Rap here," Mario rejoined evenly.

Rap rose, bowed low, and said with humility, "I apologize, Master Mario. *General Sun Tzu* has taught the cactus wren well, 'that all warfare is based on deception.'"

Rap was seated to the applause of his fellow troopers. Taylor stood before him with an official posture and challenge. "Now Officer Rap will learn from his brother, the cactus wren. You are the chosen one who will seek and find the wise wren and photograph them in the correct nest. Should you fail in this 'Operation See the Birdie,' then Master Mario may impale you upon a cactus spine and leave you in the desert sun to dry out your excess confidence," Taylor concluded to the comedic entertainment of the others.

* * *

Over the weeks of preparation, there had been as many suggestions as there were natural choices for the bird-watching logo to be selected to adorn the front sides of the two bus RVs, serving as the official covert name for the Mexico mission. Taylor was looking for a well-known bird in Mexico other than their golden eagle, the country's official bird and government symbol found on their national flag and seal. Cope's symbol suggestion of a bald eagle carrying a golden eagle in its talons over the US border was rejected for obvious reasons. The red, white, and green bird of paradise, of Mayan folklore, the resplendent *Quatzsecual* was considered too resplendent and passive to best represent the mission. Grav said he hadn't seen that much tail since Las Vegas.

"People might wonder what we're up to," he speculated. The legendary Mayan macaws were considered too flighty and festive of an image, the owls were believed to be messengers from the underworld, and the Aztec's white heron of *Atzlan* lore was "too skinny and pretty for a bunch of bulked-up birders," Eizzo contested. "Image and symbolism are everything in Mexico," Taylor exclaimed.

The long deliberation and selection process had worked, producing the appropriate mission bird symbol and broad education about the Bird Nation, Mexico, the host to over 960 species. The crested *caracara* would be their avian host and covert mission mask.

Mario officially recited the published description of their selected birder symbol as "primarily ground-dwelling falcons inhabiting open prairies. They are strong, rapid fliers with a four-foot wingspan, two feet tall, brown birds with a white throat, neck, and tail. Its distinguishing black flat crest looks like a toupee a bald eagle might covet. The reduplicative name translates to English as 'face face,' the physical explanation for its normal red face changing to yellow when excited. The *caracara* is an attack bird of prey; with a swift, single strike, its strong legs and deadly talons kill small mammals, reptiles, and fish." It was the perfect team logo, was the consensus, for the two-faced reduplicative field mission masquerade to dupe the public and the enemy. *Caracara* it was.

Following the four days it took to paint the bird of prey logo on the front sides of the two RVs, Taylor organized a christening ceremony with Mario and Campbell taking the lead. The unpretentious brand of Thunderbird wine was chosen for the bottle-breaking ceremony on the front bumpers of the RVs, officially naming them *Caracara* I and II. Campbell prepared a celebratory meal that surprisingly did not include a single can of soup. He served 14-ounce grilled OK Corral T-bone steaks with chili-lime butter, skillet cornbread, snap green beans and sweet onions, and Cookie's spoon batter blackberry cobbler. T-bird wine was not on the menu. But Dominican Robusto Opus X cigars were the promised finale. Tomorrow they would prepare to move out.

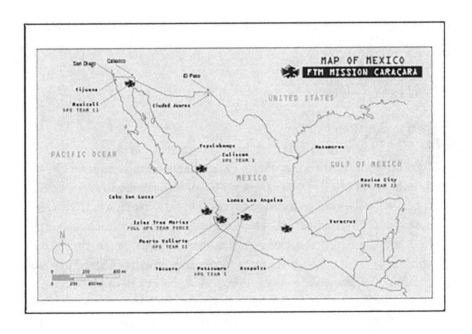

9

MISSION CARACARA

Los Angeles, California

It was time to move out.

"This will be our last briefing together as a group before heading south. Intel out of San Diego has our FTM fugitive Olivel Morales off of our Tijuana target grid—disappeared without a trace. Since his gang works as a fringe supplier for the Tijuana Cartel, anything could have happened. The gangbangers are the stolen car suppliers for the drug traffickers and money launderers, so they have exposure at both ends of the transborder movements. These guys are dispensable *pelones*. We know Olivel Morales is not in the US according to the San Diego DEA Special Agent-in-charge. Mexico's AFI was tracking him as a lead to larger fish, but lost him six days ago. Lori's in-country contact is our best source and means for finding him, especially if he's incarcerated somewhere in Mexico. If he was whacked in their ongoing drug turf war, then we'll only know about it from their local newspapers," Taylor declared coldly.

"So then our Team I will bypass TJ?" Grav asked with reservations.

"Yes, unless Olivel has reappeared by the time we reach the border. Then we'll reassess the opportunity at that time. But Team I, with Grav, Cam, and myself, will still cross the border at Tijuana. The plan is for Team II, with Eizzo, Cope, and Rap, to cross at *Calexico*,

California, into the *Mexicali* target grid along the Mexican border to apprehend their first FTM fugitive, Manual Bravo," Taylor confirmed.

"He's still in his grid, I assume?" Eizzo asked.

"Very much so. It gets complicated along the Mexican side of the border. You have local police pretending to chase down the *Coyotes*, the people smugglers sneaking the illegal migrants over the border. Add to that the US subsidized undercover Mexican Border Patrol surveilling the *Coyotes*."

"Random surveillance, or 24-7 coverage?" Cam asked.

"Around-the-clock, according to our latest intel: cameras, eye-in-the-sky balloons, drones, night-vision goggles, wiretaps, tagging, tailing—all potentially putting Team II in the same crosshairs as Manuel Bravo, if not careful," Taylor cautioned. "The good news is that he is our only FTM fugitive who left a forwarding address. We know where Bravo lives and operates," he continued.

"And our first coastal rendezvous with Nep and the *Sea Cat* will be where?" Eizzo asked.

"Once you have TA (target acquisition), you'll continue south to the Sea of Cortez along the mainland coast. I'll explain in a minute the options you have for your captives' transport and transfer," Taylor paused.

The Delta team members were aware of the modifications made to the two custom RVs since their mission into Canada to seize two Hong Kong Chinese fugitives. The changes were minor in mechanical engineering terms. They simply duplicated what was already in place as a single hidden holding pen in the rear of the RV, to comfortably and quietly sequester their criminal captives for an extended journey.

"While Team II is in *Mexicali*, Team I will proceed directly from Tijuana down the mainland coast of the Sea of Cortez to *Culiacán*, Sinaloa, known as *Tierra Blanca*, the drug traffic capital of Mexico." Taylor quoted the Mexican media's popular appellation for *Culiacán* as the "White Land—*Tierra Blanca*" because of all of the cocaine spilled there due to the pervasive drug trafficking—illegal shipments from Colombia, Bolivia, and Peru. It was landed on the *Sinaloa* coast and stashed in *Culiacán* until shipped to the Mexico/US border, Tijuana Cartel and Juárez Cartel with Los Zetas in play in the northeastern end as distribution platforms. Mexico's marines, local and state police, and government officials at multilevel would take a monetary *mordida (bite)* along the way.

"So now we know who put the *sin* in *Sinaloa*," Cope declared

"Our planned destination is the *Culiacán* grid—where we grab FTM fugitive Lionel Mario Madrid. We face other risks there as well, the rival Guadalajara cartel," Taylor warned.

"A high probability?" Cam asked with measured concern.

"Last year in *Sinaloa* alone, cartel members were being killed at a rate of two per day during their six-month-long turf war. And because Lionel is one of the *Sinaloa* Cartel *sicarios* (assassins), there will be an *ajuste de cuentas* (retaliation) target on him," Taylor declared.

"From any one in particular?" Grav asked.

"Only from the Gulf Cartel, Juarez Cartel, Arelliano Felix, Tijuana Cartel, Los Zetas, and the government's elite drug-fighting forces *du jour*," Taylor replied flippantly.

"It's nice to be so popular," Eizzo exclaimed.

"We have to grab him first to protect our interests. His enemies won't stop their pursuit until they see him dead," Grav stated emphatically.

"When we make him disappear, it might throw them off his trail and ours," Cam offered.

"Let's seize and secure Lionel first, then we'll determine if a red herring follow-up is required," Taylor agreed.

He emphasized again the seriousness of the *Sinaloa* drug traffickers' danger zone, the "hottest grid" in their overall mission, called by the media "the killing fields."

"Remember who we're up against, a lowlife group of trigger-happy narco-terrorists who not only shoot their enemies execution style, they suffocate them with clear plastic bags while one of their *el gordos* (fat men) bounces on their chest. Then there's the savage *carne asada* (barbecue), executing entire families, then tossing their corpses on a bed of burning tires," Taylor said with disgust.

"*Capos* (drug lords) rule by terror. It's referred to in *Sinaloa* as the 'metal mentality—silver and lead rules.' If silver can't buy influence and cooperation, than lead bullets will get rid of those who won't or don't," Taylor added.

"Don't forget the 'Colombian necktie,'" Rap interjected, referring to cutting an informant's throat beneath the chin, then pulling his tongue through the wound as he chokes to death—the grizzly penalty for talking to the wrong people.

"Lionel Mario Madrid is doubly dangerous because he's sloppy. He shot at and missed his intended target in Santa Barbara and killed an innocent bystander, fled to Mexico, stopping along the way to kill a drug dealer client in Los Angeles who hadn't paid, only to learn later that he had," Taylor recited from Lori's intel.

"These enforcers are paid for quantity, not quality," Cope opined.

"The worse screwup was in 1993 when the Arelliano brothers made a retaliatory hit attempt on rival drug lord Chapo Guzman at the *Guadalajara* airport and mistakenly killed Cardinal Juan Jesus Posadas Ocampo, who arrived in a similar car to Chapo's," Taylor continued.

"Damn! Imagine hearing the shooter's plea for forgiveness in the church confessional: 'Forgive me, Father, for I have fucked up big time. How was I to know that the man two feet away wearing a long black cassock and a large pectoral cross wasn't Chapo Guzman?' 'Say ten trillion, "Hail Marys," and then go directly to hell, my son,'" Eizzo dramatized in a mock tone of reverent reconciliation.

"As they say, the only thing worse than a professional assassin, is an amateur one," Cam contributed, to the collective nods of his partners.

"Should Team II remain on standby in case you need backup in *Culiacán?*" Eizzo asked.

"Nep will be close by, off shore on the *Sea Cat*, should we need back up or a quick exit. Team II, when you leave *Mexicali*, you'll have to get into your second grid, ASAP, with our elusive target, Juan Diego Leon. He's our only FTM fugitive target with a GPS tracker fixed on him, tagged on his pickup truck to be exact. He has been working the entire US border, from the Pacific to the Gulf of Mexico near *Matamoras*, constantly on the move, doing what exactly, we can only imagine. Currently he's headed to the southwest forest lowlands near the pueblo of *San Jacinto*, just above *Puerto Vallarta* near the Pacific. You'll receive an updated, detailed briefing on Juan Diego

Leon once you're in country. That will determine your route from *Mexicali*, south into the interior of Mexico. Of all of our six FTM targets, Juan Diego Leon is the most mobile, a moving, tagged target," Taylor declared craftily.

"Still considered dangerous?" Eizzo asked.

"He beat and stabbed an old woman to death in Santa Barbara for her ATM card PIN number and now is packing a .45 revolver. So the answer is yes, more than ever," Taylor responded with polite sarcasm.

"Do we hold Manuel Bravo on board Caracara II while proceeding to our next target grid, or make the transfer to the *Sea Cat* first?" Eizzo inquired

"You'll be close enough to the coast to make the Manuel Bravo transfer to the *Sea Cat*. Nep will tell you where to rendezvous along the coast, you tell him when. Remember, the catamaran will shadow us along the western mainland coast, from midway up in the Sea of Cortez near *Culiacán*, sailing south past *Mazatlan, Topolobampo, Puerto Vallarta, Zihuatanejo,* and if necessary, to *Acapulco*, directly south of Mexico City."

Taylor fingered the map of Mexico to review all of the road routes marked as Primary, and the alternates marked Secondary and Clandestine, the latter designated for emergency evasion options. Their travel strategy was to be overt, hide out in plain sight in such an obvious manner as to defy all logical and reasonable cause for anyone to be suspicious. Especially of something as large and slow as a giant RV identified with birder logos transporting a bunch of geeky, gringo birders inside. They would be the antistealth travelers known to all in route as common *touristas*.

"When you transfer Juan Diego Leon to the *Sea Cat*, Nep will give you a special delivery of electronic equipment from Lori. You'll make a clandestine dead drop of the crated equipment in Mexico City to her covert contact there. You'll be given the drop site before entering that grid. Then you can commence with your search and seizure of FTM fugitive Jose Taboada, an urban grid of only twenty million people," Taylor underscored with a grin.

"That's not a needle in a hay stack, that one in a whole damn hay field," Cope countered lightly.

"Well, Jose Taboada thought he could hide among the masses in the largest city in the world. But he made two rookie mistakes. One, he assumed that the citizens of Santa Barbara would forget about his slitting his wife's throat, and two, that no one would come looking for him in his protective country. In his criminal mind, he's home free—no worries," Taylor stated flatly.

"The last thing he's thinking is that he'll be kidnapped right off the streets, his streets, in his nation's capital," Rap condescended with a tone of irony.

"Well, shit does happen, even to the worst of us," Cope punctuated Rap's comment.

"From Mexico City, you head due south with Taboada to the fishing village of Zihuatanejo, west of Acapulco. At the same time, Team I should be in the *Patzcuaro* grid initiating the OODA on Pedro Barajas. He was dumb enough to return to his home surroundings, but smart enough to hide behind the protective cloth of the church. We'll have eighteen churches to choose from in the area. In one will be the devil himself," Taylor said contemptuously, remembering his nearly cremated son, Miguel.

"Where will Team I make the Barajas transfer to the *Sea Cat*?" Rap questioned.

"South of *Puerto Vallarta*. Nep will pick a secluded cove. Team II will meet us there. By then, Lori should have a current fix on our last FTM fugitive, Olivel Morales," Taylor projected hopefully.

"We should still be in a good position geographically, assuming he remains in western Mexico, possibly back in TJ," Cam speculated.

"We'll just have to wait for new intel from Lori's in-county source. But we are not leaving Mexico without Morales. Any number less than six captures will be a failed mission," Taylor exclaimed resolutely.

The ranch training was completed. The detailed criminal case-by-case and individual fugitive profiles had been covered repeatedly so that each team member had their FTM targets committed to memory. No documents or notes related to the fugitives or the mission in particular would be aboard Caracara I or II. The onboard laptop computers were only loaded with information on migratory and indigenous birds to Mexico. Common travel maps of Mexico and RV park locations were on a CD-ROM.

Concealed in secret onboard compartments were custom CDs with the photographs of the six fugitives with computer-generated facial variations as a positive ID aid. They would be loaded into the operations laptop during the initiation of each OODA phase and deleted at its conclusion. They all knew Delta Force stealth meant internal as well as external: "If nobody knew they were there, then it didn't happen."

Taylor had paused for his fellow troopers to process all of the information and collect their thoughts about the final instructions that would soon carry them in to harm's way. They were seasoned enough soldiers to realize that what appeared in a briefing room or on a map was far removed from the harsh reality of the true lay of the land and the hidden, proverbial "landmines." They were all mindful of the *Sun Tzu* tactical disposition, that "The thing is to see the plant before it has germinated."

Taylor continued with the Mexico mission summary, standing now before his comrades with the official countenance of the commander that he was. "Teams I and II will cross into Mexico the same day, same time, Team I from San Diego into *Tijuana, Baja Norte*, Team II from *Calexico*, California, into *Mexicali, Baja.* Communicating only on our closed-circuit Casper cells, we will synchronize our entry time. As of today, the planned sequence of our dual team, six 'search and seizures' are as follows:

Manuel Bravo	*Mexicali, Baja*	Team II
Lionel Mario Madrid	*Culiacán, Sinaloa*	Team I
Juan Diego Leon	North of *Puerto Vallarta, Jalisco*	Team II
Pedro Barajas	*Patzcuaro, Michoacán*	Team I
Jose Taboada	Mexico City, DF	Team II
Olivel Morales	Grid to be determined	Team I

"And what are our three tactical dispositions?" Taylor asked openly. "Conceal the disposition of your troops, cover up your tracks, and take unremitting precautions," he recited crisply. "Secure success by modifying your tactics to meet those of the enemy. Cope, recite the general's third tactical disposition."

"The opportunity of defeating the enemy is provided by the enemy himself."

"And if not, gentlemen, we don't wait for opportunities, we create them," Taylor stressed to the ops team one last time.

With those familiar words, the men knew it was time to move out into *terra incognita*. Mission *Caracara* was under way.

The white, 85-foot long, 42-foot wide catamaran was well-known along the southern and central Pacific coast of California by its namesake, the *Sea Cat*. Along the Mexico, *Baja* peninsula, from Ensenada in the north to Cabo *San Lucas* on the southernmost tip, it was referred to as *El Gato del Mar*. Christened as the west coast's largest charter catamaran, it had sailed the same coastal routes for scores of private parties ranging from ten to twenty. Always crewed by its owners, the captain, and first and second officers. Additional crew boarded on an as-needed basis, ranging from galley cooks to mechanics.

Delta Force member Nep, short for his field handle, Neptune, was the yacht's principal owner and captain. This would be his second private ops mission at the helm of his catamaran, chartered by Taylor for Mission *Caracara*. His first charter ops mission one year earlier was into Vancouver harbor to pick up the two extracted Hong Kong Chinese that Taylor and the Delta team had captured in Montreal and Toronto. Nep off-loaded the two captives in San Francisco to Taylor's receiving team. The current Mexico mission would be the *Sea Cat*'s first Delta operation south of San Diego, although every Mexican nautical mile was familiar chartered water for the entire crew.

Nep boasted that with the aid of the ship's state-of-the-art GPS, radar, and MAPTECH navigational computer software, the *Sea Cat* could travel entirely on autopilot from San Diego to *Cabo San Lucas*, seven hundred miles down the *Baja* Coast. The highly sophisticated marine software system displayed NOAA nautical charts, USGS topographical maps of land and sea floor, navigational photos in 3-D, as well as aeronautical photos, covering every nautical square mile of the *Sea Cat*'s operational territory, including diversionary options and open water escape routes if needed.

Nep calculated a 48-hour journey to the Cape (*Cabo*), accounting for a couple of whale watching deviations into the warm water lagoons of San Ignacio and Magdalena in Baja Sur. That was, after all, their seafaring guise of masquerading as a charter, gray whale science cruise.

Following the same southerly coastal route as the annual migrating grays would be a natural cover for the clandestine prisoner ship. The *Sea Cat* would fly the blue and white pendant of the *American Cetacean Society* at the masthead and aft flag pole. Special seaworthy cameras with deck mounts both stern and aft would film these gentle giants all the way into their ancestral birthing waters of the environmentally protected bays and lagoons of *Baja Sur*. The return trip north would again trail the grays' coastal voyage. The *Sea Cat* would drop its live catch off in Santa Barbara, California, well short of the gray whales' migratory destination of Alaska's Bering Straits.

Nep spent only two weeks at the Sun Ranch with his fellow troopers, sufficient time to learn what his role in Mission *Caracara* would be. He participated in all of the initial briefings and preliminary extraction plans for the six FTM fugitives. His task now was to have the *Sea Cat* modified to meet the new mission demands and to be optimally prepared to set sail upon Taylor's command. This voyage would be far more complex and challenging than the Canadian mission. The exposure to suspecting Mexican eyes would come during their proximity to the Mexico mainland along the coastal drug traffic routes where South American smugglers dropped their shiploads of contraband. Reentering US waters with the prisoners on board would pose the greatest risk under the vigilant presence of the US Coast Guard, more watchful than ever with their new Homeland Security mandates. People-smuggling from Asia and Mexico by sea had also increased in the last few years, making every vessel along the California coast, large or small, suspect.

Nep's orders were, "To be one with the whales," to migrate round trip, "slow as she blows," Taylor advised.

Mad Mary 1

McKinney was now boarding his *Conch II* yacht twice a week, every Wednesday and Sunday mornings. Seven weeks had passed since Taylor and his team had visited Santa Barbara, so he was becoming most eager for the first coded message to arrive from Mexico confirming that the mission was proceeding as planned. Although he would never know what the tactical plans were, he and his associates had a vested interest in its ultimate objective, bring the bad guys to justice on our side for the world to see.

Taylor had spoken with McKinney once since their Santa Barbara meeting, and only for a brief moment. It was a secure call, field-testing McKinney's high-tech encrypted cell phone, one that displayed no caller number or record of origin or destination, what McKinney termed "ghost calls" into thin air without a trace. The prototype cell phone model name was Casper "because it is user-friendly," McKinney touted with amusement. The entire Delta team and support group had twelve Caspers, all programmed with a matrix of caller codes, blockers, scramblers, and deciphers on a closed-circuit, dedicated network that was "more secure than any phone system has ever been," McKinney's technicians guaranteed. "Not even mental telepathy is more secure because your wife can always read your mind," they claimed.

Taylor's call had been as cryptic as was brief. McKinney was told that he would get progress reports at the Harbor Market, unbeknownst to the store workers. It was a tiny, compact convenience store specializing in snack foods, cold beverages, and ice for the harbor workers and sea-going boats out of the Santa Barbara Harbor. The boaters liked its location, twenty-five feet from the docks, and opened daily at six o'clock every morning. McKinney wasn't given a chance to protest the choice of location for message pickups. As convenient as the Harbor Market was, every boater dreaded going in to face its irascible owner, Mad Mary, or Mary Malcontent, as McKinney called her for her mean, nasty, negative attitude whom all who entered must endure, "and that was on a good day," the harbor patrolmen would warn. Her bitter, bitchy disposition motivated boaters to shop well at their neighborhood grocery stores so as to not have to "enter the harbor house of horror" and deal with the "witch with a *b*," it was said.

Her self-proclaimed moniker was Cash-and-carry Mary, no checks, no credit cards accepted. "On a bad day, Mary will even question cash," a customer once declared. Her retort to anyone who dared question her payment policy was, "If you can afford a fucking fancy yacht, you've got cash."

McKinney entered her store only if some necessary item from his grocery store list had not been purchased, and if he couldn't find some willing dockworker to go in for him, his generous tip being worth more than the store item. For his recent visits to the Harbor Market with expectations of receiving Taylor's coded message, McKinney had made single purchases of a small bag of ice, paying with three one-dollar bills, and never waiting for change as he dashed for the exit door. Any waiting message would have been broadcast loud and clear by Mad Mary. Absent of any, he never hung around to be made a target of her acerbic tongue.

"Damn Taylor," McKinney groused as he reluctantly set foot into the little market for the fifth time in over two weeks, always buying a bag of ice on the run.

This morning was different, greeted surprisingly at the entrance by the thin, pale complexion, middle-aged woman with short, burlap-brown, uncombed hair, and a smoker's smile of stained teeth with tobacco odor to match. It was Mad Mary, one foot in front of his startled face. She snapped at him before he was fully in the doorway. "McKinney! Some broad called, said to tell you to pick up a six pack of Corona beer, her exact words, like I didn't know Corona was a friggin' beer, for Christ's sake," she snarled.

McKinney bolted directly to the beer cooler along the back wall without responding, paid with more than enough cash, commenting, "Keep the change," while exiting in the same motion. Outside the store, he heard Mary yell, "What? No ice?"

Aboard his yacht, he sat alone in the galley staring at the carton of six Corona beer bottles, waiting for his five regular passengers to arrive. "*Corona—Cerveza Fina de Mexico*," it read in a white, gold, and blue design. Taylor knew that McKinney never carried beer on board the *Conch II*, only a well-stocked wet bar that catered to the more sophisticated and pampered palates of his wealthy, discerning friends. It was all too simple, McKinney pondered, no mystery to why Taylor ordered beer, that it was Mexican, and to why the quantity of six. The six beers would never have been intended for the six Santa Barbara associates, he was certain of that. They represented the six Mexican fugitives, but way too soon to have been captured, he safely surmised. It could only mean that the team had now entered Mexico in pursuit of the six killers, that the intel and preparation phase of the mission was completed, he deduced. Every symbolic bottle was in its place, sitting there, waiting to be lifted up, out, and opened, McKinney analogized.

Later that morning, the mission backers on board would agree, "Taylor would never send a six-pack of beer for us to drink, but would do so as his subtle signal from Mexico that they have all their bottles lined up, ready to consume." McKinney removed a large bottle of Moët & Chandon champagne from the galley refrigerator to make room for the six bottles of Corona, a fair exchange he felt for their foreign investment thus far.

As they enjoyed their celebratory champagne, they speculated with increased eagerness as to when the next secretive signal would be sent, and how.

10

MINI G. I. JOE

Los Angeles, California

The *Caracara* I RV rolled to a lazy curbside stop on the Wilshire Boulevard side of Lafayette Park in Los Angeles, six blocks away from the Shriners Hospital for Children. Taylor remained on his Casper cell phone with Lori for her latest confirmation of his visitation appointment, a visit he felt compelled to make before entering Mexico. The arrangement made with the hospital's Director of Public Relations, Barbara Harris, was for him to go directly with her to burn victim Miguel Bravo's room, bypassing reception, waiting rooms, and nurses' stations. It was to be, after all, a surprise visit with direct access to young Miguel.

His orthopedic surgery the day before was postburn treatment on his right foot. The toes had fused together from the acute burn damage resulting in contractures interfering with his mobility. Miguel had spent over three years of reconstructive and rehabilitative care at the Galveston, Texas, Shriners Hospital for Children with acute burns. His first year there was in the positive pressure isolation room and state-of-the-art hydro-bariatric chamber, undergoing fluid resuscitation of burn shock. The scarring and deformity of his face had been treated there through surgical debridement, skin harvesting and grafting, as well as plastic reconstructive and restorative surgery, a total of twenty-three to date.

Cam remained in the driver's seat while Grav detached the Kawasaki-650 from the RV's underbelly metal platform on the curb side. Taylor holstered his cell phone.

"We're on schedule. The PR director will meet me in the lobby in ten minutes. Expect me back in an hour," Taylor exclaimed. He strapped on his backpack outside and then mounted the Kawasaki. "Lafayette Park may not be birders' paradise, guys, but make like it is if a police patrol comes around," Taylor forewarned them.

"They'll be at MacArthur Park a few blocks away where the drug action is. They won't hassle a bus with a big bird on the door," Grav said confidently.

"Remember, you're in LA now," Taylor countered over the muffled roar of the bike's 650 engine. "They'd pull a hearse over in this town."

"Good luck. See you in sixty," Cam said sincerely.

Taylor headed slowly onto Wilshire, where he changed gears, accelerating rapidly over to Virgil Avenue. Within a couple of minutes, he arrived at Geneva Street where he circled the hospital from Commonwealth to Fourth Street. There he stopped at the underground garage entrance to press a red security button on the black metal voice box to announce his appointment with Ms. Harris.

The hospital was an attractive, red brick two-story building with a Williamsburg peak roof in front that hid the back rooftop playground in a parklike setting. Lori's background briefing of the Shriners Hospital was an impressive story of children's care and recovery from some of the most horrific burn injuries the human body could suffer. Not all survived. The forty-three physicians, eighty nurses, and four hundred staff of employees and volunteers were an amazing personnel-to-patient ratio for a 60-bed hospital that provided comprehensive postburn care at no charge.

Standing at the lobby check-in station talking to the security guard was a light-complexioned, medium height, young-looking woman in her early thirties with short, curly, red hair and light-blue eyes. A navy-blue blazer snuggly framed her well-filled white silk blouse. Her abbreviated, gray flannel skirt complemented her curvaceous figure. The professional pose she struck was dignified, a perfect first impression for a hospitable hospital.

Taylor's appearance from the lobby elevator interrupted her conversation with the younger, stocky, Afro American security guard whose brass nametag read Maurice Robinson. She saw exactly what Lori had advertised from their phone conversations: a supersized version of G. I. Joe in the flesh. The impressive display of the military's finest, only ten feet in front of her, gave her flesh a warm flush. She gazed unabashedly at the tall man with the granite build, a model stock soldier, as though rolled right off of a recruiting poster. He was dressed in a form-fitting sand-colored T-shirt, which accentuated his cut, muscular build and massive arms. He wore desert camouflage army pants tucked into tan, laced high-top combat boots. Her eyes went to his bulging right bicep with the *Sempre Fi* tattoo flexing large as he lifted off his brown backpack. He grew ten times larger in her eyes as he approached her. The top of her beautiful red head only came up to his chest-high dog tags as he stood before her with his hand of greeting extended.

"Ms. Barbara Harris, I presume?"

She remained still, starring upward in silence when the guard answered for her with an amused smile, "That would be her," pointing to the mute director.

"Yes, yes. I'm sorry. I'm Barbara Harris. It's that your assistant said to expect an ex-Special Forces soldier, not an entire platoon in one package. Welcome to Shriners Hospital. I apologize for my awkwardness, Captain Taylor. I'm used to small, helpless children. And, boy, will little Miguel sure be surprised," she exclaimed gleefully.

"I hope not frightened. I understand he's quite shy, introverted. My visit was cleared by your medical staff and his guardian, correct?" he said, knowing the answer to be yes.

"Absolutely correct, and considered to be the best medicine for his social needs right now. There's a definite social reticence, a reluctance to play with other children, even those with similar physical deformities. His Galveston medical rehab report stated that his most favorite recreational toy there was the G. I. Joe action figure. Our psychosocial service staff leader believes that it made him feel safe, secure."

"I understand that he remains frightened of his father after all these years," he said, verifying what he was told repeatedly.

"Very much so. The night nurses say that he has a recurrent nightmare, cries out, '*Papi, no—no, Papi!*' almost every night."

Taylor felt his first pang of emotion come forth in a flurry, which he was determined to keep in check publicly. He signed the visitor register and asked the guard to please keep his bike helmet at his station for him.

Ms. Harris ushered Taylor down a corridor of clinical offices and examination rooms. He was struck by the nonhospital-like atmosphere and great number of medical and volunteer staff active throughout the floor.

Before entering the medical staff's wide chrome elevator, she stopped to say softly, "Miguel only knows that someone special asked to see him. If I was surprised, he'll be stunned." She gently placed her hand on his forearm. "And, Captain Taylor, thank you."

"Please, the pleasure is all mine, I can assure you." This sentiment was more heartfelt and purposeful than he could ever reveal to her, or anyone. They rode the elevator to the second floor in silence. The double doors slid open to the soft-colored corridor the length of the building. Patients' rooms and nurses' stations lined both sides. The walls were decorated in young children's themes of uplifting fantasy.

"Miguel's room is at the end, facing Fourth Street." She gestured as they stepped onto the pediatric care floor. He couldn't help but subtly glance into the open doors where parents or medical staff were visiting or attending to the needs of small girls and boys of different ages. He heard English, Chinese, Spanish, and even Russian spoken. He had emotionally prepared himself to see accidental burn deformities, scarred bodies, and hairless kids, which appeared from nearly every room in one degree or another. He had seen photos of Miguel's early stages of burn damage and had dealt with the initial shock and horror of his disfigurement. What he would never get past was the fact that Miguel's damage was deliberate, done with malice of forethought and heinous intent to maim or kill, not accidental. He knew the scars would be deep psychologically and socially. That's why Taylor was there, not with the capacity to heal his external scars, but possibly with efficacy to help mend the internal suffering. He was eager to meet the child within the body of scar tissue. He wanted to connect with the person, not the problem. He was determined to help Miguel heal himself. He had finally arrived at his door and that opportunity.

Miguel was seated in a cushioned armchair facing the window when Barbara Harris entered. His guardian, maternal grandmother was reading a story to him from a corner chair. Alongside her was a handsome, middle-aged woman with wavy, short, black hair and Latino features. The black and white nameplate on her blue blazer read Dr. S. Saragosa, Psychosocial Services. Both women stood to be introduced to Taylor, who gently shook their hands. Miguel was now sitting erect, looking up in awe at this huge man filling the doorway. A plastic-covered footstool supported his bandaged right foot. He was dressed in light-blue hospital pajamas and his own green robe. His only functioning eye was opened wider than any of the women had ever witnessed before. The normal-sized aperture that had been artificially created for his compressed mouth and synthetic lips expanded wider now than ever before, a smile that was all genuine.

"Miguel, this is the special visitor I said wanted to visit you. He's special for many reasons, but the important one for now is that he was a highly decorated member of the United States Special Forces, a Delta Force trooper, Captain Taylor. Captain, this is Mr. Miguel Barajas."

Miguel's only immediate utterance was, "Jesus. G. I. Joe?"

"Miguel, your manners!" his grandmother admonished above the light laughter of the others.

Taylor stepped up to Miguel and took his weak, scrawny, seared hand into his. He slowly shook it as Miguel witnessed the stranger's massive hand make his disappear.

"Thank you, Miguel, for the privilege to meet you. May I sit down?"

"Yes, sir," he replied softly, sizing up Taylor from his square jawed face to his hard-toed combat boots, awestruck by this real live action figure in front of him. Barbara provided a chair for Taylor, at arm's length from Miguel.

"You see, Miguel, we soldiers are connected in a secret way to those G. I. Joe action figures that are all around the country, like the one you played with over in Texas, Galveston, I believe. The word got to me that these Shriners didn't have one for you to play with, so I rushed over here to correct the problem." Taylor reached into his backpack and produced the 12-inch, Hasbro, G. I. Joe plastic action figure, attired in the identical military outfit he was wearing. He placed it in Miguel's left hand with official pomp, saying, "This is yours to keep, young man, take him with you wherever you go. He will protect you in here. And I, and my other Delta Force troopers, will protect you out there, okay?" he stressed for acceptance as much for understanding.

Miguel's polished-looking hand gripped the toy soldier with possessive affection, forcing his synthetic face to form a joyous smile. Inside, his heart was pounding with excitement as his attention went back to the big man. "Thank you, sir. Thank you so much, sir. He's so cool."

The three women were beaming with delight at Miguel's effusion. The elderly, white-haired grandmother, to date, had only witnessed his daily pain and suffering since the loss of his mother, her daughter. Taylor knew better than to look at the women for fear of reacting to their outward emotions. He stayed on his "Miguel Mission" by pulling out a rectangular, black, plastic envelope from the backpack. "I thought you might want to see photos of some real G. I. Joes—my Special Forces Delta troops."

Miguel nodded enthusiastically, "Sure. Please, sir."

Taylor patiently explained each picture in detail, naming the troops by name and rank, the various armed vehicles and armaments. He described what it was like to "fast rope" down from a hovering helicopter, to paraglide into enemy territory, and to run a training obstacle course. He again reached into his backpack to retrieve two medium-sized boxes.

"Miguel, your G. I. Joe will need these after I leave." The first box he handed him contained a variety of toy size soldier outfits and field accoutrements, including a poncho, helmet, M4 rifle, and pistol with holster, field glasses, radio, and phone, all made to scale.

"Sir, this is way cool. He's a total soldier, sir. Thank you."

"Well, now's he's complete," he said, handing the ebullient child the larger of the two boxes. He opened it with manual difficulty. Taylor was pleased to see that none of the women attempted to aid him, a lesson learned, he was certain, from the physical therapists.

"No way! It's an army Jeep and Apache helicopter," he exclaimed with glee, both proportioned to scale for his action toy soldier. He raised both high in the air for the women to see. Taylor saw the grandmother dab her eyes with a tissue, causing him to avert eye contact with her and the other two observers.

"It's like Christmas. You've given me so much, sir. Thank you."

"Miguel, I have seen many good soldiers, great men, injured in combat. They all suffered in some way, yet survived to lead normal, happy lives. But all of my Delta Force men have agreed that none have suffered and survived with such strength and bravery as Miguel Barajas. Therefore, as a very special and courageous young man, we hereby make you a 'Honorary Delta Force trooper.'" From his pant pocket, Taylor drew a chrome metal chain with two metal dog tags attached. Both read the same title just bestowed upon Miguel with his full name pressure-stamped beneath. Taylor rose from his chair as he draped the chain over the boy's scar tissue neck. Miguel fondled the two tags, rubbing one smooth, shiny finger back and forth over the relief letters. "I can't believe it sir. I'm a G. I. Joe. Does this mean I have to run that obstacle course?" he said, provoking laughter from everyone.

"No, Miguel. You've already run one far more difficult than ours, with extraordinary courage and success."

He then turned around to the three smiling women. "Ladies, would you all please join me standing," he requested politely without explanation. As they rose, he reached into his backpack one final time. He held a square, polished black leather jewelry case in the palm of his left hand. He placed his feet firmly parallel against one another, standing erect, as though at military attention.

"Miguel Barajas, it has been recognized by your fellow Delta Force members that for the last three years, you have distinguished yourself with a limitless capacity under the most painful of circumstances to survive against all odds, a heroic achievement which, as of this proud moment, is again recognized with the awarding of the US Military's *'Bronze Star Medal with Valor.'*" With solemn ceremony, Taylor gracefully opened the hinged leather case. He slowly exhibited the medal for all to see briefly before removing it from its royal purple satin interior. Miguel placed both hands to his wizened face in mute astonishment. All three women emitted differing pitches of excited gasps. "*A Dios mio!*" the grandmother involuntarily blurted out.

The five-point bronze star was 1 ½ inches in circumscribing diameter, suspended from a red scarlet ribbon, 1 ⅜ inches wide and 1 ¾ inches high, with a thin white border and a narrow, vertical, ultramarine blue line running down the center, bordered in white. In the center of the large bronze star was a relief of a very small star with a *V* engraved upon it for "*valor.*"

Taylor leaned forward to pin it on the left breast pocket of Miguel's robe, when suddenly he uttered firmly, "Sir, in your pictures, weren't the soldiers standing when you pinned medals on them?"

"They were."

In unison, the worried women protested, "Miguel, your foot!" pleading that he remain seated. He answered with the proud uplifting of his new dog tags, saying, "Delta Force troopers stand," silencing his well-meaning protectors. Taylor's heart pounded with a pride he had not felt for some time. Miguel rose with considerable corporal strain. A painful grimace appeared on his mask-like face.

Taylor stood firm, thinking, *This young man has heart enough to heal a hospital full of kids.* Seeing his severe discomfort, Taylor quickly fastened the ribbon with its shiny brass medal to his robe. He stepped back one pace and then crisply saluted. "Miguel Barajas, it is with the highest honor, pride, and distinction that your fellow Delta Force troops confer this medal on you and salute you. Congratulations!"

Miguel saluted back with a strenuous extension of his torso, and then dropped gently into his cushioned chair. In an agonized voice, he responded with a humble, "The Special Forces make this special."

Congratulations were echoed from the proud women as they lightly applauded the special moment. Miguel was beaming with joy, still overwhelmed by the momentous occasion, never taking his sight off of his fellow soldier and new friend. Taylor turned to the women and diplomatically asked if they would please step out of the room for a few minutes "while we men discuss matters of classified importance." The ladies exited, smiling at the thought, leaving Taylor to be seated face-to-face with his little friend. While the grandmother left for the ladies' restroom, Director Harris and Dr. Saragosa remained standing at the nearest nurses' station, sneaking an occasional peak into the room. Ten minutes later, Taylor was at the doorway waving to the women to return.

"Ladies, you are in excellent hands now with Trooper Miguel. We've said goodbye for now, so I'll do the same with you lovely ladies as well." The grandmother stepped in to kiss Taylor on the cheek. Leaning down to receive it, she thanked him profusely for his kindness.

"I wish we could bottle you, Captain, as the perfect medicine for our little ones. Do come again," the doctor implored.

Barbara Harris insisted on accompanying Taylor down to the lobby. He smiled at Miguel affectionately, and then saluted. "I'll be seeing you, soldier."

"Thank you, sir. Thank you so much," he replied with a cracking voice.

As Taylor and Barbara started back down the long corridor, they both stopped at the queer sight before them. A gauntlet of people lined both sides of the hallway, two and three deep, all staring at the brawny soldier in uniform. Barbara estimated eighty to ninety people gathered, children in wheelchairs, held in parent's arms, on crutches, with nurses, plus orderlies, and doctors. He looked quizzically at Barbara for an explanation.

"Don't look at me—I don't know what's going on," she remarked with a bewildered expression on her blushed face. "Maybe the grandmother said something," she hazarded a guess.

They resumed their normal paced promenade past the curious onlookers who exhibited warm smiles and random, reserved waves from the children. He saw the kids close up, each one with a personal horror story to tell, if asked. He walked at Barbara's pace, who was expressing greetings to those she knew best. The elevator doors opened upon their arrival, allowing them to end their public parade with a quick *duo exodus* inside. With the doors sliding closed,

Barbara turned to Taylor with a serene smile and tearing eyes she had fought hard to control. The doors were closed. "I can think of only one way to sincerely thank you, Captain Taylor." Standing high up on her toes, she reached with both arms fully extended to embrace him around the neck, drawing her face to his in a prolonged, warm kiss, stopping only when the elevator door opened on the first floor.

"I can't think of a better way either," he replied with a grateful grin. "Take real good care of my boy soldier up there, and I'll be thanking you, Barbara." He winked, stepping off the elevator alone. The doors closed as he walked toward the lobby security station.

"Would you please sign me 'gone' on your log there, partner?" he waved to the guard. "And my helmet, it goes upstairs to a special friend of mine, Miguel Barajas, room 260."

"You got it, sir," the guard responded, watching Taylor disappear into the garage elevator.

Barbara walked briskly back to Miguel's room, trying not to make tearful eye contact with the few people remaining in the corridor. She blotted her eyes dry before entering his room, finding Miguel kneeling backward on his chair facing toward the window, flanked on both sides by the other two women.

"What are we looking at?" she wondered aloud.

"Taylor," was the doctor's simple answer, pointing to the street below.

Barbara leaned up to the glass to see. A soldier straddling a long, thin motorcycle came roaring out of the underground garage to the street entrance, sliding the bike to a sideways stop. He looked up at the window and gave an animated, farewell salute before standing the Kawasaki slightly up on its rear wheel as he launched himself off into the Fourth Street traffic with roused spirits.

"I told you grandma he'd wave up here," Miguel said excitedly. "He said he'd take me for a ride on it one day."

"*Si, mi amor* (Yes, love)," the smiling elder replied.

"And, Miguel, tell Ms. Harris what Captain Taylor also shared with you," Dr. Saragosa requested.

He held his G. I. Joe up for her to see. "He told me to place him under my pillow at night when I lie down to sleep so that I won't have any more scary dreams," he stated with confidence.

"And show Ms. Harris the back side of your bronze star, Miguel," she prompted him again.

Barbara leaned in close to read the engraved obverse of the medal, "*In Honor of Captain A. Taylor.*"

Barbara placed her hand up to her mouth with a quick gasp of shock. "This was his Bronze Star medal of valor!" she marveled. Her heart quickened, racing with her emotions about this selfless man, wondering why he would relinquish such a coveted memento of honor and prestige to an unknown child. She did not want to ask why out loud. She simply turned quickly toward the door and departed silently in tears.

11

CAUGHT ON VIDEO

Mexicali, Baja Norte, Mexico

Like Siamese twins attached and codependent of each other, yet of independent minds, the contiguous border cities of *Calexico* in the United States and *Mexicali* in Mexico prospered quite well as good neighbors. Their respective names reflected their parochial pride of place while admitting to the geopolitical dependency with each other. The prefix of *Calexico* denoted the California dominance over the Mexico suffix and *Mexicali* the same over California.

Calexico, California, needed the Mexican day laborers and consumers crossing over into their Imperial Valley soil rich agricultural fields and shopping malls. *Mexicali* needed the hybrid seeds, fertilizer, pesticides, farm machinery, and water channeled through *Calexico*. There was never enough of the latter to satisfy the *Mexicali* Valley's expanding needs for farm and domestic consumption. They relied on every last leftover drop coursing west from the Colorado River through the 84-mile long All-American Canal that eventually connected with the tail end 123-mile Coachella Canal in upper Sonora and Baja Norte, California. The vast majority of their gravity flow irrigation water came from that main American artery. The rest came from seepage in the US soil leaking its way into the *Mexicali*

Valley aquifers. From there, it was pumped from farm wells into their thirsty fields of cotton, wheat, alfalfa, onions, asparagus, and squash.

By the time the 1,450 miles long Colorado River reached its last brief stretch in Mexico, 90 percent of its annual flow had been drained away in the US. It was referred to in the US as the "American Nile," in Mexico as the "American denial."

The capital of *Baja Norte, Mexicali,* was a big sprawling city, two border crossings connected the sister cities. The most heavily traveled was the *Calexico Garito–Mexicali I.* The *Calexico East–Mexicali II* crossing was much quieter and less crowded. *Caracara II* crossed the latter at 0935, *Caracara I* crossed 118 miles to the west into Tijuana at 0935. Navigating from the driver's seat, Eizzo pointed to the *Mexicali* welcoming sign that proudly stated, "The City That Captures the Sun."

"Well howdy from the Sun Tzu boys here to capture FTM Manuel Bravo," Cope responded with a courteous wave from the window.

Bravo was the only FTM fugitive among their six man capture list who had actually left a forwarding address. Santa Barbara homicide detectives had even attempted to interrogate him in *Mexicali* months following his stabbing Rosio Fuentes to death, the housekeeper of Stan Laisum, member of the Six-Pack. When Bravo was told that his crime was caught on video tape, he coolly replied, "*Y que?* (And so?)" then defiantly walked out of the *Mexicali* police station the way he walked in, a free man.

Lori's current intel on Bravo confirmed his same address two years since the attempted police interrogation. What had changed was his occupation as a *Coyote* (people smuggler), which was of no concern to the Delta team. Their role was not as crime fighters in Mexico to bust up smuggling rings.

"We just want to bust a move on Bravo." Rap had best described their purpose there. They also understood they couldn't just snatch him up off of the street where *Los Halcones* (lookouts, street level informants) roamed freely. A cunning strategy and stealth would win the day. But they must start the day on the street.

They observed how modern and clean the city was, absent of the tourist traps and seedy bars found in other border towns like

Tijuana and *Nogales*. It was an important business center, a wealthy agricultural powerhouse considered the breadbasket of northwestern Mexico. Their entry plan was to tour the outskirts of the eastern edge of the city along the main *Canal del Alamo* flowing east to west parallel to the US-Mexico border. Eventually it would intersect the *Boulevard de Las Americas,* where they would see their first phase OODA landmark, *El Pozo del Campo* (The Well of the Field) restaurant. It was a popular barbeque eatery and watering hole for the locals and visiting *gringos*.

El Pozo was Manuel Bravo's hangout because of its close proximity to his home two blocks away. His place of work was along the border providing contraband and facilitating their staging areas and eventual illegal movement into the US, albeit carried by smugglers willing to make the risky crossing. Supply and demand was always there, it didn't matter what. But "the greater the risk, the greater the reward" no longer applied to the fugitive from US justice. What mattered to Bravo was easy cash, and can it be easily carried.

The team's initial task was to get into his loop and determine how to best play off of his game. Location and detection were completed. They now needed identification verification before the execution of their plan, and do so without being detected. "Plan what is difficult while it is easy, do what is great while it is small," Master Sun Tzu would remind them.

Eizzo drove into the white crushed gravel parking lot of El Pozo just as the noon lunch rush of customers was beginning. He parked the long RV at a distance and angle that would provide the best view of the front door. He would remain in *Caracara* II with the recon radio on and his binoculars at the ready. Rap and Cope would enter the restaurant as common tourists hungry for some good old barbecue *Mexicali* style.

They knew Bravo would be inclined to choose the bar over the family dining room of large tables and booths. They perched themselves upon the high stools around the raised round cocktail table. It provided the best overview of the long rectangular room of gray paneled reclaimed barn wood. More than a dozen old fashion cast iron hand pumps were displayed along the midsection of the walls like antique trophies. A wide flat TV screen was up high in the center of the bar for all to see. The smell of mesquite smoke with a whiff of fresh cilantro, garlic, and lime marinade flavored the air. A light skin young waitress with flaxen hair and blue eyes greeted them with two laminate menus and a welcoming invitation to visit the salad bar first if they desired.

"My name is Blanca, and I'll be your waitress. May I start you off with a beverage?" she offered with a perfunctory patter and smile. Needing to buy time, they only ordered iced tea and chips with salsa for the moment. They immediately began their methodical visual coverage of the growing crowd of lunch customers. Small percentages were *gringos*, elderly snowbird tourists and male commercial reps wearing US agribusiness logos on their jackets or caps. No one yet matched the photos they had memorized of FTM fugitive Manual Bravo. It was still early by Mexican late lunch customs. But after two bowls of chips and salsa, they thought it prudent to order.

Blanca recited the signature house special of *carne asada* (barbecued meat) in exotic detail, "A thinly sliced skirt steak tenderized in sweet papaya juice, marinated in spicy jalapeño juice, fresh cilantro, garlic, toasted ground cumin seed, vinegar, sugar, and olive oil, grilled over mesquite fire along with char-grilled green onions."

"Without all that, you'd take the 'Mexico' out of the meat," Rap editorialized approvingly.

After ordering, Cope headed for the restroom near the entrance on the off chance Bravo had entered the dining area unnoticed. When he returned, he saw Rap focused on one familiar looking man seated at the bar.

"No prospects in the dining room," he commented casually, taking his seat.

"We might have one, six stools in from the far end of the bar, gray shirt, black pants, white straw cowboy hat," Rap whispered.

Before Cope could respond, a man passed by with a similar commonly handsome facial appearance that turned their heads with interrupted interest. Both prospects had dark-brown eyes and skin, trimmed black mustaches and dense, dark stubble over their lean squared jaws. The shape of their eyes and nose were identical, even the convexity of the cheek bones.

"Too bad our target has no distinguishing features, tattoos, scares, moles, because these two could be clones," Rap complained.

"Tell me about it. Look around. There are at least a couple of others here with similar looks." Cope pointed out the ethnic physical descriptors in frustration.

"Do you think we *gringos* all look alike to them?" Cope questioned sincerely.

"For our purpose, let's hope so," Rap answered seriously.

"How is that a newborn zebra can instinctively find its mother within a thousand head herd of adult zebras?" Cope wondered aloud.

"Easy. They use a bar code," he chuckled. "But humans aren't pure species of oneness. Even identical twins aren't identical in the eyes of their parents. We have subspecies called races and the intermingling of races." Rap attempted to explain the similitude of one man to another, whether Mexican or American. "That's why God created DNA," he concluded with a sigh.

They continued to scrutinize the several suspects until their meals arrived. Cope took the third *carne asada* they'd ordered out to Eizzo in the RV.

"Good news, bad news. The barbecue is a winner, and Manuel Bravo is an amoeba who has split into six carbon copies of himself," he reported lightly.

"I believe it. I've seen at least three look-alikes entering, and I've got his photos right here on the laptop."

They discussed the fact that the one helpful element missing from Lori's intel on Bravo was a definitive ID on his vehicle. They knew that smugglers constantly changed vehicles and license plates for obvious reasons, making it impossible to get a reliable fix on his. It was decided that Eizzo would write down the makes, models, and plates of the top three prospects selected by Cope and Rap as they left the restaurant. Cope would then drive by Bravo's address on the bike to hopefully make a match.

The three-man team left the *El Pozo* forty minutes later, Cope riding the Kawasaki 650. The RV headed east, Cope two blocks away to the address they'd been given. It was an older weathered apartment complex with common landscaping and parking. He cruised around the lot twice looking for any one of the three trucks Eizzo had ID, all of them pickups. What he discovered were eighteen pickups, mostly white, all like the three he needed to ID.

Cope reported disappointedly back to the *Caracara* II by radio. They agreed to meet south of town a short distance on Highway 5 at an RV park named *Delta Numero Uno*.

"I know we're supposed to hide out in plain sight, but this is a bit too much!" Rap exclaimed jokingly, aware that the valley was part of the Colorado River delta flowing into the gulf of Cortez.

Although they couldn't ID Bravo on their first attempt, they had come prepared with plans B through Z. Before early morning, the Delta team had brazenly completed the second OODA phase of their new recon ID operation, incubated during the evening hours and hatched at night. The decisive execution of the fledgling plan would take place that afternoon. They would flush their quail out of *El Pozo*, separated from the rest of the look-alike covey. This time the bird dog would be Eizzo.

The second thing the pretty *El Pozo* waitress noticed about the new male customer waiting to be seated was his blue-billed cap logo that read "Rain for Rent." The first were his broad shoulders centered by a thick neck and steel cut head of an athletic-looking man under the cap. He wore bronze tinted aviator sunglasses with gold frames. His large tan hands were callused, leading her to assume he was in some line of agricultural work.

"I'd like to see the soccer game," the man stated emphatically, pointing to an empty stool in front of the raised flat TV screen in the center of the bar.

"Certainly, help yourself. But tell me, if you don't mind, what is Rain for Rent?" she asked seriously with a flirtatious smile.

"Field irrigation systems," he simply answered.

"Interesting. Do you also rent thunder and lightning?" she questioned peevishly.

"No, but our competition does," he replied dismissively.

"And who would that be?" she continued her coquettish banter with a sassy grin.

"Mother Nature unlimited," he smiled, turning to take his seat at the bar.

Eizzo was not there to socialize. He was there to initialize the identification process of Manuel Bravo, who was known to hang out at the *El Pozo* bar in the afternoons and ply his illicit trade by night. That was his known loop, and Eizzo was there to interrupt it.

National arch rival soccer football teams were always popular sports television in Mexico, in particular at bars. Today the televised opponents were *Los Chivas* from *Guadalajara* versus *Las Américas* from Mexico City.

"Got a favorite?" the tall, thin, middle-aged bartender asked Eizzo. "Team or beer?"

"Both if you care to share," he answered with an accommodating grin.

"I prefer my football American smash face, hands on NFL, my beer Mexican. *Dos Equis* if you would please," he grinned back.

The bartender laughed, adding, "That reminds me, another *gringo* once told me that playing soccer football without your hands is like fucking without your dick, why bother!"

"Then you do understand," Eizzo rejoined with laughter.

Waiting for his beer, he immediately saw two men in the bar who fit Bravo's description, although possibly too young. He would be thirty-four years old by now, still within the age-appropriate profile they had on their laptop photos. He also noticed that the machismo mentality of the Mexican *campesino* wasn't much different from the southwestern US cowboy who considered the cowboy hat an essential extension of their physique and persona, nondescript and incomplete without it. He theorized that was the reason they refused to take them off at a bar among men, which now made his task of identifying Bravo all the more difficult.

With his beer came another Bravo clone that joined two other men at a tall cocktail table. Shortly after Eizzo had ordered more chips and salsa, one more Bravo look-alike entered with a young-looking woman on his arm. Each of these likely prospects wore a white straw cowboy hat atop a five-foot, eight to nine–inch tall, slender frame. It was as though they all wore Manuel Bravo masks, one size and look fits all. Fortunately, for his plan to work, they all showed interest in the soccer match projected on the large flat screen twelve feet in front of him. He also took mental notes of the timing of their respective consumption of drinks and food, careful to calculate the projected timing of their completion. He had to act before any one of them exited of their own volition.

The soccer match was heating up, tied two goals apiece with less than four minutes to go on the game clock. He looked around the bar and saw all sets of prospective Bravo eyes on the TV screen. Now was the time to strike. His right hand drifted down to touch the key pad on the radio–cell phone attached to the right side of his belt. He pressed the top center button three times, sending a signal to Cope in the restaurant front lot on the Kawasaki 650. Rap picked up the signal in the RV parked out of sight a half block away from Bravo's apartment.

Eizzo then slowly raised his right hand over to touch his inside left wrist covered by his long sleeve blue denim shirt. Taped inside was a remote control that transmitted a dedicated signal to the Delta team's Sony DVD player tucked inside the air-conditioning vent five inches above the TV flat screen. The DVD player's red play light illuminated on the black faceplate display but was not visible behind the vent screen strip of black tape.

Instantly the wide flat TV screen displayed a silent, mono-chrome video film of a Latin male struggling with a Latin woman outside a back door to a modern house. Plastic bags of groceries are dropped and kicked around on a concrete patio as he begins to strike her repeatedly with his fists, each blow more violent than the last. He grabs her long black hair from behind and presses her face against a wall-mounted security key pad. She kicks and fights to escape, but is stunned when he slams her into the brick wall.

Eizzo looks around the bar to see all eyes on the screen, many protesting the disappearance of the soccer match, others he assumed, believing they were watching an old black and white movie. That belief quickly shifts to disbelief and confusion when the male attacker on the screen pulls out a knife with a shiny six-inch-long blade. He stabs the woman in the shoulder then waves the bloody blade in front of her pleading-yet-stoic face. He then begins to stab her repeatedly about the face and upper body until she drops to her knees, blood pouring out of her left eye. Just as she begins to fall on her face, the man grabs the top of her head by the hair, jerks it back while slashing her throat in an abbreviated sweeping motion.

The bartender is too shocked to change the channel, as mesmerized as the rest of the bar audience of more than thirty people. The protest turned into demanding questions as to whether or not this was a breaking news report or just a bad movie. The bartender ignored the questions and negative comments to concentrate on all the remote control buttons in his shaking hand, none of which could manipulate the unwanted screen content. Gasps and profane groans could be heard when the gruesome scene began all over again, as though locked in on a repetitive play loop.

Eizzo was focused on the multiple Manuel Bravos, ignoring the crowd's growing outcry. Suddenly the one prospect seated with the two men at the tall cocktail table stood up. He said something briefly to his table mates while gesturing toward the entrance restrooms. He briskly strode out of the bar in a shrinking posture, head down, hat tipped low in front. Eizzo pressed his radio-cell button, this time holding it down for five seconds. He then tossed a ten-dollar bill on the bar counter and casually but quickly headed for the entrance. He looked over his shoulder to observe the other Bravo prospects remaining in their seats, turning their heads uncomfortably from the screen.

"Our quail has bolted, outside now wearing an olive green, long sleeve western shirt, dark brown pants, black field boots, white straw cowboy hat," Eizzo radioed to his partners. He could hear the growling re-jetted muffler of Cope's Kawasaki bike fire up before he saw it.

"Subject is entering an old model white Ford, F-150 pickup in the northwest corner of the lot," he continued his play-by-play account of their hot target's movements while remaining out of sight. He observed the truck speeding onto the side street with Cope a nonthreatening, surveillance distance behind. Eizzo called Rap, who reported that he had a visual on the white pickup now double parking in front of Bravo's apartment. The prospective target left the motor running as he ran into a first-floor apartment numbered as the domicile of one Manuel Bravo, as per their intel. They had the ID confirmation they were looking for, the determining dots were now connected.

Bravo reappeared two minutes later carrying a long white canvas bag and a change of cowboy hats, this one black, which Rap deemed more apropos. While entering the pickup, Rap was able to focus his close-range binoculars on the target's face. He was now convinced he was the one and only suspect in question.

Bravo made an awkward U-turn in his pickup to go back to the main highway. Remaining out of sight, Cope picked up his moving visual tracking him on the highway from a nonconsequential distance. Rap met Eizzo curbside in front of *El Pozo*. He had just reentered and exited the restaurant briefly to surreptitiously click off the remote DVD player from an inconspicuous location, leaving the stunned patrons chattering angrily among themselves.

"Were the customers revolted with the show?" Rap asked Eizzo as they drove away.

"Absolutely, even more so when the soccer match came back on with *Los Chivas* having already won 3 to 2 in the final six seconds."

"Had it been a Broncos-Cowboys game, I could understand the anger," Rap rejoined sarcastically. *If only they had known the killer was in their midst, what then?* he pondered privately.

The RV tracking monitor showed Cope heading eastbound on Highway 1 with a two-mile gain on it.

"Classic fright and flight. Bravo must have the ghost of Rosio in his rearview mirror and his pedal to the metal trying to outrun it," Eizzo exclaimed.

"Well, Cope is the ghost rider on a hundred mile per hour bike, so that's not going to happen. Whether he's headed to a safe house or underground somewhere, we know it won't be into US territory, especially after a public showing of his 'Made in America' murder," Rap proclaimed confidently.

"His grid will parallel the border, that's where he plies his illicit trade, that's what he knows best," Eizzo safely speculated.

They had to determine the range of Bravo's grid for planning purposes. They supposed that the farther away from *Mexicali*, the better, and the farther south of the border, all the better. Knowing his televised crime of murder in the US was now in local replay, Bravo considered the possibility of fleeing south, not only away from suspecting eyes, but from any avenging hands that would do him harm. The team knew that he didn't fear extradition to the US. All attempts to do so had failed. He would more likely suspect a hit man seeking family retribution. That would motivate his desire for deep cover locally or south, out of sight and hopefully out of mind among those who wanted him dead.

Cope's voice came over the radio. "Target has turned onto a dirt road a half mile off Highway 1. He's entered an unmarked property with perimeter cyclone fence and surveillance cameras. There's a one-story white concrete building in the center of two acres approximately, either a warehouse or factory. He's parked in back, over."

"We copy that. Was there a name or marker to your dirt road, over?" Eizzo asked.

"Affirmative. *Canal 13*, a service road along an irrigation canal, goes for miles. If he stays inside, I'll get closer for a GPS fix, over."

"Copy. We'll pull off along Highway 1 near the *Canal 13* road exit and wait. After GPS transmission, scout the area and report back, over," Eizzo ordered.

"Copy. But one more ID note on the white pickup. It has a black letter motto painted on the tailgate, '*Caballo, Machete Y Mujer. Tener Bueno, O No Tener* (Horse, machete and woman).' Have a good one, or don't have one," Cope recited.

Laughing, Eizzo replied, "I'm sure he's complaining, not bragging. Over and out."

There were more numbers than names assigned to the 1,500 miles of canals and service roads networking throughout the *Mexicali* Valley. A flowing canal's size declined and increased by width and depth like the human circulatory system carrying blood throughout the body. From the main artery of the *Coachella Canal* to the veins of the zone distribution outlets to the small capillaries of the crop rows soaking up the water for crop production, the water rolled on and on at differing seasonal levels.

The team had been supplied with an official *Mexicali* Valley water management map among Lori's intel briefing papers for the purpose of road navigation. With Cope's computed position coordinates transmitted on the white mystery building, Eizzo would request day and night satellite photos from Lori for their operational map overlay.

Cope rendezvoused with the Caracara II on canal service road 14, which ran four hundred feet behind the mystery building. On board the RV, he reported that he had successfully planted one of their hidden miniature duo-surveillance cameras for daytime as well as nighttime infrared vision of the gated entrance. Posing as a field tech maintenance man servicing the area's water gate controls, he covertly attached it to the irrigation control panel pole across the road.

"If you look through the binocs here, you'll see Bravo's white pickup parked behind the building. I'll install the same duo cameras back here on the 14 for rearview coverage," Cope stated.

"Any clues as to what's inside?" Eizzo questioned.

"My guess is that it was formerly a produce-packing warehouse with the high loading dock in back. It's too overt for drugs or firearms trafficking. If it was a legit business, it would promote itself with at least a company logo somewhere, even if it was a false front for an illegitimate biz."

"Well, with Bravo inside, its illicit. All we need do is watch the surveillance monitor for movement," Eizzo declared.

With the second set of cameras in place surveilling the back side of the building, Eizzo drove around to a secluded corner of a rectangular pond by Canal 13. He eased the long RV off the road and parked between the pond and two large Guadalupe cypresses with broad buttressed trunks.

"This not only gives cover for the RV but can serve as a natural bird-watching venue," Cope offered as a poser explanation to anyone who asked.

"Perfect. Rap, you set up an advanced spotting position with a bird blind. Stock it with camera equipment and place the bike inside it after dark. You'll take the first watch there in rotation. After today's scare, Bravo will unlikely leave his new hideout, but we want to be ready if he does," Eizzo reasoned.

"Determining what the building is all about should give us better insight as to his loop and next move," Rap projected.

Eizzo picked up the encrypted Casper cell phone and called Lori. He would give her the P-code (precision) GPS fix of the mystery building, requesting a max background intel report. Cope prepared their bird-watch list of resident and migratory species. The emphasis would be on freshwater birds given the pond and multitude of canals and reservoirs in their grid. They had already noted the white-faced ibis, lesser yellowlegs, and whimbrels in flooded fields, and the unmistakable four-foot tall double-crested cormorant around the waterways. By Canal 14, a half dozen white cattle egrets were trailing a tractor mowing a one-foot stand of alfalfa for their own opportunistic insect harvest. Willets, mourning doves, and Inca doves were added to the list. All were edited together from their photo archives to create their *Mexicali* Valley watch list, and none too soon.

An hour before sunset, Rap radioed Eizzo and Cope aboard the *Caracara* II from his bird blind, blended into the high reed growth on the northeast shore of the pond. "You have a black and white stopped on the 13, shoulder eyeballing the RV. I see only a driver, over."

"We copy. Copes going to exit the RV off channel. I'll follow if necessary, over," Eizzo replied.

"Copy that. I'll stay on channel and visual. Out." Rap signed off with his binoculars fixed on the dusty police Jeep SUV. It slowly turned into the same rutted path the RV had entered onto when leaving service road 13 for the pond. Cope was now outside setting up a long lens camera on a tripod facing the pond fifteen feet away. The backup partners watched as the black and white Jeep pulled alongside their geeky-looking partner sporting a bright yellow visor, a white T-shirt with large red block words "Don't Feed the Birdwatchers," and bright lime green shorts while strutting in baby-blue flip-flops.

My god, thought Rap, *if this is the fashion police, he's so busted. How Nancy can he get?*

Eizzo watched from inside the RV side window as Cope approached the squad car. Cope leaned into the driver window for a face-to-face conversation. It lasted for under a minute with the cop car quickly exiting back to the 13 in reverse all the way, as though fleeing from the line of fire. Once out of sight, Cope entered the RV. He went on the radio to share with Rap what he was reporting to Eizzo.

"He asked in English if we were hunters down here for the seasonal white-winged dove, Hilota dove, or black Banta, goose, pheasant, duck, quail, rabbit, hare, *et cetera*, and wanted to see our hunting licenses. I told him we were vegetarian bird-watchers who were afraid of guns, here only studying the pesticide and heavy metal contamination from selenium and baron found in their valley water, poisoning all of the birds and animals he mentioned. I invited him to come in for some pumpkin blossom quesadillas and corn fungus crepes, a cool glass of blush wine and Marc Antonio music. That's when he put it in reverse and left, like, so rude!" Cope summarized with mock bruised sensitivity.

Laughing aloud, the two partners told Cope, "You just don't have it any more, man. You've lost that loving feeling."

"By the way, was that your Siegfried or Roy wardrobe?" Rap asked rhetorically with amused snickering.

With darkness upon their camp, they made additional surveillance preparations. Rap moved the bike into his hide and took the uneventful night watch shift. His first daybreak sighting was a two-foot tall white-faced ibis at the charcoal-colored water's edge. It had a salamander wiggling helplessly in its long gray downward decurved bill. Its head, neck, and belly were a dull gray-brown streaked with white, its back and wings an iridescent purple-red color. Rap quickly snapped two photos. The bird's breakfast reminded Rap of his field survival training when he partook of the same natural menu after two weeks of no prepared food.

He radioed the *Caracara* II. "Eizzo, tell the cook, sweet pants Cope, I'm coming in for some of his quesadillas and hot coffee. Over and out."

He was greeted in the RV to the late breaking news from Lori's overnight recon report.

"Our mystery building is a mystery no more. Lori's intel comes from our US. Border Patrol and confirmed by customs agents. It's a derelict CD duplication plant for bootlegged Latino music. They import blank Chinese discs for a quarter each, burn them with pirated fan favs of Latino pop and traditional Mexican music, and seal them in fifteen-cent jewel cases with counterfeited cover art and liner notes. They sell for around a buck apiece in the estimated fifty thousand street stalls around Mexico," Eizzo reported.

"Why don't the locals get their music the American way, steal it off of the internet by downloading pirated shareware," Rap offered sarcastically.

"Lori believes that this place also assembles pirated CDs for the US Latino market, underground of course," Eizzo speculated.

"That's where Señor Smuggler here comes in, I take it. The dupe plant is his home away from home, now his FTM hideout," Cope stated.

"There are dozens of these illicit plants around Mexico. Last year they cranked out an estimated 250-million bootlegged CDs throughout the country. That's why he's stuck around *Mexicali* all this time—for the pirate's booty," Eizzo concluded.

"Well, it's a nocturnal operation, explaining no traffic by day, *mucho* by night. Cops must be on the take this close to town," Rap projected.

"True. But that doesn't mean they won't be around again. They're as predatory as the bad guys, always sniffing around for the next free meal, hot or cold," Eizzo interjected.

They agreed that another twenty-four hours of surveillance was necessary to establish a fixed pattern of FTM Bravo's routine activities. They hoped that their target's unsettled nerves would keep him sequestered inside until they were ready to execute their plan of extraction, now in the making. The RV remained out of sight behind the natural screen of *Guadalupe* cypresses.

The TA (target acquisition) decision phase was now in play, how best to contain, capture, and extract safely target Manuel Bravo. Their military experience told them it was now all about the lay of the land, the ground they shared with their target. Tactical field training taught them that diverse grounds drove their decision for tactical execution. Master Sun Tzu taught them that "light ground, ground of contention, heavy ground, bad ground, and dying ground" were measured degrees of difficulty from having the operational advantage or fatal disadvantage. "The ground" to a warrior meant the location of opposing forces, "the place of confrontation—gain the advantage and you live, lose the advantage and you die." Therefore it was imperative that they examine it, "the way, qualities of terrain, configuration, distance, difficulty or ease of travel, relative danger and detection, and how to disperse." The minimum risk route was the common denominator, hit and run the simplistic sum of their strategy.

Examining Lori's recon satellite photos, topography maps, water irrigation distribution network for the vast agricultural valley and Rap's scouting notes, the three planners concurred; they were confronted with the challenge of flatness, followed by more flatness. Theirs was an unwelcome "ground of contention."

From above the land appeared to be a patchwork quilt. The canals incised the flat land, demarking diverse crop production zones in perpendicular patterns where size mattered not. They could not hide behind hills or in forests, or escape beyond mountains and shores. The fields of farm production were modern by Mexico's national agrarian standards, "maxed out" for high yields per hectare with a minimum of homes and outbuildings allowing for large mechanized field equipment to work the land efficiently. This all translated into the team's disadvantage. Hiding out in plain view had its limitations. It worked for early reconnaissance and innocent bird-watching, but not for sustained surveillance and extraction execution. They needed the element of surprise that only a surprise location could provide. "Victory is gained by surprise," Master Sun Tzu would not need to remind them.

"The flat, open land may be to our disadvantage, but its open aquatic network can be to our advantage," Eizzo suggested.

"Meaning the irrigation canals?" Cope offered.

"Not if they're full of water. We can't fight the flow and still remain fluid on our own terms," Rap contended.

"True. But we can if one of them has no flow, totally dry so that one of us can come and go at the point of planned extraction, hidden below land level," Eizzo proposed.

"Explain how? They're controlled remotely by wireless signal transmissions," Rap declared.

"Yes, but the transmissions are random, dictated by the soil moisture sensors throughout the fields. When dry, they tell the block irrigation control transmitter to relay information to a remote irrigation control," Eizzo explained.

"So it's a wireless valve activation device?" Cope asked rhetorically.

"A cell phone call can manipulate the flow at the stop gates," Eizzo added.

"Awesome. We've got the search scanner to intercept the cell signals, the recorder to capture the receiver transmission, and our encrypted cell phones to manipulate it at will," Cope summarized.

"We can trigger the control attached to the solar panel pole where I planted the cameras in front of Bravo's building," Rap interjected.

They all concurred on the final plan of execution and that Canal 13 would not be Bravo's lucky number. They dubbed the plan's first phase "Operation *Zanjero*," one who is in charge of water distribution. The second phase name was also to the point, "Operation Roadkill." Master Sun Tzu's wisdom was with them, "Know all possible adaptations to take advantage of the ground—know how to adapt advantageously." They had created their own opportunity for TA. Now they had to execute it with the precision timing of a Rolex.

They put their high-tech telephonic gear in place. It would receive, record, and retransmit the necessary cell signals managing the irrigation waters, in particular those flowing from north to south on Canal 13 across the service road from their target's dupe plant hideout. By 1900 hours, the north end of Canal 13 had its stop-gate shut down in a fully sealed position. The adjacent southern section would fully drain out by 0400. They would execute the Roadkill phase at sunrise, 0600.

The three Delta members were in their predawn tactical positions waiting for Eizzo's go signal from the *Caracara* II still tucked out of sight off the 13. Rap was the closest to the building entrance in hiding, straddling the still bike on the north end of the pond. Cope had made his way down the drained section of the canal south of the entrance. Their Operation Roadkill objective was to get TA (target acquisition), Manuel Bravo, out of the building, into his truck, and off of the property heading south. If he tried turning right to the north, then Rap would enter the center of the road on the bike at a perpendicular stand still, like a cowpoke herding a maverick steer, to intimidate Bravo to U-turn around to the south.

Dawn was easing up on the horizon with little skyward illumination. That was Eizzo's self-imposed signal to place his encrypted cell phone call to Bravo's cell, his number courtesy of Lori's latest intel. There would be no conversation, only a cryptic, succinct message in English designed to stimulate their target's final motivation of fright and flight. "Good warriors get others to come to them," was his Sun Tzu *modus operandi*.

On the third ring, a groggy Bravo answered the phone with a raspy voice. "*Dime* (Talk to me)!' he snapped.

"Manuel Bravo, I understand there's a bloody video show of you. Can you make DVD copies of it there for me to pick up?" Then quiet. Eizzo hung up, not expecting or wanting an answer.

"Target connection made, ready for Roadkill phase, over," Eizzo radioed his partners in waiting who confirmed their preparedness.

Cope left the four-foot deep dry canal to cross the dirt service road. He carried a canvas-wrapped road spike system commonly used by US law enforcement officers. He carefully unrolled the six-teen-foot long spike strip in the plowed field then returned to the seclusion of the empty canal. He firmly held on to its thirty-five-foot long nylon recovery rope.

"We have movement. Hot target just started his truck, now exiting parking lot with no lights on. Hold for exit direction," came Eizzo's calm report to his partners in waiting.

"He turned left, heading south. You're up, Cope, over."

Cope was not surprised to see the truck traveling without its headlights on, Bravo's naive notion to sneak away undetected. *All the better to snare you,* Cope snickered to himself. He then pulled on the recovery rope hand over fist toward his hidden canal position until the sixteen-foot long, half foot wide nylon leader filled with hundreds of two and a half–inch long, three cornered hollow spikes extended across the two lanes. He estimated the truck speed to be forty miles per hour in the semidark dawn. Only his eye-level head was exposed above the canal edge. The truck's front tires struck the long spikes with a faint metallic clang as some of them spit upward against the truck's underbody. The rear tires were then stabbed with the remaining spikes that bore deep into the rubber and radial belt. The air immediately began to seep out of the tires through the deeply imbedded hollow spikes. Its hissing escape was loud enough for Cope to hear as the pickup slowed down fifty feet away. He pulled the spent spike strip back to his canal position.

Bravo angrily guided his four deflated wheel pickup to the soft shoulder of the road alongside the irrigation canal. It rolled to a dead stop like a rolling rock on hot tar. He beat his black cowboy hat repeatedly against the dashboard before springing open the door with a hard shove.

As he circled the truck, the sight of each additional flat tire elevated his ire until it reached a pitched fever of fury punctuated with invectives in two languages. Cope could make out every profane word fifty feet away as he gradually skulked his way down the open canal towards his target's position.

"Roadkill ready for pick up. I'm on the move, ETA one minute. Road open and clear, over," Cope radioed his teammates. He continued his crouched forward movement below the land level of the canal. He paused to look back at the RV appearing on the northern end of the road. It traveled at a leisurely pace with only Eizzo aboard.

Bravo was now in rage mode from the discovery of several spikes stuck in all four flat tires. He starred in disbelief, screaming as though his ranting would blow life back into them. Cope was now near the disabled truck keeping an eye on his agitated target. The team's expectation was that he was completely on his own, trusting no one at this point, not even in a road emergency. Four blown tires at once could not be a coincidence, Bravo pondered looking all around the empty road and nearby lifeless fields. For as far as he could see, he knew he was all alone. He attempted to process in his muddled mind the possibilities that would cause the spikes to be carelessly lying in the road, layered with his limited options for solving his sudden dilemma. Maybe a Good Samaritan would happen by, he wished for. If not, he was ready for the worse, and in the wrong frame of mind to take it on if necessary.

"In position, road clear. Ready when you are," Cope radioed Eizzo.

"Copy that. I'm on approach, target in sight, ETA twenty seconds. Are you loaded? Over," Eizzo responded.

"Affirmative. Copy, out," Cope replied as he adjusted his crouched posture to an advanced state of readiness for TA approach.

Rap's brief radio call confirmed a clear road behind them. The RV did not slow as it closed in on the target and purposefully passed him by one hundred feet before stopping. From his right-side mirror, Eizzo saw Bravo standing with his arms akimbo, cautiously checking out this mysterious, large RV with a US license plate. Eizzo's tactic was to lull his target into a comfort zone believing that this modern bus-like RV with a tourist-like appearance was indeed the passive, friendly Good Samaritan he had wished for.

Eizzo was thinking nothing less than deception. "Hoodwink the enemy so that he may be remiss and leisurely while you are tactically maneuvering," Master Sun would profess, he recalled as he backed the RV slowly to where Bravo stood apprehensively. Just feet away, Cope noticed a small bulge in the back of Bravo's shirt above the belt line and prepared for any unwanted surprise he might have for his partner.

Eizzo took his time opening the door, casually stepping down to the entrance bottom landing. Bravo slowly pushed his cowboy hat back off his forehead like an old western gunfighter before a high noon showdown, taking measure of the stranger while giving him a baleful gaze. He then placed his fingers into his front belt line, his right hand behind his back, bewildered by the goofy looking *gringo*. Eizzo was dressed in blue Bermuda shorts, yellow cotton bucket hat, open leather sandals, and a white, baggy T-shirt imprinted with the words "*Bird Watchers Are Peeping Toms.*"

"*Que paso amigo?* (What happened, friend?)" Eizzo asked pleasantly with a concerned countenance.

Bravo paused archly. "*Las pinche llantas ya estan fregadas, todos jodidos!* (The crappy tires are messed up, all fucked up!)" he replied, flushed with anger.

"*Lo siento. Yo puedo llevarte a un taller si quires.* (I'm sorry. I can take you to a garage if you want.)" he offered sincerely.

Bravo disregarded the offer, moving directly in front of the RV open door. His manner was cold. He tried to look inside but the large Good Samaritan in the baggy clothes obstructed his view. He pulled the tail of his western shirt out from his belted blue jeans. From behind, Cope saw the black revolver tucked into his exposed thick belt, now only a rapid reflex away if this explosive tempered killer cared to draw it.

"*Donde va usted?* (Where are you going?)" Bravo grunted with a stressed attitude.

"*Cerca de Puerto Vallarta para estudiar los pajaros.* (Near Puerto Vallarta to study the birds.)" Eizzo responded with his consistent insouciant attitude. He suddenly saw Cope rise from his empty canal hiding with both arms extended out in front of his face in a locked position. Eizzo spoke quickly to further engage his nervous target.

"*Estoy viajando solo. Yo puedo darte un venton si quieres.* (I'm traveling alone. I can give you a ride if you like.)" he offered with a hospitable smile.

Bravo's tense expression did not relax.

Cope was now looking down the six-inch short barrel of the high impact black polymer housing of his X26-ECD taser stun gun. He slowly depressed the trigger, silently releasing compressed nitrogen that instantly deployed two small probes attached by insulated conductive wires. They traveled like arrows fifteen feet, penetrating Bravo's shirt and shoulder muscles. He winced with an abbreviated groan. The fifty thousand volts from the taser transmitted electrical pulses along the wires and into his body for a five-second cycle at a pulse duration of one hundred microseconds. The arching voltage affected Bravo's sensory and motor functions of the peripheral nervous system. He was completely immobilized. The debilitating effect on his muscle control was complete, his face contorting and his knees collapsing, causing him to drop gently facedown to the ground following a brief high pitch cry of pain. The cycle ceased when Cope engaged the safety lever, even though the electrical force was not considered lethal.

Eizzo looked down on their dropped semiconscious target and saw the .38-caliber revolver tucked inside his backside belt.

"Did you know he was packing?" he asked Cope with a tone of surprise.

"Yeah. But I wasn't worried. He would have shot you, not me," he retorted with a smirk.

"I feel the love, partner," he said, not the least concerned, packing his own .357 mm SIG Sauer P229 pistol into his rear belt. "Let's get him inside before Triple A comes to change his tires," Eizzo said hurriedly.

"They're only flat on one side," Cope wisecracked unsympathetically.

"TA of Roadkill complete," was the radio message to Rap on the north end of the 13. His orders were to open the stop gates on the closed canal section with his wireless phone code transmission triggering its valve activation device. The open flow control would flood the dry section of the canal back to its original level, leaving no signs of human entry. Cope had already tossed Bravo's cell phone and empty revolver into the canal along with the retrieved spike strip in anticipation of the coming water burial. Rap remained behind as a rear position sentry to make sure the Caracara II and its prize inside were not followed. They had left the scene of abduction as quickly as they had arrived. Cope had placed their ashy pale FTM fugitive in the secret cell restraints of his reclining seat before reviving him completely. The only early dawn traffic was north bound, two flatbed trucks loaded with large bags of fertilizer.

"How's 'sparky' doing?" Eizzo asked Cope.

"Fine. I think he got a charge out of it," he replied with a straight face. "He can blame Tom A. Swift for the stabs in the back," referring to the fictional sci-fi, inventive character of the popular serial books that inspired the TASER name, Tom A. Swift Electronic Rifle.

Rap received radio instructions to follow them as planned from an inconspicuous distance. The RV traversed the east-west dirt service roads to connect with southbound Highway 2. Daybreak had borne a clear blue sky with the winter sun absent of any warmth at that early hour. There was little traffic for the season and Sunday morning. Ten minutes down the paved highway, Eizzo eased the RV into a gradual curve, losing sight of Rap now a quarter of a mile behind. He accelerated up to his 60-mile per hour cruise speed while Cope radioed Rap.

"Bring it up and in now, open road ahead, over."

"Copy. I've got an unknown following three quarter miles behind. Ready the nest for arrival on the fly, over," Rap replied.

"Copy that. Will hold at 60-per," Eizzo answered. "Copy and out."

"Rap rode the lean Aztec red bike hard into the curve on the tires edge, leaning in and out at eighty miles per hour. The RV was now only one hundred feet ahead. Eizzo saw him coming up fast and brought the *Caracara* II over to the center line, steering a course Rap could count on. With a push of a button, the right side lower center cargo door opened, and a black steel platform glided out eight inches above the blurred gray asphalt pavement.

Cope monitored Rap's approach from the right side rearview mirror, calling to Eizzo to maintain his alignment. The road remained open, his speed steady at 60.

"On your ready," Eizzo signaled to Rap to execute.

"On approach," was his succinct response, bringing his bike inches away from the extended platform, his motion practiced, his manner calm.

With synchronized down strokes of his wrists, his road-tested hands adroitly shifted the fifth gear and accelerator to cause the 340-pound bike to rear up like a green stallion. The Kawasaki lurched upward off the ground and forward sufficiently to overreach the platform for a calculated instant before making a soft landing on the hard steel. With a griping application of the disc brakes, the bike and rider were one with RV. Rap's boots slammed down on the platform, his left hand grabbing the raised door to secure his body and bike's balance to the rolling RV. He dismounted to the left in a low crouch into the cargo hold, bringing the bike down on its side with him. He was now completely inside radioing to Cope to electronically draw in the platform and drop the cargo door.

Eizzo was eyeing the left side rearview mirror when he called out to Cope. "Please tell me he's all in and door down. Our unknown just cleared the curve, now in plain view."

"Affirmative," Cope confirmed confidently.

The RV had returned to the right lane riding the country road as normal as any tourist bus traveling into Mexico. Eizzo identified the vehicle in the rear as a white panel truck closing in on their 60-mile per hour pace.

Rap appeared through the center floor trapdoor, welcomed back on board to the pumped-up volume of Bruce Springsteen's "*Born to Run.*"

The three quickly discussed whether or not their unknown was an unfriendly, observing the panel truck's speedy gain on the RV's rear camera monitor mounted on the dashboard. They saw two figures seated in the front of the truck. It suddenly jolted over to the passing lane with increased speed. When it passed the RV, Eizzo made sure to smile and wave, angling his head down to the left for the observing passenger to notice his casual twisted sea grass straw safari hat with a rainbow pattern band. The nondescript passenger glanced up at Eizzo briefly before observing the large *Caracara* logo and small Audubon Society seal. The Delta team felt secure in their assumption that any suspicious eyes cast upon them as abductors of Manuel Bravo would be instantly dismissed when seeing their southbound RV with bird insignias on it and a geek at the wheel. A US bounty hunter would have hustled Bravo north across the border in the trunk of a car, Eizzo surmised.

The panel truck sped far ahead, slowing in the distance to make a U-turn at a dirt cross road and come back their way without even a glance from the occupants.

"They just might be looking for a stranger on a red bike," Cope contended.

"He's now the ghost rider in the sky," Rap countered.

Their incursion into the valley of the flatlanders concluded, the Caracara crew and reluctant passenger would travel south through Hermosillo and Ciudad Obregon in Sonora to arrive at Los Moches, Sinaloa along the Gulf of Cortez by dawn the next day. There they would await Nep's radio call to rendezvous at night at a secluded spot by the mountainous bay of *Topolobampo*. There FTM Manuel Bravo would be secretively transferred to the *Sea Cat*. The long road journey would begin with the stereo sound track of Martha and the Vandellas serenading the now alert captive to "*Nowhere to Run.*"

Mad Mary 2

McKinney's Wednesday morning visits to the *Conch II* were usually alone, an opportunity to tinker around his toy boat, polish a brass bar or two, and catch up on his magazine reading he never found time for at home. As a matter of routine, he wanted to duck into the Harbor Market for his bogus bag of ice on the off chance that Taylor had sent a second message. Three days had passed since Sunday's first exciting signal from Taylor regarding the presumed initiating pursuit of their six Mexican criminal targets. It was too early, McKinney speculated, for any new news. But he was determined to remain disciplined with his routine visit to the Harbor Market, albeit a dreaded duty because of the "troll that lurked within," he had told his five associates.

He was sure that not even the morning's cool overcast weather would mollify Mad Mary's intense mood. He took an extra deep breath of ocean air to bolster his courage as he stepped inside the store. It took Mary only three seconds to knock it out of him with a full verbal assault greeting of "Jesus f'in Christ, McKinney! What's with this lame dame callen here with Corona orders? This time she's sayin' to sell you a five-bottle carton. I said, 'Honey, there ain't no thing as a friggen five-pack.' She says, 'Sell you five and you'll pay for the whole six-pack.' Is this broad a blonde, or what? I know you got money, McKinney, but are you as dumb as you are rich?"

McKinney recovered his breath and composure to reply, "I'll gladly pay for the six-pack and carry out the five as instructed. You can have the extra bottle, Mary. Resell it or drink it if you like, on me," he offered with indifference.

"I don't sell individual bottles and this ain't no bar, no drinking in the store, California liquor law!" she stated firmly with a red, furrowed forehead.

McKinney really wanted to tell her what to do with the bottle, but opted to pay for the whole six-pack while placing the single, orphaned bottle on the counter. Wanting to exit quickly, he declined her sarcastic offer to put the five-bottle carton in a paper bag.

"Are you sure you want people to see you carrying a five-bottle pack for the price of six? At least put the bag over your head, McKinney."

He forced an insincere smile and darted for the door.

"How friggin' embarrassing!" her words trailed after him.

Seated in the yacht galley with the five Corona carton the center of his attention, the message from Taylor was all too obvious. One of the six Mexican murderers was captured and in Delta team custody. In the broader scheme of the mission, he understood which fugitive it was did not really matter. The totality of the mission's success was predicated on six successful extractions from Mexico, not one or even five. He was struck by how really great it felt to see one less bottle in the six-pack carton.

If Mad Mary really knew the truth of the matter, he mused, she would want to wear a bag over her head. On second thought, McKinney wondered how many times a bag had been placed over her head. That thought put an unforced smile on his face.

12

OPERATION DOUBLE SNATCH

Aquaruta, Sinaloa

Driving into *Culiacán, Sinaloa,* to extract FTM fugitive Lionel Mario Madrid was the equivalent of medieval knights riding into the cave of the flame-throwing dragon. You knew there was a high probability of getting smoked. After all, *Culiacán* was the home field of the infamous Pacific/*Sinaloa* drug cartel, better known as "the killing field." It was the principle transshipment point for drugs coming up from the *Silver Triangle*, the South American region of Peru, Bolivia, and Columbia, a major illegal drug production area, then on to the *Golden Triangle* drug export platforms along the Mexico/US border. Although it used to be that drugs flowed from the Andes to America direct, US drug enforcement records show that 70 percent now flows through Mexico. *Sinaloa* was the new, bigger, badder Medellin, Colombia, of the 1980s.

The *Arellano* Felix cartel in *Tijuana* is where Lionel Madrid initially operated as an enforcer for the *Sinaloa* cartel in the southwest Pacific state, collecting and couriering trafficking money for his cartel kingpins. The drug traffic violence that claimed 268 lives in one year alone in *Sinaloa* in the unending fight for control and fear-mongering had made *Sicario* (hit man) Lionel Madrid trigger-happy. The Delta team's intel on Madrid reported his involvement in several killings throughout the Pacific coast trafficking corridor with no precise number noted. He was the trigger man in the assassination of the state police commander in a hail of more than sixty shots from an automatic rifle. The rap on Madrid was that of a compulsive killer whose *modus operandi* was, "Unready, shoot, aim," explaining the drug deal gone bad in Santa Barbara where he shot an innocent bystander.

Taylor and his team knew full well what they were up against, going into an out-of-control shooting arcade like *Culiacán*. To make matters worse, they would most likely have to draw Madrid out of the cartel's impenetrable compound protected by a guarded bridge crossing the *Tamazula* River. Not even the paid-off police dared to enter. This licentious no-trespass turf was well known as *Tierra Blanca* (White Land), so named for the excessive amount of cocaine spilled there over the years. There was a popular story in the region that the young sons of the cartel fathers didn't have any chalk powder to mark their home baseball field. So cocaine was used by the groundskeepers thanks to their proud cartel sponsors, proving once again that they controlled their own boundaries.

Taylor awoke to the beeping "New Mail" alert from their computer. He had been anticipating Lori's latest intel on the *Culiacán* grid and the latest known whereabouts on fugitive Madrid. Recent turf wars were causing new alliances to be formed among the rival gangs, making it difficult to get a fix on the players in such a fluid situation.

Taylor groaned at the first paragraph of Lori's e-mail update. "Eleven dead in *Culiacán* shootout yesterday. Most victims' members of the *Juarez* cartel. Local police, as always, claim no known link to *Sinaloa* cartel. Expect Madrid to go into hiding following incident, whether involved or not. Check location of no-name cantina/brothel near village of *Aquaruta*, twelve miles west of *Culiacán* on north side of river, popular with cartel operatives, Madrid known to go there regularly as his normal loop."

The profile of their target noted his weakness for prostitutes, even though he fancied himself as a real ladies man on the street. "I guess with so many enemies on his tail, old lover boy Lionel can't risk chasing local tail—is now on the lay-away plan," Grav speculated lightly.

"Money is no object for a cartel bag man. A hundred pesos says his *putas* are all coked up anyway, paid in white powder, not green-backs," Cam conjectured.

In less than an hour, they had departed the RV park and Highway 15, heading down a well-traveled rural road that bypassed the state capital city of *Culiacán* three miles to the north. It paralleled the westward flowing *Culiacán* River toward *Aquaruta*. With Grav driving, Taylor and Cam began the prep work for their protective cover, traveling birdwatchers hoping to sight freshwater fowl like long-billed curlews, spotted sandpipers, ruddy ducks, and buffle-head ducks along the riparian habitat of the river and nearby lagoons. R&B singer Al Green entertained them with *"Take Me to the River."*

Once the cantina-brothel was IDed, they would devise a plan for day and nighttime reconnaissance of its perimeter and its patrons. The hope was that Lionel got horny sooner than later so they could catch him with his pants down. They named it *Operation Double Snatch*. They would have to snatch Madrid secretively from inside the *Casa de Putas* (Whore House). They appreciated the fact that time was on their side. Yesterday's gangland shootout would have all of the *sicarios* (triggermen) lying low until the dust at the "Not OK Corral" settled down.

"Madrid won't be mobile for a few days, no business as usual with his narco money pick-ups," Taylor conjectured.

"Yeah, and whacking people as usual. So I'm guessing he'll have an itchy trigger finger in a few days as well," Grav added.

Taylor e-mailed Lori asking a three-part question. "Any way to ID Madrid's vehicle: make, color, plates?" He knew he was asking a lot in a city where the police were corrupt and the region was one constant crime scene. Every male between sixteen and sixty was suspect, if they lived that long. The government's anti–drug trafficking agencies depended primarily upon informants, not honest detective work, the latter considered an oxymoron. Many secretly provided damaging information on their enemy rival gangs with the hope that they'd be eliminated. A gang member's true loyalty was predicated on money in hand. Ratting on your own cartel *Chapos* was worse than a death sentence; the penalty was torture, followed by death if you were fortunate to succumb quickly.

The *Sinaloa* cartel's torture of choice was to place the informant's head inside a vise-mounted workbench, ten inches long and six inches high. Then slowly close it to watch the eyes and brain ooze out in front of his eyewitness operatives. Once the head was the shape of a pancake, the corpse was then tossed out in public for all to take warning that the *Sinaloa* cartel had its own vise squad. Most recently the cartel ordered the beheading of three uncooperative police officers from *Rosarito* Beach.

The *Caracara* I caught the attention of a traveling busload of school children entering the city on their passing lane. While most of the kids gazed at the RV's large bird logo, a small group of boys amused themselves by flapping their arms up and down in mock flight.

The city was small by comparison to other state capitals with a modest population of 743,000. The region had severe labor shortages during the spring planting and fall harvests of corn, having to bring in thousands of farm workers from as far away as *Oaxaca* in the southeast corner of Mexico, indicative that Mexico had lost sovereignty over its own labor force with 25 percent of its active population working in the US.

This cool, overcast winter morning saw light commercial traffic on the two-lane highway with aging rural, diesel buses setting the black polluting pace. From a distance, the city appeared to be a mix of modern buildings contrasting with ornate, white colonial structures dating back to the 1500s when *Culiacán* was founded by the Spanish.

The waters from the western slopes of the *Sierra Madre* Occidental mountains to the northeast fed the rivers of Tamazula and Humaya, which wound their way into the city to form the *Rio Culiacán*. Nine urban bridges crossed the three rivers dissecting the capital into a serpentine delineated north and south city. The Delta team realized what a nightmare it would be to extract anyone from such a jigsaw grid. They were hopeful that Lori's intel was right on, putting Lionel Madrid in an open rural grid. As the RV followed the winding Rio *Culiacán* highway west, they became more and more interested in the fact that it emptied in the Pacific Ocean where somewhere nearby their *Sea Cat* shadowed the coast. The river bridges became fewer and farther apart, connecting to the ever-decreasing size rural *pueblos*. The narrow strips of riparian growth were getting denser and deeper with diverse trees and thick bare bushes. The team was pleased that there was an invisible river running alongside. The territory opposite the river was a vast expanse of harvested tan corn fields reaching to the horizon. They were populated with modest sharecropper houses every half mile or so.

Taylor called out to Grav to slow down as they approached *Aquaruta*. The right-side video camera was activated. Cam viewed its interior monitor while Taylor oversaw the GPS finder.

"The river bridge is coming up on the right. Get a fix on my count," Grav forewarned Taylor. "Three, two, one, fix."

The little farming village was no larger than six blocks wide and six blocks deep with the PEMEX gas station and farm implement dealer dominating the town's entrance across the concrete river bridge. Commercial hybrid corn seed signs of Pioneer, DeKalb, and Asgrow brands competed for attention along the highway and into the town.

"Everybody, eyeball the right side for what looks like a cantina-brothel just beyond the pueblo," Grav alerted them. They knew not to expect any outward signs of a brothel no matter how wide open and wild these outlaw traffickers were. "Where there was booze, there were broads," was the stereotypical indicator. The other was the absence of a town church, equating to the absence of the eyewitness of God and guilt.

The team's only expectation was that the cantina-brothel location would be inviolable in order for its class of clientele to feel safe, not from unwanted witnesses to their indiscretions, but from enemies wishing them harm while their guard and pants were down.

Three quarters of a mile west of the town bridge, they found what they were looking for. A stone-throw from the river's edge was large, light-brown stucco, flat roof building with no windows. Its only architectural feature was a central double door of ornately carved dark wood with a lit neon sign above for *Cerveza Superior*. They noticed the large empty gravel front parking lot bordered by a chain link fence around the front and sides with a single lane entrance. The smaller lot in the back was for deliveries and employees who accessed the building by a single door overlaid with a protective wrought iron outer door. Taylor took a GPS position fix while the camera continued to roll. A midsize *Tecate* beer truck was parked by the rear door while its driver exchanged cases of bottled beer for empties. Forty feet beyond the back lot was an enormous oval-shaped lagoon fed by the river's rivulets and seasonal rain.

"Who got a count of the vehicles on site?" Grav asked.

"Not including the beer truck, three, all in back," Cam replied.

"Got anything to add to my P-code GPS vectors to Lori?" Taylor queried his partners.

"Yeah. The satellite photos have to be day- and nighttime. And we need to see details of the roof. The outer walls are giving us little to work with," Cam stated flatly as the RV continued its slow pace westward. They began to scout for a natural spot for birders to camp and for clandestine Special Forces to establish a beachhead for their special ops. The former had to foreshadow the latter to maintain their cover as geeky birders.

"We have to find someplace between the river and the highway. We can't cross the *Aquaruta* Bridge and risk being trapped within Madrid's loop. If he's in there, we'll have to go in by land and water," Taylor declared to the nodding agreement of his team members.

"Look for a sizable pull-off on the right side that will give us a deep cover departure area. It has to hug that river," Taylor emphasized with no need for explanation. They all understood that their extraction strategy would have to involve the river—both in and out of their hard target grid. But first things first, they all concurred. The right campsite was now crucial to their success. Operation Double Snatch would begin and end there.

It was a half mile from the cantina where the highway abruptly veered away from the *Culiacán* River. They observed a broad grassy terrain on the right with approximately five acres of densely wooded growth beyond. Grav slowed the RV to a stop on the highway shoulder. He had spotted a narrow, worn area ahead where vehicles had entered the grassy area. The men looked at each other in silent agreement to enter the expansive pull-off. Grav maneuvered the *Caracara*

I over the shallow tire ruts that carved out the direction it was to follow. He decided not to second guess its destination, knowing that anyone venturing inward had only the river in mind. Where the thicket of willow and ash trees began, he stopped.

"Cam, walk down to the river and report back how close can we get to the water, and what wiggle room, if any, do we have for big bird here?" Taylor ordered.

In less than ten minutes, Cam returned to report no obstacles, only a few low branches that might scrape the RV roof. "You'll have to back it in. There's no turn around room. Twenty-five feet from the shoreline is your stop point, Grav. It slopes quickly from there. Taylor and I will guide you back in."

With the aid of his partners and a rearview camera, the RV squeezed into the woods, two hundred feet from the grass clearing. They could not see the highway traffic from their new camp, nor could they be seen by the modest stream of farm trucks and occasional rural buses. For safe measure, a camouflage net was placed over the front end of the RV. Atop the roof, a mélange of antennas and two satellite dishes rose to their calibrated positions, one locked into Lori, the other to the *Sea Cat*. They would first settle in as "birders," binoculars and cameras at the ready. Cam put on his new T-shirt with the large, bold inscription, *"Bird Watchers Do It in Natural Habitats."* Taylor offloaded the bike, Grav inflated the water raft, and Cam attached and tested its 5,000-rpm electric motor. They returned to their new base map inside to discuss the reconnaissance phase of the operation. Grav jokingly selected the background music of Simon & Garfunkel's *"Bridge over Troubled Waters."*

Although the talk of entering a cantina-brothel provided some levity, the planning was deadly serious. They were acutely aware that this particular operational grid had the greatest potential for a fatal firefight within the overall *Caracara* mission. They understood the consequences of operating in the infamous "killing fields," among the most murderous cartel in Mexico. Taylor put it in perspective when stating grimly, "Only *Kabul* could be more dangerous than *Tierra Blanca*." They didn't have their Delta uniforms, but they definitely had on their Delta faces. They were about to enter Lionel Mario Madrid's lethal loop and a vespiary of loaded weapons.

Their ground reconnaissance would be in two parts, one by land and the other by water. Taylor would ride the bike into *Aquaruta* as a tourist in search of a cold six-pack of beer. The bike's hidden video camera would record the bridge, the parking lots entrance and perimeter. If it was considered safe, he'd enter the back door of the cantina on the pretext of buying beer, preferably *Cerveza Superior*. There he'd take still photos with his clandestine button camera chest high on his shirt. He would not socialize, not speak Spanish, and quickly leave.

Grav and Cam would test the river flow by taking the raft upstream to the lagoon by the cantina-brothel property line. They'd openly display their photography equipment and shoot photos of anything with feathers. Their objective would be to measure the river current, note water obstacles and shoreline landmarks. Arriving at the lagoon, they would scout for potential hiding places for their nighttime recon and advanced base, should they become operational. Taylor would remain in the RV recording the daytime recon.

"Take those bird photos first and fast. We need them in the cameras and computers to establish our legitimacy to be snooping around as birders, should we be challenged. Add to this morning's list of migratory ducks, the pintails, gadwalls, shovelers, redheads, and scaups, they're all wintering waterfowl. The residents are the herons, egrets, cormorants, anhingas, and lily walkers. Consult your field guide book," Taylor spoke academically, asking, "Does the redhead work nights?"

"Only as a two-bit hooker,'" Cam responded.

"That's a 'low-cost provider,' for the politically correct," Taylor rejoined.

Broaching the 120-foot wide river would not be a challenge, but finding a safe hiding spot would be. Motoring against the current provided them with ample time and opportunity to observe the landscape of the river and large lagoon beyond its upstream left side shore. The river banks were thick with two-foot high grass and water reeds, taller yet. A variety of trees followed the riverbed, only a few lined the lagoon side, allowing them a panoramic vista of the entire broad body of water. Their first avian sightings were four tall, slender snowy egrets feeding along the bank one hundred feet ahead. The solid white, graceful plumes on their heads, neck, and back made the field-marking identification easy compared to their much taller white heron cousins. They stood their ground on long black legs as the birders cruised slowly by their riparian habitat with their cameras capturing close-ups of their striking yellow eyes and long, pointed, black beaks.

Grav found a flat landing spot on the left bank next to a rivulet, which permitted the width of the rubber raft to dock itself. Cam leaped ashore from the front to tie it down to a large woody bush. They were inconspicuous naturalists in the natural aviary environment standing on the high ground grassy border of the lagoon only 150 feet from the cantina. A couple of nearby ducks scudded away across the still water. Cam spotted a small flock of ducks dabbling in the gray, calm water of the lagoon 20 feet off the reed-lined shore. They were now in short lens range.

"If these guys were right along the shore, we'd probably miss them with those natural brown and gray camouflage feathers," Cam commented, looking through his camera view finder. "This is an easy ID I'm saying, northern pintail, by the looks of the male's long pointed tail and back feathers," he confirmed.

Grav consulted their *Peterson Field Guide*. "Does the male have a chocolate-brown head on a narrow white neck and a slim profile?"

"Affirmative on all marks, the female a perfect beige and brown mottled pattern over her body and a pale beige head and neck, would be impossible to see if in the weeds," Cam stated with professional respect.

They took their time photographing the pintails with different lenses. Grav spotted a smaller paddling of ducks floating in the middle of the lagoon as though in a holding pattern, awaiting their turn at the shoreline feed trough.

"I'm going to try out our bird call sounder on these guys, see if they respond. If they give us a heads up, they'll be redheads," Grav speculated confidently.

He set the sounder selector to number 31, redhead duck, and aimed the small speaker in the direction of the idle birds. A strong, clear, spectacular call of a male redhead greeting broadcast across the water. "Whee-ough, whee-ough!" A second series of the redhead call turned their curious attention toward the interlopers. "They're all looking this way, but the pintails aren't. The male definitely has a bronze red head and neck, black breast, and smoky gray body. This female is beige from head to tail, also well protected in the weeds," Cam noted with his eye on the 600-mm telescopic lens.

"Yeah, well, she's not that way in order to protect her nest. The lazy bitch, according to the guide, lays her eggs in the nests of other duck species who become unwitting foster parents who raise the redhead's abandoned brood," Grav related with a groan of disapproval.

Their cameras loaded with water fowl photos, the birders returned to the RV, this time taking snapshots of downstream landmarks. They were all transferred to the dedicated birder laptop along with the other feathered family album members. Their attention again turned to the tactical planning of their target fugitive's extraction from the "no-name."

"In that well-armed den of thieves, we can't just rush in and pull him out. We have to surreptitiously push him out," Taylor expressed the obvious. He had already spoken of the drug cartel's weapon of choice being the *cuerno de chivo* (AK-47), responsible for thousands of cartel killings.

"I'm thinking 'Military Malodor number 3'—stink him out with rotten egg odor," Grav offered.

The Special Forces was familiar with the chemical cocktail the US military designed during World War II for use by the French to humiliate the German soldiers.

"Almost. It will only actuate with moisture, hydrolyze, causing hydrogen sulfide to release. That is what we had the displeasure to experience during our Fort Bragg LET (live environment training)," Taylor recalled.

"Master Sun Tzu stated that, 'The flavors are only five in number, but their blends are so various that one cannot taste them all.' What we have now is more effective, a vile mix of eight chemicals that requires no water catalyst. Their putrid stenches resemble human feces, vomit, burnt hair, rotting carcasses, wet garbage, spoiled milk, rotten eggs, decomposing fish, and spoiled fish, a blend that can bombard all of the human senses. And Lori put a small supply on board just in case," Taylor advised proudly.

"You just described Grav's morning breath," Cam snickered.

"Yo mama didn't mind," Grav rejoined to loud laughter.

* * *

Six hours had passed when Lori's satellite photos of the suspected fugitive hangout, the no-name cantina-brothel arrived. Finding Madrid's different hideouts could take weeks. They had no choice but to go with what they were handed. Given their fugitive's primal history of whoring around, it was likely to be a solid lead. "We create opportunities," Taylor repeated once again.

From above, the one-story no-name building looked like a square donut. Its center had a large square opening for the alfresco central courtyard below and what appeared to be a multitiered stone fountain. Grav speculated aloud that it flowed with tequila.

"For our recon entry into the building, that's our answer," Taylor exclaimed. "For our push of Madrid out the door, we have something else just as significant." He jabbed his finger at the twelve large air coolers spaced irregularly over the roof.

"We're going to need interior digital motion cameras to monitor our execution, real-time 'when and where.' We already know 'who and what'—and I don't care to see the 'what' on camera in a brothel," Taylor stated with disgust.

Pointing to the laptop, Cam suggested, "Take a look at these night time stills—all time-stamped. Most all of the vehicles on the lot are gone by 0200, all by 0300."

"Check out the two white minivans parked in back. They arrived in the evening and left at night at the same time with all women," Grav noted.

"They had to be carpooling *putas*. Very sensible young women," Cam speculated sarcastically.

"We'll request the same time period set of photos for the next two nights from Lori. Tonight, we'll go in to scout the building layout and place the nanocams. We're still assuming Madrid is laying low until the streets are safe or he gets a boner, whichever comes first," Taylor conjectured.

"Remember Willie Nelson's country song, '*I hate every bone in your body but mine*,'" Grav chuckled along with his partners.

"I think Grav needs a night down there with the brothel, boys," Taylor grinned. "We have a lot of electronic prep to do. Cam, you plot out your entry and exit for the camera recon. Grav, you ready the river and entry equipment. I'll contact Lori on the satellite photos."

Cam studied the existing photos taken from the ground and overhead. Entry was a "no-brainer," he quickly concluded—onto the roof, down the center opening, and into the center courtyard. Placement of the nanocams was always a challenge. As tiny as they were, they still required the perfect concealment, especially where women would be around the subject area. Field experience taught them that men were oblivious to the particulars of their immediate surroundings in sober times, blind to them when imbibing. Women, however, were naturally observant as to what flowers made up an arrangement, to a girlfriend's newest gold chain among the set of twelve old ones around her neck, to a child's untied shoelace, and to a spider the size of a pinhead in the dark corner of a room from forty feet.

The no-name would have over twenty sets of 20/20 female eyes familiar with the norm of their nightly work environment. Invisible placements would have to be creative and abnormal to pull off this covert on-site recon and extraction operation. "Turn to your feminine sides when in there concealing the cameras," Taylor suggested with tongue in cheek.

"What are you saying, we're part *puta*?" Grav protested.

"We know your male side is," Taylor shot back.

It was unanimous, no cameras placed in the *putas'* bedrooms. "We don't need to be watching real-time porno shows of a bunch of narco-nymphs and their beer-swilling, limp dick drug dealers," Grav declared emphatically.

"Cam, give me one wide-angle and one close-up camera placement with nighttime aperture on the roof's edge in front and back over the two entrances. I'll need to view the vehicle traffic and hopefully ID our horny toad as he hops in," Taylor requested.

Moments later, he shared an e-mail message from Lori with disappointment in his tone. "She came up empty on a vehicle ID for Leon Madrid. The bad boys here can buy a car or truck with no plates, no registration, as in, 'It's nobody's damn business what I drive,'" he informed them.

"What?" Cam asked in confused disbelief.

"The bad boy buyer receives a hard copy official paper demonstrating irrefutable ownership of that vehicle, but neither he nor the seller has to register it with state or federal motor vehicles departments if they don't care to," Taylor explained with a sigh.

"And miss out on that warm and fuzzy DMV experience?" Grav interrupted.

"I guess not carrying plates is a sign of prestige and power. 'I'm not only above the law, I'm an outlaw, you gotta problem with that?'" Cam dramatized.

"Oh, and Lori said not to be surprised if our fugitive and half of his posse are driving black trucks and cars with tinted windows as well," Taylor added.

"Henry Ford would be happy," Cam added.

"Well, I'm glad we've narrowed down the field," Grav added sarcastically.

"All the more reason to place those outer edge cameras on the roof. And while you're up there, you'll set up the stink bombs on the air coolers, twelve total. We'll sequence them after you return with the interior layout."

"So we go in tonight?" Cam asked for confirmation.

"Affirmative. Lori's future photos will serve to establish definitive time-sensitive population patterns for our final tactical planning," Taylor clarified.

* * *

Persistence and patience were imperative in a recon operation. The hurry up and wait *modus operandi* was the norm in the field, set up quickly and sit around slowly. The team's recon prep work was completed with all spy devices tested and ready. The only device they would not test for obvious reasons was the stink bomb. They had all experienced the older version of rotten eggs stench during Delta training camp and prayed they'd never have to use one. Taylor assured them that the military's newly created antidote pill would inoculate their brain's natural smell receptors for the same eight chemical odors emitted from the stink bombs.

"Remember, if you can't breathe, nothing else matters," Taylor underscored the tactical premise of the horrific fetor bombarding of the "no-name" guests.

"*Sun Tzu* said that?" Grav asked quizzically.

"No. The American Lung Association," Taylor corrected him.

For now, they'd continue to play the part of birders for the afternoon before setting out at 0100 in darkness for their recon ops.

By 0215, Grav and Cam were atop the no-name flat roof. Their inflatable river raft was well hidden a hundred feet away near the bank. Taylor remained in radio contact from inside Caracara I, this time patching in the work environment sounds of the Drifters, singing "*Up on the Roof.*" As standard procedure, he had contacted Nep aboard the *Sea Cat* and Lori by encrypted phone regarding their pending entry into an enemy grid. Although out of immediate reach, Taylor's team now had backup at the ready for an emergency exit or rescue, if needed.

It had been a slow weekday night at the no-name. Only one white van had parked in the rear, and all vehicles had departed by 1:20 a.m. Looking down the center square opening in the flat roof, they could only hear the monotone hum of the bar coolers. The interior was dimly illuminated from widespread multicolored neon beer logo lights plugged into the flamingo pink–colored walls.

The recon duo silently went to work setting up the four roof top cameras, two in front and back over the entrances. Taylor activated and tested them from the RV recon control center, communicating to his field operatives that he now had "eyes" and would report any outside activity. The two men next opened the side panels on the twelve air coolers to insert the battery-operated triggering devices that would set off the stink bombs. Each one had its own radio frequency numbered sequentially in order of placement. They would later coordinate that sequence with the physical position of the nanocams throughout the building. With all of the small stink bombs armed and attached securely to the triggering devices, the cooler panels were replaced with only a thin, indiscernible wire antennae exposed on the outside.

Taylor radioed that he had active reads on all twelve bomb devices. That advisory was their go-ahead order to enter the building. Cam confessed he subconsciously was more concerned that his mother would disapprove of him entering a brothel than its owner knowing.

They fast-roped down into the small courtyard, landing softly to the side of the four-tiered carved stone fountain. Its basins were filled with still water, the lowest one with purple flower petals floating on top. The men separated in silence, moving in opposite directions, clockwise and counterclockwise around the inner perimeter of the building. Their wide-beam flashlights fully illuminated the walls from floor to ceiling, permitting comprehensive mental note-taking. The first observation of interest was the large amount of festive garniture adorning the walls and structural supports. There were multiple colorful paper festoons webbing across the long bar room ceiling, alternating pennants advertising *Corona* beer and the name of some unfamiliar soccer team.

The one feature of greatest interest throughout the cantina for the recon team were a series of large rectangular framed paintings of scantily clad, voluptuous young Latin women in seductive poses. What caught their professional eyes, beyond the exposed cleavages, was the fact that they were painted on soft, black velvet cloth.

The brothel bedrooms in the rear of the cantina numbered ten by both counts as the men converged in the middle of "romper room row," as Grav would label it. Together, they very deliberately checked out each bedroom, commenting on the air vents, door knobs, locks, lighting, and individual proximity to the single back door. It was located in the far-left corner on the river side of the building, opposite the storage room. Cam pointed to the exposed light bulb on the ceiling by the black metal, jail bar–style screen door. Grav made a mold of its Yale bolt lock keyhole.

Cam shone the light inside the open store room door to discover two key elements of their recon search, the electrical circuit breaker control box and air cooler controls.

"Make a mold of this lock keyhole too. It's open when they're closed, but surely closed and locked when their open to the boozers and losers," Cam speculated.

Cam inspected the air cooler controls. As he had hoped, it was a multipurpose ventilation system that both cooled and ventilated the building, extracting smoke and stale air while drawing in fresh outside country air on a continuous circulating basis when open for business. The control panel showed all twelve coolers by zone from the front of the building to the rear, the last three ventilating the ten bedrooms. Cam now knew how they would program the gradual sequence of bomb device activations. The building's twelve zones of air quality, or lack off, could be determined by the Delta team's hand-held radio controls.

Their recon focus returned to the cantina bar, lounge area where they carefully surveyed the layout, speculating on the flow of patrons and *putas*. Their singular concern was target acquisition—on capturing Madrid's image on one or more cameras in order to capture the man. Grabbing the wrong man would be beyond embarrassing, although they knew that most all patrons there could also be convicted in an honest court of any number of crimes of their own. They sought the one they knew to have the bloodiest hands and serial killer mind, Leon Mario Madrid.

The Delta duo summarily agreed upon the tactical placement of the nanocams. The first one was done together to test its practicality. The camera's tiny lens protruded the velvet cloth from behind secured by duct tape. Its precise frontal protrusion was determined by profound artistic interpretation among the two art critics, whether to have its pinhead-size, nonglare lens coming out through the painted subject's beaded necklace at the bottom of her ample cleavage, or from the matching jeweled earring on her left ear lobe. The critics concurred, in spite of popular opinion, that men aren't observant, their discerning, albeit perverse eyes would always be drawn first and foremost to a woman's cleavage. Grav believed that the *putas* would be more focused on the cheap costume jewelry their real rival *putas* were wearing than what some over-accessorized, two-dimensional fantasy floozies were exhibiting on paintings.

The earring won out. It was the placement of choice for nine cameras secreted behind nine vixen paintings with a vista of both moving and seated clients. The remaining three cameras found clandestine coverage behind assorted wall hangings near the passage to the brothel bedrooms. They would be their last literal window of opportunity to ID their FTM fugitive.

The array of camera placements received radio approval from Taylor for viewing quality and layout numbering. The final phase of the recon ops had more to do with the actual extraction operation. The men turned off their flashlights and began to move about certain areas of the interior in a manner they anticipated the planned extraction to go down in darkness. They repeated their improvised, choreographed "scheme of maneuver" in dress rehearsal fashion, each with his assigned role. They had given themselves only thirty seconds to pull it off, two men in, three men out, without incident.

Taylor gave his safe exit clearance for the men to leave the building, which they did without any trace of entry or espionage. Their one-half-mile planned return by river was timed by Taylor, meeting them on the bank by the RV.

"Well done, mates. Your mothers would be proud of you, your first time in a Mexican brothel and still virgins," Taylor proclaimed, smiling, patting them on their wet backs.

"I never thought I'd be the one crossing a river in Mexico," Cam chuckled.

"Well, if the *putas* in there are like the sexy honeys in the framed paintings, we just might do a prisoner exchange, me for Madrid," Grav suggested to loud laughter.

Back in the RV, the three worked together to assign camera numbers to their layout of the building. They would commit them to memory. Taylor was the fugitive ID man relying completely on the long-distance nanocamera transmissions. Cam and Grav would have the final opportunity to verify the ID up close and personal. Taylor knew he'd have to be right on, or get his men off the outer property and wait for another day. They could not afford to snatch the wrong captive, abort the mission, and run. The camera recon ops were their one best chance for success.

* * *

Once again, the Delta team turned their public personas back to birders for the next two days, finding numerous waterfowl to photograph. They saw two hunters who appeared to be Americans walking with their shotguns on the opposite side of the lagoon. Cam sighted the larger of the two hunters in his long lens, noting out loud the inscription on his green sweat shirt, "I'm a Bird Watcher—Through My Gun Sight."

Cam waived his camera at them in an insincere greeting, knowing the hunters would avoid contact with "us wimpy, geeky, non-NRA, pussy photographers," he proudly characterized themselves out loud to the laughter of his partner.

"They likely have been lectured by US birders about killing birds for the blood sport of it and don't need to hear it again in Mexico," Cam guessed, to the grinning agreement of Grav. He only wished they could coincidently read his T-shirt's large, bold inscription, "Kill Two Bird Hunters with One Stone."

Each evening, they'd take turns reviewing the camera monitors more for technical correctness than with expectations of sighting their target. If so, they were ready to initiate their operation within an instant.

On the third day, they received their requested nighttime satellite photos. Taylor had been right. There were definite people placement and pace patterns formed from opening to close on a predictable basis. The patrons parked in front, the *putas* in back, they met in the middle, drank booze to excess, screwed in the back bedrooms, and all left as they arrived during an almost identical passing of time. "A big bang for their buck," Taylor admitted. His most cogent observation was the fact that in all of the photos, there was never a bouncer at the front door or guards at the parking lot entrance.

"That tells me three things. One, every patron there is packing a sidearm, two, who needs a bulked-up meathead at the door when everyone is packing, and three, there's honor among thieves," Taylor surmised.

His partners grinned in agreement, Grav commenting, "I guess little ole bouncer Booby Gump need not apply."

It was Saturday night. The camera monitors began to fill up with pickup trucks, new model cars, men of all sizes and shapes, mostly appearing to be in the age range from thirty to fifty, and of course the resident *putas du jour*. The men were dressed in a mix of casual sportswear including US football team logo jerseys, baseball caps, blue jeans, and polished cowboy boots. The macho wardrobes they wore were more to impress their fellow womanizers than the women.

"I guess they don't have to impress the women here, do they. They're paid to tell them how macho they are, regardless," Cam opined sarcastically.

They had never planned on entering the cantina in military field gear and black face. Their overall strategy to hide out in plain sight would carry over to the actual entry site in order to not stand out as an infiltrator, even though their presence would be in darkness and for thirty seconds only. "We don't tempt fate. When in Rome, do as the Romans. In *Sinaloa*, as the sinners," Taylor exclaimed. Cam and Grav quickly sorted through their travel wardrobes like quick-change artists. Blue jeans were a must along with long sleeve cotton jerseys above and rough hide boots below. Cam selected a green cap with a John Deere tractor logo. Taylor tossed Grav a Cincinnati Reds baseball cap to wear.

"I'm not so sure about this Reds cap. The first thing men think when they see a guy in Reds gear is, 'He must throw like a girl!' They'll want to kick my ass."

"Yeah, well they'll have to do it in under thirty seconds, in the dark, up against a 230-pound Special Forces commando while puking their guts out," Taylor rejoined laughing.

"Well yeah, there's that," Grav grinned knowingly.

"I have a strong feeling about tonight being 'body snatch' night. We don't want to hang around another week waiting for Madrid to get a woody, so let's hope this is it. Are you ready to roll?" Taylor questioned his field ops teammates.

"Affirmative!" came their firm joint response. The river raft was loaded with their operations equipment. The recon work and entry, exit prep completed, they only needed a positive ID of their fugitive target to "green light" the extraction ops. Taylor's instincts on the timing being right came from the assumed animal instincts of Madrid having to have a woman in the absence of a good kill. Both were power plays to a psycho, macho, egomaniac as Madrid. The safest place to exercise that power in dangerous times was a brothel, a known, safe environment where he'd be in control from the moment he entered, or so he'd assumed.

Taylor anticipated the challenge his men faced entering a hostile environment of horrific odors bombarding their olfactory receptors to the point of convulsive vomiting. Gas masks would be counterproductive for their *modus operandi*. He handed them military issue olfactory neuro-deadener pills to anesthetize them from the eight chemically replicated fetid smells their stink bombs would introduce. Grav and Cam swallowed the pills with gusto.

One hour later, they synchronized their watches to Taylor's at 2100 and shoved off up the *Culiacán* River aboard their raft under a cool, overcast sky. They would remain hidden under a camouflage cover on the *Aquaruta* shore side behind a knee-high wall of water reeds. A direct 75-foot unobstructed distance from the cantina's rear door, they waited in radio contact with Taylor for his "Execute" order. He was all eyes on the spy monitors with gallery photos of Madrid framed on a separate laptop screen for instant reference.

Taylor had committed to memory all of his fugitive's salient features: small head, tall, thin frame, light complexion, thick, straight black hair with boyish bangs, squinting dark eyes, and his signature, long, Pancho Villa–style mustache. Taylor described his composite profile as a person you would instantly stereotype as an "asshole."

Roof top camera number 1 validated Lori's prediction; half of the vehicles so far were black pick-up trucks and new model SUVs with a couple of Escalades to piss off the have-nots. The most recent one to arrive caught his attention because it pulled up to the front door instead of parking, idling as though waiting for a valet attendant. Taylor studied every face that entered, circulated, or sat down.

The romper-room activity was starting up; the provocative *putas* were actively working the growing crowd of male patrons. The men entered in twos, threes, and fours, all collegially greeting others inside.

Finally the driver's door on the black Escalade opened. The tall, thin driver exited, carrying a black, shallow briefcase. The high camera angle could not frame the man's face for ID. The first interior camera picked him up laterally passing the courtyard fountain, showing the man to have a small head on a thin body. The next camera captured the first frontal frame of what appeared to be Madrid, a squinty-eyed man with long, black bangs and thick, bushy mustache. He had passed a dozen men without a salutation, all avoiding eye contact. The camera near the bar framed his face in close-up as he spoke with the bartender. It exhibited all of the features Taylor comparatively viewed on his laptop, including his signature scowl.

"I'll be a son of a bitch! I do believe we have target ID," Taylor unofficially radioed his field team.

"Is that a confirmed?" Cam replied.

"Hold for TA," Taylor responded with calculated hesitation.

The same side wall camera showed the subject lifting two uncapped bottles of beer with his left hand while gripping the briefcase under the arm. He walked over to an unsmiling, sexy looking *puta* in a tight knit top who appeared uninterested in Madrid's presence. Taylor could now see all of his subject's salient features in full frame. The *puta's* unhappy face and dismissive demeanor confirmed that she too recognized an asshole when she saw one. He placed his free right hand behind her neck and firmly guided her toward the brothel end of the cantina.

"Our prize is inside, a positive ID, and he's in a fever, headed directly to a bedroom with a *puta*, hatless, all white V-neck jersey, blue jeans, shoes unknown. The wardrobe won't matter in a minute. He's packing a semiautomatic holstered on his right-side belt. I'm guessing a 9-mm Glock. I'm watching them now enter room number 6. Be ready for my 'Go' in three minutes," Taylor forewarned them.

"We're ready on your go," Grav copied.

"One more thing. Madrid left his black Escalade parked right by the entrance door and entered carrying a shallow black leather briefcase. Bring it with you," Taylor strongly ordered.

He closely watched all monitors with one eye fixed on room 6. The field team crept closer to the rear of the building under the cover of their camouflage blanket. The back door was closed. Grav had his two replicated door keys ready if needed, cut earlier in the RV. They crouched down behind a large metal dumpster at the edge of the parking lot. They realized then that their anti-stink pills had kicked in when the dumpster didn't offend them.

Knowing his men were "danger close," Taylor arrived at the decision point and radioed, "One minute and counting, over."

"Copy, out," Cam responded.

The men began their visual sweep of the entry zone and saw no one. The white minivans and two old foreign, med-size cars gave them left flank defilade. The absence of exterior lights on an overcast night gave them an extra blanket of cover.

Taylor radioed, "Prepare for sequential rooftop pops in thirty seconds, full execution over three minutes. 'When he is united, divide him.'—Sun Tzu."

"Copy that," Cam replied.

They knew that all twelve stink bombs would detonate with a slight popping sound in a predetermined sequence from the front to the back of the building. It was orchestrated so that panic and disorder would not occur with a single, overwhelming putridity. The stench would flow evenly from the front lounge area to the middle bar and lastly impregnating the air in the ten rear romper rooms. The strategy was for more than just crowd control. Those closest to the front door would be affected first and exit first, followed by the bar area crowd, leaving the romper room's repulsion for last with little traffic and potential resistance to deal with.

"My current count has four of the ten bedrooms occupied, number 6 still ours," Taylor reported.

The exterior antennas on the front three rooftop air coolers received a simultaneous radio signal transmitted from *Caracara* I. The triggering devices silently activated miniature metal capsules, causing them to emit light concentrations of "Military Malodor #8," the foulest odor on earth. The putrid vapors entered the ventilation ducts, blowing what was to be fresh air from outside, in. Within seconds, the people in the front lounge area turned their noses up in revolting curiosity. Those closest to the door exited immediately, followed by those seated near the walls. By then the second set of three air coolers were venting their retched vapors to the middle bar section, causing the same quick negative reaction. When the third set of three coolers triggered, the most heavily populated area of the bar had already received a strong vile whiff of the previous waves of vapors that now permeated the entire area. This group quickstepped in anger for the entrance, shouting profanities at the bartender and *putas*. They joined the gagging masses, now covering their faces with cocktail napkins and handkerchiefs, clustered out in the front parking lot where many were vomiting between the cars and trucks.

When the final set of stink bombs detonated above the brothel area, Taylor radioed the decisive engagement order to "Execute!"

"We're in approach," Grav radioed. With fourteen long, quick strides to the back metal door, and a precision-inserted turn of a key, they achieved entry. Cam stretched high in the air to loosen the ceiling light bulb, darkening the small area between the back door and storage room door. A quick glance around the corner told him that the cantina was now empty. Grav entered the locked storage room with the second replica key, pulled the power grid handle down to the off position, placing the building in total darkness with no extraction of air. He closed and locked the storage door behind him. They now heard a chorus of raw, deep coughing and swearing coming from the bedrooms along the brothel hallway.

Taylor monitored the confused, discommoded, and angry crowd of teary-eyed patrons and *putas* in the parking lot laboring for fresh breaths of air and relief from the fetid assault on their senses. Suddenly the front passenger and back doors of Madrid's black Escalade opened. Three medium-sized men in tight, white T-shirts stepped out, hurriedly heading for the front double doors. All three wore shoulder-holstered handguns.

"Fuck me!" Taylor exclaimed aloud. "Listen up. It's good you've gone dark because you have three armed unfriendlies entering the front, Madrid's men from his SUV. Hustle up!" Taylor ordered with urgency.

Standing now in front of bedroom number 6, Cam whispered, "Copy that." From inside the room, they heard a duet of his and her coughs punctuated with a terse, strained outburst of "*Que mierda es esto?* (What the shit is that?)"

The Delta intruders could not wait for Madrid to exit voluntarily. They prepared for their forced entry when the door opened with the *puta* bent over slightly, her lower face buried in a towel. She quickly shuffled barefooted in a pink satin robe down the hallway and out the back door. Cam and Grav covered their nose and mouth with a handkerchief more as a mask than as a filter, and then stepped determinedly into the bedroom. Madrid was struggling with his belt, trying to cinch it closed with one hand while the other pressed a towel against his mouth and nose. In his best Spanish, Cam shouted, "*Ven, ven afuera!* (Come, come outside!)"

He firmly gripped one arm to guide his captive into the dark hallway. Grav followed with the secured shallow black leather briefcase and holstered pistol from a candle-illuminated nightstand. He grabbed Madrid's other arm and held him still while Cam stabbed him in the side of the neck with a syringe. His body coiled tightly for second then relaxed as he mumbled, "*Conjo—que fue esto?* (Fuck—what was that?)" His startled, raspy voice trailed off.

"*No se—vamanos a fuera* (I don't know—let's go outside)," Cam spoke through his muzzled handkerchief.

The other bedroom doors were opening behind them with disoriented, gagging patrons and *putas* choking for fresh air. Grav shot a wide screen of pepper spray behind him head high to cloud the visual air of detection. They heard the receding footsteps of the unfriendlies back to the front entrance. Now by the rear door, the Delta duo heard the unfriendlies' distressed voices swearing loudly as they exited the front door. Without interior lights, the camera monitors were dark except for the front parking lot now partially illuminated by a half dozen vehicle headlights. Taylor's attention was on the rear parking lot, straining to discern shadow shapes as those of people.

"Standing by for evac. Are we clear?" Cam radioed to Taylor.

"The rear is clear, but the unfriendlies are coming around to the river side of the building toward the back. Go now!" he advised with alarm.

They burst out of the doorway holding their now subdued, limp prey by his belt and upper arms, destination dumpster. Out of sight behind the dumpster, Cam placed a precut piece of tape over Madrid's mouth. Grav unsheathed a long, black SP-1 marine combat knife from his ankle nylon holster as he kneeled in an attack crouch. Cam unholstered a .357-mm, 12-round SIG Sauer P229 pistol from his right ankle for backup. It alone had enough stopping power for every bad guy on site. Their rules of engagement were very clear: "Kill only if about to be killed. Guns and knives were not to be engaged unless a Delta member's death was imminent." And then it would have to be "a kill shot."

After laying their limp, mute captive on the ground behind them, they observed the shadow shape of three men finding their way to the back door and entering with their guns pointed upward, the leader shouting, "*Cortar cartuchos* (Weapons cocked)." Grav waited to the count of five, and then sprinted to the rear door. He silently key locked the outer door, trapping the unknown adversaries inside the dark, wretched smelling cantina, searching for their man who had just disappeared into thin, albeit putrid, air.

The casually dressed commandos dragged their drowsy captive to the bank of the river draped in the camouflage blanket. He was placed face up in the center bottom of the raft with Cam fore and Grav shoving off aft. They quick paddled ahead of the river's modest current, disappearing into the cover of night below shore level. In the now distant background, they could see headlight beams going in all directions from the chaotic aftermath of the cantina snatch.

Taylor was waiting on shore to aid his teammates offload their catch of the day. They immediately stored their FTM fugitive in his secret suite under lock and key. The RV's diesel engine was idling, warming up for their hastened departure. They had already decamped in anticipation of the extraction getaway with only a quick change left of their fetid field wardrobe to be buried in the belly of the cargo compartment.

It was 2310 when they rolled slowly onto the westbound highway to the upbeat sounds of Nirvana's "*Smells Like Teen Spirit.*" As expected, they found a cash stash in the briefcase. A quick count amounted to "One fucking hundred thousand dirty dollars!" announced Grav in the voice of a game show host. Taylor radioed the *Sea Cat* to confirm their *Topolobampo* coastal rendezvous two hours away. Only the *Rio Culiacán* knew their secret. Only the river was going their way.

Mad Mary 3

McKinney hesitated momentarily at the entrance of the Harbor Market having seen two fellow yacht club members inside. He wondered if they might serve as a buffer for Mad Mary's verbal abuse or as further incentive for her having an audience to play to. *Damn Taylor.* If only he didn't have to buy the beer, he wished, but merely hear the coded message, then run out empty-handed. But he knew Mary. If he stopped buying the ordered beer, she would tell his code caller to "Piss off" the next time she made her *Corona* call. *It's a small price to pay in the big scheme of things*, he reasoned. "But damn Taylor anyway," he grumbled to himself as he stepped inside.

The yacht club members acknowledged McKinney with pleasant smiles and nods of the heads while Mary glanced up from the register with a peevish grin. "Hey, McKinney. You on some sort of six-step program to dry out, or what? Like six, five, now four beers at a time. Jesus, man, it's only beer. Why not just quit cold turkey?"

"Are you saying that there's a phone order for four *Coronas*?" he asked, reacting more irritated at Mary's lack of clarity than embarrassed by the quizzical looks from his fellow yachtsman.

"Jesus, man. Mexican beer causes diarrhea, not deafness. I said *four beers*, McKinney. You know the drill. Pay for six, take as few as you like. It's your McMoron payment plan, not McMine," she said with stinging sarcasm.

Now McKinney was irritated. Grabbing his six-pack of *Corona* from the back wall cooler, he leaned down behind a tall rack of potato chips, pulled two bottles from the carton with one hand, and shook them vigorously. He then tossed a ten-dollar bill on the counter while handing one of the selected bottles to each of his club compatriots. "Here, have a beer on Mary," he said absently as he dashed out the door.

Outside, he heard Mary shouting, "No! Not in here, you idiots! Ah Jesus, now look what you've done!"

Back on the *Conch II*, McKinney counted only four days since he last looked at a carton of *Corona* on his galley table, this one high-lighted by two empty slots. He knew that he shouldn't be surprised at the rapid repetition of events with Taylor's field reputation for swift action. They had weeks of required reconnaissance and tactical planning under their belts. Now they were out of the hunting mode and into capture and carry maneuvers. The Santa Barbara backers realized that two seizures were far from a successful mission and that the Delta team was now immersed in the most dangerous phase for themselves, where they could be the hunted, or worse, the captives.

It was a clear blue sky, cool Sunday morning, and McKinney was excited to soon share the latest message with his associates. Waiting for their arrival, he was struck by the amusing irony of sit-ting aboard his million-dollar yacht paid for by the profits from his high-tech telecommunications empire that provided the Delta team with his state-of-the-art Casper cell phones while he personally had been reduced to depending upon the most crude means of commu-nicating, via a simplistic gesture of counting beer bottles symbolic for bad guys, sold to him by a crazy woman in a second-rate snack shop, who unwittingly receives coded messages over an old landline phone from some unknown caller. So much for leading-edge technology, he sighed. This, he mused, was not too far removed from the elementary grade song of "ninety-nine bottles of beer on the wall. If two of them should happen to fall, four bottles of beer in the carton."

Later that morning, he would laugh about it with his mis-sion partners while they sang the "beer on the wall" song, drinking Bloody Marys, and raising their glasses to Taylor and his team while the quantity of unopened *Coronas* mounted in the galley fridge.

13

JOE CROW IS AN AMIGO OF MINE

San Jacino, Jalisco

"Eizzo, I've got some promising intel on your killer, street drug dealer Juan Diego Leon," Lori was calling in on their Casper cells. "It turns out he is now just a common smuggler who got burned on the Santa Barbara botched drug deal. In the years since he escaped capture in the US, he's tried his bad luck with contraband of all sorts, most recently exotic birds."

"In which states?" Eizzo asked.

"Texas, Louisiana, and burned again in California."

"Caught?"

"Yes, but released with fake papers. His gringo, San Diego buyer, a pet wholesaler, was raided after buying ninety exotic parrots, Lilac-crowns and red-crowns that Juan Diego had trapped in the lowlands of Mexico and delivered himself on the US side."

"Where exactly did he cross?" he asked, attempting to plot a pattern of his border movements.

"At the San Ysidro and Otay Mesa ports of entry. The parrots were squeezed into large plastic women's hair curlers with their beaks taped—found in the side panels and under seats of two cars, only fifteen out of the ninety still alive. Sadly, that's the normal survival rate," Lori lamented.

"Juan Diego's victim survival rate in Santa Barbara was zero. So where is Porky now?" Eizzo replied with disdain.

"Porky?"

"Yeah, his a.k.a.—Porky *Porcino*. You have his file photo. It's Porky Pig with a mustache. Some call him Poncho Pig," Eizzo stated sardonically.

"My god, yes! I have it here. His nose is beyond pug—like a dollar pancake with two holes. No wonder he turned to a life of crime—only way he could bring home the bacon," Lori giggled.

"Cute. Where's Porky now?"

"Deported to Mexico, not even processed. US Border Patrol is more concerned and consumed with drug and people smuggling. Besides, they know that bird trapping and trading is legal in Mexico, only restricted somewhat by season and harvest quotas. But the US buyer will probably get five years, off in two," she recited knowingly.

"Jesus. They actually call it harvesting?" Eizzo questioned gloomily.

"Oh yeah. More than 100,000 painted buntings were trapped and exported from Mexico between 1984 through 2000, that's over 5,800 per year."

"You mean that they even keep numbers on this harvest?"

"Exactly, but this does not include numbers on the illegal bird trade by the Juan Diego Leons of Mexico. It's estimated that five million wild birds in Mexico end up in home cages somewhere in the world every year," Lori reported statistically.

He quickly ran a search on his laptop Mexican bird-watching program for painted buntings, remembering the brilliant, multicolored, robin-size bird from his orientation. *Colorin Sietecolores*, the Seven-Colored One, it was called in Mexico, the computer reminded him. *This bird would make a peacock blush*, he thought to himself.

"So he was smuggling painted buntings as well?" he asked, now understanding the bird's popularity.

"To Texas and Louisiana where they make their way to Europe for seventy dollars a pair. His field cost is only six dollars, including a small wooden cage. Our intel plots his next most likely field of operation to be in southwest Mexico, following the southerly migration of the painted buntings to their Pacific lowland wintering range."

"That's quite a ways from the US border," Eizzo expressed concern.

"There's an Asian market as well, Japan in particular. The bird's considered a real beauty everywhere. Its French name is the *nonpareil*—without equal."

"Well, it's soon going to be a rare beauty at this rate."

"In thirty-five years, the known population has declined 72 percent, and still dropping," Lori stated with disgust.

"Trapping the trappers might help some. But where do we find Juan Diego among the birds?" Eizzo asked testily.

"We don't. We have a Mexican contact who will after he teams up with you as a birder guide. He doesn't know it yet. He knows the migration wintering grounds, which we'll be tracking as well via the Partners in Flight Watch List. He'll unwittingly lead you right to Juan Diego Leon," Lori offered confidently.

"Where did you find this guy?" Taylor asked with pleased curiosity.

"Where else, the Audubon Society, Mexico chapter. He's an active member of all the Mexican wildlife watchdog organizations, even paid by a few of the more aggressive groups. He's considered a lone ranger, extremist, yet well-respected and loved by most. He knows Juan Diego Leon is a trapper and smuggler so will chase him if given the opportunity and motivation," Lori emphasized.

"As the birds fly, so does their predator, which becomes our prey. Sort of our own Bermuda Triangle with a Latin twist," Eizzo synthesized the developing scenario.

"We have good reason to believe that our birdman will take you right to our pig man, Juan Diego Leon. Surreptitiously, of course. But we can't reclassify him as a soft target. He is still armed and dangerous—with a nervous trigger finger connected to a mean temperament," she said, citing her official files on their target.

"'When the strike of the hawk breaks the body of its prey, it is because of timing.'—*Sun Tzu*," Eizzo recited with purpose, knowing what their field tactics would entail.

"So, what's our contact's name?" he asked, wanting to get down to what mattered most, the pursuit and capture of their FTM fugitive.

"I've been saving it because it's too good to be true—Jaime Falcon, pronounced 'Hime Falcone'—his Mexico a.k.a. Jose Cuervo, because his calling card for the bad guys is a miniature bottle of Jose Cuervo tequila. Logically his US alias is Joe Crow. My kind of hero," Lori personalized.

"I thought I was," Eizzo feigned.

"Old Crow comes to mind."

"Ouch!" he grimaced.

"Falcon could become a liability if he gets close to Juan Diego before we do. What's his MO, money?" Eizzo assumed the norm.

"Surprisingly, no. He's an eco-activist maverick, with a Greenpeace mentality when it comes to protecting his little feathered friends."

"In other words, he's effective," he pronounced, positively speaking.

"Embarrassingly so. While these organized defenders of birds raise funds, he's raising hell with the offenders, disrupting their illicit operations or exposing them to the public or powers that be, who unfortunately don't have much of it. His victims are trappers and smugglers," she exclaimed flatly.

"Victims? He not knocking them off, is he?"

"There's no proof he is, but there is proof that they don't continue in the same line of crime either. So yeah, he's damn effective, whatever he's doing. And we know that he has Juan Diego Leon in his sights," she stated with assurance.

"Now we have to prevent him from pulling any kind of trigger before we pull ours. How did he earn an American alias?"

"Fascinating background. His father is a well-to-do cattle rancher in *Chihuahua*, who was US-educated and married to an American gal from New Jersey. At age fourteen, Jaime was sent to study in the US, living with his maternal uncle, the butcher Guseippi Lombardi in Jersey City, working in his small Italian neighborhood meat market."

"So what he really gets is a Jersey education, right?" Eizzo adds knowingly.

"And attitude, accent, and brass balls to boot. He did exceptionally well in school, spent summers back on the ranch except for the one following high school graduation."

"He wanted to become a butcher?"

"Only of a particular Jersey mafia hit man named Louie 'Bagels' Daidone."

"Did you lift this out of a Mario Puzzo novel?" Eizzo asked skeptically.

"True story, I swear. We got it from FBI files and newspaper clippings. It so happened that one *Gaetano* 'Three Fingers' Luchese, godfather of the Luchese organized crime family, ordered Vittano Anso, the Luchese acting boss, to put a contract out on a family informant for the Feds named Bruno Facciola. Anso hired a family gumba known in the underworld as Louie Bagels. Louie shoots Bruno Facciola in both eyes, kills a canary, and stuffs it in Bruno's breathless mouth for 'singing to the Feds.'"

"Was it Jaime's canary?"

"No. But when he read the story in the newspaper, he went nuts, couldn't care less about a murdered mafioso, but an unknown, innocent, whacked bird, forgettaboutit. It put him over the edge," Lori stated dramatically.

"What, he put a contract out on Louie Bagels?"

"Worse. The police had no hard evidence to prove that Louie was the hit man, but the incriminating rumors around the butcher shop were pretty loud and convincing. So Jaime took it upon himself to track down Louie and discovered his favorite neighborhood restaurant, hangout, DeLuna's, in Jersey City."

"You mean it wasn't a bagel shop?" Eizzo asked sarcastically.

"You'd think, but no. Jaime scouted the place for days. At the right moment, he managed to place a small gift box on the driver's seat of Louie Bagel's Caddie Seville."

"A stale bagel?"

"No again. From his uncle's butcher shop, he had packed a chicken's head, severed below the neck with bloody feathers, and crest, along with a threatening note. I'll read it to you. 'Louie Bagels—you pecker head, chicken shit. Kill one more canary and this will be you. *Coppice?*—Jaime the Hawk.'"

"The Hawk? Afraid to use 'Falcon'? I wonder why?" Eizzo chuckled to himself.

"It wasn't quite the horse head in the bed. But what the hey, he was only eighteen at the time."

"He showed promise early. How old is he now, and more important, where is he?" Eizzo wondered with growing curiosity and concern.

"He's thirty-two and we don't know exactly where, but that's not difficult to learn with the tracking connections we have on him."

"I have to say, Lori, we've lucked out so far on this one—it plays right into our bird-watchers guise for now, so we'll obviously play it as such. But you'll have to be oblique in how you have Jaime Falcon connect with us. Use a Mexican birders group. Say that we're in need of an experienced guide, that we're photographing threatened species without mentioning the painted buntings. He needs to know that we're aggressive chasers with some tech toys that might pique his interest in us. Oh, yes, and that we have plenty of money for the right guide with the most adventurous plan. To further motivate him, add a little edge to our past birding exploits," Eizzo summarized.

"Like antimuseums, antihunters, and antitrappers—not afraid to challenge those who are?"

"Precisely. With that fringe profile, the Mexican bird organizations will know to connect us with their bird Zorro, Joe Crow himself. Try and make it happen sooner than later, Lori. We might be facing a limited window of opportunity here," he said, exhibiting his professional drive to act.

"I'll get right on it."

"Oh, and, Lori, whatever happened to Louie Bagels? Did he come after Jaime?"

"No. Uncle Guseippi feared retaliation and sent his nephew back to Mexico. Our FBI boys had Louie under close surveillance at DeLunas. Their file says that after he received 'Jaime the Hawk's' chicken head threat, he stopped ordering his favorite dish at DeLunas, *Petti di pollo forciti*, stuffed chicken breasts with fontina cheese, dry sherry, and capers."

Laughing, Eizzo suggested, "He should have ordered stuffed canary, tastes just like chicken."

Chuckling, Lori said, "Tell that to Joe Crow when you meet him."

* * *

The *Plaza San Jacinto* was typical of hundreds of small *pueblos* throughout Mexico. The open air, town center square was framed by four, one-block-long, single-story colonial buildings of eighteenth-century architecture. Their high arched colonnades provided the multitude of entrances with covered *arcada* portals that staged and protected the *tiangusas* (daily market stands) from the cool winter rain and hot summer sun.

Eizzo and Cope sat on the woven straw seat, ladder back chairs around a small wooden plank table on the outer edge of the designated café, easily visible to their new bird guide. Through the Audubon contact, Jaime Falcon had arranged to meet them at ten that overcast morning. They made sure to appear as the bird-watchers they claimed to be, Audubon poster boys, wearing their beige, soft canvas caps, forest green wind-breakers, leg pocket pants, and brown, high top Timberline hiking boots. Only Eizzo had a camera strapped to his body, presently being used as a monocular to scout the busy Saturday morning crowd of plaza shoppers.

They had arrived early to secure a prominent place at the tiny plaza side café to allow for observation and orientation of their new environment, albeit, a soft target area of operations. Cope tried to get the attention of a short, white-haired, craggy-faced old woman twenty feet away standing over a small tabletop propane stove. It supported a large red clay pot that emitted a strong coffee aroma infused with spices. He watched her meticulously stir in *piloncillo*, raw brown sugar, cloves, dried orange peel, and cinnamon bark before covering the pot. Noticing his curious stare, she began to make her way through the crowded tables of local customers to ask the two strangers, "*Buenas dias. Como puedo servirles?* (Good morning. How may I serve you?)" Her smile was welcoming and sincere, displaying toothless gaps in her aging mouth, which caused a distinct impediment to her slow speech. Her *buenas* became a *fuenas*, with a slight whistle.

"*Dos cafés, por favor,*" Cope requested.

"*Esta bien café de olla? Esta muy fuerte con sabor de dulcito.* (Is coffee from the clay pot okay? It's strong with a little sweet taste.)" Her *bien* sounded like a musical *fien*.

The two American birders accepted the pleasant old lady's offer then turned their attention back to the active commercial plaza. Eizzo's elbows on the table became his camera tripod as he steadied his long, 650-mm lens and focused on the opposite side of the cobblestone plaza, 150 feet away. He scanned the buffet of market *tiangusas* one by one, starting from the right-hand end of the block-long archways. The lens was powerful enough to actually count the flies on the sign of the fresh vegetable stand that read, "*Aquacates, alcachofas,* and *nopales* (avocados, artichokes, and cactus paddles)."

The *tiangus* to the left allowed him to sharpen his focus on the vast variety of fresh and dried chilies displayed in enormous open bulk burlap bags. He could identify them by their array of colors, shapes, and sizes, recalling their distinct degrees of heat, the small, bright-green *serrano*, the dark, blackish green *poblanos*, the small orange and green *rocotillos*, the medium deep green *jalapenos*, the dried, faded red *chipotles*, the unmistakable *giiero*, a long, triangular, blonde *chili*, and the infamous bright orange *habaneros*, hottest of the *picante capsicum* family.

His scalp began to tingle sharply with the total recall of their fiery flavors. He quickly moved his viewfinder to the neighboring *tiangus* on the left. It cooled off his memory with a soothing show-case of vivid-pastel colored *aguas frescas de frutas,* blended fresh fruit pulp water dispensed by a ladle from large, clear glass barrel bee-hive-shaped jars. The cool, cloudy morning was keeping the customers away, permitting Eizzo to view the jars' contents with ease. The first in focus was the scarlet colored *aqua de Jamaica*, made from the ruby red hibiscus blossom, the brownish *aqua de tamarindo* made from the fuzzy, pod-shaped tamarind, and the pinkish white-colored rice, milk, cactus juice, and almond combination drink called *horchata*. The less exotic *aguas frescas* sighted were the *sandía* (water-melon), *limón* (lemon), and *guayaba* (guava) flavors, better known to Eizzo's gringo palate.

Eizzo pulled away from his camera upon hearing the whistling words of their elderly coffee maker. "*Muy fien senores. Tengan cuidado, esta muy caliente.* (Very well, gentlemen. Be careful, it's very hot)," she said with care as she placed two small clay mugs on the wooden plank table. She observed with interest the American's reaction to her classic Mexican brew. Both men blew over their cups to avoid scorching their tongues. The first sip of *café de olla* produced pleasant surprise and satisfaction from her newly baptized Mexican caffeine customers. She proudly leaned in with the learned question, "*Mejor que su Estarfucks, verdad?* (Better than your Starbucks [with her impeded whistle], right?)"

They nodded in amused agreement with her sapid assessment. Cope responded with a grin, "*Esto es estarfantastico, senora, la otra estarfucks sucks,*" causing her to expose her checkered set of teeth with a wide, grateful smile.

Their eyes were back on the casual-paced foot traffic around the plaza when they suddenly noticed a dirty, thin, off-road motorcycle enter on the left side of their block traveling counter clockwise around the square. The young male rider seemingly acknowledged their presence with a turn and nod of his head, which was topped with a black baseball cap turned backward, covering his long black hair. He rolled to a slow stop at the far-left corner of the opposite block, directly in view of Eizzo's tracking lens.

Eizzo asked Cope, "I didn't make out his cap logo, did you?"

"Me neither. He fits the description, but we need verification that a bird logo is there, or he's not our birdman," Cope replied, reiterating their instructions.

"Well, he did park right in front of the caged bird stand, whether that's a sign or not," Eizzo said, referring to a wide metal table in the far-left archway stacked with approximately fifteen crudely made wooden cages containing pairs of different species of local, wild songbirds for sale.

"Probably a bad sign, given this guy's reputation," Cope said with reservations.

With his long-distance lens trained on his subject's every close-up and personal moves, Eizzo reported, "He's moving away from the birds, to the right past the *huarache* sandals stand, now in front of the pots and pan seller, and now stopped. "*Come on fella, turn around,*" he ordered under his frustrated breath.

"There you go, didn't he just turn the cap bill to the front, pulled over his forehead?" Cope interjected, gazing across the open square at their subject who was looking cautiously about, like a deer tentatively entering a forest clearing.

"Got it—right on, an NBC logo, proud peacock feathers in living color," he said, sounding relieved.

"I guess the all black crow thing gets a little boring after a while," Cope speculated in jest.

"Did Lori mention that he was a smoker?"

"He's not. Why?"

"He just lit up and is now removing something from the side pocket of his backpack," Eizzo said, reporting like a play-by-play sportscaster.

"Can you make it out?"

"Negative. He's blocking it. Now he's inspecting a kettle hanging from an overhead display wire."

"I can see that from here. Is Jaime the Hawk going to prepare some chicken head soup?" Cope asked, being jocular.

"He just dropped whatever he had into the center hanging kettle," Eizzo mentioned with more curiosity than concern.

"He's walking back to the bird cages. Do you see the vendor, a young boy in a yellow jacket?" Cope offered for perspective.

"I'm staying on Jaime next to the cages, you watch the boy who is—"

Suddenly, sharp, successive crackling bangs and loud popping sounds erupted from the far side of the plaza, causing people to scatter from the pots and pans *tiangus*. Small puffs of white smoke and metallic echoes of the bangs rose from the hanging kettle overhead, creating bollix among all in the vicinity.

"They're just a string of firecrackers," Cope confirmed, noticing Eizzo's head rise above his fixed camera position.

"Stay focused on our man. What's he up to?" Cope spoke urgently.

"No good. He's opening up all of the cage doors—blowing cigarette smoke at the birds inside. There must be a couple of dozen birds or more on the wing now. He's putting something in the bottom cage—can't make it out. Where's the boy in the yellow jacket?" Eizzo asked with urgency, now worried about Jaime being caught.

"He's facing the fireworks show—his back is to crazy Joe Crow. Jesus, what are we getting into?" Cope asked, finding Jaime's freedom fighting antics partly threatening to their presence, but at the same time amusing.

"We'll soon find out. He's back on his bike—headed this way," Eizzo alerted his partner.

"Check out the boy—see if he noticed Jaime drive off," Cope wondered, hoping for a clean getaway for their man.

"Negative. He's mesmerized by the snap, crackle, and pop show—just staring at the kettle—waiting for more, I guess."

Cope looked around the plaza at the people turned toward the origin of the brief and harmless excitement. None appeared to be following the movement of the clandestine cause of the Saturday morning mini-pyrotechnics, nor his high jinx at the birdcages.

"The bird Zorro has struck again! Are all of the cages empty?" Cope asked enthusiastically.

"Oh yeah. Everyone has flown the coop—a real Mexican *coup*, I'd say," Eizzo announced proudly in parody. "That's some great Jersey *chutzpah* for a guy from *Chihuahua*."

"Put the camera down, Eiz. He's headed this way," Cope said as a quick warning from the corner of his mouth.

Jaime parked his Kawasaki 400R dirt bike behind the Delta red Kawasaki 650. He shed his large backpack with the single pull of a front Velcro strap. He carried it to the table in his left hand as he extended his right with an introduction. "I am Jaime Falcone. Call me Jim if you like," he offered with a confident smile, displaying a model set of white teeth, which Cope thought were false for their absolute perfection. His face was of Spanish progeny with the lineal lighter skin and angular nose and jaw. He was much taller than the average Mexican male and dressed like an American, which Eizzo thought might be only for his bird-guiding gigs.

Knowing their large military physiques to be telling and intimidating, Cope and Eizzo rose only halfway to extend their hands in greeting their new guide. They would use bird-speak with Jaime in order to mask the Special Forces demeanor. With a wide grin, Jaime's attention immediately went to the large, bold inscription on Cope's T-shirt, "Bird-Watchers Are for the Birds."

"I'm Eizzo and this is Cope, and Jaime will do fine, as well as Spanish or English, which ever you prefer," he offered as a courtesy.

"Please sit down. The *café de olla* is fantastic here," Cope advertised.

"Thanks. For me this is a hot chocolate day. And it will help get rid of a nasty cigarette aftertaste," he said, revealing that smoking was not a habit.

"Just think how the birds feel. They probably have emphysema by now," Cope poked at him in fun.

Laughing, Jaime responded, "Busted! So you saw it all? The caged birds are too frightened at first to leave with the firecracker noise. So a little smoke makes them take flight. A necessary evil, if you know what I mean." His New Jersey accent came out for the first time.

The old lady server appeared with her warm greeting, asking, "*Café, señor?*"

"*No gracias, señora. Yo prefiero un champurrado atole–chocolate caliente. (No thanks, señora. I prefer hot chocolate with cinnamon, please.)*"

"*Con gusto, señor.* (With pleasure, sir.)"

"*Esta fresca, señora?* (Is it freshly made, señora?)"

"*Claro. Ni amor recomenzado ni chocolate recalentado, señor* (Of course. Neither rekindle a love affair nor reheat chocolate, sir)," she politely declared with a slight blush on her sweet worn face.

"*Solamente para usted, señora* (Only for you I would, señora)," Jaime proclaimed with a wink, causing her blush to deepen, and then departed smiling to her kitchenette.

Turning his attention back to his visitors, he asked bluntly, "Did it bother you that I set those birds free behind the vendor's back?"

Cope was the first to respond, "Absolutely not—most liberating to watch, quite frankly. I'm sure it pissed off the owner though."

"Owner? That boy and his bird-trapping father don't own those birds. They stole them from me and you and all Mexicans who enjoy them in the wild, in their natural habitat. Nobody owns them, so I committed no crime. I was returning stolen property to Mother Nature, so what can they do?" he challenged confidently in his defense.

"No need to convince us, my friend. We were happy to see it. We'd like to do the same in our country with the buyers of the caged birds. Do you do that everywhere you go?" Eizzo asked expectantly.

"At every opportunity I can get away with it—not because of the present challenge, but simply said, the wings on birds are for flight, not to please man's sight. It is flight that defines a bird, what makes it a bird—they were created, born to fly. Deny them that and you redefine it to nothing more than an animated body of colored feathers, no longer a bird by definition," Jaime said authoritatively.

"So why then possess something that no longer is, that you can no longer have as it was intended to be, originally, a wild bird or beast? An incarcerated body is an incarcerated spirit, now reduced to a virtual version of itself, of nature's intention," Eizzo professed with sincerity.

"Most illogical," Cope contributed, "are those people in Thailand who capture birds to give to Buddhists to release because it will give them good karma. Isn't there one enlightened Buddhist monk among them who can recommend cutting out the middleman and say, 'Hey, folks, want really great karma? Let the birds be and you will reach Nirvana. Fuck with the birds and bad karma will darken your life for an eternity and a plague will befall your family, hum-mmmm," evoking laughter from his two fellow birders.

Jaime drew his wooden chair in closer to speak as though sharing a deep secret. "What you saw me do across the plaza, I call the modified da Vinci walk. Often when Leonardo da Vinci was walking past markets in Italy where birds were sold, he would pay the price asked, take them from their cages, and let them fly off, giving them back their lost freedom," he related with great pride in his voice.

"And you've modified it by not paying, right?" Eizzo confirmed.

"No disrespect to my hero, da Vinci, but it's counterproductive to pay the bastards—they'd be rewarded for trapping and incentivized to go out and capture more wild birds. Take away their profit incentive and replace it with punishment, I say."

"As should be done with any criminal—make them pay, one way or another," Cope said supportively.

The old lady returned with a wide clay cup of the spiced hot chocolate served with a flirtatious smile and in her signature whistling elocution, "*Fuen provecho señor,*" then slipped away before Jaime could reply.

"What were the birds you just set free across the plaza?" Cope asked casually.

"Mostly grassland yellow finches, and red warblers, some barred parakeets, and two pair of painted buntings, which concerned me the most," he said ominously.

"How so? Are they threatened?" Eizzo asked innocently.

"Soon to be, yes, because Mexican conservation groups know them to be vulnerable to permitted mass harvesting for export. Their population have plummeted in recent years, so yeah, they're threatened."

"Aren't they called colorine seven colors here?" he asked looking at his Peterson Mexican bird field guide.

"Right on, Eizzo. The early Spanish colonists called them *mariposa pintada*, 'painted butterfly,' because there is no blending of its colors on its coat. The demarcation of its brilliant red, yellow, green, purple, and other colors are precise and well-defined. A writer once described them as a kaleidoscope of colors, which over time has been their curse," Jaime said with a sullen expression.

"Because they're so attractive?" Eizzo asked.

"Exactly. People buy them as though they were decorative porcelain figurines to adorn their homes."

"Why would those two pair of painted buntings in the plaza be of such concern?" Cope asked, attempting to focus the conversation on their target of interest.

"If this bird vendor and his son have captured these buntings locally, then the western migratory flocks have arrived—which means the mass trappers are here too."

"Not good?" Cope agreed rhetorically, speculating that the boy was left to sell the caged birds while his father was out trapping more buntings.

"I was told of your birding backgrounds but only a hint about your interests with me as a guide. Whata we talken here? And don't tell me you're contract hunters for some kill 'em and stuff 'em natural history museum!" Jaime implored as he looked alternately at Eizzo and Cope. "I just dealt with one of those sonofebitches last week. Put my own contract out on his sorry ass." He sounded more like a hit man from Jersey than a benign bird guide.

"No, no, never. Quite the contrary, my friend. We're collecting field photos of endangered and threatened species throughout the US and now Mexico. Bird-watching is hunting without a gun," Eizzo declared, handing Jaime a small piece of paper drawn from his shirt pocket. "Take a look."

Counting five species on the Mexican endangered list, Jaime asked, "And how many have you sighted so far?"

"Only the two jays, the tufted, and the black-throated mag-pie…in the north, northwestern Mexican states," Cope answered.

"You realize that for the *Tamaulipas* pygmy owl, you have to go there, and to *Socorro* Island in the Pacific for the *Socorro* mocking-bird. Their indigenous dove is already extinct, killed off when they brought domestic cats to the island, and the mockingbird is next unless the coyote is introduced there," he stated with a rueful expression on his face.

"That leaves the grey-breasted woodpecker. This is his range. Can you help us here?" Eizzo asked with a tone of resignation.

"Maybe, if we're not too late. The imperial woodpecker died out a couple of years ago because of the 'list paradox.'"

"Please explain," Eizzo asked with a confused expression on his face.

"It works like this. When a wild bird becomes officially placed on the endangered bird list, then the natural history museums and private collectors have anxiety attacks, fearing they will be denied a last chance of ever processing one. The demand immediately goes up, the competition to get the last remaining specimens goes up, the price per head goes significantly up, the bounty hunters' motivation to kill the remaining birds goes up, and finally the species' popula-tion goes down and out. That's the list paradox. While its intent was to help save the species, in the end, it spells the end, a death warrant, if you know what I mean," Jaime said sorrowfully.

"Supply and demand can be deadly, for the birds that is," Eizzo admitted.

Jaime pulled a folded sheet of paper from his backpack and opened it between his two American birders. "Does this look familiar?" Jaime asked sourly. The two novice birders bent forward to read the identical five endangered Mexican bird species list that they had just provided for their guide.

"So this is common knowledge then," Cope offered.

"All too common, I'm afraid. This piece of paper I took from an endangered bird hunter's camper truck last week before it burned. It was his bounty hit list, not conservation program," he said caustically.

"Burned, huh? That's unfortunate," Eizzo exclaimed with false condolence. "Anything else saved from the fire, by you that is?" he asked, definitely out of curiosity than of concern.

"Only some files, cash, credit cards, passport, driver's license, gun, and ammunition. Oh yeah, and only one of his dozen or more stuffed bird specimens he had just picked up at his taxidermist's shop in *Toluca*."

"Let me guess," Eizzo asked quizzically, "a Mexican crow?"

"Man, you're good!" Jaime said with a surprised look.

"A little bird told us a little of your birder background as well, *Señor Jose Cuervo*," Cope confessed with a grin of acknowledgement.

Jaime hesitated with a reciprocating grin and then proudly continued with the fire damage report as though he was describing a mercy killing. "I can't say how many more stuffed birds were lost in the shop. Probably fifty more," he said dryly.

"You mean the taxidermist shop caught fire too?" Cope asked in disbelief.

"Well yeah. The hunter's truck was parked inside the shop's garage when it burst into flames. Unfortunately, I had no time to rescue anything from the shop, a total loss I'm afraid."

"Was anybody hurt?" Eizzo asked, afraid to hear the answer.

"Burned? No. But the hunter did break his trigger finger trying to rescue his personal effects," Jaime reported with a furtive smile.

"Like money, passport, gun?" Eizzo's words trailed off sardonically.

"That would be my guess," rejoined Jaime.

Cope was fighting back the urge to burst into laughter, not sure yet if they were dealing with a real whack job, an eco-terrorist, or potential Special Forces officer. Whichever he was, Cope believed that Jaime deserved some sort of medal for bravery under fire, even if he set it himself.

"Hunters we are not, unless there is a hunter to be hunted, if you know what I mean," Eizzo attempted to get on the same playing field with their much-needed bird dog, *Jose Cuervo* himself.

"You're welcome to visit our RV," Cope interposed, "where we'll gladly show you our photo collection of rare birds. Also, you can hear our aural birding tape, now at seventy-four voices of Mexican birds we recorded with our parabolic field mic," he boasted, in his best geek birder-speak.

"You're not bustin' my chops here, are you guys?" Jaime replied with excited incredulity.

"You'll hear all kinds of chatter, chip notes, beep-buzzing, chirping, crackling, grinding, metallic notes, flute notes, sweet solos to songfests," Cope said coaxingly.

"Do you even have the famous Mexican *chachalaca's* namesake sound?" Jaime asked with growing enthusiasm.

"Even!" Cope rejoined confidently.

Eizzo was reading Jaime's countenance as he absorbed all of their unexpected and enticing offer, sensing that the hook was now firmly set. Jaime had taken the bait, the intrigue of technology as a birding tool as well as a new birder toy. What real birder in the chase could possibly resist? Eizzo decided to reel him in.

"Our RV is only a few blocks away on the south end of town by the Del Valle meadow. Follow us over there, and you'll see and hear for yourself. You'll meet our third birder, Rap. There we can plan for the next couple of days of bird search and rescue, *de acuerdo* (agreed)?" Eizzo asked for confirmation.

"*De acuerdo!* (Agreed!)" Jaimie confirmed emphatically.

* * *

The high grass meadow sloped slightly downward toward a small nearby stream. It was a habitat for the small seed-consuming birds that Rap was photographing. As the two motorcycles noisily approached, they caused his subjects to take flight. Dismounting his bike by the side of *Caracara* II, Jaime stood with both arms raised high in the air, declaring, "*Que bruto! Esto es el pajaro mas chignon gue yo a visto en me vida!* (What a brute! This is the most badass bird that I've seen in my life!" staring in amazement at the door side painting of their mission logo, the crested *caracara*.

"We chose it to honor one of Mexico's most interesting indigenous birds. Hello, I'm Rap. You must be Jaime," Rap commented hospitably as he approached the new guide sporting his oversized, baggy T-shirt that read, "Bird-Watchers Are Stool Pigeons."

"Right on. Pleased to meet you," Jaime responded, still admiring the large *caracara* logo.

The three hosts wasted no time in bringing their guide on board and into their archived birding world of hundreds of photos and Cornell Lab of Ornithology songs for auditory birding. They demonstrated the calls and chip notes of the seventy-four recorded species they had promised Jaime, the painted bunting in particular. In awe of the high-tech archives of both residential and migratory Mexican birds, he reacted with equal enthusiasm, offering his services gratis if they would assist in a simple matter of mutual interest. Would they help him drive off and put out of business a wild bird trapper in the area known as Juan Diego Leon.

"I've been trying to catch up to and destroy this sonofabitch for more than three years. Maybe with your help, I can put him out of business and the painted bunting back in the sky where they belong. Are you with me?" he asked with sincere determination.

Responding with the same high-minded allied attitude as the famed Three Musketeers, the covert Delta team answered in the affirmative, "Let's do it! Let's bust the sonofabitch!"

Leaning over a local map provided by Jaime the four-man team reviewed their options given his knowledge of the target and area. It was agreed that a recon trip to the bird-trapping area in question would be conducted by Eizzo and Cope with Jaime as their guide. There Jaime would break off from his two field mates to make contact with target, Juan Diego Leon. His objectives, to make him an offer he couldn't refuse for his illicit merchandise and gain his confidence as a trusted contraband coconspirator.

Leon was infamous for his volatile, quick temper and trigger finger. And they knew he would not be alone. Jaime's weapon of choice would be cash money, large visible wads of it to buy the caged birds and his safety. His real safety net would be unknown to him, the two field mates hidden out of sight but within reach in case Leon lost his temper or decided to take the money and run. "To overcome an army without fighting is the best of skills," Sun Tzu's words had taught them.

In the hard targeting operation cycle, they were at the identification verification point, having accomplished detection and location. Cope and Eizzo would have to get close enough to the target to ID him unquestionably as FTM Juan Diego Leon. From there, the decision to extract or not would soon follow. Jaime's enthusiasm to have like-minded partners plus his heated passion to eliminate a formidable trapper was enough for the Delta team to initiate the recon effort that afternoon.

"The longer Leon is allowed to operate his trapping expedition here, the greater the loss of painted buntings. He just got started. We have to finish it soon before he takes flight," he implored his new partners.

They would follow Jamie to his truck camper not far from their entry point to their target's trapping location. In route, Eizzo would call Lori for satellite photos to be sent ASAP after they had transmitted the GPS coordinates. The backpacks carried by Eizzo and Cope would conceal a laptop and collapsible Special Forces crossbows. Their field radios would be activated as soon as Jaime was out of voice range. He would be shadowed to the target ID spot, never knowing of their presence. If in clear and imminent danger, the crossbows would also come out.

Rap remained in the driver's seat of the RV parked behind Jaime's solid grass green truck camper. He watched as his large partners squeezed themselves inside the camper portion behind Jaime. He insisted on showing off his humble mobile center of operations. He had offered certain field objects the men considered mission-essential material, at least for Jaime's cover. What came as an interesting surprise was not his requisite library of books on birds but an impressive number of poetic classics as well. Eizzo fingered the spines of Shelley's *To a Skylark*, Keats's *Ode to a Nightingale*, and Emerson's *The Titmouse*.

Profound curiosity interrupted Eizzo's thought process with a sincere question. "My friend, tell me what in your young life made you become an advocate and activist in the protection of wild birds? What set you off on this dedicated journey, if you don't mind me asking?" Eizzo queried sincerely.

Although surprised by his partner asking, Cope too was curious as to why a man makes a life decision to pursue such an unusual passion of crime-busting of bird trappers and killers.

"No, I don't mind. It came to me as early as the age of six when my American mother read to me the book of *Alice in Wonderland*. When she got to the part where Alice is invited to play the lawn game of croquet with live, upside down flamingos as mallets, I became incensed. It might seem silly to most, but to youngsters in their formative, not to mention sensitive years, it just plain seemed wrong. It pissed me off so much, I refused to hear or read the rest of the book. The thought of such a thing made me focused on all abuses of birds as I matured. I realize now it was the creative license of a children's fictional author, but it nevertheless can subconsciously desensitize people to such behavior over the long run."

"When we should be sensitizing them, like with Emerson, Keats, Shelly?" Eizzo questioned rhetorically, not wanting to pursue his curiosity beyond what he considered an understandable answer, albeit an unorthodox genesis for such a passionate life pursuit. *Maybe he should wear a cape and become the masked hero, Jaime Falcon by day, Joe Crow by night, protector of all birds, wild and caged,* Cope imagined. But for now, he was their trusted guide on a mission against the arch enemy, smuggler, killer, FTM fugitive Juan Diego Leon.

The entry point into the woods was not common ground to the public. There was a faint path that only trained eyes could pick up. The three men had changed their wardrobe to become one with the woods, yet not total camo coverage. More than a mile into the woods of mature trees and scrub brush, Jaime waved off his teammates, fearing exposure to their target and helpers. Cope had discreetly placed a tracking tag in the bottom of Jaime's small backpack as a back up to the tight visual they planned to have on him. Rap remained in radio contact from the RV, although expected communication only in case of an emergency.

Contact was made by Jaime with the bilious Juan Diego Leon within fifteen minutes. Ten minutes earlier, the Delta duo knew they were close with the unmistakable symphony size sound of hundreds of birds. More specifically, they were the song chirps they had listened to on the digital recording in the RV, of painted buntings. The trappers used expansive tree locked mist-nets not seen by the birds until impact, when it's too late. Their initial harmless bounce onto the net snared them with a covering of micro threads that entangled their feet and feathers, rendering them immobile until harvested by the trappers. The plain-looking females were released into the air, their lack of commercial value their freedom pass.

The two-man team had remained stealth one minute behind Jaime's pace, unable to witness his initial encounter with the trappers. He first came across Leon's two workers, who appeared neither startled nor interested in the surprise visitor. Eizzo and Cope separated by a distance of fifty feet in order to flank Jaime's position standing next to several long rows of crudely made wooden cages housing the captured male painted buntings. Cope chose a surface level hide of fallen deadwood with direct line of sight to the trapper's camp. Eizzo easily scaled a large old oak tree providing the best overview of the scene below. From there, he sighted a small roughened man wearing a dirty white cap kneeling behind a pile of empty cages with a curious eye on Jaime. After a minute of cautious observation, he emerged with his .45-caliber pistol drawn in more of a precautionary fashion than threatening.

To be sure it would not be a threat, both Cope and Eizzo had their crossbows drawn and loaded with steel head bolts within three seconds of Leon's appearance. The unsightly man's Porky Pig trademark face was a positive ID giveaway of Juan Diego Leon, that *even a blind cyclops couldn't miss*, Cope mused to himself. Eizzo knew it was a no-brainer bingo, *a hell of a lot easier to ID than the carbon copy Manuel Bravos in Mexicali*, he recalled. They were close enough to hear their voices but concentrated on their physical beings, their animated body language telling the story unfolding before them.

Leon pocketed his pistol at the sight of Jaime's large roll of US dollar bills funded by his birder buddies. Money on the table abbreviates any negotiation, and this one came to a quick conclusion with the two men shaking hands. The business deal took no more than five minutes with Leon receiving a satisfactory down payment for his caged buntings and a promise to have the agreed upon balance later the following day at dusk.

Jaime exited the way he had entered with an increased pace. Eizzo and Cope were standing at the spot where they had separated earlier. They returned to the RV cautiously, checking periodically that they weren't being followed by an even more cautious adversary.

Rap had explored the surrounding area in the RV, assessing the minimum risk routes for post-operation exiting the coming evening. The satellite photos received that night augmented the planning process and helped in the ground assessment. They realized that Leon knew his terrain best, which was a plus for the enemy. Photos and further scouting would soon give them the terrain advantage, not to mention the devious plan of execution they were about to conjure up. "A military operation has no standard form—it goes by way of deception," Master Sun Tzu would have told Jaime Falcon if he had any clue of what was really about to take place. His three new best friends had told him only to rest well that night.

The new day's dusk was upon them in the deep woods. At the first sight of Jaime entering the clearing wearing his Baltimore Ravens sports cap, Juan Diego Leon waved his gun with one hand and his dirty white cap with the other. He shouted fiercely, "*Por fin, cabron! Quedamos pensando que nos han abandonados!* (At last, you bastard! We thought you had abandoned us!)" Jaime immediately saw a small red laser beam dot appear on Juan Diego's left temple, glowing like an imbedded firefly.

"*Nunca. Ya se ve que soy hombre de mi palabra.* (Never. As you see, I am a man of my word. I came by a different way to avoid being followed. I didn't want any crooked police with their crooked eyes on me.)" Jaime served up his inventive excuse.

"*Pinche policia. Siempre pidiendo mordidas, hasta que un hombre honesto no se puede sobrevivir.* (Damn cops, always wanting a piece of our action until an honest man no longer can survive.)" Juan Diego glowered, returning the revolver to his hip pocket. The small red dot disappeared from his head.

Laughing to himself, Jaime handed Juan Diego the thick wad of money. "Here, count it, 1,500 in US dollars. You'll get the other half when the caged birds are on the truck." The two other bird trappers neared Juan Diego as he counted the stack of one-hundred-dollar bills. Jaime actually thought he heard Juan Diego make a swinish snort as he fingered the greenbacks.

"And when will it be here? We don't want to spend another night camped here," he exclaimed in an inconvenienced mood.

"As I said before, later tonight, when there's no traffic on the road. By midnight, you'll be out of here rich men," he replied, cajoling the three birdnappers to be patient in order to buy time for his plan to work. "*Mientras compañeros, mataremos el tiempo con un brindes al exito del negocio* (In the meantime, we kill time with a toast to our successful business)," Jaime offered, opening his dark-green backpack. Upon seeing the four, one-liter bottles of *Jose Cuervo* silver classico tequila, the two workers became jubilant, more so than with the dollars Juan Diego Leon had just tucked into his right front pocket. At that moment, the tequila meant more than money. After working in the deep woods for days, they were now ready for a taste of their world, the wet spirits of happiness, followed by the expectant numbness, an anesthetic for their dismal and sordid lives. Tequila was the ticket, the transport of escape from a drudgery of day-to-day survival to a place of neither here, nor anywhere but the happy unconsciousness of nowhere. Intoxication provided a suspension of awareness of a world of want, to one of care not, a perfect world after all. Jaime and *Jose Cuervo* were new friends of the trappers, so they believed.

Each man eagerly reached forward to receive his bottle of *Jose Cuervo* while Jaime made certain to hold back the one with the cap seal broken. That special bottle he lifted with care, spinning the plastic cap off with a single swipe of his open palm, raising it high in the air like the winning trophy of World Cup Soccer, unflinching with his charade.

"*Caballeros. Un brindes al Colorin Siete Colores. No son Agelas de Oro, pero para nosotros, les significan oro puro.* (Men. A toast to the painted bunting. It's not the golden eagle, but for us it means pure gold.)" His long swallows of the clear liquid punctuated his exclamation. The three bonding partners in crime unsealed their bottles and instantly competed for the longest sustained ingestion of the silver spirit. Jaime was impressed that not one of them grimaced with the alcohol shock, or even coughed at the raw texture of the single distilled *agave* taste. Their experienced palates knew it as nothing more than pure spirited refreshment. They were most likely weaned on the raw, undistilled *pulque*, the poor drinking man's milk in Mexico, Jaime presumed.

"*Quines quieren limóncito?* (Who wants some lime?)" the youngest worker, Bulmero, offered, gesturing toward their small campsite. They sat on large fallen tree sections for benches, each quartering a whole lime for their tequila accompaniment. Jaime intentionally sat with his back to the three hundred wooden cages of trapped, quivering, chattering painted buntings. He could not stand the sight of one caged bird, let alone six hundred. He tried focusing on his target subjects and their tequila consumption, now one quarter of their bottles consumed. For his plan to succeed, he needed them to continue drinking to at least the halfway mark as the assumed "pass out" level.

"For me, my *Jose Cuervo* is a required ritual after every caged bird deal. A superstition maybe, but I don't take any chances," Jaime said, planting his seeds of curiosity and concern.

"Chances of what, getting caught? You just pay the cops or customs their cut and go on or go home," Juan Diego said flippantly.

"*Ya lo se, asi es* (Yes, I know that's how it is), but experience has taught me that there is truth to the Mayan myth of *Upcep*, the *Nahuatl* word carved in stone hieroglyphs discovered originally in *Uxmal*," Jaime spoke as an academician.

"In *Yucatan?*" Bulmaro asked.

"Yes. And later found in *Kabah* and *Xpujil*, telling of the *Upcep* god's punishment to anyone who captured and caged any of nature's creatures of flight, birds, bats, insects, but especially birds," Jaime stressed with a voice of authority.

"I know that the Aztec chiefs would execute those who killed a sacred *Quetzalcoatl* bird of paradise, but *Upcep* I've never heard of," the older worker, Trinidad, admitted, more innocently than challenging.

"Years ago, I, too, thought it was only a silly Indian legend, that the *Upcep* god would punish bird captors by changing them into crows. I actually knew some men at different times that disappeared after caging birds. One was the *viejo* (old man) in the *plaza of San Jacinto* who sold caged canaries and finches. One morning, his customers discovered the small birds gone from the cages. A crow was found in one cage whose gate was too small for the big bird to enter. The old man was gone, vanished, without a trace," Jaime exclaimed hauntingly.

"*No juegas* (You're playing around)!" Bulmero exclaimed, followed by a large nervous gulp of tequila and lime squeeze.

"*En serio* (Seriously)?" Juan Diego challenged, wanting to disbelieve in front of his partners.

"*Te lo juro* (I swear)!" Jaime responded without appearing defensive. "I actually knew the old man. The town's people say that from the moment they broke the cage open to let the crow out, it would never leave the plaza. The people gave it cracked corn that no other crows would compete for."

"And this has happened before, elsewhere?" Juan Diego questioned with skepticism.

"I've heard of other cases, all involving crows. That's why I drink my *Jose Cuervo*, Joe Crow tequila before I take any caged birds," Jaime said with a sense of self-comfort.

"Just because of the *Cuervo* name?" Trinidad dimly asked, confused, fumbling with his bottle.

"No. The *Upcep* gods become confused when our bodies receive the *Jose Cuervo* spirits, an earthly connection with the other world spirits. My *Veracruz* bird partner taught me that the consuming of the distilled earth spirits represents the black crow, which will protect us from the *Upcep* gods. They become confused when our bodies receive the *Jose Cuervo* earth spirits. If it's worked for me before, why stop now? *Salud!*" Jaime toasted to his *Cuervo* canard with self-satisfaction. The others followed with their own *brindis* (toasts) to the mythical Upcep gods and their new best friend, *Jose Cuervo*, as the drinking continued unquenched through the sunset.

Eizzo and Cope maintained radio silence from their hides while ever vigilant of the fugitive hard target. With one hand on their cocked crossbows, their eyes never left Leon's right hand and pocketed pistol.

Jaime told a few more "missing persons" stories with symbological references to reinforce his subterfuge, propagating cautionary tales about the dangers that exist therein. The ominous high shrill crow sounds of *creows, creows,* repeated from the opposite sides of the campsite further motivated the hexed birdnappers to imbibe in drink, reaching the half bottle level all the sooner.

Trinidad had heated some *queso Montego quesadillas* over the campfire for everyone, and then tossed two armloads of remaining firewood on the hot embers, brightening the clearing like a Boy Scout Jamboree. Bulmero sipped on his bottle while tossing the last of their birdseed into the cages, proclaiming it to be the *colorin siete colores*, "last meal before the road." Jaime silently disagreed as he drank from his half bottle of *Jose Cuervo, reserva classico, aqua pura* (a.k.a. classic plain water).

The *aquave* spirits had taken their predictable effect on the ignorant tequila trio, pervading their besotted minds and entire bodies. They all struggled to speak, not babble, walk, not wamble, and see clearly, not double. Well into the bottom half of their liter bottles, all three men had slid down from the fallen tree benches onto the pine-covered forest floor as nature's mattress for "*un breve descanso antes que llega el camion* (a brief rest before the truck arrives)," Juan Diego slurred before passing out next to his inebriated, sleeping partners. Jaime whispered an exasperated sigh of relief, "*Por fin* (at last)," as he quickly relieved himself behind a large standing pine.

At the bottom of his backpack, Jaime pulled open a Velcro hidden compartment and took out the walkie-talkie radio Eizzo had lent him. He immediately depressed the Send button, speaking with excitement, "Joe Crow is an *amigo* of mind." Instantly Cope's Texas accent drew over the speaker, "*Jose Cuervo* is an *amigo* of mine too, partner. Copy and clear."

Within five seconds, two very large men abruptly appeared at opposite sides of the campsite in camouflage clothing with backpacks and Barnett commando crossbows strapped over their broad shoulders. Jaime froze, partly from the suddenness of their arrival and partly because of their awesome presence, nothing like he had expected from his laid back, *gringo* bird-watchers. Cope waved toward the two long rows of wooden birdcages stacked six high and twenty-five deep. "You know what to do. Go!" he demanded of Jaime who was still awestruck at the swift and deft movements of his real partners. He saw Cope bind the arms and legs of Bulmero and Trinidad with the rapidity of a rodeo calf roper while Eizzo did the same with Juan Diego. Eizzo picked the wad of dollars from his shirt pocket then wrapped bandanas tightly over his eyes and mouth. *Ah, the subtle art of the double cross*, he thought to himself.

"Damn, these are a couple of badass birders," Jaime murmured to himself. He ran to the stack of cages filled with flitting birds. He quickly opened the hand-sized gates, one after the other, shouting as though in their bunting bird lingo, "*Libertad!* (Freedom!)"

"The caged songbird's freest song comes not through bars and wires, but in the open air," Jaime paraphrased *The Prophet*, Kahlil Gibran. In the first two minutes, the air above began to sing with scores of painted buntings in search of a song of freedom, a melody of gratitude for flight. Soon there were hundreds reclaiming the sky and trees above, filling the surrounding woods with song. Jaime was now opening the cages on the back row, glad his two fellow birders out in front couldn't see the gleeful tears in his eyes. The light of the full moon and campfire illuminated the painted bunting's full palate of brilliant colors, radiating like a rainbow on the wing with the free air its fresh canvas.

The Delta duo was smiling at the sweet irony. The FTM fugitive from US justice was captured and soon to be caged, the hard target mission accomplished. Juan Diego Leon was tightly bound to a brown canvas field stretcher that was brought out from the nearby bushes. His signature filthy white cap was tossed near the firewood. Eizzo called out to Jaime, "We'll return in twenty minutes. Keep the radio with you," as he and Cope disappeared back down the main tree-lined trail.

In the bottom cages of the last row, Jaime started to find dead and dying painted buntings, apparently the first birds captured six to seven days earlier. With all of the buntings released, he returned to collect the weak, dying birds and placed them into two empty cages. He then tossed in some seeds from the trapper's exhausted larder along with tin cups of water. He gathered a total of twenty-two dead buntings and placed eleven each on the reposed laps of Bulmero and Trinidad, still bound and asleep on their earthen beds.

With three hundred cages now empty, Jaime seized the two machetes by the firewood and began his ritual dance of destruction. He flailed away at the flimsy cages with the Mexican field swords while stomping one foot at a time upon each cage, collapsing them with a single blow, then jouncing to the next, and the next. He flounced down the two rows with a rhythmical cadence that prompted him to hum a jerky, heavily punctuated version of "The Mexican Hat Dance," with each cage flattened out like a Mexican *sombrero*. He noticed on his watch that twenty minutes had gone by when his radio sounded with Eizzo's voice. "We're two minutes away. Everything okay? Over."

"Okay here. The dirty birders still dreaming of dollars—when they wake up, the dollars will still be a dream. Over, out."

"And tonight, it's not the caged bird that stands on a grave of dreams," he paraphrased his favorite poem out loud with delight.

Cope and Eizzo reappeared to find Jaime atop a broad mound of shattered sticks, the cage demolition completed, rendering all unusable. Eizzo removed the arm and leg bindings of the two-grounded captives.

"They'll be out until sunrise, if not longer," Jaime declared with pride.

"Perfect. But we have to move out now," Eizzo said with urgency.

Cope delivered the large covered birdcage Jaime had given him earlier, setting it at the feet of Bulmero and Trinidad. He removed the cover and inserted Juan Diego's soiled white cap in the center next to the big stuffed black crow. "Are we all set—ready to move out?" he asked, turning to his partners, motioning them toward the path.

"Ready here," Jaime responded as he placed his signature miniature bottle of *Jose Cuervo* in the special cage.

Eizzo glanced one last time at the two reposed drunks, then suddenly stopped, and leaned in closer. Examining the heads of the two men, he questioned with muffled laughter, "Is that what I think it is? Come look." Starring at their black heads of hair topped with dollops of thick, white substances, the three overhead birders verified with delight, "Bird shit!" Shining his flashlight on the two small mounds of bird droppings, the official Mexican bird guide verified that indeed it was *cacca de pajaro*. Cope couldn't contain himself, laughing out loud, "Damn! These poor bastards got dumped on twice tonight. Right on!"

Giving the new cage one last look with *élan*, Jaime proclaimed, "I love it when a legend comes to life." They quickly turned in unison and headed down the trail with haste, carrying their accoutrements, the two cages of weakened buntings and all ten packed mist nets. Eizzo, in the lead, turned to ask Jaime, "*Upcep*? Where in the Mexican history books did that come from?" he questioned with raised eyebrows.

Chuckling, he answered academically, "*Upcep* is actually the titular god of idiots. *Unicamente pendejos crein en pendejadas.* (Only idiots believe in idiocies.)"

The exit plan was predetermined by the Delta team's need to reestablish their independence from a third-party player. Jaime knew there would be no time allotted for a post-operation celebration or assessment. He had achieved everything he wanted and then some, including a digital copy disc of the bird calls with a wireless player. Eizzo gave him his coveted St. Louis Cardinal baseball cap. He even scored the unexpected roll of dollars the American birders had bankrolled the bogus bird buy with. "Use it to further fund your good work for a good cause, Jaime," was the team's message to their surprised, appreciative associate. With a firm pat on the back, Cope handed him one of their birder T-shirts that Jaime read aloud with a wide, proud smile, "*Bird Watchers Look Up to Birds.*"

Jaime carefully placed the weakened buntings in his camper following his brief farewell to his birder friends. The team's prize catch was placed with care in the rear clandestine compartment of the RV. Jaime was satisfied that his bird-trapping, smuggling nemesis was to be deposited on the remote Pacific island of *Socorro*, two hundred nautical miles from Mexico. Juan Diego Leon could only dream of such an exile.

The last thing Jaime Falcon heard from his brothers in anti-crime came from the *Caracara* II's loud stereo as it rolled southbound onto the deserted country road, the high-spirited sounds of Lynyrd Skynyrd's "*Free Bird.*"

Jaime headed north as would the free migratory painted buntings.

14

GIVE THE DEVIL HIS DUE

Lomas de Los Angeles, Michoacán

C am didn't quite know where to begin. There had to be over a hundred *ex-votos* displayed across four long, narrow tables that stood waist high along the left side of the church's central altar. The area was well illuminated by the ambient light and scores of stubby votum prayer candles lit by the worshippers that morning.

Most of the *ex-votos* were the traditional tin trinket *milagros* (miracles), symbols of a heart, arm, leg, or infant in the miniature cast image of the baby Jesus offered to saints as expressions of faith and gratitude. A kneeling figure acknowledged a prayer answered. The figures of cows marked either their recovery from disease or its fertility in producing calves. There were a few wallet-sized photos propped up near a candle, mostly of children. There were brief hand-written notes of thanks to the Lord, or a prayer requesting He grant some wish from the fervent prayer giver.

Cam felt awkward viewing the *ex-votos* close-up and personal, trying to appear only passively curious. His instructions were to look for a silver cross with the attached directions to their target's where-abouts. There were a dozen or more crosses of different sizes and ornamentation, but none he saw attached to or near a note. Most lay before a photograph, but none with the face of the FTM fugitive Pedro Barajas. He began his third pass over inspection of the wide array of *ex-votos,* wondering now if the intel tip was credible. Suddenly from behind, he sensed an approaching figure and quickly turned to see. To his relief, it was a tall, lean priest he guessed in his late thirties with a Romanesque nose and blue eyes smiling warmly at him. Presenting a hospitable countenance, the priest spoke English in an audible whisper.

As though rehearsed just for the tourists, he explained, "Most visitors to the church view these simple offerings as nothing more than folk art. But in Mexico, the *ex-votos* are a personal message to God, a votive offering, a voice for the faithful to heaven."

"What exactly does *ex-voto* mean?" Cam quickly queried innocently, working to remain in character.

"The Latin meaning? 'Out of a vow, a promise.' They are most commonly given or dedicated in fulfillment of a vow or pledge, not just expressing a wish."

"They're very public, yet a few I've seen, very personal, for health restored, wounds healed, dying infants surviving, even one for a missing mule," Cam offered.

"Yes, many are open for anyone to see, and others may be a simple private message told only to our Savior's holy cross. Others are wrapped in mystery, a private message perhaps. Miracles do come to the faithful, or so we pray. Am I interrupting you from any personal moment of your own?" the priest asked sincerely.

"No, no. Not at all. I'm just one of your curious tourists fascinated by your culture and customs," Cam responded with a wave of his hand past the display of *ex-votos.*

"Well then, if you will, allow me to share possibly one of the more interesting *ex-voto* examples known. This practice goes back hundreds of years in our church. And in 1527, the Spanish conquistador of Mexico, Hernán Cortéz, suffered a near-fatal sting on his arm from a scorpion while inspecting a property of his in *Yautepec, Morelos.* Grateful to God that he had survived the near-death experience, he commissioned a renowned goldsmith to create a gold *ex-voto* of a scorpion. It had a mosaic of forty-five inlaid emeralds on the body and pearls on its pinchers. Encased within the gold scorpion was the actual dead scorpion."

"You mean that after surviving countless bloody battles in his conquests, Cortéz is nearly taken out by a bug? Amazing!"

"So true. But then there was the amusing *ex-voto* observed by a priest where a written prayer on paper by a husband asked that his missing wife not be found. A few weeks later, a different handwriting appears on the back of the paper giving thanks to God for granting the husband's wish—signed by the wife," the priest grinned widely.

Cam chuckled, saying, "The Lord does work in mysterious ways."

"Indeed he does. And I will now leave you in peace and wish you well in your travels," he said with his two open hands pressed together prayerfully.

"You are very kind, Father. And thank you for your stories and insight."

"God bless you," were the affable priest's parting words accompanied with a slow genuflection.

Cam knew he couldn't spend much more time reviewing the *ex-votos* without seeming overly curious as a common tourist. He then recalled the priest's comment about private prayers, or messages before the Savior's holy cross. He now scrutinized the diverse crosses spread out across the long tables, one by one. *Surely no one would engrave directions on a metal cross. There had to be more to it,* he reasoned.

Around the tenth or eleventh silver cross examined, one caught his attention as nothing more than odd, radically different than all the others for its ultra-simplicity. It was made of rolled aluminum foil the diameter of a cigarette, three inches long and two inches across. He discreetly lifted it for closer examination but saw no message on either side. Ready to return it to its place on the table, he suddenly hesitated with further recall of the priest's conversation, something about wrapped in mystery and the dead scorpion encased within an *ex-voto*. Could the flimsy foil cross hold the answer to their much-needed directions? he wondered. He looked over his shoulder to see if he was in anyone's sights. He was not. The clumsy-looking cross was all he had now to go on. Confident no one was looking, he quickly slipped it into the waistband of his pants out of view from the sanctuary visitors. He then walked casually back down the center aisle with the pretended lost gaze of a tourist, not knowing if he truly had the covert message, or some worshipper's prayer note to God, in which case he knew he'd have to find Pedro Barajas in hell, because that's where he'd be headed.

The aluminum foil cross remained secreted away in the waistband of Cam's pants until he boarded the RV four blocks away. What he removed was now reduced to a tight wad of foil, which he placed on the table for his seated team members to examine.

"Taylor, you do the honors. I'm the mere courier," he said, suggesting anyone but him should remove the foil. From his open mic in the church, they had heard the priest's *ex-voto* stories. Returning to the RV, Cam had filled in the rest of the details of his search for the clandestine intel drop.

Taylor removed the horizontal portion of the cross, which was twisted twice around the vertical portion. He unrolled the shortest section first and found it empty. "If the second part is empty, Cam, then Lord have mercy on your soul, brother," Grav exclaimed in an exorcized evangelist's "hellfire" manner of divine pronouncement.

"Well, you two heathens will join me in hell for defiling a holy cross," Cam countered as Grav picked up the longer piece of foil. He took great care to unroll it when he sighted a white paper edge inside, peeking out along the length of foil. Careful not to tear it, his thick fingers adroitly pulled it open, like a surgeon tying sutures. There was a collective sigh of relief as though their prayer had just been answered, the secret directions that would lead them to FTM fugitive Barajas. They were aware of his "known whereabouts," but "abouts" wasn't good enough, Cam had stated. Only someone very close to the church could give him up, Lori had predicted, as though having an inside track.

The paper showed a pencil-drawn map of a rural road leading to a remote, high hills Augustinian monastery approximately twenty kilometers away in the *Lomas de Los Angeles* (Hills of the Angels), in the state of *Michoacán*. On the obverse side was a simple layout of the monastery compound showing a chapel, monks' residence, courtyard, and large garden with a shed as an outbuilding, all protected within a walled structure with no additional details as to size. The one word they were looking for on the layout they found above a small arrow pointing to the shed. It read, "Barajas."

Though they didn't expect to see the sender's name, they were concerned to find written at the bottom of the paper, "*Nunca se sale* (He never leaves)."

"Don't fucking tell me he 'found Jesus' just to hide out in a monastery. What is he, a born-again monk?" Grav sarcastically speculated.

"I guess when you're 'on the lam,' you're willing to lie down with the lambs," Cam added generously.

"Whatever he's up to, someone wants him out of there. Lori's intel came from inside the church, a highly credible source, she said. 'Born-again,' or protected by 'the cloth,' we don't care. With this animal's history of violence, we must make this extraction happen sooner than later," Taylor stressed.

He text-messaged Lori: "Stand-by; top priority; will transmit GPS vector from within target grid in one hour. Send satellite photos ASAP. What intel do you have on the Augustinian monastery in *Lomas de Los Angeles*?—Taylor."

Lori would understand the plural of *photos* to mean the macro coverage of the broad ops grid with decreasing area coverage down to the micro photos, to include the shed itself and its door handle if necessary.

The team's forty-five-minute journey up to *Lomas Los Angeles* was a gradual accent along a serpentine, hilly, wooded country road. Following the map directions, they pulled over on a wide spot of the road's shoulder intended for rural passenger bus stops. Opposite the bus stop, perpendicular to the RV was an unpaved road that rose quickly out of sight into the hillside's thinly forested pine oaks. The entrance road to the monastery had no identification signs to announce its presence. Taylor took a GPS fix while Grav offloaded the bike. Cam mounted a wide-angle video camera inconspicuously positioned in the front, hidden among the chrome fixtures on the handle bars. With no traffic in sight, Grav preset the trip odometer and accelerated up the dirt road. He would not activate the camera until the monastery was in clear view, taking a new GPS fix when he was at his closest distance to its outer wall. "If anybody there questions my presence there, I'll just say the devil made me do it," Grav had projected with a naive gesture of his shrugged shoulders.

The camera would remain on until after his descent back to the RV. During this time, Taylor drove the *Caracara I* one mile farther up the country road to scout anything that might serve to complicate or compromise their mission. He remained in radio contact with Cam, who was out of sight by the monastery road entrance. His first duty was as an early warning sentinel reporting on any threatening traffic. His second was to mount a special video camera high in an open spot of a *Montezuma* pine aimed at the entrance to the monastery. Cam would radio in only if he foresaw a problem.

Their return trips were coordinated by radio to rendezvous at the bus stop within seconds of each other so that the bike could be loaded on the RV with no one in sight. Exactly fourteen minutes had expired when Taylor eased the RV on to the westbound roadside bus stop. With the team back onboard, Taylor instructed Grav to text message the two GPS vectors to Lori and to load the DVD player with the fresh recon disc of the monastery.

"From on top of the monastery hill, I noticed another hillside road to the east. Did you see it off to your left, Taylor?"

"Affirmative. I used its entrance to turn the RV around. Anything significant about it?"

"It's likely to be our best direct access to the mountain bluff one hundred feet behind the monastery."

"*Bluff!*" his partners groaned in unison. "How big of a bluff are we talking about?" Taylor questioned with concern.

"Well, what makes for a beautiful picture postcard backdrop for the most reverent monastery is equally a most ugly 200-foot high, 10 percent vertical recline, smooth rock bluff. I filmed the whole enchilada, you'll see."

They viewed the freshly shot photos of Grav's recon bike run. All were impressed with the fortresslike structure of the humble monastery in terms of the high, gray stone walls and single front, sheet metal gate entrance, which was closed to the public.

"Is the rest of the perimeter all woods?" Cam asked.

"Yep, and with a couple of foot paths, probably for prayer walks," Grav surmised. "But the only access road is the one I took. I couldn't see inside because of the high stone wall."

"That leaves us with the top of the bluff for an overlook," Taylor concluded.

"Just as well. We'll have to maintain surveillance of Barajas at some point until we decide how to get him out," Cam offered.

"'Supreme excellence consists in breaking the enemy's resistance without fighting,'—*Sun Tzu*. For now, we'll search out a bird-watching camp to the east and ascend the bluff from there. From above we can assess what resistance we'll face," Taylor decided.

The *Caracara* made its second trip up the country road to the one-mile turnoff Grav had referred to. This time he stopped in front of the turnoff, waiting for a four-donkey caravan laded with cut firewood to saunter on by west bound on the opposite side of the road. The wood cordage was as thick on both sides as it was high, bundled tightly with burlap wrap and rope. The donkeys were linked together with light rope harnesses led by a grizzled middle-aged-looking thin man wearing torn brown work boots laced with twine; his upper torso was wound around with a long gray and white wool *serape*. His soiled, frayed wide-brim straw hat was turned down to allow for any moisture to run off. His eyes never left the road directly beneath his feet. All traffic would have to negotiate around the carefree caravan; beasts of burden had the right of way in third-world countries.

Turning left onto the dirt road, they noted that its rise up the wooded hill, lined with high altitude *Ocote* and *Michoacán* pines, was not as steep as the monastery road. It was also wider and deeper into the pine woodlands, which satisfied their concern for recon cover. The road's end was a convenient, a wide circular turnaround with a lone, large yellow oak in its center. The RV came to a stop on the far end of the turnabout with thicker woods behind them and the bluff a quarter mile away. Grav made the observation that the bluff here was shorter, less challenging, estimating a 160-foot rise with a jagged face.

"We'll set up the birder camp here. I'll research what local feathered friends we should be looking for. Grav, prepare the equipment for the assault of that rock. Cam, you'll assemble the recon gear," Taylor ordered with nods of acknowledgement from his partners.

The satellite dishes and antennae rose from the *Caracara* roof top. The monitors were turned on and adjusted for the remote surroundings.

"Take a look at this. The deadwood donkey train is turning up the monastery road," Taylor reported, pointing to the monitor receiving the camera transmission from its hidden treetop placement set up by Cam earlier.

"Well, it does make sense. I saw no power lines around the monastery, and I'm guessing we won't see any propane tanks inside that wall," Cam speculated.

"Their vows of poverty and sacrifice go back hundreds of years, so heating rooms and ovens with firewood is the norm. Let's find out what size wood stockpile is in there, and we can calculate the frequency of donkey deliveries," Taylor requested.

The two recon men made a quick ascent of the bluff and trek over to their best vantage point above the monastery two hundred feet below. Their instructions were to take mental notes and photos of what was inside the parapet, verification of their FTM target and all movement until he retired for the night, returning to the *Caracara* immediately after.

Covered by a green and brown camouflage net, Grav and Cam concealed themselves in repose among the common scrub brush atop the *mesa,* one foot from the bluff's edge. Grav opened his powerful 7X50 binoculars while Cam assembled his two cameras for wide-angle viewing and telescopic close-ups.

"In place," came the first radio transmission to Taylor situated at the *Caracara* base camp.

"Copy that. What's the status of our traveling woodsman?"

"All four donkeys are unloaded, and he's helping a man stack the wood in a protected holding area next to the building's side entrance. Cam's trying to ID the man now," Grav reported.

"Is he dressed as a monk?"

"Negative, long sleeve beige shirt and pants, sandals, and hatless. No facial description yet. We'll call back when we have one, over."

"Copy and out," Taylor replied.

With the uniform cut faggots of firewood neatly stacked, the worker opened the large metal main gate for the woodsman and his relieved, bareback burros to depart. He returned to the broad court-yard, where he slowly walked across a narrow, diagonal garden path to the gray wood plank shed alongside the far east high stone wall, sweeping as he went with a long twig broom.

"That's the shack drawn on our *ex-voto* map of the monastery. If he enters, he's likely our man," Grav declared with guarded reservation.

They had Pedro Barajas's head photos in front of them waiting for a visual match. With a thin overcast sky, the desired lighting was a concern for optimum visuals of their subject. The ID had to be an *absolute*, a *probable* unacceptable, was the mandate of all extraction operations. Cam steadied the 600-mm lens on the stubby mono-pod. He found his subject approaching the shed and adroitly focused tightly on his face, which was focused on the footpath below. As though scripted and rehearsed, Barajas stopped suddenly and looked upward toward the sky. The two recon spies quickly hunkered down low on their elbows out of sight.

"Look straight ahead," Grav ordered urgently. "He's watching those two passing green birds at twelve o'clock, our eye level over the courtyard. They're chasing off a hawk in front of them, a territorial counterattack," Grav asserted rapidly to his attentive partner.

"No bird shots today. My ground subject is posing pretty. That's it, my man, look at the birdie. Work with me, work with me!" Cam muttered excitedly as his camera shutter clicked repeatedly, capturing the facial images of his subject of interest below.

The hawk and interceptor birds had left the monastery man's range of view and interest. He shouldered his broom and entered the shed. Cam and Grav huddled in front of the camera view finder to review the fresh photos alongside the still pictures they had of FTM fugitive Barajas. Every facial detail was examined comparatively to verify the mandatory match: flat flaring nostrils, thick mono eye-brow, thin pursed lips with one corner turned up, the other down, a full black mustache growing to the corners of his crooked mouth, three deep forehead furrows over a broad, flat front with high reced-ing hairline, and straight black hair combed over his ears and down to his neck. The most distinguishing feature was the large dark mole by the corner of his left drooping eye, giving the impression that nature had given him two separate identities, albeit, both sinister-looking.

"Bingo! We have a winner!" Cam declared with more relief than exuberance.

"That's a look that only a makeup artist could create for a 'slasher' movie," Grav editorialized.

Grav returned to his Bushnell 7X50 binocular observation of the man who just changed from a subject to a target with a few clicks of a camera. Taylor received the radioed, target confirmation, repeating his orders for his recon team to remain in concealment position for further entry into their target's loop. They would take mental notes augmented by relevant photos of Barajas's movements within his courtyard workplace. His only entry into the actual monastery was to deliver firewood, returning once with food, which he consumed in his shed before nightfall. The Delta observers commented on the irony of their ability to identify their target by his becoming the accidental bird-watcher. They had two green birds and a hawk to thank, although they couldn't agree on the species of either. They did agree that the Augustinian monks must really be saints to allow this "Antichrist" into their holy sanctuary.

It was a few minutes past eight in the evening when they observed the dim light in the shed go dark. The last lights shining from the monastery refectory windows were extinguished shortly after. In less than an hour, Cam and Grav entered the *Caracara* base camp. The digital photos were loaded into the laptop where the three men viewed Barajas's description and loop. The slightest detail was covered and tactically analyzed, including no lock on the shed door to the forty-eight-second average time spans for Barajas to arrive at the monastery entrance. They would not call it a routine until after another full day of overhead reconnaissance. But a template was beginning to form that would set their plan of extraction in motion. Lori's satellite photos had arrived earlier, which Taylor had formatted on the screen for side-by-side layout comparison with the recon photos.

"We have no layout of the monastery interior building, but won't need to know with our target living and working in the outer courtyard," Taylor stated to delineate their ambit.

"The *ex-voto* map note said he never leaves, so it's up to us to motivate him to do so," Cam emphasized, having ruled out physical force extraction.

"Lori's background intel on the Augustinian monastery might give us some ideas," Taylor interjected.

"How so?" Grav asked.

"Friars were sent from Spain to establish Christianity in the New Spain, Mexico, back in the early 1500s. The first to arrive were the Franciscans followed by the Dominicans and the Augustinians. They all built fortress monasteries that identified them symbolically as a spiritual fortress. In reality, they wanted protection from hostile Indian arrows during their spiritual conquest of Mexico. There are twenty Augustinian bulwark citadels of Christianity across the country," Taylor explained.

"That's why the high walls and hilltop position," Grav underscored the challenge.

"Their basic desire is for solitude. Monks are hermits, the consistory Order of the Hermit Friars monk coming from *mono*, 'one—alone.' They haven't locked themselves in, they've locked the world out so that they can dedicate their lives to prayer, study, and meditation," Taylor continued.

"But not preaching to the masses," Cam challenged.

"No, guiding fledgling priests rising in the priesthood. The friars made a monastic vow for life to be the keepers of the faith, the moral and Christian compasses for the priesthood, which are the teachers and shepherd of the faithful. The monastery is the bastion of the faith. This monastery has been so for over 450 years," Taylor stated in awe.

"That would cover about twenty-two generations of monks existing here without a single change in their lifestyle. For sure they've never heard of ESPN," Grav interjected in sympathetic disbelief.

"Then how can they follow Notre Dame Football?" Cam wondered in jest.

"It wouldn't matter. They haven't won a national championship in 450 years," Taylor chortled with the others.

"So where does this put Pedro Barajas in this cloistered scenario? He's not a member of the friar fraternity. So he must stay to himself except when delivering firewood inside and collecting his simple meals to eat outside," Cam summarized his rusticated lifestyle.

"Tomorrow is Sunday. We'll see if the loop is any different, if he goes to the chapel inside," Grav questioned.

"Did you ever see him in prayer or meditation?" Taylor asked.

"Negative," Cam answered.

"Lori described a series of religious murals in and around the chapel walls. One in particular I'm sure has haunted our killer Barajas. There are large-scale scenes of hell with devils torturing sinners," Taylor related with interest.

"Lots of fire I bet," Cam conjectured.

"Let's hope. Because what I think we might have here is a sinner who's trying to confront his hellish fate now in hopes that by hanging with and serving the good guys, he might avoid it," Taylor speculated.

"Kind of community service credits?" Cam offered.

"Or time served for good behavior?" Grav asked rhetorically.

"For sure he doesn't want to confront the consequences of his sins here on earth by hiding out in a fortress monastery in a secluded forest in the middle of Mexico," Taylor stated confidently.

"What if he had to confront the devil sooner than later, here and now?" Grav asked seriously.

"Like spook him out, make him think the devil found him?" Cam projected further.

"That it has breached the spiritual fortress and is after his spirit," Grav continued the proposed plot.

"Well we can't just show up at the gate like trick or treaters dressed in devil costumes. What would spook him more than anything is the one thing that has surely haunted him...his son, Miguel," Taylor exclaimed.

"The prefire Miguel or post?" Cam asked.

"Both. I know that he's never seen his son's scorched face, nor would he recognize him if he did. But we can make that happen, delivered by the devil himself," Taylor proposed emotionally.

"Tack up photos of Miguel in the shed?" Grav asked.

Taylor knew that would be the simplest way but much too pedestrian. It should not have the human touch, he believed, nothing slick and polished that would smack of man against man. It had to be more spiritual, downright demonic, he decided.

"No photos. We should give the devil his due…let him make a demonical delivery stamped with the fear factor. Barajas has to be frightened to the core where flight is his only natural option," he declared decisively to the supportive nods of his team. They would proceed with their devilish plan immediately following the recon phase.

"Speaking of flight, what do you make of the three mystery birds' flyby we witnessed?" Cam inquired.

"My avian research turned up very few regional species, all unusual and interesting, not just the black-throated sparrows we see everywhere," Taylor reported. He then pulled up laptop photos of his findings.

"We weren't exactly sure of what flew by us, but it was two green birds chasing a much larger white one, a hawk perhaps," Grav guessed.

"Well if what you see here is what you saw on the fly, then you witnessed two very unique species," Taylor stated as he exhibited what he thought they briefly observed.

Grav and Cam leaned in to examine the images of green jays perched and in flight. Its body plumage was a dark olive-green above, yellowish green below with yellow outer tail feathers.

"Weird. Its head is bright blue with a black facial mask and throat, as though it started off as a blue jay but changed its mind," Grav commented with curiosity.

"It's not easy being green," Cam snickered.

"Was the green jay's call like this?" From the laptop speaker a "cheh-cheh-cheh-cheh" sound repeated when Taylor clicked on the bird's screen picture.

"Right on, both birds bitching out the hawk for its flyby," Grav confirmed.

"It's a family flock thing, very aggressive in the defense of their territory. But the hawk was actually a laughing falcon, and was no threat to the green jays. The falcon feeds mostly on snakes and other reptiles.

"Poisonous snakes?" Grav asked excitedly.

"Yeah, the coral and others. Its legs and toes are covered with small, rough, hexagonal scales—an adaptation to withstand any poisonous bites," Taylor recited from his research.

"Now there's an idea for a patent on a new boot. I'll name it Bite Me!" Grav suggested with exuberance.

"You'll laugh all the way to the bank, my man," Cam joined in the joke.

The mountain top birders stared at the digital photos of a medium-size white falcon with short rounded wings and tail. A broad black facial mask extended around the back of the neck in a narrow white bordered collar. The crown feathers were stiff and pointed forming a bushy crest.

"Did you hear the laughing falcon's call?" Taylor inquired.

"No. Apparently the chase was no laughing matter. But I don't think he was too concerned if he takes on venomous snakes," Cam conjectured.

While viewing the bird of prey's intimidating screen image, it's laughing namesake call played on the speakers to the amusement of the RV audience: "hahaha-herher-harhar."

"This proves that God does have a sense of humor, especially if the snake represents evil," Taylor guessed.

The three men continued their review of the day's recon information and planned the next day's operation of the same. Cam and Grav would be in position atop the bluff before sunrise to account for the target's early morning activities. Taylor would gather additional information from Lori for the base map and their "devil his due" plan. In twenty-four hours, it would be in place. The *Caracara I* team would decamp late evening and drive into the night to reach the town of *San Luis Potosi, Michoacán,* before dawn.

15

MASK MAKER–MASK MAKER

Tácuaro, Michoacán

The doors to the *Museo Nacional de Mascuras Folkloricos* (National Museum of Folk Masks) opened at ten in the morning at the edge of *San Luis Potosi*. The national collection of masks was housed in an old historical stone house with high ceilings and vibrantly painted walls bordered with hand painted *Talevera* tiles. Tall euphorbia cacti in folk art pottery filled in the corners of the open, bronze-colored wooden floors. The walls were adorned from floor to ceiling with the most unusual-looking masks Taylor had ever seen, live or in photographs. The faces depicted ranged from the mystic to the playful, the saintly to the diabolical, the aristocratic to the village idiot, and the spooky to the angelic. The range of materials used was as diverse as the thematic faces, noting primitive coconuts, sophisticated glazed ceramics, simple *papier-mâché* and finely carved wood. He stood in awe near the entryway, where he was greeted in English by a handsome looking older woman dressed in a white cotton dress with multicolored flowers embroidered across the collar.

"Welcome to our national mask museum, sir. I presume you speak English?" she politely asked.

Taylor was dressed in the most *gringo*-looking outfit from the team's wardrobe of tourist and birder costumes. He looked like the poster boy for Teddy Tourist, Grav had joked. From his Dallas Cowboy cap to his oversized, baggy T-shirt that read, "*Bird Watchers Are Empty Nesters*," and worn blue jeans down to his white Nike shoes, he "reeked of apple pie," Cam had exclaimed.

"Yes, I do, ma'am. From Texas actually. Here in Mexico bird-watching but wanted to pick up some fun masks to take back to the kids," he responded with a west Texas twang.

"We don't sell masks here, only exhibit what are considered to be the finest examples of our country's long history of regional folk masks," she proudly clarified.

"I can see that. But can you direct me to somewhere nearby where I can pick some up?"

Lori had directed him to the *San Lois Potosi* museum with that question precisely in mind. For the team's plan to work, it would require the best mask maker possible in the closest proximity and compressed time line. Second best was not an option. Long distances and protracted time was not practical.

"Well you're in luck on both counts. The reason *San Luis Potosi* was selected for the national museum was because of its close proximity to the best and most prolific makers of masks in Mexico... *Tácuaro, Michoacán*. It's one hour west of here," she explained with a smile.

Taylor was relieved, pleased that Lori had come through again.

"I'd be happy to point out their work exhibited here and write down their names for you as well," she offered graciously.

"That's mighty kind of you, ma'am. Do you have their addresses as well?"

"It's a tiny town. Just ask anyone for directions. *Tambien el ciego si sabe* (Even the blind man knows)," she quipped smartly.

Taylor toured the small museum with sincere interest and genuine amazement at the artistic quality and creativity of the myriad masks from all over Mexico. The new list of artisans now in one hand, with the other he reached into his pocket to fold up a one-hundred-dollar bill, which he placed inside a small wooden donations box, a bargain he thought for actionable intel. It was commensurate with the gratitude he felt and expressed to the nice lady upon departing. It was now on to *Tácuaro* to find their mask maker.

* * *

Passing the lakeside village of *Paztcuaro*, Grav cranked up the
sound on the RV stereo with U2 performing "I Still Haven't Found
What I'm Looking For."

Tácuaro was a tiny rural village known for its folkloric artisans.
Its population of six hundred welcomed fifty plus shoppers per day
the week leading up to the Day of the Dead (Halloween), when tourists arrived to purchase local artisan–made masks for the occasion.
Mexican and foreign tourists passed through *Tácuaro* year around,
especially before Christmas when a mask or two was on someone's
gift list. It was not an uncommon sight to see RVs with US license
plates come down the five blocks–long, no-name main street.

There were no commercial shops displaying the artisan's works
of art. Taylor knew that he would have to go house-to-house asking
for the mask makers by name from the mask museum list. He parked
the RV at the far end of the stone street by a large grove of cotton-
wood trees.

"Grav, you'll take bird-watch patrol starting in this grove. Cam,
you'll take monitor duty in the RV. Remember, I'll have a live mic,
but no earpiece. Grav, both of yours will be live. This is not a target zone, so we're all casual tourists for a day of mask shopping and
bird-watching. Everybody clear?" Taylor asked, looking the two partners in the eyes.

"All clear," they responded in unison.

Dressed as touristy as practical, Taylor walked the first block
of faded sherbet colored, flat roof, concrete houses. He approached
a fenced yard gate with a hanging white wooden sign. Its artistic
blue letters read, "*Se Vende Mascuras* (Masks for Sale)." He pulled
on a thin gray rope attached to a brass cowbell, and waited. A boy,
approximately twelve years of age, dressed in a white-buttoned shirt,
black pants, and white athletic shoes appeared at the front door of
the light-blue stucco house. He waved to Taylor to come in. The
front room had no furniture on its hardwood floor, allowing visitors
to view the dozens of masks on all four off-white walls in a well-
lit gallery environment. Taylor thought he was back at the *San Luis*

Potosi National Mask Museum as he admired the same top-quality masks made mostly of wood, the rest divided equally between clay, *papier-mâché*, and leather. He saw the popular horned demons, hairy witches, the white faced, Spanish mustached nobility, the exaggerated eyes on clown like faces, and the village idiots expressing their blended innocent ignorance.

"This is great work. Whose masks are these?" Taylor asked the boy with genuine interest.

"My father's, Juan Orta Castillo. Do you see anything you like?"

Taylor couldn't believe his good fortune to find the country's most celebrated mask maker on his first try. No wonder he recognized his quality of work from that of the museum. "What I'd like to do is pay Señor Castillo to custom-make two masks for me taken from the images of two photos here," he said, raising the large manila envelope.

The boy raised both hands in a halting manner, politely refusing the envelope, saying, "First, let me ask my father. I know he is very busy." He turned and walked down a short hallway, disappearing behind a bright-green door with dark-blue trim. He reappeared within seconds to face Taylor apologetically. "I'm sorry. With the Christmas season here, he won't have time. Perhaps sometime in January if you're not in a rush."

Taylor was tempted to play the wealthy, ugly American and make the artist an offer he couldn't refuse. But obviously Sr. Castillo was not a "starving artist" if he could afford to turn away business. In the back of his mind, he admired that. Besides, this was *Tácuaro*, the mask capital of Mexico. There were others on his A-list of top artisans. Pulling a small piece of paper from his shirt pocket, he asked the boy, "I am in a rush. Could I trouble you to please direct me to the workshops or homes of Gustava Horta, Felipe Terra, and Felipe Anciola?" showing the list to the boy.

"I'd be happy to. My school is out for the holiday, so I have the time to take you if you like. Everyone is a neighbor in *Tácuaro*. My name is Juan Jr., by the way," the boy said, extending his introductory hand toward Taylor.

* * *

Juan junior accompanied Taylor to all three home workshops within a short three block radius where he received the same negative news of holiday season backorders. His offers of cash in advance payments were to no avail. Juan junior took him to seven other local masks makers whom Taylor rejected for lack of confidence in their quality of work compared to the A-list artisans. This element of the mission demanded the very best image recreations or his plan might not work. He did not want creative interpretations of the images. They had to be right on the money, the real deal, or not at all. And money was no obstacle for that high standard.

Juan junior sensed Taylor's growing frustration. "Forgive me for asking, señor, but out of curiosity, would you mind showing me the images you want made into masks?" he asked pointing to the large envelope.

"No offense, Juan, but there's no point now. You've been kind enough to introduce me to the entire town's mask makers. And I want to pay you for your time. I do appreciate it." He pulled a one-hundred-peso bill from his pocket.

"Thank you, señor—but no thanks. What I'd really like though is an opportunity to see the two images you have, if I could please," Juan junior persisted.

Taylor paused silently, reluctant to expose the innocent lad to such a shocking and repugnant image of his scorched young friend Miguel. It was difficult enough for hardened adults to view them. But what Taylor had observed of Juan Jr. was a very mature and sincere boy who had surely witnessed the hard times in his little Mexican village, exposed at an early age to the good, bad, and ugly of impoverished rural life. The children of Mexico, by necessity, grew up faster than their affluent, insulated, American neighbors. Most rural Mexican kids didn't have the luxury of diversions from the raw realities of life. They were exposed to them early and often in a transparent society that sheltered no one from communal warts and scars. Taylor thought that just maybe Juan could handle it. If not, then the kid would be exposed to yet another ugly reality, that even across the border, shit happens, recalling the evil man responsible for these altered images.

"You are not going to like what you see, Juan." He pulled the two 8×10 photos from the envelope. "They are of the same boy, Miguel. The second one here is not a mask. It's Miguel one year after his accident," Taylor gently forewarned him. He chose not to tell the tragic circumstances for the so-called accident.

Juan junior held one photo in each hand, side by side. Taylor watched his expressionless face. He studied the photos with quiet eyes that never blinked. Taylor stared at the boy for some sign of revulsion or shock. He saw neither. No words were exchanged. Several seconds later, a cascade of tears fell from Juan Jr.'s big brown eyes down his reddish tan cheeks. Without commentary, he handed Taylor the photos. Then he said firmly, "Please follow me," as though it was a command, one which Taylor curiously obeyed. Juan junior briskly walked off of the main street on to a rough surfaced dirt side street. Immediately, the quality of homes became more and more dilapidated, commensurate with the degrading appearance of the rugged, potholed road.

Remaining several steps behind his fast-paced guide, Taylor spoke in a low murmur, describing the area and the direction they were traveling, still not knowing his destination. In abbreviated terms, he commented on the brown mud stucco and stone church one hundred feet ahead. No matter how small, poor, and humble the Mexican country church, it always had a bell to ring. This quaint little church was no exception. A thick, broad, arched *campinela* rose above the church's centered, tall wooden doors hinged by massive black wrought flat iron. The bell was modest in size by comparison to most Catholic churches in the country. For the size of the town, Taylor was certain the bell's ring would match those of Norte Dame, all things being relative, he presumed.

Juan Jr. arrived at the church entrance several steps ahead of Taylor. He opened the door and then turned to face Taylor with a look of solicitation. "Would you mind waiting here for a few minutes, *señor*? I'll return right away." Deciding not to probe for details yet, Taylor nodded yes.

Always in a reconnaissance mode, Taylor casually walked over to the left exterior corner of the narrow church. The side of the building was lined with young trees. In back of the church appeared a large garden of vegetables, flowers, and fruit trees. The only movements of life were from butterflies and a pair of blue grosbeaks chasing insects. He took the same exploratory walk to the right side of the church where the scene was the same. The only movements there was more blue grosbeaks and a single, perched Cassin's kingbird, all being ignored by a bird-watcher with binoculars one hundred feet to the far right of the church garden. Taylor raised his hand to his right ear and formed the OK sign with his fingers for the bird-watcher to see, then returned to the church entrance to wait for Juan Jr. Five minutes later, he appeared.

"Would you please come inside, *señor*?" he asked, stepping back into the candle-illuminated church. A single aisle divided over twenty rows of highly polished blonde wood pews. The rough-hewn beams on the high ceiling augmented the linear look of the rectangular sanctuary. Taylor was ready to ask why they were in a church looking for a mask maker, when the possible answer appeared before his eyes. Mounted between two lit candles each on both side walls were twelve masks of heavenly, cherub-like angels, equidistant from one another. As he walked slowly down the center aisle, Taylor noticed that all twelve angelic faces differed except for one common quality. They were all lifelike, perfect woodcarvings of children's faces with real human facial color tones and highlights painted by the hand of a master. Their realism and workmanship quality exceeded those of the masks he had seen in the national museum and *Tácuaro* workshop galleries. *These masks were surely a gift from some benevolent priest or bishop from Rome or maybe Spain*, he thought curiously to himself.

He found himself at the end of the aisle standing before the church altar. It was a simple structure consisting of a single step, dark wood platform supporting a wide, narrow table covered with lit prayer candles. Taylor didn't notice the dozens of *ex-votos* leaning against the candles and wall. His eyes were drawn to a tall, rustic, gray wood Christian cross hung low on the back altar wall. It was well illuminated by the scores of prayer candles below. On the exact center of the cross was a mask of Jesus Christ staring down directly at him. When Taylor moved a few steps to the left, the eyes of Christ followed. He found the beard and other facial features so realistic as to believe it could have been an actual "death mask" molded from some Christlike person. He became mesmerized by its realism, in awe of its superb Michelangelo quality. Abruptly his fixation on the Christ mask was interrupted by Juan Jr.'s request to join him in the left corner of the sanctuary. He was standing in front of a door that led to a room behind the main church building. In front of the door was a black, plain-looking confessional with ornate screen windows on all sides and a small white cross on the vertical frame dividing the two front doors. Taylor looked around the sanctuary and saw no one but Juan Jr.

"I have to confess, Juan, I have nothing to confess. Can you tell me what this is all about?" he asked, growing a little impatient with the mystery mask maker tour.

Gesturing toward the left door of the confessional, Juan Jr. said, "I might have someone to make your masks." Pointing to the right-side door, he said invitingly, "Please step in here, *señor*." Taylor barely fit inside his half of the confessional, thinking that the *Tácuaro* citizens were either really small people or they had really small sins to confess.

"*Señor*, would you be so kind as to slide your photos beneath the divider screen window?" he asked while standing midway outside the narrow closet-like structure.

Taylor did so without questioning out loud, all the time wondering why so much mystery over one mask maker. Was it the parish priest who wanted to pick up some cash on the side as an agent without openly competing with the town's artisans? Maybe it was a woman who was wise enough not to compete overtly with the males' artistic and commercial domain, he speculated to himself. Suddenly a candle was lit on the other side of the interior screen window. He could not see any details of the person seated there, only the small silhouette of the head. It remained motionless as it stared at the two photos. Taylor waited for the typical reaction, but none was forthcoming. Then the candle went dark. Some soft-spoken words in Spanish were exchanged between Juan Jr. and the clandestine viewer. Juan junior then turned into Taylor's half of the confessional with a smile. "He said he will do it. He needs two days."

"But I need to see his work first," Taylor demanded with a slight edge of protest.

"You already have, *señor*." He waved his arm out toward the masks on the sanctuary walls and altar cross.

"He's the one? They are magnificent. I thought they might be from Italy or Spain. Why doesn't he have his own display shop if he's this good?" Taylor asked out of confused curiosity.

"Because he has never sold his masks before, *señor*. He is only my age and has only given his work to this church," Juan Jr. said flatly.

Taylor couldn't believe what he was hearing. If he weren't squeezed into his half of the confessional so tightly, he'd be on the floor with the news, he thought to himself. "Then this will be his first sale. I'm willing to pay him cash now. How much for the two masks in two days' time?" he asked cheerfully.

There was more whispering and then, "He says for this very special assignment, it is not considered work. He cannot charge you. It is gratis, *señor*. He considers it an honor and thanks you."

Taylor thought for a second that maybe something was lost in the translation. He felt a tinge of embarrassment to accept the generous offer challenging his gesture. "Free? I'm sorry. No disrespect to your father, Juan, but this is the best mask making I've seen and I can well afford to pay him for it," Taylor insisted.

There was more whispering from the other side. Juan turned to Taylor with a look of exasperation. "I'm sorry. He says it is gratis or not at all, *señor*."

"Well, the Lord does work in mysterious ways. I guess I now know what I'm doing in a church," he said with a sigh of surrender. "Can I meet this mystery mask maker, Juan?"

"His name is Miguel, Miguel Urbina. He says he's pleased to know you. You'll have to excuse his shyness, *señor*. We should go now so that he can get started right away," he said with a courteous insistence. Taylor hesitated for a moment, still reflecting on the coincidence of the same first name and age of the mask maker and the photo subject, as well as the change of bad fortune to good.

Outside of the church entrance, Juan junior commented, "I'll deliver the masks in two days from now. Where will you be, *señor*?"

"Right here in front of the church," Taylor confirmed. He then patted his new young friend on the shoulder with words of sincere gratitude as he said goodbye.

* * *

Once aboard the RV, Taylor briefed Grav and Cam beyond what they had heard through their earphones. Cam asked, "So, who was that mask man?"

They all chuckled as Taylor interjected, "For all I know, he could be the son of the Lone Ranger. I do know that he's twelve years old, very shy, one heavenly talent, and is a very compassionate, generous kid."

"And he doesn't like money," Grav added.

"We can't force it on him. But for one, my conscience won't allow me to leave *Tácuaro* with Miguel's two masks and not compensate him in some way," Taylor declared.

"I might have an idea," Grav offered as he held up his bird-watching Minolta 400 digital camera. "Take a look here." He pointed to its picture monitor. I took these from the backside of the church when this old priest came out the back annex rear door into the garden."

They looked at a series of digital pictures of a stoop shoulder man of medium height and build with short, gray hair, dressed in a brown flannel smock. He walked with a garden hoe for weeding, and at times for support. Of interest was the small size of the church annex. "So you think the priest and boy live in that postage stamp–size room?" Taylor asked Grav.

"And work in there as well. But take a look at these two handmade ladders. One goes up to the roof of the annex, the other from there to the top of the flat church roof." Grav pointed out with curiosity.

"It would be interesting to know why, as well as more information on our mask maker. We have to march in time for two days anyway. We might as well do something productive, like find out how we can compensate the young master artisan without his backing out of the work for gratis agreement. Plus, there are a couple of mission matters to attend to," Taylor said.

"The top *Tácuaro* mask makers are charging a few hundred dollars for their masks. Why do you think a kid, who literally lives like a church mouse, would forego a windfall opportunity like this?" Cam questioned with sincerity.

"We're about to find out, Cam. Grav, did the old priest notice you bird-watching?" Taylor asked.

"Yes. I made sure he saw my binoculars and camera."

"Perfect. Then this is what we need to do today. We'll decide later about tomorrow," Taylor stated as the team huddled over the dinette table.

* * *

Tácuaro was like any other small rural Mexican *pueblo* with its traditional one o'clock late lunch hour followed by a brief *siesta*. By three in the afternoon, the town showed some signs of life with children in the yards and streets and adults in the neighborhood *abarrotes*. Mostly everyone took their time going from place to place on foot or bicycle with the exceptional pickup truck rolling down the main street at twenty miles an hour. An occasional car with out of state plates would pull up in front of one of the mask makers' home workshops, where people of all ages, dressed in nice urban clothes, would make a purchase. They would not travel all of the way to *Tácuaro* and not buy a mask, even if it meant a bargain one for fifty dollars.

The casual Delta trio spread out over the town with a plan, to be as public as possible. Staying in the RV or perimeter groves and not make a public purchase would arouse curiosity. Taylor remembered Juan junior's comment that "Everyone is a neighbor in *Tácuaro*."

Cam chose the *La Poloma* café, the larger of the two central avenue cafés because of its counter service that was in close proximity to the ten Formica top dining tables. A young woman in her early twenties with two tightly bound pigtails, high, tan cheek bones, obsidian eyes, and a welcoming smile greeted Cam with a gesture to sit anywhere in the near empty café. Two, heavyset male lunch diners in dirty work cloths sat at the nearest table eating *enchiladas en chili verde* and drinking *Superior* beer from bottles. She stopped her counter cleaning to ask Cam if he'd like to see a menu. He replied in Spanish that he'd just take a bottle of what the two men were drinking. When the waitress returned with his bottle of beer topped with a small lime wedge, Cam got right to the point in a voice loud enough for the two table customers to hear. "*Senorita*, excuse me, but where could I go in *Tácuaro* to find a building designer and some reliable construction workers for a small project?" He knew that an architect and construction company was out of the question in this rural *pueblo*. It was Romans who built Rome, he reminded himself. The Delta trio had decided that keeping everything local was good business all around. Besides, Cam had a feeling that "what happens in *Tácuaro*, stays in *Tácuaro*," a good neighbor policy for any community, he thought.

"The Maldonado family, father and sons, are the best known here, *señor*, not that there is a lot of building going on. Mostly maintenance work. You know repairs upon repairs."

"And how can I meet the father Maldonado?" Cam asked politely.

"*Oye, Gordo. Por donde anda su padre?* (Listen up, Fatso. Where's your father?)" she demanded of the portly, midthirties man seated closest to Cam.

Maintaining his focus on the fast disappearing food in his mouth, on his fork, and on his plate, Gordo replied in Spanish, "Out there as always, looking for work so his sons can afford to pay your tips."

"What tips? He needs to look harder then. I got a tip for him. There's an American here who has a work project to discuss with him," she responded with the same demanding tone.

"He'll be here this evening at 6:30," he answered before finishing his beer in a single swallow. Gordo then rose, displaying the dimensions of a short sumo wrestler, with as much girth as height. Without another word spoken, he walked out the door with his hefty friend close behind. Cam noticed the now vacant table with no tip.

"So, Gordo is one of the sons, I presume?" Cam asked rhetorically.

"Yes. *Señor* Maldonado's most skilled carpenter sons are working in the United States, sending money back home to support their own families. Gordo here tried to make it across the border but had to return."

"Where did he try to cross over?"

"Not over, *señor*, under, *a pico y a palo* (by pick and shovel), from *Mexicali* to *Calexico*."

"You mean tunneling under the border into California?" he asked for clarification.

"*Si, señor.* The tunnel was seven hundred feet long, five feet deep, and three feet wide, but not wide enough for Gordo."

"Will he try again?"

Cam was aware of the tunnels discovered by the US Border Patrol, "*110 subterranean incursions into the United States since 9/11*" was the official statistic he recalled.

"Unfortunately not. He's bigger now than when he tried two years ago. I would try it myself if I didn't have his eighteen-month-old daughter to care for," she said with resentment in her young voice. Cam now understood her source of sarcasm with Gordo. But he wanted answers to other questions for the time being.

"So, is mask making the biggest source of income in *Tácuaro*?"

"Among the local workers, yes. But now there are over sixty people from here working in the USA, all sending half of their income back to *Tácuaro*. That's the number 1 source," she said with a reserved sense of pride.

"Your town has quite a few established mask makers already. Are there any young, new generation artisans coming along who might add to *Tácuaro's* fame?" Cam asked, fishing for the catch of the day, information on Miguel Urbina.

"Every local artisan looks at his sons as possible apprentices. But most of the young men here want to leave for the big cities or go to the USA." She shrugged with a resigned attitude. Cam knew from his country briefings that the futures of the small *pueblos* that depend upon popular handicraft were in jeopardy. Not for lack of demand, but for interested young people willing to take over the folk art traditions of their ancestors. In most cases, it pays only a penance to the artisans while the middlemen and retailers make a fat profit in the name of art. The *Tácuaro* artisans were different. They charged full retail. The big buck started and ended here. Except for Gordo.

Cam watched as the short, plump waitress cleared the men's table, noticing how mature she looked for a young mother, how quickly the young girls have to grow up in rural Mexico. She seemed pensive during the table cleaning, and then paused to look at the American seated nearby.

"There is one such apprentice here studying under the maestro Juan Orta Castillo. He lives and works at the church with our priest, Padre Montes. The boy, Miguel, makes masks only for the church. They are quite amazing for an artisan of any age. But only a few of us in *Tácuaro* have even seen him since he arrived here two years ago," she stated with certainty.

"Why does he keep to himself?" Cam asked with a sense of relief that he was finally going to get some answers about the recluse Miguel.

"Because he is embarrassed about the loss of his face and hair. He has neither, only a layer of rough scar tissue that looks like a poorly made *papier-mâché* mask for the Day of the Dead. *Pobrecito* (Poor kid). When Miguel first arrived at the church, the padre said it was as though the devil himself had laid his hand upon the child," she said sympathetically.

Cam was stunned by the news. The coincidence of the same name of Miguel was one thing, but two identical male burn victims at that age were bizarre, *like living in parallel worlds*, he thought. Fearing that the coincidence might also include a murderous father, Cam asked cautiously, "Was it an accident?"

"A real tragic one, I'm sorry to say. The faulty propane tank at his home in *Patzcuaro* exploded, killing his mother who was the nearest and melting poor Miguel's face standing nearby. He was in a *San Lois Potosi* Social Security Hospital for several months. With the mother gone, the father could not care for him as well as for three other younger children. So his church in *Patzcuaro* made arrangements for him to come here and be cared for while learning a trade, you know, for his future livelihood."

Cam was shaking his head in sympathy and continued amazement. It was no longer a mystery, but a good old-fashioned church miracle, the coming together of the two scared Miguels. There had to be a reason for this happening beyond the mask making, he speculated, but didn't want to ponder it now. He continued his probing. "You say you've met him. How, if he's so shy?"

"The padre had to leave town for a day, and so I took food to his room behind the church."

"I've passed by there. It's hard to imagine living and working in such a small space, especially for two people," he declared.

"Miguel also works up on the church roof when the weather is right for him."

"When is it right for him?"

"Cloudy. He can't be in the direct sunlight. The Padre says that if it's not windy, Miguel will work at night on the roof by candlelight. Before our *pueblo* got electricity twelve years ago, all of the artisans worked that way. They claim that it adds to the aesthetics of the masks. If you ever see Miguel's masks, you'll think that it's because he works closer to heaven, you know, up on the church roof."

Cam was struck by that image and made a mental note to discuss with his team. He expressed his gratitude with kind words for her time and a very generous tip that would more than make up for Gordo's lack of gratuity. He then set out to purchase a specific mask Taylor had seen at the home gallery of Juan junior's father, Juan Orta Castillo.

* * *

Grav arrived back at the church immediately after lunch to set up the tripod for the special, wide-angle digital camera. To assure a laid-back tourist look, he wore a floppy round brim khaki hat, a T-shirt that read, "Ornithologists Are Bird Brainiacs," and well-worn blue jeans. This time he moved visibly to the edge of the garden near the back-right corner of the church. He stayed to the right side of the assumed property line, yet close enough to get a good shooting angle for his picture taking of the blue grosbeak, now in larger numbers than in the morning. Through his powerful Zeiss 10×40 binoculars, he could appreciate their full plumage. The male was a striking, brilliant indigo blue with blackish wings, two chestnut wing bars, and a thick conical bill, giving it its namesake. The female was less spectacular with a two-tone tan appearance, lighter below and a rump tinged with blue. He had lowered the binoculars to follow the birds' flight when he saw the same old priest from the morning walking slowly toward him. The garden was divided into multiple large sections of diverse vegetation by well-paved, hardened pebble and sand paths for the purpose of walking while in prayer or simple meditation.

"Good afternoon, Father. I hope you don't mind my picture taking, but this is the only place we've found so many blue grosbeaks."

"You are most welcome here. It's up to the birds to give you permission to be photographed. Some are shyer than others. Are you an American ornithologist?" the priest asked politely.

"American, yes. Ornithologist, no. We're just members of the Audubon Society, amateur photographers on vacation. We're here admiring the local species as well as the migratory birds from the United States."

"Well now. You bring up an interesting question. You say the birds migrate from the United States, wintering in Mexico, I presume."

"Yes, Father, a couple hundred species, and millions of birds, every year without fail."

"Remarkable. But couldn't it be said that these birds are really from Mexico, summering later in the US?" he asked with a grin.

"Well I guess it really depends on where they were hatched and raised."

"So, they actually reside in both countries year around until they die. Correct?"

"Correct."

Grav studied the old man's eyes trying to determine how serious he was with this unexpected topic of conversation. Or was the priest studying him, perhaps to see where this American was really coming from, he wondered.

"But where do they die? Do we know?" He was asking sincerely.

"In both places, from predation, accidents, diseases, and old age."

"Do you think it matters to the birds?"

"As to dying, I'm sure it does. It's instinctive. As to where, I doubt it. They are not like African elephants," Grav said jovially.

"Then it wouldn't matter to them where they are born either, do you suppose?"

"You ask interesting questions, Father. But only the birds have the answers."

"Maybe not," the priest asked reflectively.

"And why not?" Grav asked respectfully.

"Because they probably don't ask the question. For a bird, why should it matter? For a bird, the question is of survival. They go to wherever they can to survive, north, south, east, west. To a bird, life, between being born wherever, and dying wherever, is all that matters to them. Right?"

"I imagine so." Grav was thinking that maybe his team should change the name on the RV to *Birds without Borders Society*.

The priest began to walk down one of the sand pebble garden paths, signaling with his arm for Grav to join him. He then put both of his arms behind him, binding them with a handclasp. Grav noticed this and thought, *My God, it's true. These guys actually do meander in the garden like this, just like in the movies.*

Wishing his philosophizing host would get to his point, Grav decided to draw him out. "Are you suggesting, Father, that all people on earth should migrate as freely as birds?"

"Birds, unlike man, don't see any borders. Man is different by nature. Man becomes his own border. It is man who binds man to one land or another. Man creates his own boundaries for himself, for other men, and from other men."

"Do you believe that 'Good fences make good neighbors,' Father?"

"It did in ancient China. I would rather hope that good neighbors eliminate fences of intolerance."

"In a perfect world, I would agree. But unfortunately, this is planet earth, not planet Utopia. We've seen birds kill other birds, invade their nests, eat their eggs, and kill their chicks. Birds don't have natural borders. But they do have their unmarked territories for defending a feeding or breeding zone. A hummingbird will attack an eagle to protect its nesting area if necessary. That, too, is in the name of survival."

The bonhomie priest stopped and looked up at his tall American guest. "It is obvious that you have been a student of nature for some time. Have you also taken notice of my flock, which has migrated from Mexico to your country in the name of survival, in search of a more hospitable environment?" he asked without taking his eyes off of Grav.

There it was, his point made at last, Grav thought. Was the priest merely being the diplomatic host by being so oblique in expressing his real concern, the freedom of his people to travel wherever they wish for a better life? Or was there a deeper frustration, maybe a fear for the well-being of his people? he began to surmise.

"Are you referring to your local parishioners who've crossed the US border, Father?" he asked, showing his own expression of concern.

"I am indeed. Those whose sweat, muscle, and skills were not needed or sufficiently compensated here chose to migrate to a better place, as we both have said, for survival," the *padre* said with emotion.

They made a short U-turn onto a perpendicular path barely wide enough for the two large men. Grav now found himself walking meditatively with his long arms clasped behind his back by his hands.

"Do they believe that the work will be easier in the US?" Grav asked.

"*Adonde ira el buey, que no are?* (Where can the ox go where he is not made to plow?) My simple, poorly educated people know their limitations. But they carry with them a strong work ethic, optimism, and hope for a better life for their children. They are your good neighbors wanting to become good American citizens."

Grav paused, not to process what the priest just said, but not to comment too quickly in the negative. This was a sore point with the majority of Americans he knew, but a topic he had studied even before the Delta team received their country briefings. He had observed the priest's "flock" for many years in the form of migrant workers and sojourners who come to the US to simply make money to send home or return home with it. The majority of Mexican immigrants, legal and illegal, he observed, come to the United States for the almighty dollar, eighteen billion dollars to be exact, sent back to Mexico last year, he had read.

Grav broke their brief silence, saying, "Americans are not so naive as to believe that the immigrated Mexicans' main motivation to come to the United States was to renounce their Mexican citizenship for that of the USA. Yet the Mexican immigrant has insisted on receiving all of the same benefits and rights of US citizens as though they were entitlements just for showing up illegally. I know that their true love and allegiance is to Mother Mexico. On face value, Americans, for the most part, don't object to one's love of their homeland. But naturalized Americans don't subscribe to binationalism. They want and expect immigrants to become new American citizens in every way, just as our early ancestors from England, Ireland, Scotland, Italy, Germany, China, and other nations did. You of all people, Father, would agree that you can't worship two gods, right?"

"Yes, I would agree," the priest conceded, appearing surprised by the American's fervent opinions on the subject.

What Grav really wanted to tell the good Father was that the twelve million illegal Mexicans in the US, as well as nationalized Mexicans, are ampersands, that they consider themselves "Mexican & American," not solely Americans. He knew that the majority of Americans feel that Mexican immigrants treat the USA as a mistress, that they use her for their basic needs, but that their real love and loyalty is with Mexico, and never will divorce her to commit to the USA as a true, loyal American citizen. He thought it best that he just get to his point and get out of the point-counterpoint conversation cycle.

"Those who know American history know that our country was founded by legal immigrants, foreign settlers who committed all of themselves, sweat, muscle, skills, plus all of their earnings in their new homeland. They made it theirs. They became the original US citizens because they wanted to commit to all of what it is to be a true, loyal American, not a binational sojourner. Because of their singular commitment, devotion, and allegiance to one country, their USA, they created a new nation for all of those to follow, willing to share their same national core beliefs and values," Grav declared with a passionate tone that even surprised himself. He had spoken from the heart as well from his own allegiance and service to his country.

The priest gazed in awe at the American's sincerity and clarity, thinking that this was not the first time he had articulated on this subject. "And you have observed this not to be the case with the Mexicans in the US?" he asked innocently.

"Daily. But let me give you just one dramatic example. During the 1998 Gold Cup Soccer game at the Los Angeles Coliseum between the USA and Mexican teams, I observed over ninety thousand Mexican soccer fans from the US dressed in red, white, and green, booing the playing of 'The Star-Spangled Banner' while throwing beer and debris on those trying to raise the American flag and on the US soccer team," he said with a forced smile on his face. He knew he could go on with more examples, but they would only embarrass his host. He didn't expect to hear any papal proclamation telling it's faithful to, "Go forth to the United States and multiply," but he would settle for some sincere admission that his church did encourage and support its parishioners to do so.

"That is shameful. I'm so sorry to hear that, and so un-Christian-like as well. Whatever their reasons for such bad behavior, there is no acceptable excuse for it. It only fuels the flame of anti-Mexican feeling among your citizens, I'm sure. And I'm sorry for that. I hope that in time, you will forgive them as they hopefully acculturate and mature," he said with his hands together in front as though appealing to heaven.

Now Grav was biting his tongue, wanting to tell the shepherd that six black sheep from his flock were about to "get flocked" big time for some really bad behavior in the US. *Forgiveness will begin when justice is served, "so sayeth the Six Pack and Delta team,"* he mused to himself.

They had walked the entire garden perimeter with their heads bowed in deep conversation when the priest stopped to look across the field of greenery and flowers.

"Listen to the sweet melodious sound of our blue grosbeak. Music to our ears," he said serenely.

"To our ears, yes. But that's the males' warning sound to other birds in defense of the blue grosbeak's territory," Grav said, not to be negative, but to stay on point.

"I didn't know that. It seems so innocent and pacifistic to one of God's creatures and yet threatening to another."

"I guess we could say it's another metaphor that my countrymen could apply to their perception of noncitizens invading their territory, would you agree, Father?" Eizzo said with a sigh.

The old priest shrugged his stooped shoulders without a reply, still viewing the long garden and open woods and brush beyond. A minute pause passed when he turned to Grav with an expression of understanding, as though he had an epiphany.

"This I do understand about nature from our blue grosbeak. In the months when the garden is in bloom with plants, we welcome the blue grosbeak because they eat the unwanted grasshoppers, beetles, caterpillars, cicadas, and even the snails. They are our friends and working partners. But when the planting season arrives, the bird is unwanted because they will want to eat all of our seeds that we have planted for the new season's crop. They are not needed or wanted here. So they are frightened away. They must be confused, I would think, just like my compatriots in the US. Would you agree?" the padre questioned sincerely.

"What I do understand is the irony of it all. If the birds were allowed to eat all of the seeds, then there would be no plants in the summer to attract the insects, which the blue grosbeak needs for survival. It all comes down to a balance of nature for all concerned," Grav tried to reason.

"A balance of nature left to nature, I presume."

"No, controlled by man, in the bird's and man's best interest, both here and by your good neighbor to the north," Grav argued, now sensing that the friendly exchange of opinions and avian analogies were going around in circles. He wouldn't feel comfortable preaching to a preacher about religion, but didn't mind doing so about national sovereignty when it came to his country's immigration laws. He sensed now that the discussion had served its purpose and run its course over the worn garden paths. He looked at his watch to politely comment aloud that he had an appointment to meet up with his fellow birders back at their RV.

"We welcome you back here to visit anytime, my friend, with or without our shared feathered visitors. And when you encounter my people back in your wonderful country, remember that we are all of the same flock. Until then, go with God," the sagacious priest offered in a prayerful manner.

Grav smiled broadly in return, wishing the Father continued peace.

* * *

He joined his teammates in the RV exchanging notes taken from their respective reconnaissance work. He uploaded his multiangle digital photos of the rear one-room wooden home Padre Montes and young Miguel shared. The matter of what to do next was a simple one, the decision easy. Spreading a large piece of paper over the dinette table, they collaborated on a building layout that would increase the size of the one-room home behind the church to five times its size. It would include a two-tiered staircase with railings that reached the roof top of the church. There a sheltered studio terrace was designed to accommodate the artistic needs of the young resident master of mask making. The pen and ink drawing would be submitted at six thirty to the *Señor* Maldonado by Cam, who would scribble a $27,000 US cash dollar contract agreement with the local builder out on a paper napkin. The prepaid materials would be delivered to the rear of the church the day of the birdwatchers' departure from *Tácuaro*. Maldonado and Son would be paid upon completion of the project with the money advanced by Cam to the waitress of the *La Paloma Café* who, in return for her services, would retain a 15 percent *propina* (tip).

The team made a brief trip to the *Banco Nacional de Mexico* in *Paztcuaro,* where Taylor entered with a shallow black leather briefcase filled with $73,000 US dollars in cash. It was deposited in a high yield certificate of deposit in the name of Miguel Urbina, of *Tácuaro, Michoacán.* Taylor would gratefully receive the packaged two masks at the appointed time and place from Juan Jr. with no questions asked nor money exchanged as was agreed upon. Following a warm *abrazo* of goodbye between the two, Taylor would place his Dallas Cowboy cap upon the excited young boy's head and a LA Angels cap in his hand for master Miguel.

16

SPELLBOUND

Lomas de Los Angelas, Michoacán

They timed the return trip to the Hills of Angels campsite for an early evening arrival. They were now entering the extraction phase of the mission cycle. Their operation readiness was a "Go." They were back on grid, now referring to the monastery fortress as the TEA, target engagement area, the shed their TC, target concentration. Paradoxically none of the tactical planning called for the touching of their actual target, FTM fugitive Pedro Barajas. Taylor employed the baseball analogy where the offense isn't allowed to touch the ball in play.

"You'll be in the TEA to motivate, to stimulate our target to react to his paranoia. Primal fear will do the rest," Taylor summarized the tactical intent of the extraction plan.

"The TEA approach point will be the eastern wall of the monastery courtyard, Grav at the north corner, Cam at the south end. At 0600, you will simultaneously breach the wall, taking your respective hidden positions at the inside corners of the wall. From there you will proceed as planned when ready. Grav will take point. Are we clear?" Taylor asked in direct eye contact with his Delta mates.

"Clear, sir," was the dual response in unison.

"At 0500, the ops team trekked the one-mile path below the bottom of the bluff that brought them to the monastery's southeast corner of the wall. They synchronized their watches and checked the radios wired with ear and mouth pieces. Taylor monitored all radio communication but stayed off air. Grav took his position at the northeast corner of the wall.

The cool, moist forest air was silent and still with a pungent scent of live pine. A modest moon glow shone in the clear sky's far horizon. At 0600, the men were atop the thick stone wall in a reposed posture, pausing momentarily to scan the courtyard for any unexpected challenges. It was the "Go, no-go" moment for the Delta ops, the assessed condition of operability for safety and success before proceeding.

"I have a 'Go' here," Cam's radio called.

"Copy that. I'm 'Go' here. On your ready, move," was Grav's ordered response.

They rapelled down the eighteen-foot high wall at the same quick pace, dropping silently behind garden bushes. They opened their backpacks to ready their packages. Cam would move first, traversing the long rectangular courtyard garden to his clandestine position behind the freshly replenished supply of firewood beside the monastery.

"In place," he radioed Grav.

"Copy. I'm on the move," he replied.

Grav made his way along the wall to within five feet of the TC. Standing near the shed door, he could hear the subtle snoring of Barajas from within. He sprayed the three rusty hinges on the vertical plank door with WD-40 oil. He pulled out his two *Tácuaro* masks from the backpack before blowing three times into his lip microphone. Cam repeated the same muted code for "Going hot," his reply signal to proceed.

Grav pulled his night vision goggles down over his eyes and carefully eased open the old door enough to peer in. Barajas was asleep on a narrow mattress with his back to the door twelve feet away beneath several layers of covers. There was a three-drawer dresser next to the head of the bed and a solitary small table and tilting chair in the center of the earthy-smelling room. Grav reached in and attached mask number 1 on the upper right side of the inner door with double-sided tape. Mask number 2 was attached to its left. Glancing around the room studiously, he was assured that there were enough candles on holders and wall sconces to provide the desired effect. He gently closed the door and silently slipped back to his corner hide. "Clear on target," he radioed his ops partners.

A large Christian cross had been formed by Cam on the pathway in front of the monastery entrance with firewood placed end-to-end. The largest cut of wood was situated upright in the center of the second step building entrance. It was crowned prominently with a red-faced, green-horned mask of the devil. A battery-operated lantern was secured to its backside and illuminated. He then returned to his dark cover behind the high pile of cord wood. He peered out to admire his work, whispering a sincere apology to God, "Forgive me, Lord, the devil made me do it."

"In position. Satan on stage center, over," Cam radioed.

"Roger that. Prize inside. Packages delivered. We wait for daybreak and awakening. Over, out," Grav responded.

Their reconnaissance told them that Barajas would rise at dawn, dress and enter the monastery with firewood for the morning fire ovens and fireplaces before exiting with his breakfast, which he'd consume in his shed.

Sameness was the one routine they could count on in an ultra-conservative, monotone monastery where unwavering tradition was a lifestyle. Their only task now was to wait. Both men would remain hidden, hoping the team had read Barajas and his loop correctly, that his paranoia would flare up with their gambit and, most importantly, fear would take flight.

Their concentration was broken by a treetop bird call, starting low in pitch, going up, then wavering up and down in sets of five-second trills before ending abruptly. This continued for several sets, creating an eerie series of screeches, causing Grav to radio Cam.

"What we're hearing is our local Guatemalan screech owl. Satan must have ordered it for Barajas's wake-up call. There's light in the shed. Stand by," Grav reported.

"Copy that," Cam replied.

The men sensed the ghostly effect emanating from the screech owl's repeated trills, a call from beyond the grave type of nocturnal quality.

They could not know the effect it was having on their target as he lit the several candles around his small abode. Barajas's attention was arrested by two unknown objects mysteriously appearing on his door. He carried a dual candle holder over to the door to inspect the two strange objects hanging there. He rubbed both eyes to wake them up and focus properly. He positioned the two candles below eye level to optimize the illumination of the foreign objects. It took several seconds for his hazy mind to process the binary images. It would suddenly register; the twin like objects appeared as split life-like images of his young son, Miguel. He now made out the two opposite halves of Miguel's face. The object on the left showed a normal half face and a horrifically scared one on the opposite side. The second object displayed the reverse, a monsterlike face on the left half, the youthful face of his son on the right. He looked alternately at them repeatedly in suspended reality.

The young master Tácuaro mask maker had unwittingly achieved the desired effect with his artistry, a perfect depiction of the juxtaposition of humanity versus inhumanity, as though from the hands of an angel to the eyes of the devil.

Barajas had not taken a breath since he first sighted the queer images, causing him to feel faint from the bewilderment and emotional shock. It was definitely his son, he noxiously concluded, wishing it not so, wishing that it was a bad dream, that he was still asleep. His trembling hand caused hot candle wax to splash on his skin. The brief but intense sting of pain woke him to a stark consciousness he did not welcome and to an awareness that something very, very bad was happening.

The screeching sound outside was now grating on his frayed nerves. Breathing now became more difficult, the room becoming smaller. The two paradoxical images now revolted him, knowing them to be nothing other than that of a burn victim, and that victim was his son coming there to haunt him.

Barajas walked backward, transfixed on the surreal scorched faces. He stopped when he touched his bed with his wobbly legs. He set the candleholder on the dresser and hurriedly gathered his clothes set out the evening before. Shaking from head to toe, he wondered if his son's images were a spiritual sign, a warning of worse things to come.

Fully dressed, he now stood in the middle of the room, shuddering with anxiety. He knew that the only way out of his shrinking room was the door past his son's spirits. But then, what awaited him on the other side, he worried for the worse. Flight might be his only friend to fend off any evil spirits after him, he contemplated. A run for the monastery would be the safest course, he considered, wiping the increasing flow of sweat from his furrowed forehead.

It then struck him, that if these spirits got into his shed, they also got into the monastery. He had no other choice than to escape the one before him and risk that there were no others outside. He lifted the primitive wooden chair like a lion tamer confronting the wild beast. He lurched forward with the chair as though it were a lance outstretched before his enemy striking the heart of the spirit door. It swung open with a jolt as he leaped outside, dropping the chair behind him.

"Eyes on target. Target on approach," Grav radioed Cam.

"Copy that. Igniting smoke capsule now," he responded as he detonated the small canister placed behind the vertically positioned log on the entrance steps.

The early dawn's glow would illuminate his rapid and safe passage through the garden paths to the monastery entrance. There he hoped to find refuge among the monks, whose strong faith would surely ward off any evil in pursuit of his soul.

The monastery remained dark inside. The entrance was only a few quick paces away for the hopeful fugitive. But for some strange reason, he found it obscured by a haze that was suspended in the air. His quickened steps were halted by a long line of firewood laid end to end before the entrance. He cautiously stepped closer to see more firewood stretching out to the left and right. Bewildered, he took a curious moment to study the wood layout. It was too simple, too obvious to miss...a large Christian cross at his feet.

Trying to catch his breath and understand the mysterious placement of a cross, his eyes were drawn to a small but intense light beyond, shining four feet above the top, second step into the monastery entryway. The sight of a cross gave him borrowed confidence to approach the light. He leaned toward it to discover the bright burning eyes of the devil glaring directly at him. His large glossy red face was crowned with green horns, the sinister shaped mouth was framed by a thin black mustache and pointed goatee.

Barajas became breathless as though punched hard in the stomach, now paralyzed with terror. The resumed haunting sound of the screech owl became an unsettling backdrop of demonic proportions, a harbinger of misfortune, most likely of impending death he sensed. The thick white haze surrounding the devil's head became the smoke from the inferno below in his frightened, muddled mind. The vengeful spirits had penetrated the spiritual fortress monastery, he could only conclude. He knew that he had to run, escape from whatever else awaited him within the possessed walls that had once sheltered and protected him.

The flummoxed Barajas instantly turned in a panic to flee the devil's stare, heading straight for the main gate. He opened it only sufficiently to escape the evil inside, closing it tightly behind him.

"Elvis has left the building," was the coded radio message to Taylor.

Grav joined Cam by the entrance, having retrieved the two masks from the shed. Cam had dismantled his stage props and was ready to move out. But first he offered a brief but sincere apology to God for borrowing the symbolic cross for the ruse. "It was to root out evil," was his simple explanation.

"The devil works in manipulative ways," Grav commented as they quickly headed for the main gate. Securing it behind them, Cam countered with, "*Sun Tzu* works in an all-knowing way. 'What is difficult about maneuver is to make the devious route direct.'"

Barajas's downhill pace was now faster with gravity and sheer fear to motor him. His flat leather bottom sandals caused him to slide on the dirt road, tumbling over into the brush. A new sound filled the forest. One of laughter from the treetops. It began sweetly with a slowly descending series of notes that ended sadly with a different pitch and rhythm, "hahahahahaha- har-har—her-her-her."

He painfully rose to his hands and knees like a track sprinter. The repeated trill of laughter served as a starting gun of a race, causing Barajas to bolt upward and onward, faltering down the hill as fast as his bruised, feeble legs would allow. Nearing the bottom of the road, he saw his first and only sign of hope and salvation since he woke up to his fresh hell fifteen minutes earlier. It was a large passenger bus at the country road bus stop parked in the westward direction. His joy at its first sight told him it was brought by a guardian angel sent now to watch over him. Its passenger door was open, displaying a warm, welcoming glow from the soft lights inside. His eyes again focused on the uncertain terrain beneath his sled like sandals to avoid another misstep that might cause him to miss the heaven-sent chariot that came to carry him away from the devil.

"No se vaya, no se vaya, ya yo vengo! (Don't go, don't go, I'm coming!)" he shouted desperately at the bus.

Sweating profusely, his damp, salty eyes didn't bother looking over the bus. All he noticed was that it was big, clean, headed west, and most importantly, it was there. He grabbed tightly onto the metal hand rails and joyfully pulled himself up and on board.

"Gracias, gracias por esperarme, señor. (Thanks, thanks for waiting for me, sir.)" Barajas struggled to express with a heaving chest, his legs throbbing as he looked across the entry aisle at the driver facing forward in the dark.

"Por donde va el autobus, señor (Where is the bus going to, sir)?" Barajas asked the driver.

"Nos vamanos al infierno con una parada primera en Santa Barbara, California, Los Estados Unidos. (We're going to hell with a stop first in Santa Barbara, California, the United States.)" Taylor nodded grimly.

The metal door closed behind Barajas with an air-sucking sound. He didn't notice the two new passengers who stepped on board behind him, wearing night camouflage clothing, backpacks, black face, and black knit caps.

Back in the nearby woods, there was an audible thud on the leaf litter floor. A white falcon with a black mask imbedded three forward talons and one rear killer talon into a three-foot long snake. The bird's thick wings spread wide for balance as it clamped its sharp, powerful beak down behind the snake's wavering head, snapping it off in an instant. One leg then lifted the limp body up for the falcon to begin swallowing its prey, tail first. The woods were silent of laughter.

Caracara I rolled away slowly westward from the bus stop. Three of the four passengers were enjoying the sounds of "*I Put a Spell on You*," by Screamin' Jay Hawkins.

Mad Mary 4

McKinney's last two visits to the Harbor Market were to retrieve his unwanted bags of ice in the absence of the anticipated coded messages he and his pack members so eagerly awaited. It did minimize the verbal assaults from Mad Mary, whom McKinney believed missed more than the extra money she made on the beer buys. It had been twelve days since the last call for Corona, which began to worry him that maybe the Delta team had hit a snag, or worse. Anything worse he believed would surely have been communicated to him in some fashion. But for now, a more immediate concern faced him as he entered the convenience store, "Miss Congeniality" herself, who was waiting behind the cash register like a lion, awaits the lamb.

"McKinney. Is the Corona caller your AA sponsor, or what? Whoever she is, she's killing you, man."

"How so?" he asked, afraid of the answer.

"She's got you down to two Coronas at a six-pack price, McKinney. She'll never make it on *The Price Is Right*. And you ain't no Bob Barker for buying it either. But hey, have you ever heard me complain?" she asked seriously.

Such a question from her lambasting lips to his honest ears seemed to burn into his brain, begging for an answer. But the covert message of two more captures halted any reply he might normally have made, positive or negative. The exciting news made it easy for him to ignore her invectives and go directly into his beer bottle maneuver with dexterity, four Coronas lifted out, two left in at the six-pack price; no problem.

Placing two five-dollar bills by her register, he would not allow her to spoil his fresh euphoria, saying, "If it pleases you, Mary, then it pleases me. Keep the change. I'll make more tomorrow," leaving with a smile as wide as his stride. Outside, McKinney heard her shout, "Well make some with Ben Franklin on them. That'll please me more!"

The last time the mission associates saw a Corona carton on board the Conch II, it contained four golden bottles of beer. For dramatic effect, McKinney set the new, two-bottle carton on a small round, white table in the center of the main deck. He covered it with a lap-size blue cotton napkin, which he would theatrically unveil when all the members were aboard. Their sights and minds would focus on the four vacant slots, not caring which fugitives they might represent. They were too close to six for it to matter now.

17

CACCA HAPPENS

Mexico City

Another sad love ballad bellowed from the dirty vagrant's battery powered boom box radio. He sat alone atop a large stack of gray foundation bricks alongside a commercial construction site in the historical *Zona San Angel* on the southwestern corner of Mexico City. Beneath the shade of his sweat-stained black cap, he observed the half dozen *obreros* moving wheelbarrows of sand, bags of cement, and bricks with their gnarly, callused hands. Their procession to the gas-driven cement mixers around the corner was a constant one, like a human conveyor belt transporting the new building piece by piece to the skilled workers inside the raw structure. Like worker bees, the day laborers had their specific duties to perform no matter how menial. Slackers were replaced by anyone willing to toil for the minimum amount of six dollars a day. There was always someone to step into the labor line for what amounted to mere subsistence money. The observant vagrant was not one of them. He simply sat, listened to his Mexican music, chewed on a hard crust *bolio* bread roll, and focused on one particular *obrero* only, known to him as Juan Taboada, a FTM fugitive from US justice.

Unlike the vagrant, the music did not go unnoticed by the construction workers. In passing, they would occasionally sing along with familiar lyrics in the song or yell out an impassioned *grito* (yell of agreement) with its forlorn theme. The workers began their lunch break with a visit to the portable toilet behind the building on Galvez Street, hidden by a large mound of concrete mixing sand. Even among these low-level laborers, there appeared to be a pecking order determining their turn to enter the porta toilet. The difference in age and seniority was not discernible for the order of their loosely spread queue. The vagrant's target of attention was always last in line during their morning work break and last before lunch, consistently looking over his shoulder in route. This noted, the vagrant dialed the radio's volume down, and then walked across Galvez Street to the Plaza *San Jacinto* Park. There he disappeared among the park's large aging trees and heavily shaded lawn, juking anyone who might have noticed his earlier presence.

This exact same scenario was repeated for the next three days without any variation. The worker bees knew their places, and their places were predictable, day after perfunctory day.

On the fifth day, the vagrant arrived at the customary hour with his traditional music enjoyed by the laborers. The only difference today was with the large golden brown *bolio* he held. He would not chew on this one. It would frequently rise to his mouth, but only for him to talk to, as though he was lip-synching the music's lyrics. This subtle activity intensified, leading up to the workers' lunch break.

Eizzo had walked about the *San Jacinto* Park throughout the morning with a studious gaze upward toward the mature tree branches, bird-watching with his recon binoculars strapped around his neck and his radio ear fob in place. He was dressed the part from his beige canvas bucket hat to his baggy white T-shirt that read, "Bird Watchers Do It All Day," down to his safari brown shorts and high-top bush boots suitable for the jungles of an urban park.

Standing by a woody vine shrub of brilliant violet bougainvillea, his attention was drawn to a flash of sapphire and a faint hum. He stepped back from the resplendent floral bracts to see a familiar sight. The rufous hummingbird was an old friend often sighted around the alpine azalea, moss heather, and wild iris at his base camp by Alaska's Mount McKinley. Its radiant, iridescent feathers were dazzling in the sunlight, its hyperkinetic wings fluttering eighty times per second in a mesmerizing three-dimensional, unpredictable, feisty flight pattern. It suspended its thumb-size, three grams body four feet in front of Eizzo as though it, too, had recognized a familiar friend. In awe of nature's wonderment, he could not resist the question, "Did you make the twenty-five-hundred-mile migration to Mexico just to see me?" he asked aloud, recalling their annual epic roundtrip journey from Alaska. The six-foot, three-inch tall, 230-pound Special Forces warrior stared with envy at the diminutive creature, known as the most durable, toughest creature in the animal kingdom. Of the 330 species of hummingbirds in the world, the rufous ruled, and Eizzo was inspired by its omnipresence.

"Fat life, little one. Summer in Alaska, winter in Mexico. See you back at McKinley." As though in tacit agreement, the flighty friend with the bright orange-red gorget bobbed its needle beak up and down before darting over to nectar at the buffet of fresh blossoms on the vine. Eizzo turned his binoculars back on the sedentary vagrant.

There was never an actual line for the porta toilet. When one worker returned to the building site, the next one would walk around the high sand pile and enter the tan, molded plastic outhouse. It sat on two thick wooden skids, which boosted its height to around six and a half feet, including its white plastic dome roof.

The vagrant turned up the volume on the radio when worker number 6, as expected, headed for the porta toilet. The vagrant placed the *bolio* to his mouth one last time. He uttered the words *Sun Tzu* before putting the oval-shaped roll in his pant pocket. On cue, a white pickup truck entered Galvez Street with a blue plastic tarp draped over a tall, rectangular hump standing in its back cargo space. It cruised slowly alongside the new building. It passed the walking worker and sand pile by twenty feet, stopping on the Plaza *San Jacinto* side of Galvez Street.

The two men inside the truck watched the approaching worker they now clearly recognized in their rear and side view mirrors. They verified one last time his ID with the photos on their laptop as their FTM target, Juan Toboada. Afro Mestizo, six feet tall, dark-skinned with black, puffy Afro hair, large black eyes, and a well-conditioned build for a forty-year-old. In an instant, he went from *obrero* number 6 to TC number 1. Once the target was inside the porta toilet, the driver spoke through his hidden miniature microphone to the vagrant. "The opportunity of defeating the enemy is provided by the enemy himself.—*Sun Tzu.*"Their wangle commenced.

The vagrant quickly surveyed the immediate area for any witnesses nearby. Seeing none, he approached the porta toilet, cranking up the volume on the radio. The pickup truck followed his lead by backing up to within four feet from the outhouse door. Two burly men emerged from the truck, wearing khaki-colored service uniforms from caps to work boots. The vagrant quietly slipped a long U-shaped bolt through the lockless door latch, securing it to the doorframe. The two pseudo-servicemen walked swiftly and quietly around opposite sides of the porta toilet, each holding one end of a long, professional mover's canvas belt. They met in the back, where they connected the two ends through a thick metal buckle. The belt circumvented the porta toilet at midlevel, preventing the door or any weak corner of the prefab structure from being kicked open from within. As they cinched the belt tightly with the metal teeth of the buckle, the vagrant reached up high to the top of the unit's vertical, gray ventilation tube. Very gently, he stuffed a dirty white towel tightly into the opening. The two men pulled the tarp off the truck's cargo, revealing an identical porta toilet to the occupied one. The truckers offloaded the new unit with ease, setting it alongside the used one.

A high-pitch, panicky male voice now came from within the original porta toilet. The vagrant turned the volume higher to drown out the increased level of pounding and shouting. The uniformed men tipped the top half of the occupied unit onto the truck's tailgate with the door facing down. The three of them lifted the bottom up, sliding it horizontally over the bed of the truck. A week's worth of bodily content erupted throughout the sealed unit as the shouting inside turned to intense screaming. Brown water began to ooze out of the unit's corner seams, creating a fetid odor. The three men hurriedly tied the tarp down to cover the entire cargo hold while allowing air to flow underneath. With the tailgate up, the vagrant set his booming boom box alongside the new cargo, muting the stream of angry profanity coming from beneath. The radio played a loud, sorrowful song about a man who was "dumped on" by his lover, engendering no sympathy from the irate target.

The vagrant watched the truck drive slowly away as he sauntered casually across the Plaza toward the small *Iglesia San Jacinto* on the south end. Once the white truck headed west on *Avenida General Rivera* toward the *Periferico* freeway, the vagrant wiped his face clean with a sani-napkin and removed his over worn cap to adopt a more tourist like appearance. He entered the large, wooden double doors of the seventeenth-century, gray stone, landmark church as he had once before, as an American tourist.

Walking from the altar up the center aisle was a short, reddish-dark, Indian-looking young priest, who recognized the tourist.

"Father, I want your church to have this for your generous accommodations and kindness." He handed him a crisp, new, one-hundred-dollar bill. "Sometimes it's more practical to be a walking tourist. You can observe more on foot," the tourist declared.

"This is so. As you Americans say, 'You should stop and smell the roses,'" the priest offered.

"I wish that had been the case," the tourist rejoined to the puzzled-looking priest. "But now I must leave your beautiful *Zona San Angel* and your historic *Iglesia San Jacinto*. Thank you for protecting my bike and backpack, Father. Is there somewhere I can change clothes?"

"Yes, of course, in the side vestibule where we stored your possessions. And where is your portable radio?" the priest asked, noticing the tourist's empty hands.

"It's with someone who needed a little cheering up," the tourist said with a tone of charity in his voice.

"God bless you for that," the priest offered with a gracious smile while placing the hundred-dollar bill in his pocket.

Meanwhile, a small group of older British tourists had gathered outside the *Iglesia* in front of a brass plaque mounted on the church wall. It told the historical account of an Irish regiment of soldiers named *San Patricia,* who fought at that site in 1847 on the side of the Mexican army against the attacking American forces. The Catholic Irish soldiers deserted their Protestant US forces to join their Catholic Mexican allies during the Mexican-American War. Led by their Captain O'Rally, the entire regiment was killed, captured, or wounded by the victorious US Army. The captain was forced to watch his captured men hanged, then to have his forehead branded for life with a *D* for "Deserter," then set free.

Concluding the reading of the historical plaque, the church's front double doors were opened by the young priest. In an instant, with a machine-pitched, throaty roar, a red Kawasaki motorbike shot out from the church entrance. Wearing an all-black rider's outfit with helmet and backpack was Cope, launching himself out of the high double door entrance onto the cobblestone street. Within four seconds, the thin power bike was on *Avenida* General Rivera heading west.

Twenty seconds later, he turned south, entering the *Periferico* freeway in excess of ninety miles per hour in pursuit of the white pickup. Back at the *Iglesia San Jacinto*, the tour guide commented to his group of stunned Brits, "That must have been the ghost of the only Irish soldier who got away."

From his radio mic imbedded in the helmet, Cope was now in direct, secure contact with Rap, riding shotgun, and Eizzo in the driver's seat of the pickup.

"I should be up with you in under two minutes," Cope reported.

"Do you have our visual?" Rap responded.

"Negative on the visual. But it's a positive on your smell," Cope chided. "How's your special passenger?" he added.

"Still unhappy. Thank God he's downwind."

"Not from me he's not. Or is that coming from Eizzo?" Cope prodded.

Rap shot back, "He just sent you a hand visual, Cope. Do you copy?"

Laughing, he shifted up into the fifth gear as the traffic began to thin further away from the city. He waited to come out of the long eastbound curve to find the white truck in the moderate traffic ahead. A quarter mile away, he spotted it merging into the far-right lane. But something else caught his attention merging onto the freeway from a side off-ramp.

"I have your visual a quarter mile back, but so does a motorcycle cop on your six at half my distance," Cope warned them with urgency.

"Copy that. If we're in his crosshairs, then it's because we're spewing water," Eizzo reasoned.

"Or we're just another random victim being cited for an arbitrary traffic violation, also known as highway robbery," Rap contributed.

"I'll slow down a little to see what he's going to do. Our turnoff is coming up soon. You can't let him pull us over, Cope, so do what you have to do before the exit and keep him on the freeway," Eizzo ordered.

"I copy. No matter what I'm doing behind you, don't take your exit until the very last second. Make it abrupt and clean. I won't be able to hold him for too long, so floor it to the ranch. I'll take a different route back. Over and out."

He eased up closer on the tan uniformed cop riding an older, heavier model of motorcycle, which Cope guessed to be a modified V-twin, 745cc, Honda Shadow Aero, cruiser class, well suited for paved highways, but outclassed by Cope's ride. His close proximity to the truck now confirmed in Cope's mind that it was his intended victim. Cope accelerated up to fifteen feet behind the cop, whose attention was solely on his prey.

"We're exiting in ten seconds," came Eizzo's forewarning as the pickup increased its speed slightly. The police motorcycle kept pace with the truck. Cope spurred the Kawasaki 650 briefly to bring it along the officer's right side. The cop turned his head toward his surprise visitor with an expression of shock, followed by a gesture of disapproval. Cope began making friendly, nonsensical gestures in return in an attempt to distract him while observing his team's truck surge in speed. Cope tightened his bike's proximity to the cop's just when the pickup lunged abruptly to the right onto their planned low-grade off-ramp exit. Immediately the cop reduced speed drastically with an authoritative gesture to Cope to get out of his way. Innocently refusing to do so, they began an alternating sequence of slow and go speeds with Cope, maintaining control of the angry cop's outside position. The siren and blinking emergency lights were activated on the highway patrol bike to both warn and intimidate Cope that he was no longer going to play his game. Cope reasoned that until the cop reached for his radio, the game could and would go on.

Frustrated and furious about his out-of-control situation, the cop swerved sharply in toward Cope with the hope of interrupting his controlled pace setting. But Cope had the seasoned reflexes of a professional bull rider and reacted in stride, moving adroitly to the side with a big grin. That in turn infuriated the red-faced cop, who now reached to his belt to draw his gun. Cope swerved hard toward him to force his gun hand back onto the handlebar and buy him time to downshift quickly to a near stop on the shoulder. As the cop continued down the highway regaining his equilibrium, the Kawasaki had turned 180 degrees, accelerating through all gears to gain as much distance away as possible from the eastbound cop. Cope stayed on the narrow shoulder with his headlight on to alert all oncoming traffic that now was not the time to get a flat tire. He saw a break in the side guard rails a short distance following the truck's earlier exit. He commanded the Kawasaki to do what Kawasaki's do best: leap through the air onto natural off-road ground, soaring up the long grassy knoll in a single bound. A few yards away, he entered the sinuous country road that branched off the feeder highway his partners were on southbound to their safe house ranch. The bike tires went from dirt to hard asphalt with a biting grip of blue smoke and rubber squeals, accelerating to ninety miles per hour into the rural outskirts of the mountain-ringed capital.

When the dairy industry died around Mexico City decades earlier due to environmental and economic reasons, hundreds of small dairy farms closed. Most were abandoned altogether, deemed unsuitable for any kind of livestock farming for the same reasons. One such farm, however, found life after death because of its remote access and hidden view in a low chaparral terrain. The Delta team never questioned Lori's many field resources, but had to assume that this rural safe house had been used many times before by clandestine US agencies, most probably CIA and DEA. For their particular interests, it was tailor-made. The *Caracara* I nested out of sight in the deserted old hay barn where Cope rolled into to store the bike back inside the belly of the RV. He had been in radio contact with his team reporting on his "flank the fool" maneuvers. "I didn't get the cop's name though," he lamented. "I wanted to tattoo it on my butt."

The all-brick milking parlor still had good, strong plumbing, where Cope found his partners washing down the still secured porta toilet standing on a concrete floor by a large floor drain. Where muddy dairy cows were once cleaned prior to milking, FTM fugitive Juan Toboada was about to receive his baptism of cold well water from two high-pressure hoses.

"Does our new best friend know that we're throwing a shower for him?" Cope questioned warmly.

"Oh, he'll welcome it, believe me. Go ahead and release the belt and pull the latch pin. Eizzo and I will welcome him to 'Waterworld.'"

When the porta toilet door opened for Toboada, they found him covered with liquid excrement, doubled over on his knees dry heaving. He crawled out a few feet before being blasted on both sides by the water hoses for fifteen seconds. As ordered to do, he stood silently and removed his cloths before being tossed a bar of soap and a small plastic bottle of shampoo. Once he was lathered up with suds, he was rinsed with another dual power blast of water. Shivering from top to bottom with lips compressed, he dried off with a large sheet towel before being handed a clean set of warm cloths. He was then instructed to gargle Listerine mouthwash followed by swallowing an assortment of pills guaranteed to kill every "cootie" known to man or animal, plus vitamin supplements from A to Z. For safe measure, Rap injected their terrified captive with a series of inoculations to ward off the worst of the possible diseases contracted by not washing your hands after using the restroom.

"So I hope this is a lesson to Juan the next time he uses the 'Juan,'" Rap smirked.

Foremost in their collective minds, the Delta team remembered the grizzly photos of Juan's murdered wife and automatically dismissed any sympathy possible for their disgraced captive.

"Well, one thing is for certain. He'll never walk into a porta toilet again. Let's get him into his private suite now with some bottled water. He won't be ready to eat for hours. We're ready to roll. Cope, you'll take the wheel. Our southbound route to the coast will be back roads only, birding if needed as we go," Eizzo declared.

In an empty grain silo, they had secreted away the wooden crate they had transported to Mexico City from the *Sea Cat*. It would be moved into the city during the dark of night to the basement location of *Mi Tio's* saloon by the owner of the old white pickup.

The narrow two-lane, brown gravel-tar highway was worn thin from years of traffic and neglect. The intermittent white center line had nearly disappeared from the bleaching of the high desert sun. The road's horizon was shortened by the constant rise and fall of the terrain, which created an undulating effect of a ribbon being whipped up and down. Unlike the neighboring, parallel, straight, flat super toll highway seven miles to the east, their old Highway 95 held true to the land, hugging the natural contour of its host hills and valleys, causing distant scenes to appear and disappear with regularity.

"Now you see it, now you don't," Cope commented to Eizzo and Rap, regarding the nearsighted horizon. "If I weren't driven, I'd be puken. The rock 'n' roll on a bull is only eight seconds," he said with a groan.

"I'm love'n it. I only wish there was white water below," Rap said jovially.

Eizzo set his sights on the hillside on the right. It was inclining gradually from the highway for a hundred yards with sparse growths of patchy grass, short, dry bushes, and large, four- to five-foot high brown boulders strewn over the high slope, ending at a steep escarpment. From there, the land rose sharply, peaking at a three-thousand-foot serrated ridge that stretched another sixty miles south.

Eizzo saw the first sign in the last hour of human and animal life, spotting what appeared to be a lone field peasant near a skinny brown steer on the rising slope. The young boy was wearing raggedy white pants, *huaraches*, a brown *poncho*, and waving enthusiastically to them with his large straw *sombrero* high over his head.

A half mile farther down the orphaned highway, the scene was repeated. An underfed steer was grazing on mountain bunchgrass near his watchful shepherd boy. The boy, taller than the earlier shepherd, began waving his large straw *sombrero* high in the air at the passing, large, rare RV rolling over the hillside road. Eizzo didn't bother waving back at the boys because of the dark tinted windows. He merely watched with growing curiosity.

Standing atop the largest boulder around, another half mile further down the road was a third shepherd, a larger young man with his solitary steer nearby. Sighting his younger brother's waving *sombrero* back to the north, he lifted his off of his head, placed two fingers in his mouth, and whistled loudly. Three slender, older, mustached men, standing in the middle of the highway looked up in his direction with interest. A dusty white cow with a rope bridling its large, short horned head stood in front of the men, motionless and obedient. They were at the lowest level of the long, deep dip in the road, completely out of view from distant traffic. Only the shepherd could follow the pace of the oncoming RV. Suddenly he raised his large *sombrero* above his head, prompting the trio below to pull on a couple of ropes, which carefully dropped the cow on her side, sprawled across the center of the highway.

When the RV began to rise over the next incline, the young peasant began waving his *sombrero* like his two brothers before him. The gradual decline from the road's peak was long enough for the RV to slow down to a safe stop in front of the reposed bovine. The three men, pretending to be frightened and desperate with their situation, stood behind the cow with their arms rising out of their *ponchos* in waves of mock frustration. Their hillside sentinel remained standing on his lookout post with keen interest as the leader of the trio approached the RV front door with a pleading expression on his unshaven, dark, drawn face. The shepherd could make out the large image of the big, black and white crested falcon on the door as it opened. He recognized it from the Balsas River region to the south. But all he could concentrate on for the moment was the belief that he could actually smell American money from within. Surely they would have lots of good food, nice clothes, cameras they could sell, and maybe liquor, which they would definitely keep to celebrate with. His imagination was racing with thoughts of riches, like how pirates must have imagined their booty when boarding a captured vessel at sea.

As planned, two of the highwaymen quickly boarded the RV with revolvers drawn. The third and smallest member, with a thick Poncho Villa–like mustache and his menacing machete at the ready, remained by the now standing cow in front of the RV. The young man watched patiently from his elevated perch for his partners in crime to appear with the booty. A voice called from the RV for the third highwayman to quickly come on board. This was a good sign, he thought. There was probably too much loot for the first two men to handle, he was hoping. His excitement was growing, but still guarded as he constantly glanced northward and south toward his fellow hillside lookouts for any signal, warning of additional oncoming traffic. The best sign so far was the silence aboard the RV. From this he judged that all was well under control. He only had to guess how many armfuls of treasure would be coming through the door, and all American-made, he presumed.

The silence continued for a minute longer. Suddenly shouts of Spanish profanity emerged followed by three naked brown bodies thrown out the front door, one by one, somersaulting over the hard pavement past the curious cow. The three highwaymen, would-be robbers painfully lifted themselves upright, struggling to run up the hill toward the refuge of the large, sun-dried boulders. Their swearing screams had stopped, saving their breath for the long, barefooted, bare-naked climb and escape from embarrassment and humiliation.

The only sound now heard by the shepherd was the slow diesel acceleration of the long RV with its door closed. It continued south with its possessions intact plus two revolvers, a machete, *huaraches*, and a pile of dirty laundry. The young sentry somberly squatted down upon his lookout boulder, his tipped *sombrero* covering his disappointed eyes, not wanting to witness the slow, sorrowful disappearance of his lost, shiny treasure, "the big one that got away."

Cope remained behind the wheel while Eizzo put the *huaraches* and clothes in a black plastic trash bag. "Man, these things reek. Those guys weren't exactly 4-H Club members," he exclaimed as he sealed the top of the bag. "I was willing to give them some food. But pistols pointed at me piss me off. They really need to take a Dale Carnegie course in public relations," he exclaimed.

Rap checked on the prisoner in the holding cell secured to his seat restraints. He was still too drugged and drowsy to pose any problem. His appearance was more of a zombie than a raging killer. With sedatives added to all of his future meals as a tranquilizing supplement, he would remain in his laid-back state for the duration of the trip, with no natural desire for flight. Juan Toboada was a captive of clinical chemicals provided by a Delta friend in the pharmaceutical business.

Looking at the GPS navigational screen, Cope reported to the others. "The next *pueblo* is *Apaxtla*, sixty-two miles southwest. No need to worry about our three *banditos* reporting this to the *Policia*. Who wants to admit to a failed robbery attempt, not to mention showing up as naked as a potential jailbird?"

Rap asked, "Was I the only one who saw that cow laughing?"

"Most definitely laughing. I think they should name a cheese after her," Cope laughed with the others.

"Those guys have taken 'cow-tipping' to a whole new level. Don't let the Wisconsin farm boys hear about this one," Eizzo said half seriously.

The RV picked up speed while Rap and Eizzo emptied the unspent rounds from the two old .38 revolvers and began to dismantle them with an electric drill. Passing the village of *Apaxtla,* they would toss the weapons' parts and bullets into the *Rio Balsas*, and then follow its winding flow westward to *Coyucas* before camping at the river basin for the night. In the morning, they would cross over the southern mountain pass of the *Sierra Madre del Sur*, serendipitously photographing their namesake crested *caracara* flying low over the land in search of prey. From there, the southern Mexico coast, *Zihuatanejo*, and the Pacific Ocean would be in sight.

Mad Mary 5

McKinney paused on his walkway approach to the Harbor Market at the sight of Harbor Patrol Officer Brian Paulson standing in the entrance. He towered over a medium built man in his midtwenties, wearing a black cap with a Bandito Spearguns logo and a blue printed T-shirt that read "Scuba Divers Go Down" in white letters.

Noticing McKinney's approach, the officer greeted him, "Good morning, Mr. McKinney. Going to stock up for your morning cruise with the boys?" knowing his Sunday morning channel cruise routine.

"Ice only, if Mary will sell it to me."

"Jimmy here will. He's subbing for Mary through Tuesday," he stated impassively.

McKinney and the young man exchanged silent head nods, the male greeting for "pleased to meet you."

"I would appreciate a couple of nasty insults with the sale, Jimmy, so that I don't forget where I am, okay?" grinning slyly.

Embarrassed, he replied, "I could never do that, sir. And don't worry about Mary. She won't be back until Wednesday."

Sensing McKinney's confusion, Officer Paulson explained. "Mary has been given an official leave of absence, an ordered cooling off period of four days because of a minor incident here Friday afternoon with a fisherman from the *Catch of the Night*."

"That's a squid boat, right?" McKinney asked rhetorically, familiar with all of the harbor commercial fishing boats.

"Right. The diver, Big Bert, came in to buy his second six-pack of beer while waiting for his night's catch of squid to be off-loaded. Jimmy was here to pick up his paycheck and then ran to us for help. Jimmy, go ahead and tell Mr. McKinney what you reported to us."

"Well, Bert had set a new carton of Budweiser bottles on the counter when Mary went off on him for being 'more stinking drunk than his own stink of fish.' He said that wasn't as bad as her, having permanent PMS. For that, she said she wouldn't sell him the beer. So he said that because of her, the reason they call it PMS is because 'Mad Cow Disease' was already taken."

"Oh jeez. Is that when she swung at him?" McKinney speculated hopefully.

"She was plenty pissed, for sure, and told him to 'Piss off!' Bert then got into her face, saying, 'The *M* in PMS stands for Mary! Psycho Mary Syndrome!' She grabbed one of the beer bottles and swung at him, missing by a minnow's breath, shouting, "I'll show you, psycho, you beer-breath bastard!" He bolted out the door with

Mad Mary twenty feet behind, throwing beer bottles at him, yelling, "For all you do, this Bud's for you, you squid-screwing drunk."

"Fortunately, she can't throw bottles as well as insults. But there were six busted bottles splashed across the walkway. Jimmy came for our duty officers, and they asked him to mind the store while they booked Mary for disorderly conduct," Officer Paulson stated with an official tone.

"Did she go to jail?" McKinney inquired with a hidden sense of wistfulness in his question.

"No. Just booked and released. She'll get off with a fine unless she gives the female judge any lip, then all bets are off. It would become a war of words with Judge Tonya 'The Tongue' Anderson tearing Mary a new one, if you know what I mean?"

McKinney knew exactly what he meant and decided to leave the matter right there, wanting to enjoy the moment of a "Mary free" Harbor Market. With an indifferent shrug of his shoulders, he went to get his token bag of ice. Waiting this time for his exact change, Jimmy asked him, "I'm sorry. Did Officer Paulson call you, Mr. McKinney?"

"Yes. Michael McKinney. I own the *Conch II* in slip D-37."

"Wow, I'm glad I asked. There's a message here from yesterday, some gal called to remind you to pick up a bottle of Corona. I explained that—"

"Yes, that you only sell six-packs. I know," McKinney gently interrupted, "and that's no problem, Jimmy. Here, this should cover it," handing him a ten-dollar bill. "Keep the five bottles and the peace with our fine patrol officers, off duty, of course." He winked at Officer Paulson.

"Of course, Mr. McKinney. Thank you," the two recipients said in unison. This time McKinney took his time exiting the store, completely unabashed by the unbalanced carton carrying a single bottle of beer. It felt pleasingly light in his hand, as though the weight of the mission was about to completely disappear at any time. He subconsciously felt that something was missing at that moment, when he suddenly realized that no strident screams, expletives, or incriminations came from the Harbor Market behind him as he gleefully walked to his yacht.

What a beautiful morning, he thought, as he set the Corona carton with its solitary bottle center stage on its customary table, which had now become a pedestal exhibiting a prized trophy for all his companions to admire. With a poetic license, McKinney began humming to himself, *If one more bottle we should happen to lack, no more fugitives from justice to extract.*

18

PADRE MADRE

Tres Marias, Madre Island

"Lori, Mattie here. All secure?"

"Secure here. Go ahead," she answered on her Casper-encrypted phone from the *Sea Cat* docked in the *Puerto Vallarta* harbor for refueling, resupply, and a rendezvous with Mattie and Angelino.

"Angelino and I have arrived in PV. And I bring good news, bad news, twofold. Are you ready?

"Hit me gently."

"The reason we urgently needed to meet you here is because I have the confirmed location of your fugitive Olivel Morales de Gutierrez. The bad news is he was in the *Sinoloa* State Prison in *Aqua Luto*. Good news, he was out last week. Bad news, he was transferred to another prison on the island of *Tres Marias Madre*. It's ninety-five nautical miles southwest from *Puerto Vallarta* in the Mexican sector of the Pacific Ocean, due south of the mouth of the Sea of Cortez, and southeast of *Cabo San Lucas* on the tip of *Baja*. That's why I said we needed to meet here ASAP."

"Please tell me more good news, Mattie. It can't get any worse."

"Only that the island is guarded by the Mexican Navy's armed marines, ninety-eight in total, and four patrol boats, not to mention the one hundred or so penal colony foot-patrol guards who are unarmed. That's good news, isn't it?"

"Yeah. Thanks. What did these prisoners do to end up on an island?"

"Believe it or not, it's a medium security prison, no walls, no bars, just open ocean with hungry sharks that love Mexican food."

"So how did Olivel Morales score an island vacation?"

"Remember I said he was on our 'Sentenced Felons' list, but not found on our daily active inmate population reports?"

"I do remember. Did he escape?"

"No. I couldn't find him in our tracking system under his original assigned inmate number for a reason."

"That number stays with them for life, right?"

"The very one, but it disappeared as though he had vaporized. Then he reappears with a new number suddenly, as though he were a brand-new inmate."

"So he has a new number—why so, and why would it matter?"

"Not why, but what. It spells trouble, as in *Los Lobos*, the code name and numbers your brainiac decoder decoded for us, 50807507. Here it gets complicated. He was supposed to be in the *Tijuana* Prison serving fifteen to eighteen years for a series of killings. Sonora State was aware of his alleged homicide in Santa Barbara, but ignored it for reasons we already know."

"But not forgotten, and not alleged as far as we're concerned," Lori interjected forcefully.

Mattie chose not to respond to Lori's comment. She realized that although they would be working at cross purposes for extracting Olivel from *Maria Madre*, they shared the same objective. Get Olivel off of the island—soon!

"You'll also recall that his record shows him to be a 'blood' member of *La Eme*, your US-based Mexican Mafia."

"But they don't operate in Mexico, right?"

"Operate, no. Exist, yes. A few members like Morales fled the US to escape California statutory capital punishment, even though killing someone, anyone, was a requirement for *La Eme* membership.

You know, 'blood-in,' their mantra for membership. Because Mexico won't extradite, we're stuck with Olivel in our system."

"How much time has he served?"

"Only five months, most of it in protective custody after receiving inmate death threats in the *Tijuana* Prison, and recently a murder attempt on him in the *Sinoloa* penitentiary."

"So that's why the prison transfers?"

"In part. Remember *La Eme's* 'blood-out' rule?"

"Yes. You're a blood member for life, or it's death to those opting out. So he's now out?"

"Exactly. So in effect, he signed his own death warrant with *La Eme*. Are you sure your guys will want him now that he's a 'dead man walking'?"

"Absolutely. Faster now than before with this 'blood-out' bullseye pinned on him. The real question is can we get to him before *La Eme* does? What do you think his chances of surviving are?" Lori questioned with genuine concern.

"He's apparently accepted a *quid pro quo* deal with somebody high up in exchange for a safe transfer out of the *Sinoloa* pen. Being given protective confinement on the remote island I believe has a life-threatening condition attached to it, his life for someone else's. His new prison inmate number could only have been assigned to him from a very high-ranking authority in the criminal justice system," Mattie declared emphatically. "That person now owns Olivel!"

"The purpose, which only a person of power can control, making him logically the leader of the pack, the *Los Lobos* pack, right?"

"Precisely. But this leader wouldn't send Olivel Morales there simply to protect his bad ass. He has to be there on a mission for the wolf pack, an experienced, unrepentant killer on a predatory mission, just like the hired killer that murdered my father," Mattie stated with bitterness in her voice.

"But who in the prison could be of such significance to warrant a hit man to be sent in?" Lori asked with genuine intrigue.

"The significance of whoever his target is, Angelino and I believe to be at the very core of what our father had uncovered and was killed for. We think Olivel's marked man has the answers to the mystery, the motive for father's assassination," she surmised with an air of credulity.

"And must be eliminated at some point, like, let's say by designated inmate number 50807507," Lori punctuated the obvious.

"Just one more of many reasons why we have to get to Olivel first," Mattie proclaimed with urgency.

"We? You're not wearing your Wonder Woman outfit as you speak, are you?"

Laughing, Mattie declared with personal pride, "No, my dear, but I have with me that secret weapon I've referred to before, Brother Angelino, better known as reverent Father."

"Brilliant. I think I know where you're going with this, my sister, enough said for here and now. Tell me where I can meet with your Colima combo to continue this conversation," Lori asked with enthusiasm.

When Mattie asked days earlier, there was no hesitation with Angelino's acceptance to visit the Pacific island penitentiary, *Maria Madre*. He was there eight years earlier as a council member of North American Priests and Ministers studying innovative methods of incarceration and rehabilitation. The Catholic Church played a major role in the rehabilitation programs. On that basis of historical precedence, the Colima siblings hatched their plan, "*Padre Madre*," to penetrate the inner circle of the penitentiary with Father Angelino as the covert advance man wrapped in the cloak of the church.

A letter from Cardinal Montenegro's Mexico City office had been composed by Father Angelino and express-mailed to the warden of the island prison. It simply said that His Eminence sends his personal emissary to *Maria Madre* with the desire to have unrestricted access to the prisoners, no reason why given. Angelino knew that a papal priest with pontifical credentials would have an unassailable pass to and throughout the prison colony. They only lacked Lori's technical support for Angelino's twenty-four-hour visit there within a five-day, do-or-die window of opportunity. The Colima siblings would rendezvous with Lori in *Puerto Vallarta* at the *Hotel Playa de Oro* overlooking the marina within the hour following Mattie's call.

* * *

The Pacific coast port of verdant *Puerto Vallarta,* where the jungle meets the sea, sits in the middle of Banderas Bay, Mexico's largest. To the south was a lush, tropical rainforest with rivers, waterfalls, and exotic birds. However, the Delta team was no longer in a bird-watching recreation mode. They were now in the business of jailbirds, caging one in particular before he took flight or reverted to his instinctive behavior as a bird of prey. They now had actionable intelligence from Mattie's contacts that their jailbird target, Olivel Morales de Gutierrez, would soon be assigned his *Los Lobos* prey in the island prison of *Maria Madre.* Who and why was of no interest to the team's mission. If they could quickly extract their FTM target for their purpose, then the purpose to prisoner 50807507's presence there had no relevance to them, only urgency.

Lori would have only a few hours with her two Mexican accomplices to come up with a plan to stop the purported murderous plot. Failure to do so would prevent the Delta team from capturing their sixth and final FTM target. The Colima siblings personally wanted conclusive evidence regarding the true motive for their father's murder. Based on reliable intelligence from their individual resources, they both believed that the definitive answer to their prolonged puzzle lay within the island penitentiary.

Angelino knew that he had to go in. His role there would only be a walk-on part; only he could get the answers and walk away. He had assembled all of the questions in his unsettled mind for some time now and would not settle for a safe and easy resolution. After that, prisoner Olivel Morales de Gutierrez's fate was in God's hands, he reasoned. Angelino and Mattie would have a different, personal conspiratorial target to deal with upon the Father's return from *Maria Madre.* His visit there would hopefully confirm the Colima siblings' suspicions. The answers should subsequently incriminate the true culprit to the unsolved crime. Their method of just deserts, *a la Mexicana,* would follow later.

Echoing in their minds were the words their mother had recited on finding the motive for her husband's murder, quoting Voltaire, "To the dead, one owes only the truth."

After checking into the hotel, Lori dialed a coded number on the private Casper phone. A woman's voice answered in English, "*Playa de Oro*. How may I help you?"

"What extension do I dial for room service?"

"Number 722."

"Thank you. I'll call now," Lori responded, proceeding directly to room 722, where Mattie was waiting with her papal priest brother, who was ready to be baptized as a Delta spy.

Lori would conduct fast track training in espionage trickery and provide Angelino with the necessary spy craft gadgetry taken from the *Sea Cat*'s vault of CIA toys. Angelino would have to be cunning, instinctively or not. Internally his biggest challenge would be to live a lie, to convey a spurious air of authenticity, a disenfranchised member of the cloth still enrobed in the cloth as well as in intrigue. That was not instinctive. The priest must be motivated by the same Delta mission to succeed. He was now a member of Lori's mission as well as his own. She would imbue him with the *Sun Tzu* stratagem of "He will win whose army is animated by the same spirit throughout all its ranks."

The reverent Father Angelino boarded the morning cargo boat for the three-hour sea journey to the penal island. Although still dressed in his travel vestments, he continued to embody a different spirit than what the church had hoped for, from a Vatican spook to a Special Forces spy on a special mission that would help conclude one operation and initiate another.

The *Tres Marias Madre* penal colony was exactly as he had remembered it: a flat, oblong-shaped lay of land rising fifteen to thirty feet from sea level, six miles wide, and nine and a half miles long. It was carpeted with short grass, ground-hugging scrub oaks, and tall palm tree–lined streets providing scant shade for the single story, white concrete buildings spread out in small clusters of five camps over the fifty-eight-square mile island. There were small peach, avocado, and lime orchards, beehives, large pastures for sheep, dairy, and beef cattle, corrals for hogs, and long, metal roof barns for the laying hens and broilers providing the 3,500 inhabitants with fresh meat, milk, and eggs.

The surrounding shark-infested waters of the Pacific Ocean substituted for prison walls, incarcerating not only 1,800 convicted criminals, but also hundreds of family members and prison staff. The omnipresent paradox of blue waters and sky for prison bars was not lost on even the most casual visitor to the open prison island. Long-term inmates confess how this island paradise quickly becomes an extramural penitentiary when the reality sinks in that they've lost their freedom to leave at will, making the concept of a "colony" an illusion, a false front for a traditional Mexican community. It soon becomes its own island country, one with impassible borders. *Island* to them was another word for isolation—out of reach, out of touch, and out of luck.

But Father Angelino harbored no pathos for the convicts, given the harsh, oppressive alternatives of incarceration elsewhere in the overcrowded Mexican penal system. The sight of a *Tres Marias Madre* inmate swinging in a hammock under two palm trees swayed by a light ocean breeze was hardly doing hard time, he felt. Alcatraz it was not, he thought, but Club Fed it was for many inmates who were raised in crime-ridden urban barrios or impoverished rural villages.

Tres Marias Madre provided a sanctuary for many of the penal population. It was to be a new safe haven for recently admitted prisoner 50807507, Olivel Morales de Gutierrez, or so he was led to believe. Like most inmates, he would work four hours a day on an assigned job, tend to his own small garden midday, and fish from the seashore in the afternoon, cooking his catch, if any, in his camp's cafeteria that evening. Not a bad life for a convicted felon and killer, Father Angelino resented. To find convict Morales was his primary purpose for coming to *Tres Marias Madre*. He would "have to get into his loop," was the expression Lori had used, not quite the secular lingo he was accustomed to. And he must do it within twenty-four hours without arousing suspicions of the inmates or the prison staff.

Most of the island inmates had never seen the ocean before and now saw nothing but ocean in 360 degrees, 365 days a year. Father Angelino believed that its novelty and beauty would soon seduce Olivel, drawing him to the shore at every opportunity. The Father's first challenge was to find out when and where to isolate him and initiate the first phase of their mission they coined as *Padre Madre*, which he had accepted with a bemused attitude.

Beyond the marine patrol boats constantly circling the island, the inmates would delight at the sight of passing pleasure boats, fishing vessels, and commercial freighters, the sight of freedom on the move, evoking emotions of envy they all learned to temper with the reality of being island locked by the inescapable world of water, water everywhere. Their visual world ended where the sea's horizon met the sky. This was a constant, creating a cage of water and air that could become suffocating to those who came from a world of cars, commerce, cantinas, and the criminal stimulus, which consumed their daily lives. Boredom could be a cruel punishment for those criminally active individuals, the drudgery of sameness driving them to desperate measures for change. "Each day is like a year, a year whose days are long," the Father had recalled the words of writer Oscar Wilde describing imprisoned convicts.

The boat patrol marines weren't concerned with prisoners swimming out to sea, which would be suicidal, but rather with surreptitious boat landings to help prisoners escape. There had been only one recorded attempted escape, which resulted in all the occupants aboard the fleeing boat drowning and consumed by sharks. The next day, a commercial fisherman from *La Paz* reported eviscerating a large blue shark and discovering a man's upper torso. It had seventeen high-caliber bullet entry and exit holes in it. There has been no escape attempts reported since then.

Lori's aerial photos of the island that Father Angelino had committed to memory were coming into focus as his transport supply boat neared the *Tres Maria Madre* dock. A quick reorientation of the penal colony would be critical in accomplishing his mission in the brief twenty-four-hour time frame. Success depended on his being in control of his agenda, a difficult task for any visiting priest in normal circumstances. The warden, colony chaplain, and needy inmates would all be competing for his limited time. He would have to diplomatically remind them that he was not on a mission of mercy or spiritual counseling. He was there in the name of His Holiness Cardinal Montenegro to assess the progress of the *Tres Marias Madre* penitentiary experiment. It could not exist without the church's spiritual, moral, and material support. He knew that Warden Trujillo had no choice but to accommodate his wishes for unlimited coverage of the facilities and private access to the prisoners. His biggest challenge would be to perform his one indispensable task unobserved in a fishbowl community by any suspecting eyes among the on shore and off shore patrol and prison staff.

Father Angelino did not recognize any of those among the small welcoming group gathered on the long, gray, wooden pier. Rope lines were tossed to four waiting inmates who quickly secured the drifting ship to the thick wooden moors. Respecting the reverent Father's status, the other few passengers stood aside for him to disembark first followed by a young crewman carrying his two-piece luggage. A portly, full faced, mustached man in his fifties removed his white straw hat to say, "Welcome to *Tres Marias Madre, Padre*," appearing embarrassed by his unintended rhyme. "I am Federal Warden Gustavo Trujillo, and this is Deputy Warden Señor Pedro Negrete at your Reverend's service." The deputy, a shorter, younger version of the warden, smiled and introduced the Father to the senior colony chaplain, Father Ignacio. He appeared to be straight out of a monastery, complete with the sunburned bald crown and monk's head of evenly cropped reddish hair, round florid face, and a wide girth. His dark leather sandals deviated from his requisite black priest vestment, providing his only relief from the hot Pacific sun.

"Was your journey a comfortable one, Father?" the chaplain asked with sincerity.

"For the most part, yes, only a brief patch of choppy water, but nothing to make me reach for my rosary," he replied, drawing laughter from the welcoming trio.

The warden motioned to a waiting inmate to take the luggage from the crewman and proceed back to the pier entrance where two armed marine guards were standing sentry and four unarmed marines stood ready to inspect all persons entering the island penitentiary, much like a customs checkpoint. The warden whistled loudly at the inspecting marines, pointed to the Father's approaching luggage with a permissive gesture, allowing the porter to pass freely.

Father Angelino felt a silent sigh of relief. The first hurdle had been cleared. They stepped on land by the prison's main guardhouse, a thick concrete structure that looked like an office building with an air conditioner window unit humming loudly on the ocean side and the metal door main entrance inland. From its size, he estimated occupancy of twenty-five to thirty guards, his first mental intel note.

The warden stopped, halting all others to say, "If you wish, Father Ignacio can accompany you to your room next to the chapel where I'm sure you'll want to freshen up, Father. Then please join Señor Negrete and me in my office at your leisure. May we serve you anything before lunch? Coffee or tea, perhaps?"

"Green tea would be great if you have it," he said, not wanting to admit to a slight queasiness in his stomach from the boat trip and uneasiness with what he must set out to do. He knew he was out of his element serving as a neophyte, covert operative for a group of seasoned professionals. It was not for lack of courage but rather fear of the unknown, especially how he would react with the killer Olivel.

"For a small island colony, Father, you'd be surprised at what we do have," the warden boasted. From what Father Angelino had observed of his ship's plenitude of supplies and the warden's ample waist, he was not surprised.

Rising inland from the pier, Father Angelino made his second mental intel note, a forty-foot radio antenna tower with microwave dishes attached near the top. That probably meant that the foot patrolmen had walkie-talkies, which were absent eight years earlier, he recalled. The four roving patrol boats were in constant radio contact with each other and with the main guardhouse. He needed to know their nighttime routine, shift changes, number of patrolling guards, their routes and frequency, plus the stationary guard posts. There was no time better than the present, he thought, stopping next to the guardhouse.

"Do those antennae dishes mean I can call the mainland on my cell phone, warden?"

"I'm afraid not, Father. They unfortunately serve only our dedicated network of colony radio walkie-talkies for the security and

staff. You're most welcome to use the navy radio to call if you wish."
He gestured to the guardhouse. His third intel note was memorized.

"Thanks. Maybe tomorrow. Speaking of the navy, the church does not want to ignore our fine servicemen here who work at sea in harm's way. With your permission, warden, I would like to board the patrol boats when they're in dock to provide a special blessing upon the crew and the vessels." He spoke with genuine interest for the marines' well-being.

"*Claro que si, Padre* (Of course, Father). They will be honored, I'm sure. They indeed feel neglected at times. Señor Negrete will arrange for all the boats to dock here together in the interest of your valuable time."

Looking down sternly at his subordinate, the warden gave the military style order, "Tell *Comandante* Maldonado to muster all of his off-duty crew and the duty boats at the pier at 1700. Parade dress is not required. And do specify why, so they will honor our reverend Father's visit with reverence," he added evenly.

"*En seguida, señor.* (Right away sir.)" The obedient deputy left directly to the naval commander's headquarters alongside the main guardhouse. Father Angelino took intel note number 4, observing the route and approximate time taken for Negrete to arrive at the commander's office.

"Will it be ceremonial in nature, Father?" he asked out of concern for the length of time the boats would be off patrol.

"No, no, not at all. Just long enough to place a holy medallion of the Patron Saint Michael in the cabin of each boat with a special blessing for their crews," he said, knowing the briefer, the better for the expedience of his mission, but long enough not to create an impression of insincerity.

"Continuing their walk along a wide dirt path to the colony headquarters, Father Angelino remembered the scene as before, similar to most small, humble, rural Mexican villages, minus the towering church. All of the buildings were white, one-story concrete edifices with plain wooden doors and window shutters painted either a pale green, blue, or light burgundy. The entire community was immaculate, cared for by the inmates whom were called interns, or colonists.

They could be seen during the daytime by the hundreds, including children, dressed as ordinary mainland citizens with no distinguishing prison uniforms, moving about freely. The foot patrolmen, however, stood out in their short sleeve, blue denim shirts and white cotton pants, crowned by the distinguished bumblebee yellow with black trim cap they were obliged to wear, day and night, easily identifiable from a distance, like a bobblehead beacon.

The interns had no choice but to perform their duties of building maintenance and grooming of the expansive, well-manicured colony landscape. Knowing the island's early 1900s prison history of savage torture and a life of hard labor, no inmate today would dare complain of being condemned to prison duties six days a week. Most were no more than four hours of simple chores before recreational time or attending to their hobby crafts, which they could sell to the general island population. No wonder the joke among outside visitors who knew about the liberal, leisurely lifestyle of the TMM prison was, *I would kill to get in there*, Father Angelino recalled as he and Father Ignacio continued on their way to his guest room.

The so-called chapel was actually a small church that was not built by the church. It was unadorned, absent the ornate trimmings the Father was accustomed to seeing on the baroque Italian churches. To his ecclesiastic eyes, this pale-white, linear structure was undressed, left bare-naked by its builders who were dependent solely upon meager government funds for its bare essentials: four walls, a flat roof, charcoal-gray concrete floor, and straight back, hard wood pews. The government wanted to save money, the Catholic Church wanted to save souls, and the inmates had a place to ostensibly pray for forgiveness, Father Angelino concluded.

His Spartan guest room was just another clerical bedroom, identical to the bedrooms occupied by the three other chaplains and two nuns assigned to the colony. Father Angelino was introduced to all five church members waiting patiently outside of his room entrance, wardrobed in their *de rigueur* vestments, welcoming him with genial smiles and a multicolored bouquet of island wild flowers. After their warm greeting and small talk, he asked them to all wait one moment while he entered his room. His two matching pieces of leather luggage were atop his single mattress bed. The largest one he opened with a small key, displaying three dozen leather-covered Bibles, thirty black and six white bound with gold leaf lettering. He returned to the room entrance where he unceremoniously presented the chaplains and nuns each with a white Bible, eliciting a heavenly chorus of "*Que Dios que vendiga, Padre* (God Bless you, Father)." When they were told that the Bibles came from the Vatican and blessed by the Pope, their eyes sparkled with delight, all automatically pressing their lips to their respective books as though it were a commonly practiced veneration, followed by more, "*Que Dios que vendiga, Padre.*"

All but Father Ignacio said their temporary goodbyes. He entered the guest room on the invitation of Father Angelino, who closed the door behind him. "My time here is limited, so I need your assistance, Father Ignacio, in procuring some important information that will help me expedite my agenda and meet my ordered objectives. You do have open access to prisoner rosters and files, correct?" he asked with hopeful certainty.

"Yes, unrestricted. It's necessary for determining how to best counsel each inmate in our rehabilitation efforts."

"As I thought. Good. Then please locate the following category of inmates for my visits today. An older male with spouse who has been here for eight years or longer, as well as a single male, same duration. Then identify all single males who have transferred here from other penitentiaries in the last two months, regardless of criminal backgrounds. I need to make institutional comparisons and assess any progress thus far," he requested with an air of clinical forethought.

"Easy enough. I can have it within the half hour. Shall I bring it here?"

"It's best that you give it to me at Warden Trujillo's office. I'll be in a meeting with him, so please wait for me there. And, Father, gather the information discreetly. I don't want the warden's office to influence or manipulate my movements here. I must maintain an objective posture in my assessment approach," he concluded with authority in his tone.

Now alone in his guest room, Father Angelino removed his shirt and Roman collar. He unlocked his second suitcase to remove a fresh, folded black shirt, which he meticulously buttoned down his long torso. He was particularly careful about the concealment of a thin wire running from the inside third top button down to below the pants' midsection. From there it appended to a miniature electronic device the size of a thin matchbook in his left front pocket with no visible protuberance. He then draped his silver, two-inch high Christian cross and chain around his neck, measured to drop precisely beneath the third button from the shirt top. Above that he attached a fresh white Roman collar. He checked his appearance carefully in the rectangular mirror above the bathroom sink. Certain that the cross would not obstruct the third button, he turned to leave, hesitated haltingly, and then, as though haunted by what he had seen, rotated back before the mirror.

He realized that he did not recognize the priest in the mirror, only the furtive reflection of a self-recruited spy on a self-imposed mission of espionage. He stared suspiciously at the unrecognizable priest with questions about the new person inside. Was this newly discovered rectitude and fortitude he possessed enough to succeed as the persona he needed to be, a fervid secret agent for the truth? Would his God recognize him now for the truth seeker he had chosen to be, or rather as an impious priest and apostate servant? Was not then the man in the mirror simply masquerading as God's servant? "He is the truth," he had been taught. That belief is all he had left to embrace and sustain him as the facade he knew he was, for right or wrong. He was committed to his cause and prayed God would forgive him, for only He could judge him in the end, not the church, and not his pernicious government.

The anguished image in the mirror was now perspiring and breathing rapidly.

Father Angelino quickly turned on the basin faucet to splash cold water on his flushed face to arrest his introspection. He must focus on his new reality, he told himself repeatedly, as he continued to put cool water over his warm head and pothered mind. He must focus on his new world where "espionage is the world of deception." Its cardinal tenet was to deceive others as they have deceived you, a primal law of the jungle, he reasoned. It was his new survival guide to ground him to the corrupt, real world around him.

"You are no longer in Vatican City, Toto," Mattie would lightly remind him. He toweled himself off and breathed deeply. Touching the third top button one last time, he whispered to himself, "This will be my 'Eye of God' to help others see the truth." With his insecurities now subsided and respiration normal, he calmly set out for the prison headquarters five minutes away. His primary imperative reenergized him: to seek the truth.

A medium height, heavyset woman of light tan complexion and a tightly wound, black hairdo bun atop her head introduced herself warmly as *Señora Trujillo*, the wife and secretary of the warden. She graciously handed him a hot cup of green tea in a surprisingly elegant porcelain cup and saucer.

"The warden asked that I bring you to his office, Father, if you'd please follow me. She led him down a short, well-lit hallway exhibiting a gallery of matted, colored photographs of four lookalike navy patrol boats, a subtle reminder to all who entered that the Mexican Marines surrounded them. A passing glance at their names captioned beneath each boat told him that they were all Cape-class United States patrol boats. They were hand-me-downs from the US Coast Guard in the name of foreign aid. Only Cape Hatteras was a familiar name to him. Capes Hedge, Carter, and Newagen were completely unknown place names.

With *Señora Trujillo's* back to him, he broke his stride momentarily to turn and square his shoulders to the Cape Newagen patrol boat photo, just as Lori had taught him. His left hand entered and exited his pant pocket deftly. He then resumed his normal gate.

The warden's office was large but plain, without any sense of aesthetics, not even a simple plant or artifact. The photographs and maps on the walls had no frames, held firm by only cardboard matting and tacks. His wide, gray metal desk was centered in front of the broad, multipaned glass window with a view of the pier and ocean beyond. The Mexican and navy flags stood in the opposite corners of the rectangular room with two ceiling fans gently circulating above. Rising from one of the four metal armchairs in front of the desk was the island's navy commander, *Comandante* Jorge Maldonado. He looked every inch of his slender six-foot frame the visage of a career naval officer in his pressed khaki uniform adorned with the brass maritime insignias and bars on the starched collar and shoulder epilates. His narrow tan face was framed with sufficient graying in his well-groomed black hair to exude the maturity of his senior rank. His spit polished black shoes came to a perfect parallel formation as he stood erect as a ruler to greet Father Angelino. He gave an abbreviated bow and firm right hand salutation welcoming the visiting priest to his ocean island, as he described his military jurisdiction, proud to be a territorial military man. *Any port in a storm*, Angelino sarcastically thought to himself, *even if it's an island prison colony.*

"*Comandante* Maldonado is here at my request, Father, to accommodate your kind offer to bless his crew and boats."

"Welcome, Father. My men will appreciate the special recognition, especially while living among a criminal population," he stated primly.

"*Cuando el sol sale, para todos sale* (When the sun rises, it rises for everyone)," the Father countered, diplomatically refusing to accept the arrogant officer's pejorative class distinction.

"But of course, Father. I only meant that your special attention to them is that, special," he apologized.

"I understand—and my apologies for such short notice for such a ceremony. But I brought something very special from my stay at the Vatican in Rome for this occasion," he announced joyously. With the simple sound of *Vatican*, the facial expressions of interest brightened demonstrably, as though being told they had won the national lottery. Anything from Vatican City, Rome, was indeed heaven-sent in the eyes of a Roman Catholic.

"You are most gracious, Father. The men will be most grateful, and at your service for anything you request," he offered with a solicitous gesture of his wide, outstretched arms expressing universal possibilities.

Father Angelino had rehearsed his questions in his head earlier so as to appear innocent and spontaneous. The complete and correct answers were critical for his reconnaissance of the island and pending *Operation A Tu Madre* to succeed.

"Well I do trust that this special occasion does not disrupt your patrol regimen too much and put your island security at risk, *Comandante.*"

"Not at all. The daytime is low risk and the boats rotate into the docks throughout the day."

"Maybe you could explain it better on the wall map, *Comandante,*" the warden gestured toward the near sidewall.

Moving to the right side of the large, rectangular map of the penal colony, the commander drew a silver pen from his shirt pocket and laid its point on the western, center side of the island's coast. He spoke as though lecturing to a war college of cadets. "*Tres Marias Madre* is twenty-six miles in circumference with a longitudinal ocean orientation of a perfect compass, the two ends of the oval island pointing due north and south. We are here, dead center on the eastern shore facing the Mexico mainland with the opposite western shore on the *Baja* Peninsula side, but facing nothing but open ocean." Continuing, he pressed his pen repeatedly on the same spot on the eastern shore port.

"It's best to think of the island as a clock which we do for patrol circulation planning. The port headquarters here sits at three o'clock on the center eastern point, six o'clock is on the center southern point, nine o'clock at the center western point, and the northern center point being on the twelve o'clock mark. Is that clear so far, Father?" He lowered his pen to his side.

He wanted to respond that for his intel notes, it couldn't be more clear, but replied instead courteously in the affirmative.

"The marine patrol boats' normal stations are at the six, nine, and twelve o'clock positions, rotating clockwise every two hours, ninety degrees until eventually into the three o'clock home port. Here they'll sit off shore for one hour, and then one hour dock side for cleaning, resupplying, refueling, and crew change."

"So crews are on their boats for eight-hour shifts," the warden interposed.

"Warden Trujillo is the expert here on the passage of time," the commander rejoined jovially to the light laughter of the others.

"And this is twenty-four hours a day, every day?" the Father asked innocently.

"Every day. Years ago, before high fuel costs and budget reductions, the boats circulated the island continuously."

"So then you need fresh eyes three times a day. That makes for a high number of sailors and marines, yes?" he probed, hoping for more precise information.

"There are always 24 crew at sea, 12 standing port side, and 30 at the ready in the quartermaster armory. That's per eight-hour shift. With officers, we will muster two full shifts totaling 155 men in attendance for your blessing, Father. The other 85 men will be resting in barracks."

"The blessing will certainly go out to them as well, Commander," he said sincerely.

"Thank you, Father. I'll be sure to tell them so. And so that you have the names of the four patrol boats you'll be blessing, here is a printed list ahead of time." He handed a half sheet of paper to Father Angelino. He looked down briefly to see that the Mexican Navy had renamed them with their own country cape names of *Cabo Catoche, Cabo Corzo, Cabo Corrientes*, and *Cabo Cruz*. He folded the paper and put it in his left pant pocket, squared himself directly before the wall map before withdrawing his hand.

"With your permission, Father, warden, I have my duties to perform so will say goodbye until this afternoon," the officer said formally with a firm, short stroke hand shake, and then turned to leave.

Warden Trujillo observed aloud that it was noontime, and then pressed his desk intercom to summon Deputy Negrete and Father Ignacio into the office to discuss Father Angelino's agenda and needs for his colony visit. It was agreed upon that Deputy Negrete's electric cart be put at the Father's disposal for his free-range tour of the sprawling colony. The warden had recalled the Father's mailed written statement that, "Spontaneous, unexpected visits to the various facilities seem the best plan for an objective assessment of the penal operations." A priest's integrity under any circumstances was beyond reproach, the warden knew. But a priest's visit under the sealed orders of a church cardinal was accommodated with the equivalence of granting "keys to the kingdom," without question, without challenge. The church was an indispensable partner in the national penitentiary system's rehabilitation program, a central player in its success or failure.

The three colonists all provided guidance to the Father where needed. He was supplied with a colony map showing the location of all the buildings and pathways, a schedule of the various classes, workhouse productions, and organized recreation. The most valuable item was his requested file copies of recent transferred prisoners and inmate resident location roster, updated daily according to a parenthetical notation. Deputy Negrete handed the Father a walkie-talkie and his keys to the electric cart with the warden's advice to stay clear of the land's abrupt edge.

"Thank you, gentlemen, for your kind assistance. Father Ignacio, I will pick you up at the chapel before going down to the dock. For lunch and dinner, I will be joining Warden Trujillo," he exclaimed preemptively to prevent any intrusions upon his late hour plans. The Father and warden were left alone in the office standing once again by the island wall map.

"I have one more question about the sea patrols that is only appropriate to ask you warden, out of sheer curiosity with no dispersions cast upon your fine military, I can assure you. But what's to prevent a patrol crew from aiding in the escape of a very rich and generous prisoner?" he propounded. "*Tres Marias Madre* is still Mexico, and such are the ways of our well-connected, wealthy criminals and corrupt country. Look at *San Pedro* Prison, ruled by the incarcerated drug cartel kingpins and narco-terrorists. And you know of the others, I'm sure." He was careful not to augury beyond the hypothetical, but enough said for the warden to envisage such a possibility. He had caught the warden off guard, taken aback by such a sinister suggestion, yet not taken as a personal effrontery when framed in the hypothetical.

Father Angelino saw the surprised expression on his host's full face as he unconsciously stroked his thick mustache. He had succeeded in planting the seeds of probability and doubt and let the warden's professional paranoia of prison breaks cultivate such an idea, no matter how remote. If a simple, God-fearing priest could conjure up such a nefarious plot, then so might an underpaid boat captain and crew, the warden would now ponder.

He regained his momentary loss of composure, but clearly still off balance in his present thought process. "Everything and anything is possible, at least that is what we are trained to think. Although we can't plan for every contingency, we do have an active system of testing the integrity of all staff involved in prison security. But then again, anybody could be susceptible to greed and corruption. As you said, Father, this is Mexico," he summed up his response awkwardly, unable to disguise his undertones of insecurity. Father Angelino had efficaciously rung the bell of suspicion, and it could never be unrung.

With the exception of a half dozen inmate trustees cleaning the tables and the same number in the kitchen, the two-hundred-seat cafeteria was almost completely occupied by the prison staff, marines, and patrolmen. Father Angelino sat at the white ceramic top table reserved for the warden, whose special seat was near an exit door, a tactical position of a well-planned emergency exit strategy, the Father sensed. As his guest, the Father sat to his right providing him with the view he needed to observe. They were immediately approached by two trustee waiters carrying what was described as a cold pitcher of virgin *piña colada*, made from fresh, island-grown pineapples and coconuts.

The warden had downed an entire goblet of the chilled fruit drink before the Father had finished his prayerful blessing of their meal, followed by the warden's irreverent amen, a loud, deep belch.

A small plate with a steaming hot *quesadilla* of chopped shrimp enveloped with *queso manchego* inside two corn tortillas, and a side *salsa* of diced mango, pineapple, onion, tomato, and cilantro was centered in front of each diner as their *primero plato* (first plate). Two large platters soon followed. The long, oval one displayed a grilled, whole red snapper with a green olive replacing its eye, and lightly bathed in a tangy sauce of orange juice, crushed garlic, *crème fraiche*, and grated onion. The round, second platter was filled to the edge with a molded, circular mound of *arroz verde con rajas,* green rice with chili *poblano* strips in the open center. The rice was enriched with cooked, blended spinach and parsley, giving it its color namesake. Father Angelino ate sparingly, politely declining a serving of *flan*, caramelized custard for dessert, offering his to the warden who didn't think twice in devouring it, followed by his own generous portion.

While the warden continued to guttle everything put before him, the Father observed that the other cafeteria diners had gone through a serving line where they were given fixed plated portions of a limited yet balanced offering of food placed on a tray. They received a less exotic beverage than what he had the luxury of drinking. Position and power had its privileges in all institutions, he reflected.

"That was a delicious and satisfying lunch, warden. Far better than what I've experienced at any other penitentiary. Do your other colony camp cafeterias enjoy the same menu as your staff dining hall?" he queried without appearing critical.

"Yes, absolutely, no favoritism among the colonists, I assure you. As our special guest, we did want to pay our respect with something a little more sumptuous. I'm glad you enjoyed it, Father. We are constantly mindful of our limited budget and try hard to be self-sufficient in many areas of local food production. But even there, we are limited to the land restrictions, fresh water supply, and of course the dry, tropical growing seasons," he stated with a resigned tone. "But I'm certain you've seen worse during your other prison visits, Father."

"Most definitely. Some more severe than others, but all money-related, not enough of it to go around. And the church can only do so much within our budgetary limitations." Father Angelino was well aware of the growing demands on the church ranging from the smallest of rural parishes to the Mexican government's pressure on them to provide more prison personnel and social services. "My tour of the penitentiaries will help us better evaluate the greater needs for the greater good," he offered as encouragement. Hearing his own words caused him pause knowing fair well that his only evaluation of *Tres Marias Madre* to be that of the double Os of OODA, to "observe and orient," for the greater needs and greater good of the future mission *A Tu Madre*. One less prisoner at TMM wasn't much of a budget reduction, he mused, but it was a start.

"Then you must already know, Father, that our cost per inmate here is three times the national average because of the obvious, supplying an isolated island population that includes families, and a small fleet of boats with an around-the-clock crew. So unfortunately, the government's focus on us is three times more intense than on the other prisons."

"In what sense?" he attempted to get to the warden's point.

"The federal budget is historically lean. The leaner it is, the meaner they become with their appropriations. Forgive my crudeness, Father, but Mexico's incarcerated population will always 'suck hind tit.' In time, it won't even be on the tit!" He leaned back in his chair with a heavy sigh.

Probing deeper to verify what he already knew, the Father asked candidly, "You're saying that they are going to close the island?"

"I see that my fellow wardens were reluctant to divulge what they've known for some time, the off-the-record, unofficial order from above to slash costs by cutting prisoners loose prematurely and permanently," he declared vaguely.

Finally the truth, he thought, the definitive word direct from a federal warden's mouth. It reminded him of the adage, "There are secrets, and then there are secrets." He knew that this was not merely a secret of convenience, but one of enormous gravity as far as national security was concerned, negative political consequence notwithstanding. But why then, he wondered, was a warden of a remote medium security prison taking such a risk in sharing the secret with him. And just as curious, what was in it for the warden, aware of how the corrupt Mexican justice system worked? With his elbows on the table and his hands twining, Angelino raised three fingers.

"Three questions immediately come to mind, Warden Trujillo. How high up when you say, 'from above'? For how long when you say, 'for some time'? And 'premature release' I understand, but not 'cut loose permanently.' I will appreciate your shared confidence even more if it comes with complete and honest candor." He addressed him with as much official attitude his pastoral position might allow under the circumstances.

"That certainly is my intent, Father, believe me. Here is what I know to be fact. One, 'from above,' there is no one higher. Two, for over five years now with incremental numbers of released inmates each year. Three, 'permanently' means released with no possibility of recidivism within the Mexican penal system at any level." He paused for effect, continuing when he saw the Father demonstrably puzzled by the latter, as though presented with a riddle. "In truth, the 'releasesees' can't possibly reenter the Mexican penal population if they are no longer in Mexico, Father."

Father Angelino's squared posture dissolved down into his chair with losses of breath and words. The warden watchfully kept his silence while his stunned guest processed the dismaying revelation with an expression of disbelief he fought to conceal, but shock would not permit. The pontifical documents he had discovered in Vatican City said as much in terms of the Holy See's *Christus Dominus 9* seal of approval blessing such a plan, should the Mexican government choose to pursue it. They knew that officially they could not and would not, so sided with the subterfuge promoted by the one powerful official of authority Father Angelino and Mattie had their sights on.

"The United States? Mexican prisoners are secretly being released into the United States on an organized massive scale?" he asked with pronounced incredulity in his voice as he struggled to regain his composure. His discovery in Rome that a few preselected Mexican criminals had been released from prison and later shepherd into the US under the consociate protection of the Mexican government, and church was one of the root causes of his doctrinal differences with the Holy See. He never presumed that it was a portent to what he had just learned from the warden. In Rome and now, he could not condone the church's ultraliberal policy of "Pastoral Care of Migrants and Itinerant People" as it related to the United States because of the Holy See's ulterior motives. But when he saw that they added the criminal element to the connivance, the papal policy became unsupportable, "a blatant moral transgression of United States sovereignty and attenuated national creed," he had concluded. *The shared border with the US had become a moral divide*, he lamented.

Why was he so surprised? he inwardly questioned himself. It was Mexico's four-hundred-year long, historical continuum of an iniquity, as he saw it, since when the Catholic Church had also been an instrument of Spain's colonialism in Mexico against the native sovereignty of the indigenous civilizations and their *mestizo* sons and daughters. That's where the church's future for growth and secular prosperity incubated hundreds of years earlier. Now he saw the church's twenty-first-century primacy was with the current generation of Mexicans migrating to the New Spain in the United States of America for the same reasons. "Roman Catholic colonialism," Father Angelino had always labeled it, yet under the papal guise of simply being "*amicus humani generis* (friend of the human race)."

"Yes, released throughout the United States," the warden continued. "The first three years were an experiment, cherry-picking from a mixture of inmates, from model prisoners to hardened killers ready and able to cross into the United States. Their willingness is not an option, a nonnegotiable condition of premature freedom, take it when offered or leave it and serve your remaining five, ten, fifteen, or more years in the overcrowded, high-risk, squalid conditions of our antiquated Mexican prisons. The acceptance rate is over 95 percent. If the guards knew the truth about these releases, they'd want in on the offer," the warden speculated with a confident smirk.

"If it's secretly sanctioned by the government, then who have they entrusted to conduct the outside movement of all these prisoners?" the Father probed.

"A select, clandestine group of *Federales*. They have their own exclusive network of *coyotes* who handle the transborder crossings. They're paid on a per-head into the US bases," he said with a sense of satisfaction.

Father Angelino knew he had to think fast, realizing at that hour he wouldn't have his new official informant's attention much longer. He needed in-depth answers to broad questions on government and church involvement in this monumental and unprecedented scheme. And more immediate was how this might affect the *A Tu Madre* mission.

"During this five-year period, how many 'releasesees' have crossed into the US?" he asked, trying not to sound indignant at such a bold and outrageously illegal international transgression.

"Only a few hundred because it's been experimental in nature to test the network, the methods, and the best border crossings. With around five thousand ordinary Mexican citizens entering the US illegally every day, the inmate numbers are imperceptible, homogenous among the masses, and will continue to be even when they're increased," he added casually.

"Increased? To how many?" he asked in a controlled monotone, not wanting to expose his outrage.

"Per year, I'd say twenty thousand," the warden stated plainly without noticing the crimson red tone on the gaped-mouth face of the overwhelmed priest who was pulling at his Roman collar to fight for air as he suddenly felt faint. "The objective is to reduce the existing Mexican prison population by 50 percent over the next ten years, realizing of course there will always be the normal flow of newly incarcerated criminals every day," he said dispassionately.

Repressing his rising ire, Father Angelino took a prolonged sip of water, a deep breath, and then with a forced smile said, "I'm familiar with the prison demographics, Warden Trujillo. You're talking two hundred thousand prisoners over ten years. How is that possible and why so many?"

"Because the US government makes it possible. They lack a realistic and effective border control policy and adequate policing. We have two thousand miles of common border that's like a sieve hit by a shotgun. American industry wants super cheap labor, so they lobby their politicians to do nothing to stop or slow the flow of *illegals*. The politicians' wives enjoy their cheap, illegal immigrant nannies, maids, cooks, and gardeners, so there's no pressure there," he exclaimed with a victorious voice.

"But, warden, we both know that the recalcitrant, incorrigible career criminals without any social or work skills will be repeat offenders over there as well as here, right?" he stated pointedly.

"Right. But as you say, 'over there.' If caught and convicted, they'll populate an American federal or state prison where there's an ample budget to house and care for them, *a su gusto* (to their liking). And remember, they've entered the US *sin documentos* (without documents), without any legal papers, which means no criminal record."

"And without an existing prisoner exchange program between the two countries, I suppose that Mexico won't be asked to take the bad boys back, correct?" The prison demographics the Father really wanted to share with him was the fact that there were presently over thirty thousand Mexicans in US federal and state penitentiaries and jails, 50 percent of them illegal aliens. But then, why would he care, it's "over there," the Father conceded disdainfully.

"Oh, they can ask, but Mexico isn't obligated by any treaty to do so. Besides, the US is expanding their penitentiaries every year. Mexico has no capital budget to build or upgrade our prisons here, certainly no need to if we lighten the load of the existing ones. And the big bonus will come with less prison population support expenses, translating into more money here for prison improvements over time."

The correct translation Father Angelino knew to mean, more money for Warden Trujillo and all of the other scheming government officials. In essence, the United States will unknowingly subsidize the Mexican penal system by serving as their surrogate wardens on US soil. The warden had said that the premature releases were thus far imperceptible, a few hundred over five years. No statistical red flag flying there for Mattie and her staff to have been alerted by. And her national inmate database had no way of tracking the "releasesees" once they're on the outside, absent a probation system of follow-up. Once out of the prison gate, the criminals were off the system's radar screen. Only local police intelligence could track the bad guys unless, of course, they crossed the US border. He knew for certain that Mattie knew nothing of the gradual and measured movement of premature 'releasesees' into the US.

Suddenly anxiety enveloped him with a desperate need to communicate quickly with his sister. Her need to know was critical on many levels, the present mission notwithstanding. But their personal requited mission remained paramount in his mind. He could not pressure the warden further for fear of signaling an abnormal curiosity outside of his purview. He had to get on with his reconnaissance tasks and then get off the island quickly, he reasoned.

The warden's attention had been placed on an approaching tall, thin, and elderly man attired in nicely pressed casual sports clothes and polished brown leather shoes. A smile of approval on the warden's face signaled that the intruder to their private table was a "friendly."

This was verified by his introduction as the prison's head school master, Alberto Estino, referred to respectfully by the inmates and staff as Albert Einstein, he would learn later.

"Your office has informed me, Warden Trujillo, that we have the pleasure and honor of the Father's good company," Professor Estino exclaimed with a convivial smile.

"Thank you," the Father said humbly, still standing from the introduction. "The pleasure and honor are mine. Unfortunately, I'm limited on time, so I apologize in advance for its brevity, maestro," he said graciously.

"Brevity of time is a concept not readily understood by our inmates, but certainly wished for. If I can be of any service, Father, please ask," he offered with a sufficient bow of respect. The warden dismissed him with a pausing smile, and then drew his chair closer to the table. "What you would observe in Maestro Estino's class, if you attended one, are his English studies and United States orientation. It's our unofficial preparatory course for those early 'releasesees' soon to cross over the border, a primer for street survival during those critical first ten days on the other side," he stated in a worrisome whisper. "The 'releasesees' need to penetrate as deep into the States as possible for success from detection and deportation. That means safe houses and safe transportation throughout the US."

"And those are established now, I presume, with twelve million Mexicans illegally in the States?" he asked, wishing to reprove vehemently.

"Yes and no, Father. For our early release program to be successful at the increased numbers, we need more safe houses in place on both sides of the border, staging areas in Mexico and receiving stations on the American side, ten, twenty, up to one hundred miles into the interior of the country, for their first day of entry."

This the Father smelled coming. He was finally going to hear why he was being made an unwilling party, in part, to this scheme. The Father was already ashamedly aware of the church's duplicity in the transborder, illegal migration of ordinary Mexican citizens. His earlier pontifical council discoveries in Rome sadly had exposed their involved hands on both sides of the border. Its present success thus far was merely a trial platform for the real deal soon to come: the mass exodus of Mexican prison inmates into the United States, integrated into the American society for better or for worse. *God bless America,* Father Angelino thought. *God help America,* he prayed.

The Father's mind was mounting high and heavy with questions for the warden. So many, that to ask them all would seem like an interrogation of a crime suspect, which was how he now viewed his hypocritical host. He thought it prudent to cease with his probing questions on the pretext of time concerns. This he knew would give him some needed cover for not appearing unduly concerned about the warden's newly introduced criminal emigration scheme. He remembered well the historical accounts of the infamous Mariel Boatlift of 1980. Cuban dictator Fidel Castro allowed 124,000 Cubans to migrate to Florida, 25,000 with criminal records including 2,746 released prisoners as a "thumb in the eye" of the US government. That would soon pale by comparison to what the warden was forecasting, Father Angelino ventured.

Pointing to his watch, the Father declared, "In the interest of time and duty, warden, I best be on my way if I'm to accomplish all that I told you. If you care to tell me more of the inmate emigration plans over dinner, I'm always willing to listen. That's what we do best," he said smiling as he rose. For now, he needed to enter into Olivel's loop.

Father Angelino steered the electric cart onto the main pressed pebble pathway leading to the southern tip of *Maria Madre*. There he would find Olivel at his assigned workstation unaware of the pastoral visitor's arrival, which would soon place his fate in motion. The prison colony had not developed much beyond what he had recalled, clusters of private dwellings interspersed with camp cafeterias and diverse work stations, which supported the colonists' daily needs. Food production and processing was the largest user of the workforce. The incentive to work was simple. If you didn't, you didn't eat. The only real punishment dealt out was for the habitually misbehaved who were exiled to a remote, solitary sector of the island with no electricity or contact with fellow colonists, only weekly visits by the guards. His trip would be focused solely on special inmate number 50807507. So far he had not misbehaved. According to the freshly compiled file, he could be found working at the tannery. There inmates processed the hides taken from the newly slaughtered cattle raised on the island. They were then further processed for the making of sandals, shoes, belts, and jackets for the colonists.

Father Angelino parked the cart at the near entrance of the long, narrow, rectangular wooden building with plantation shutters opened wide from corner to corner for ventilation of the fetid odors from within. The strong stench of the raw hides and chemicals caused him to imagine an amalgamation of wet road kill, sewer methane, and his old, sweaty gym bag. He glanced one last time at Olivel Morales de Gutierrez's dark dossier and then set it back in the file behind his seat. A preview of two prison mug shots would not prepare the Father for what he was about to view in full frontal stature. A colony guard greeted the Father with a combined smile of surprise and pleasure, inviting him to enter the tannery, which he politely declined. He introduced himself as Carlos Pazaro, a middle-aged man with a wrinkled face beyond his years due to a chain-smoking habit. He puffed on a filter-free Camel cigarette in front of the priest without apology, exhaling like a fire dragon. The Father could understand his bad habit as a natural defense from the wretched smells of fresh animal blood, dehydrating skin, and chemically cooked hair, the repugnant byproducts of the crude tannery.

"Good afternoon, Father. Are you here for a tour?" the security officer offered cordially.

"Oh, thank you anyway. I understand the tannery process. I'm visiting various colonists today, nothing more," he replied.

"We have eight colonists working here, four on the morning shift, the same on the afternoon shift, four hours each. That's the most the nose can take. Anybody in particular or the whole group at once?" Pazaro inquired.

"For now I'm only meeting with the more recent arrivals to the colony. I was told you have one here, is that so?" asking innocently.

"We do. Olivel Morales. He's not what we would call a 'great conversationalist,' but he will tell you how he really feels," Pazaro forewarned.

"Nevertheless, my instructions are to visit newcomers. Could *Señor* Morales and I visit out here?" He pointed to a green picnic table shaded beneath two broad Canary palm trees.

"*Claro que si* (Of course you can). I'll bring him out. *Con permiso* (with your permission)," the guard responded, entering the tannery. Father Angelino anxiously awaited in the cool shade of the palms. He realized full well that the meeting with Olivel would be the defining moment of his mission, determining how to position this so-called target for extraction from a heavily guarded island prison. He took a deep breath and focused on what would be Olivel's LOOP.

The sound of the building screen door slamming shut caused him to look up at the approaching sight of the most terrifying image of a human being he had ever witnessed. A tall, white, shirtless, muscular man tattooed from below his chin down across his chest advanced toward him with scowling, obsidian eyes that didn't blink but stared straight through the Father like a laser beam. His head was hairless, resembling the radical Aryan gang members known as Skinheads. His file had noted his Mexican-American border background, son of a Tijuana prostitute and an unknown gringo client, explaining his size and light complexion.

Father Angelino thought better than to extend his hand out in greeting to this imposing creature. Instead, he forced a sincere smile, all the more difficult to do after observing the red tattoo words across his thick throat that read, "*Corte Aqui* (Cut Here)." There were three small, black teardrops tattooed beneath his left eye, his gang-earned medals for his three murders committed in the name of gang loyalty. A "Dove of Peace" imprinted over his right chest had a long, bloody dagger stabbed through it. His left breast had the illustration of a large red valentine shaped heart with the blue lettered words inside, "*No Hay* (There Isn't One)."

He did not see the definitive Mexican Mafia tattoos that would confirm his ID as the FTM fugitive Olivel Morales de Gutierrez. To get him to turn around, the Father called out to the guard standing by the tannery entrance. "*Señor* Pazaro! No need to stay. Please be more comfortable inside if you care to."

Not hearing a response, Olivel turned around ninety degrees to check out the guard's presence. In that brief moment, the identifying marks he needed came into plain view. A one-inch high blue "XIII" was tattooed on the back of his broad neck, signifying the thirteenth letter of the alphabet, *M*, pronounced in Spanish as *La Eme*, for the Mexican Mafia, his abandoned criminal gang from the California border territory. On his right shoulder blade was the black hand tattoo, *La Eme*'s official pat on the back of acceptance after having made his first gang initiation kill. The Father squared his shoulders and put his left hand in his pant pocket where it remained for a brief moment longer after Olivel faced the Father again.

The deep furrowed frown lines on Olivel's sweaty forehead appeared to be permanently tattooed on as well, as though he was forever angry. When he finally spoke, the Father's presumption seemed validated.

"If you're here to make me a fucking Christian, *Padre*, it ain't going to fucking happen! I ain't asken fucking forgiveness for nothing. So, you still want to speak with me?" Olivel asked in a harsh baritone.

Expecting the worse from this repellent human being, Father Angelino was not shocked by his intimidating rhetoric. His brutish persona was a different matter.

"No, my son. I'm not here with any message from the Lord. This is my second visit to the colony on behalf of the church to determine if our work here is well served, that's all," he said without breaking his benign smile.

"First off, I ain't nobody's fucking son. Second, what's your message if it ain't from your Lord?" he insisted with an uncompromising stare.

"I was hoping you would tell me, señor. What do you ask someone who's here to help you?" he posed while staring back.

An expression other than anger appeared on the big man's face, one of bewilderment with a smirk of skepticism. "What help can a poor priest give to a condemned man imprisoned on an island, unless you know how to fly a fucking helicopter," he rejoined with bitter sarcasm.

With a broadening smile, Father Angelino extemporized. "And if I could, where would you want me to fly you too?"

Olivel's blank eyes turned in the direction of the outer island toward the mainland of Mexico. After a pensive pause, he sat on the end of the table top. "There is no place I could go to," came his empty response.

"Then I see that I can help you. If you need to think about it some more, then we can talk later. For now our visit is finished. I'll return to this sector of the colony this evening to visit with others. I'll stop by your shelter then. Thank you for the visit, Señor Morales. *Hasta la proxima* (Until the next time)," Father Angelino concluded, turning and walking to the cart with the same smile he arrived with, feigned sincerity.

Olivel remained seated on the table wondering what had just happened, and all so quickly. And above all, he wondered what he was supposed to do about it. The Father knew, because it was his plan of calumny, and Olivel Morales was the unwitting player in it.

* * *

The Father kept a close watch on his passing time, aware that he had more ground to cover before returning to the docks for his blessing of the boats and crew. The island map the deputy warden had given him rested atop the steering wheel guiding him toward the southern edge of the island. He had not been that far south before taking mental notes as he neared Olivel's shelter. It was part of a nine-unit cluster of single bedroom apartments called shelters. He intentionally drove slowly past the cluster, assessing its layout and degree of difficulty for entry. He turned left to circumvent the cluster via the rear path forty feet beyond the individual gardens of each shelter. The ocean came into view mere eighty feet away. He stopped at the rear of the middle shelter, where an elderly man had exited to wave down the Father.

"*Que milagro. Un Padre perdido en el paraiso de prisoneros!* (What miracles! A priest lost in prisoner's paradise!)" he shouted excitedly to the sky as though addressing the heavenly angels.

"*Muy buenas tardes, señor* (A very good afternoon, sir). I'm orientating myself to the area during daylight so that I can return safely this evening to visit. What is your name, sir?" the Father asked courteously while he stepped from his cart.

"*Me llamo Emanuel Encarnación, pero todos me conocen como, Abuelito. A su orden Padre.* (They call me Grandpa, at your service, Father.)" He bowed his head respectfully.

"Do you live here, Emanuel?"

"Yes, Father. In the center shelter, which means I'm the group proctor looking out for the others alongside me," he announced proudly, standing erect to demonstrate his communal stature. He was in his sixties with thinning white hair. His slender sun-bronzed body struggled to hold up his cut-off beige shorts. His oversized *huaraches* could be compared to clown shoes without the humor.

"I'm in a bit of a rush for now but would like to visit with you and a new colonist named Olivel Morales de Gutierrez. Can you please point out his shelter for me?"

"*Con gusto* (With pleasure). It's the last one on the end because he's the latest arrival here, and probably will be the last one to ever leave," he stated unsympathetically.

"Thanks, Emanuel. Until this evening then." He waved politely as he sat back in the cart. He casually steered the cart down the path deliberately to where Olivel's small garden ended. Stepping to the left side of the path, he took measured strides to the land's end. The sea cliff dropped sharply thirty feet to a narrow pebble beach below. He studied the terrain for notable landmarks, which might be visible from the sea. To his disappointment, it all looked the same for hundreds of feet to the east and west. Nothing stood out that could be seen by even the most observant sailor in a crow's nest, he speculated. He looked back at the off-white, one-story cluster shelters and realized that they, too, would be impossible to see from sea level. His concern grew as he recalled the word Lori used to describe this phase of his recon mission as *crucial*.

Father Angelino noticed the old man still standing outside staring at him. He now wondered what he wondered and suddenly felt his time at the bluff to seem conspicuous. He had to hurry and find

STEPHEN M. RINGLER

some landmark soon before becoming completely suspicious in the eyes of an old convict.

The Father directed his attention to the long shoreline. It was a narrow band of sameness, small, smooth, light gray pebbles carpeting the forty-foot-wide slopping shore. He saw no paths made by man or Mother Nature that would access the beach. He felt he had no choice but to get down on his knees and look directly below along the bluff's wall. On its face in both directions was a barren landscape of eroded dirt rising and falling in a corduroy pattern designed by ocean storms and Father Time. Discouraged, he bowed his head straight down at the beach below. There it was, literally beneath his nose, a big beautiful landmark for all to see from afar. To him it was as big as life after death, a colossal, bleached white, fully articulated whale skeleton. The torpedo-shaped body appeared whole, from its elongated skull to its massive vertebrae down to its once powerful fluke. The animal must have become beached during high tide, he surmised, to have ended parallel, tucked in against the bluff's base.

The large white skeleton's incongruence with the dark-brown backdrop of the bluff created a three-dimensional focal point of orientation, even for the most unsophisticated of seafarers, easily visible with amateur binoculars.

Father Angelino was more than satisfied with his find and somehow felt there was a greater intervention in his discovery. He quickly returned to the cart, ignoring the old man's presence. He sped down the path he entered on rounding the end of the nine-unit cluster. He stopped suddenly out of sight before turning onto the front path. He reached into his pant pocket to remove what Lori called a tag. He carefully placed it behind the building's vertical rain drain alongside Olivel's shelter. He then flipped a tiny switch, activating a transponder signal that would instantly be picked up by a US flag catamaran cruising in the Sea of Cortez, named the *Sea Cat*. They would immediately signal their ground operatives on the Pacific coast of Mexico: Operation Your Mama, now pending. Their target grid had been tagged. They anticipated other tag transmissions to follow within the same general vector of *Tres Marias Madre*. The Father drove straight for his guest room where he would gather the special medallions for

320

blessing the patrol boats, sailors, and marines. He'd go directly to the dock with Father Ignacio, who would assist in the blessing ceremony.

Comandante Maldonado had mustered his men in uniform as promised, promptly awaiting Father Angelino's arrival by 1700 on the dock. Over 150 men stood in parade formation according to rank and branch of service. The closest to the four docked patrol boats were the sailors, followed by the marines and security guards. Two boats were tied to both sides of the long wooden dock facing ocean side at the ready to launch at a moment's notice. Each had their respective crews aboard, pleased to be recognized by a Holy Father from Rome, they were told, especially one who worked for a Mexican Cardinal. Father Angelino's arrival was punctual and unceremonious as he had wished. Warden Trujillo and Deputy Negrete escorted him from the entrance of the dock to the gangplank of the first patrol boat; the *Cabo Corzo* moored on the right where *Comandante* Maldonado waited on board to greet him. He stiffly introduced him to the boat's captain, and first and second mates. There was no room for the warden and his deputy, which pleased the *comandante*. These were, after all, his boats, his men, and his moment, not those of a mere prison warden's. He called his men to attention long enough for them to bellow out an *esprit de corps* greeting of welcome to the special guest, "*Bienvenido nuestro eminente Padre* (Welcome, our eminent Father)." He immediately returned them to parade rest, standing at ease in the near twilight afternoon. A comfortable ocean breeze picked up from the southeast, sufficient enough to lift the small Mexican flags from their stern staffs at the same time, as though signaling the ceremony to begin.

The *comandante* was in his moment as he exercised his full rank and ego, standing in starched dress whites before his men as though it was a call-to-arms. Following a brief but respectful introduction of Father Angelino, he stepped aside for him to address his audience. Determined to keep his promise of brevity, he got right to the purpose of the special gathering.

"For those of you in the service of your country stationed on this island named for our Holy Mother Maria, it is befitting that the church bestows a special blessing upon you and your boats. The church honors are invoked as patron and protector, the archangel

Saint Michael, the leader of the forces of heaven in their triumph over the powers of hell. Saint Michael is your patron of danger at sea for all mariners and for the police on land."

Father Angelino paused to lift one of the four silver medallions from the leather case Father Ignacio held up to him. He elevated it above his head with his index finger and thumb for all to witness with pride as though the saint himself was present. It was the circumference of a fifty-cent piece with double the thickness. The engraved relief depicted Saint Michael as the open winged archangel holding his sword of truth raised high in his right hand with its point penetrating a large serpent below. Father Angelino read the perimeter inscription to his attentive audience, "Saint Michael—Protect Us—Pray for Us."

"The image of Saint Michael will be with you on all four of your patrol boats. I offer them to you with this prayer." He bowed his head. "Patron Saint of mariners and police, the archangel Saint Michael, who this day and forever placed before you with this sacred medallion of his Holy's likeness, who carries the sword of truth, serves to remind you that he is your friend and protector. Saint Michael, the mighty, loving being who uses his sword of truth to create a safe place on earth and within the cosmos for you, we call upon this day as we serve the Lord in all we do. The book of Revelations reminds us that Michael is warring against negative spiritual forces of Lucifer. When you are faced with fear, insecurity, and by the dark forces, call on Saint Michael for protection and peace. He is with you always. Call on him often. He is waiting for your call. In the Lord's name, we pray, Amen."

The sailors and marines followed the Father's genuflection, respectfully remaining silent in their "at-ease" stance. He entered the pilot's cabin with its duty captain and first and second mates. Father Ignacio joined him to assist in the placement of the medallion on the pilot's front instrument console. His duties were neither ceremonial nor reverent as he assisted by peeling off a wax paper from the back of the medal, exposing the adhesion it required to stick permanently. Father Angelino pressed hard with purpose upon Saint Michael's torso, activating a miniature battery cell within. Silently a seminal encoded signal was transmitted. It would be picked up instantly by the *Sea Cat* ten nautical miles off of the coast of *Puerto Vallarta*. Unlike his gifts of bibles from the Holy See in Rome, the medallions came from "The Farm" in Langley, Virginia, United States CIA headquarters. But his focus remained in *Tres Maria Madre*, where he proceeded with the ritual sprinkling of holy water throughout the cabin, chanting the appropriate blessing in Latin. He would repeat this formal ceremony on the remaining three patrol boats without flaw, the act of fraud notwithstanding.

Concluding his fourth medallion blessing aboard the *Cabo San Lucas*, he stood on its bow to face all of the uniformed men who were now "about-faced," smiling proudly at the Father. He blessed them with a brief prayer of praise and gratitude for their service to God and country. For the final time, he implored them to call upon their patron Saint Michael for protection. He closed with a slow, sincere blessing from God, asking for safe seas and patrols. Silently he asked God to forgive him for the deception, although he couldn't recall a commandment that said, "Thou shall not tag thy neighbor or navy."

Father Angelino walked down the dock feeling guilt-free. Privately he would ask Saint Michael to protect those aboard the *Sea Cat*, whom at that moment were picking up four fresh signals from GPS tags in the Pacific. In the smiling company of Warden Trujillo, he returned to shore past a dozen or more pleased sailors who lifted small Saint Michael medallions chained around their necks. This caused his mind to wander to his deceased father who, as a federal police officer, also wore a Saint Michael medallion around his neck. He recalled the grim, official report from the first police investigator to respond to his father's murder: silver Saint Michael medallion on a silver chain was found inside the mouth of the corpse. He was convinced that it was put there on orders from the shooter's sponsor to send a not-so-subtle message to other police investigators that not even divine intervention can protect a cop who opens his informant mouth.

Father Angelino now wanted Saint Michael's sword of truth pointed at the warden. He wanted the full truth about the church's involvement with the government regarding Mexican prisoners' illegal immigration into the United States. Is that what his father had discovered and died for?

Arriving at his electric cart, he turned to the warden. Speaking in an insistent tone, he stated, "My evening's schedule remains quite rushed, warden, if I'm to finish my visits with the remaining colonists on my list. May we meet privately for a light supper and conclude our earlier conversation?"

"As you wish, Father. As our special guest, we remain at your service," he responded sincerely.

"Thank you. I'll see you then at the cafeteria in thirty minutes. I'll go through the serving line and join you at your table," he insisted, maintaining his lead role as planner and executioner.

"Until then, Father," the warden said with a modest bow of his head, parting company at the main pathway.

The Father hurriedly returned to the privacy of his room, where he prepared for the next phase of his "pastoral espionage." With the five transponder tags in place, he felt more confident in his new unsanctioned, undercover role. He was invigorated by the successful conclusion of the earlier phases. Yet he was more concerned now than twelve hours earlier, with the reality that his past devious deeds could be discovered, or at the very least create suspicions. He admonished himself to remain focused and alert. After all, he was now a full-fledged spy in enemy territory posing as a priest.

Following a quick sponge bath, Father Angelino changed his shirt, adding a wireless sound recorder alongside his hidden miniature camera device. The next to the top button looked the same as the others but for the fact that it was a microphone capable of recording the warden's voice from twenty feet away. He had no need for it with Olivel since he planned to do most of the talking. With a fresh Roman collar in place, he left to join the warden in the cafeteria.

One chicken enchilada and a fruit salad satisfied the Father while Warden Maldonado guttled a complete sampling of the cafeteria's evening offering, never saying, "*No gracias*," to any of the five servers. Amazingly he started and finished eating at the same time as the Father. Perspiring profusely from the Olympian effort to consume, the warden broke his silence with stunning candor.

"You are the closest man of the cloth to a Cardinal that I know, so permit me to plead my case to you of mutual benefit. There is growing pressure on me from my superiors to transship over eight hundred prisoners per month from *Tres Marias Madre* to the US. They're sent here for two months for a fast-track orientation of the US, survival English, how best to travel throughout the country, an address list of all Catholic churches in the national network of safe houses for undocumented immigrants, as well as how to avoid being caught, which includes obeying the simplest laws like not jaywalking. *Por fin* (In conclusion), I can say it will be impossible to achieve successfully if I am not provided with greater resources from the church. The government won't give me one *centavo* more than what little I have today," he expressed with deep frustration.

Father Angelino's taping of the warden's confession of complicity in the monumental scheme of illegal immigration of Mexican prisoners to the US was what he wanted. But he needed more dark details in order for Mattie to respond effectively.

"For your message to the Cardinal to be credible, you must say who your superiors are," he declared flatly.

"But Cardinal Montenegro already knows them, and of the entire plan. He'll tell you."

This was his first outside confirmation of the Cardinal's involvement in the scheme, the *Christus Dominus 9* sealed deal Father Angelino had surreptitiously brought from Vatican City to show to his sister and *Tio Chuey*.

He concentrated hard on his response while concerned about his body language expressing the disappointment he felt. He possessed all of the official sealed *Christus Domunus 9* documents from the Holy See necessary to implicate Cardinal Montenegro and the entire Pastoral Curia of Pastoral Care of Migrants and Itinerate People. These fresh revelations would be the first real confirmation of the connection between the Catholic Church and Mexican government regarding their actual clandestine ground operations of prisoner trafficking into the US.

"I could do that, warden. However, by your identifying them specifically, you will prove to the Cardinal your privileged position in the operation, verification he will insist upon. No names, no message. Otherwise, the Cardinal will consider your request just another

appeal among the thousands received daily," he rejoined with proba-
tive frankness.

Warden Maldonado saw that the Father was serious, absent his
amicable countenance. Considering his options, he acquiesced.

"Señor Enrique Paez, Director of Federal and State Penitentiaries,"
the warden offered with reservations. He hesitated nervously, seeing
that the Father would not be satisfied with only one name. Realizing
that indiscretion in disclosing one name was equal to disclosing one
hundred, he opened up with four more, all known to the Father by
name only. More importantly, he knew that all four were known
to his deceased father: three fraternal members of the same Federal
Judicial Police force in Mexico City, one fingered earlier by Mattie in
a group photo.

Mattie had asked her brother to look and listen for one name
in particular, which he was now hearing among all of the others as
though they didn't even exist. Pasqual Diego Lazaro, the man Mattie
fingered in the group photo on her office credenza, the same man
in the newspaper photo *Tio Chuey* had discreetly sent to her had
recently become Mexico's new Attorney General as they had feared.
If he was dangerous before as *Director de La Policia Federal Judicial*
(PFJ), Mexico's FBI, then Pasqual Diego Lazaro's, a.k.a. PDL for
Protector de Ladrones (Protector of Thieves), rise to top attorney in
the Federal Justice branch would make him virtually untouchable.

Again, Father Angelino fought hard to remain focused on his
line of questioning, elated that Lazaro's name finally surfaced in the
context of the government's nefarious scheme. *This is one very significant black dot that will connect many times in our discovery of the truth*,
he mused confidently to himself with Mattie in mind.

"Do you have a list prepared specifically itemizing your short- and
long-term needs? he queried formally with a new tone of cooperation.

"I do. I was presumptuous enough to prepare it in hopes that
you'd be so kind as to carry it personally to the Cardinal."

"Please organize it in order of priority to help his eminence make
a more pragmatic judgment," the Father proposed with false interest.

"Indeed, Father. I'll have it ready before your departure tomorrow," he said, smiling broadly at his new personal courier to Cardinal

Montenegro himself. If his high-level solicitation paid off, as he had hoped, then his stock would rise with Attorney General Lazaro. He had been warned that failure to reach his prisoner immigration goal would mean he would not reach the mainland of Mexico in his lifetime. Not known to the gullible warden, the covert "Leader of the Pack" Lazaro had personally foisted prisoner 50807507 onto *Tres Marias Madre* to personally make good on that promise. Olivel represented *Los Lobos'* wolves in waiting. He only needed be told who the lamb was.

"It would be helpful, warden, to give me a synoptic explanation of this immigration operation in order to put your list of needs in the proper context," he requested within his own self-serving context of pure pastoral espionage.

"Certainly. Prisoners will arrive here from all over Mexico in groups of sixty through the most isolated port on the western coast, *Topolobampo*. On *Maria Madre,* they'll receive a crash course in survival English and rudimentary orientation on how to survive in the streets of the US. Because they're coming directly from prisons, we must provide them with a small wardrobe of work and street clothes, hygiene items, as well as pocket money. These are not your average poor immigrants, Father. They possess absolutely nothing, less than a donkey. *Por lo menos un burro tiene trabajo* (At least a burro has work), he philosophized.

"I understand. Please go on," the Father prodded impatiently.

"From here, they're transported by one of our unmarked boats to the very top of the Sea of Cortez to where the mouth of the Colorado River flows into the sea next to the upper east coast of the *Baja* Peninsula."

It all made sense now to Father Angelino, why all of the water locations for staging, housing, and transporting of convicts. The obvious was that out on the ocean, they would not draw attention from the general public. But the main reason was to prevent prisoner escapes. The water served as their chains and shackles. A strong incentive to escape existed in Mexico where it was not against the law for a prisoner to escape, nor additional prison time served if caught doing so. So why not try it, again and again, unless of course it was over deep seawaters.

"How far is it from the mouth of the Colorado River to the Mexico-US border?"

"Only seventy-five miles to the border town of *San Luis Rio Colorado* with Yuma, Arizona, on the other side. They'll travel over land on remote, unpopulated roads in secured buses manned by special Federal Police."

The Father was familiar with the riverine area as once being a vibrant river delta. Now only two hundred to three hundred indigenous Cocopa Indians remain in the lower reaches amid what are mere mudflats interspersed with a few salty wetlands.

"They'll be dropped off at a protected area east of Yuma along the California border. It's the closest point to the US Interstate Highway 8."

"I assume the border crossing is via tunnel, right?"

"Well-lit, ventilated, and standing up," he reported with borrowed pride of ownership. "From there, they'll be distributed to over four hundred munincipal locations in forty-eight states."

"Staying at Catholic churches or their safe houses throughout the national network, correct?" he asked rhetorically for what he already knew. He possessed the official *papal Curia* documents on immigration into the United States by Mexican illegals. It was the church's principal contribution as indispensable enablers of the illegal transborder scheme. Except now it would be on a grand scale and with real illegals, Mexican convicts set free on American soil. The US was truly "*the land of the free,*" the Father sadly admitted.

"With your familiarity of the church's participation in the US, we ask that more of the same cooperation take place on the Mexican side with his Eminence's approval of our list of needs," the warden solicited again out of insecurity.

"But of course, but with no assurances of the outcome," he responded earnestly.

With the warden's nod of acceptance, the Father excused himself politely from the table to continue with his visitation of colonists. He would not see the warden until his departure the following morning from the dock. But he would have his recorded, self-incriminating voice secreted away in his secured luggage until meeting with Mattie and Lori at the *Playa de Oro* Hotel in *Puerto Vallarta* that afternoon.

With his hidden miniature camera again buttoned down, he left the cafeteria for his evening rendezvous with Olivel. His first stop would be at old man Emanuel's shelter to show on the surface that his visits were legitimate interviews with the colonists.

The evening ocean air brought cooler temperatures than he had wished for. Riding in an open cart added a wind chill he wasn't prepared for either, aggravating his anxiety. He wanted this final phase of his mission to begin and end more quickly than ever. But the single headlight on the cart wouldn't permit him to speed any faster than what he could safely see twenty feet in front of him. The quarter moon on the horizon served only as a navigational point of reference. His pace was slow, arriving at the center shelter of the southern cluster camp thirty minutes after his departure. Old man Emanuel was waiting like a worrisome mother outside his front door with the lonely countenance of a deserted old cur.

"*Buenas noches, Padre*. God must have guided you here on such a dark night."

"Indeed, as he does in daylight as well."

Father Angelino's first observation of note was that every shelter had a single yellow light bulb illuminated above the screen door entrances. The lone exception was number 9 on the end. His first thought was that loner, Olivel, was sending a subtle "Do Not Disturb" message.

"Do front lights on mean the colonists are at home?"

"Yes, unless the bulb is burned out like at the shelter of Olivel. He refuses to replace it," he explained with a resigned acceptance of the occupant.

The Father had to adjust part of his plan and take his photos of Emanuel's front door with a close-up of the handle and key hole. Being invited inside was easy with the lonely old man. When asked if the interior layout of all the shelters there were the same, his affirmative reply caused the Father to make a slow revolving, omni-rama series of snapshots from the center of the single room, capturing the full perspective on the inner shelter. He covered his actions by commenting that it was a great deal more comfortable than caged in a prison cell.

"*Gracias a Dios* (Thanks to God)," the old prisoner concurred.

"Are you normally allowed visitors?"

"Yes, but they're expected to be back in their own shelters by ten."

"I didn't see any guards on the way here. Don't they visit?"

"They don't come by until ten o'clock at lights out and throughout the night. I'm asleep, so I can't say when."

"So the guards aren't much company."

"No. I don't even know their names. They're gone by six o'clock sunrise," he spoke with the lament of a lonely old man.

"But you do have your cluster neighbors. They must provide some companionship, right?"

"Four of us play dominos some evenings. Most are my age, so we're early to bed, early to rise. But not Olivel. He's much younger. He never visits, a real loner, he is. He walks back and forth along the edge of the sea cliff until late evening. Doesn't like the indoors, I guess."

"Aren't you permitted to walk on the beach?"

"Oh yeah. And fish there on your free hours. It's a long way from here to the path down to the beach though. Is that what you were looking for this afternoon, a path?"

"Yes, because I wanted to see the whale skeleton up close," he answered in half-truth, knowing it would negate any suspicions his old criminal mind might have. Reaching into his jacket, the Father pulled out a black book and presented it to the old man.

"Here is something that will always keep you company, my friend."

The old man was so surprised with the leather-bound Bible from the priest that he was rendered speechless, his wide eyes expressing his thanks.

"Bring it to church every Sunday. There you will find friends and fellowship. Remember, Emanuel, your soul is not in prison."

The Father gave him a brief and sincere blessing and bid him farewell, suggesting that he not come out in the chill of the night, and then departed. Just as abruptly, he drove the cart over to Olivel's shelter. There with his target subject, he only needed to get into his loop for no other reason than to know how to disrupt it at some future date. A quick, well-crafted conversation would tell him when, where, and how Olivel passed his free evenings. He took a real deep breath and knocked on door number 9.

The repugnant remnant odors of the tannery resurfaced to again violate his senses. Olivel had left his inner door and screen window open to ventilate his shelter, Angelino assumed. The darkened room didn't stop him from knocking again. He knew it was too early for Olivel to have gone to bed. The tannery smell intensified, causing him to step backward a couple of paces. He suddenly realized that the odor's origin was directly behind him. He instinctively turned around to be startled by an imposing, large white male two feet away staring silently at him. The Father retreated once again, this time from the frightening sight, not the odor. It was Olivel dressed in all black looking intensely at him as though he was a target of interest. His silence scared him as much as his unreadable, expressionless face and unblinking eyes.

"Señor Morales. You startled me in the dark. Did you forget our visit for this evening?" he asked, attempting to mask the fright he felt. The dim yellowish illumination from the cluster lights created a menacing special effect, which exaggerated the intimidating tattoos seemingly animated on his bulging body. It all served to highlight Olivel's assailant persona in his preferred environment, the dead of night. Father Angelino wished now that he knew nothing of this man's record of homicides. He retreated one additional pace in order to view Olivel's hands in the weak lighting. *Thank God they were empty*, he thought to himself, aware that a weapon could still be concealed.

Olivel broke his silence without moving a muscle. "How long are you going to be? I've got places to go to!" he snarled.

The Father wanted to chuckle at the comment but restrained himself knowing he stood alone before a humorless psycho, stone-cold killer.

"Then we can go together, Señor Morales. You're my last visitor for the evening, and I could use some exercise and fresh ocean air," he spoke with inviting tones. Again there was silence. This time the Father would wait him out. He needed to force the situation to his favor or his interview would stop before it started. Olivel was communicating with his searing eyes. Father Angelino wondered if his Roman collar was possibly preventing his throat from being slit.

"You can't see in the dark like I can. What's the fucking point?" he charged with a condescending grunt.

"We don't need to see to hear one another. And yes, I can see in the dark as well as you, if not better. Come along with me if you can," he boldly challenged his nemesis. He didn't wait to see Olivel's facial reaction as he walked away from him slowly to the corner of the shelter, and then stopped.

"Señor Morales, several feet south of us is the edge of the island as you know, with a thirty-foot drop to the beach. Side by side, step by step, walk without a word. Neither of us will tell the other when we've neared or reached the edge. If you're afraid to join me then stay here," he dared to expose Olivel's cowardice. Turning to assess his body language response, the Father was surprised to find a furtive, cocky grin appear on his stone face. This improvised game of double-dare was apparently appealing to a man who always lived on the edge. His obstinacy dissolved, the proud convict stepped alongside the priest.

Without a word spoken, they walked slowly yet deliberately toward the sea cliff. Father Angelino was motivated by the thought of Olivel's mute acceptance and assumption that a challenge of this nature by a pussy priest was child's play to a street-smart criminal. After all, he was on his own turf, literally in his own backyard.

The ocean side of the building was without the yellow illumination of door lights. The thin crescent moon that helped the Father's safe navigation earlier had risen slightly on the horizon. It served again only as a point of reference. The Father had only his wits and good memory to guide him. All else was truly blind faith substituting for bad night vision. Once he stepped upon the pebble pathway that paralleled the back gardens, he knew to commence his measured count off of steps. The dual crunching sound of Olivel's boots on the pebble path echoed those of the priest's.

Ahead was a solid sheet of blackness, void of demarcations or perceptions of place. He would not worry about Olivel's visual acuity, or lack of. He concentrated on his best recall of strides taken that afternoon from the land's end back to his cart parked on the path. Reconnaissance was the purpose then for such notetaking. Its practical application came sooner than he imagined, necessary now to paradoxically gain the advantage and trust of his unwanted adversary. He had to turn him, get this refractory man-beast to listen and trust what he had to say as believable, more importantly, as possible. He had to get Olivel to buy into the possibility that he might soon have somewhere else to go.

Twenty-two was the day of the month his father was murdered, easy to associate with the same number of steps he took before from the edge of the cliff to the path. With eight more to go, he had to decide if they were the same length of strides taken earlier. Was he overthinking his marked paces now that there were consequences to their totality? he worried. He was still going forward in complete darkness with only an imagined goal line in sight. Had he been traveling in a perfectly straight line? he wondered. He sensed Olivel's presence only by his casual breathing. One step too few wouldn't matter. One too many would matter to the many depending upon him. He stopped at twenty-one paces as did Olivel at the exact same instant.

"Are you sure you've arrived? Because I am!" Olivel declared with defiant certitude, as though victorious in his claim.

"Only one way to know." Father Angelino ignited a flame from a thick, silver Zippo lighter, sheltered by his other hand against the updraft of ocean air beneath their feet, only four inches away from the land's end.

"Here. Have this on me." He compressed the sides of the flaming lighter hard with his index finger and thumb before handing it with a cigarette to his unwitting competitor. The robust flame beneath his taut, tattooed neck and face illuminated a quiet expression of gratitude. He took two deep puffs on the cigarette, stalling the smoke with prolonged delight as though it would be his last. Father Angelino fantasized that it was indeed his last fateful cigarette.

"So talk," he demanded lightly.

"It's quite simple. From where we stand, you can go no further, ever! I can. And that's that, unless you listen and believe in what I'm going to tell you." He paused for effect.

"Get to the fucking point, *Padre*!"

"You see that little slice of moon left in the sky? It's now in its decline, getting smaller by the day, called 'old crescent.' Quite commonly people only take an interest in the moon when it's full, big, bright, and beautiful. But when it's totally on its dark side, the 'umbra shadow,' does it cease to exist, fallen from the sky?"

"Never thought about it. It's just fucking darker, that's all."

"True. But the moon is still there. In fact, when it appears to be gone from the sky, fully darken, it is called a 'new moon.' Have you ever looked for it when it's gone, when it's on the dark side?"

"Of course not. Why fuckin should I, or should anybody? Nothing's there."

"I can't answer for everybody. But I can answer for you. Sometimes we see what we want to in total darkness. Others wait for a perfect moon to see. If you say nothing is there, then why is nothing called 'new'? Because from nothing, we can create something new, a new moon from total darkness. If you can make it in the black of night, maybe you can make it further without any moonlight, in total darkness. Just maybe you can see farther and go farther than tonight."

"Like where? Where in the fuck is farther? I don't know where I would go."

"There are only two places on the planet, here and there. There is anywhere you want it to be. The important thing to think about is not being here."

"Why in the fuck should I trust you, priest or not?"

"We trusted each other this far tonight. Trust me when there is no moon, at this very spot. See if you can see it in total darkness, then ask your question of, Where to? First, you must see to believe for yourself."

It was difficult for the Father to read his face from the small glow of the cigarette. More importantly, the cigarette was relaxing the man-beast past the point of aggressive posturing to that of passive acceptance.

"I'll be off the island tomorrow. I'll say no more. What I have said is for your ears only," he stated emphatically. He then handed Olivel four packs of Camel cigarettes with the intent to temporize the circumstances by creating a continuum in his subject's simple programmed behavior. He needed his target on target at this hour for the next four nights at the very least.

"This is a good place to light up before lights out and think about where to? I'll say good night. Stay here, Señor Morales. You now know I can find my way back in the dark. And remember, follow the moon, you never know when. Until then, *adios*."

Olivel's response was silently noted in the dark by the red-hot cigarette tip moving up and down in positive pantomimed agreement.

Father Angelino returned the way he came, this time with the long glow of yellow lights rising above the opposite side of the building roof line as his horizon. Olivel had not spoken since his last question, a sign the Father confidently interpreted as one of passive acceptance. For now it was all he could hope for. For the sixth time that day, the *Sea Cat* was receiving a new GPS transponder signal from the same area in the Pacific, this one virtually on top of the first. They expected no others.

19

A TU MADRE

Tres Marias, Madre Island

Mattie had kept both hotel rooms, even though her brother had not occupied his the night before. She had entered his early in the morning to toss the bed covers and fake the use of the shower and towel. Lori had trained her in the nuances of a spy not creating suspicions. She picked up her brother from the marina upon his early afternoon return from *Tres Marias Madre* and went directly to their hotel. He was debriefed by Lori and Mattie in his room, which elevated their eagerness to hear the recordings and download the photos. That done, Lori would wait for nightfall to board the *Sea Cat*. Onboard she would participate in the final planning phase of Operation *A Tu Madre* (Your Mama), the extraction of penal prisoner, FTM fugitive Olivel Morales de Gutierrez from the heavily guarded island prison. Father Angelino's intel would play a pivotal role in that definitive plan.

Angelino's buttonhole photo taken in Warden Trujillo's outer office of a US Coast Guard patrol boat was now on Lori's laptop. It became the focus of their planning session, its revealed identification driving the tactical plan for the team's entry, seizure, and exit from the island target grid.

"The photo gives us confirmation. Our satellite pictures only told us they were former US cutters. They're now IDed as 95-foot, Cape-class, 102-ton cutters," Nep stated with certainty.

"Nice hand-me-downs. A few of those craft class served briefly in Vietnam, three-man pilot watch, three marines at the ready, sixteen knots, short-sea gunboat," Taylor added.

"What armament are we looking at?" Eizzo asked.

"A couple of M-60 light machine guns, handheld small arms, M16s, .45-caliber pistols at best," Taylor speculated.

"The best news is that Cape class are 1960s vintage, electronically unsophisticated from the keel up with limited maneuverability," Nep critiqued with a smirk of superiority.

"We'll be operating in their maritime domain with their maritime quantitative superiority, but we bring qualitative superiority to the game," Taylor added, confident the *Sea Cat* was "mission capable." He and Nep had made certain that the ship had mission-essential materials for operational readiness to accomplish the Caracara mission as well as for emerging contingencies, such as the unforeseen sea-basing operation they would soon execute.

Lori positioned all four patrol boat photos on the laptop monitor. She read the former US Cape class names of "Cape Hatteras, Cape Carter, Cape Hedge, and Cape Newagen, now the Mexican Navy's *Cabo Catoche, Cabo Corrientes, Cabo Corzo,* and *Cabo Cruz.*'"

"Well, meet *Cape Sea Cat*, high-tech king of the high seas. We come in peace, and leave in a hurry," Nep declared to the amusement of his teammates.

"Now we know what we're up against. *Master Sun Tzu* taught, 'Act after having made assessments, the one who first knows the measures of far and near wins.' Let's do it," Taylor ordered as he downloaded the base map datum of the island grid now overlaid upon the six active GPS fixes, dot light signals with individual tag codes on and around *Maria Madre*. Their state-of-the-art GPS system used four satellites instead of three for its 3-D waypoint navigation fix and grid true perspective. This would provide measurement and signature intelligence, critical information for the landing team's safe and accurate entry. Even their GPS Precision P-Code, the most accurate of all, was encrypted as a "Y-Code," unknown to any foreign vessels, most of all, *Cabo*-class cutters. The precise position of all tagged subjects would be known within a three-foot margin of accuracy. Every step Olivel took was tracked, as long as his cigarettes lasted.

The following morning over breakfast on their seventh-floor balcony, Mattie and Angelino viewed the port's activity, primarily with the boarding of the *Baja* Ferry and disembarking of the cruise ship, *Princess Dawn*. The commercial and sport fishermen had left hours earlier from the marina for their hopeful catches. Gone was the *Sea Cat*, casting off after midnight, heading southwestwardly toward *Tres Marias Madre* with the entire Mission *Caracara* team onboard.

The Delta team considered the capture and extraction of all six FTM fugitives of equal importance for the mission's success. Only Taylor and Lori would privately consider Olivel as their "high-value target," given his added importance to their companion in-country operators back in Puerto Vallarta. Lori personally felt the pressure to succeed in the island operation in order for her friend's mission to succeed. The Colima sister and brother team would fly directly to Mexico City, where they would meet secretly with *Tio Chuey* to finalize a fateful clandestine plan of their own.

Caracara I and II would be crossing into the United States sometime the next afternoon at the *Ajo*, Mexico, entry point below Tucson, Arizona, far away from any curious *Tijuana* Cartel eyes. They would be driven by "Ghost Riders," designated Delta member drivers handpicked by Taylor. They had been emptied of all mission-related devices and equipment before departing PV. They would go directly to the Nevada Sun Ranch, where Monster Man would strip the RVs of all bird references and holding rooms, the big birds' round trip migration to Mexico complete.

The Delta team's sixth and final tactical operation began in a calm sea fifteen nautical miles east of *Maria Madre* Island in the late afternoon under a blue sky accented with rice paper-thin, cirrostratus clouds high above. Their Raytheon radar arch spotted the normal ocean freighter traffic to the north. Within their immediate radius of sight, they were all alone, Cummins engines on idle. All hands were on deck for the mission's maiden launch and voyage of the *Figment*, the stealth superspeed, state-of-the-art boat, designed for challenges such as the one they now faced. After months of training, Lori was at the helm with marine-mate Cope as navigator, both wearing all black, all-weather seagoing gear for their stealth operation.

The *Figment* was lowered by an electronic cable feed from the twenty-foot wide, eighty-five-foot long, open belly of the catamaran to rest on the ocean's surface. A thumbs-up and crisp salute was Lori's signal for the *Sea Cat* to slowly pull away, exposing the *Figment* to the open air and sea. She would tailgate the *Sea Cat* to within eight miles east of the island at its three o'clock midpoint, where the *Cat* would abandon her. There the *Cat* would peel off ninety degrees port heading due south, where she would round the southern tip of the island heading due west over the horizon for safe anchorage. They expected to be seen in route by two of the *Cabo*-class patrol boats, demonstrating their casual innocence and good intentions as a scientific seafarer flying the colors of the American Cetacean Society. The *Figment* would sit idly until sunset, invisible to the human and electronic eyes of the enemy. They would watch the patrol boats rotate like clockwork around the island prison. Two shrimp trawlers had been sighted several miles to the north, breaking the monotony of their boring vigil.

Three nautical miles off the island's southern coast, Nep would slow down for a measured look at the beached whale skeleton landmark mentioned in Angelino's debriefing. Rap held the Canon 600 mm, image-stabilized, all-weather viewing scope, off the starboard side on a monopod. He picked up its clear, fifty-foot long white image with ease. He called out the sighting to Nep for his sea-based waypoint marking. He then exchanged the scope for a Bushnell 7×50 marine binocular with a liquid-filled compass built into the viewing optics. The compass scale was aligned with a vertical, reticule range-finding scale that allowed him to estimate the slant range of objects to a known size, such as a dead, beached humpback whale. His findings were called out to Nep. The *Sea Cat*'s course at that moment would be due west, resuming its twelve-knot cruise speed until they were beyond the horizon of any watchful patrolmen, a distance of ten nautical miles. There the *Sea Cat* would drop its eighty-pound Bruce anchor until sundown.

This would be the *Figment*'s first true test of its invisibility in a true danger zone under the vigilant watch of the enemy. The Mexican patrol boat crews would have several sets of binoculars searching the waters for unbidden inbound traffic. Other than their supply boat, there was no reason for any other vessel to approach the island within three miles unless of course for clandestine body snatching of prisoners. The *Figment* had passed the first hour successfully only three hundred feet from the *Cabo Corrients*, unseen. Lori was about to brag about this notable accomplishment to Cope when they felt a silent bump against the port side. Together they leaned over to investigate. Floating perpendicular to the forty-six-foot long *Figment* was a black, seven-foot long sea turtle with its extended thick head swaying back and forth as though wondering whether to zig or zag.

"What the hell—we've been torpedoed by a friggen sea turtle," Cope exclaimed with disbelief.

"It's a leatherback turtle to be exact, largest of all the turtles, around two thousand pounds, fourth largest reptile in the world," she recited with encyclopedic recall.

"Endangered, aren't they?"

"Critically! The leatherback goes back to the dinosaur era, but might now suffer the same fate. And if we'd been hauling ass, he would have lost his. I think he surfaced for air and didn't see us, Mother Nature's first testimony that the *Figment* is out of sight," she proudly boasted.

The enormous sea turtle's shiny leather-like shell was barrel-shaped, elongated into a streamlined teardrop, with seven two-inch high serrated ridges running down its back, converging at the rudder-like rear flipper. His broad fore flippers served as powerful oars, propelling him thousands of migratory miles per year in the open ocean. His bobbing head continued to explore its invisible obstacle, his eyelids closing to a vertical slit.

"What makes you think this leatherback is a *he*?"

"If it was a female, 'Gucci' would be stamped on it," Lori grinned peevishly.

"Cute. We'll see if the *Cabo* crews can see any better than Mr. Magoo here," Cope wondered aloud.

"Well I can assure you that the female leatherback is adept at beach landing deception. She lays her fertile eggs deep in the sand, covers them, then lays a second clutch that are yolkless for predators to find and satiate themselves with, allowing the first hidden clutch to incubate and hatch safely," Lori cited with female pride.

"You're not yolking?"

"Cute."

"Raise anchor," Nep commanded from his captain's chair. He had already plotted their course due east, back to the southern tip of the island, ten nautical miles off its coast. Their ETA, 2000 hours. Grav was studying the latest satellite weather photos and reports with keen interest in northerly wind velocities. The current report was positive news predicting clear skies until 0400 tomorrow. A slow sweep of the sky with his naked eyes saw shining stars without the moon center stage. It was completely on its shadow umbra.

Rap paced the port side wing walk observing the sea's surface, the estimated distances between the water's high crests and low troughs. "No chop, no hip-hop. So far, so good," he shouted into the pilot house for all to hear, expressing his concern for potential choppy, white-cap waters.

Eizzo monitored the six transponder signals now superimposed over a detailed satellite map of the island and its perimeter coastal waters. All signals were active, none ambulant at the moment.

Arriving at their plotted sea base staging point ten nautical miles south of the island, Cam took over the reading of the GPS monitors and Furuno true color radar. Target trails displayed in the form of synthetic afterglow on the color monitor reported that the four marine patrol boats were coming into the quarterly clock nautical positions at the of top of the hour: quarter after, half past, and quarter until the top, surrounding the island at perfect ninety-degree distances from one another: twelve, three, six, and nine o'clock, just as Angelino said they would. Cam locked in the map datum of destination bearing with distance, track, and speed references, then time-stamped it. Lori and Cope remained floating patiently, undetected six nautical miles off shore below one o'clock. The prison headquarters was at the three o'clock position, where the *Cabo Corzo* had just left the dock for its three nautical miles off shore initial patrol position.

"All signals active, all players in position. Figment team ready, shore team ready, ground team ready, mother ship ready. Waiting for your order, sir," Nep reported to Taylor.

With his immediate crew mustered before him and Lori and Cope in radio contact, Taylor stated with sincerity, "'All you need to do is throw something odd and unaccountable in their way,' *Sun Tzu*." Diversion was the name of the game, deception their Delta claim to fame.

The sun had dissolved into the western Pacific forty-five minutes earlier. Taylor wanted a pitch-black sky before commencing debarkation operations and creating the desired seaborne diversion with his *Figment* crew.

"Count fifteen minutes to 'Go' for the *Figment* team initiating from present position. All others, standby for my command," Taylor stated by radio.

With the countdown at "Go" for the Figment, Lori had readied the boat for its stealth mode, impervious to visual or radar detection and reduced audible pickup. She piloted the boat to intersect the positions of the *Corrientes* and *Corzo* currently at twelve o'clock and three o'clock, three miles off shore. The strategy was simple: to enter enemy waters and retreat within three minutes, on the order of a feint marine "drive-by," throw something odd and unaccountable in the enemy's way.

The *Figment* had slipped audaciously into position between the two marine patrol boats in under two minutes and settled into idle while Cope deftly prepared his packages. He offloaded several flotation objects loaded with flares of various sizes attached to miniature electronic devices. They bobbed gently in the dark waters over a two-hundred-foot long lineup. The boat moved a safe distance away before Lori idled the engines again. "Go on your ready," she ordered Cope, seated in the back with a black metal control panel on his lap. He extended its antennae, aiming them in the direction of their wide buffet of floaters.

"And a happy Fourth of July to all," Cope declared as he pressed a red plastic button. Instantly, pyrotechnic rockets soared vertically above two inner-tube flotation platforms. At two hundred feet altitude, a dozen bright white flares lit the sky amid a broad gray cloud of smoke. Before the wide spans of silver tinted illumination dissipated into the ebony air, Cope pressed a yellow plastic button that caused the remaining six floaters each to ignite a single, ten-inch emergency flare standing erect at one end. The six sparkling Roman candle-like red and white tips brightly cascaded upward, visible for three miles. Immediately Cam came over the *Sea Cat* radio. "We have movement, one coming south and three northbound, *Cabos Corrientes* and *Corzo* closing in. Confirm with visuals, over."

"Copy that," Lori replied as Cope joined her in the copilot seat fitted with binoculars.

The first to arrive at the scene was the *Corrientes* from the north, shining two spotlights back and forth on the six floaters. Lori and Cope could hear loud, confused voices punctuated with shouts of profanity. The *Corrientes's* six-man crew lined its ninety-five-foot port side rail gazing dumbfounded at six naked inflated rubber women, two each with red, black, and blonde hair, supporting in their round, red, open mouths a long, burning emergency flare. The Corzo arrived a minute later. Lori understood the loud Spanish description of the floaters given by one sailor to the newly arrived ones, "*Son unas putas del mar, y bien buenas. Y nosotros nos encontremos los primeros!* (They're all whores of the sea. And we saw them first!)" Some even referred to the written beer brands on the blow-up dolls in the first-person possessive. "*Mi Tecate, mi Sol. Mi Bohemia. Mi Superior. Mi Modela.*"

As the exchange of shouted claims continued, the *Figment* moved to the south to encounter the fast moving *Cabo Cruz* coming up hard from its six o'clock position. They would wait near the dock at three o'clock to observe and report. Lori radioed Nep, "The floating beer babes were a big hit. I think *Dos Equis* was the favorite."

"I'm also partial to *Dos Equis*, they're the first two words I learned in Spanish," came Cam's subjective rejoinder. But they all knew that the inflated floating sirens of the sea would quickly deflate and sink into the sea when the Roman candle burned to a predetermined height, causing an instant internal burn penetration of the rubber becoming nothing more than wet dreams for the marines.

The Delta team was not naive to the reality that on paper, their paradrop, island entry plan appeared simple, but that in actuality it was a death-defying feat. Capture of the land operation's four commandos would be catastrophic. Reality was here and now for the team. Grav and Eizzo, pilot and navigator respectively, were strapped into a double harness attached by riser lines to a 42-foot wide black parasail canopy. They would be launched off of the *Sea Cat's* foredeck by the *Sea Cat's* 15-foot modified Zodiac Mark 3 inflatable rubber boat. Its hard hull and large buoyancy tubes allowed it to plane quickly, giving it the swift surge required for rapid ascent of the parasail. The reinforced transom made it compatible with its two 90-hp, quiet 4-stroke Mercury motor capable of 45 miles per hour speeds. Augmented maneuverability provided by a stern thruster and propeller of Navy G bronze placed the special Zod into a "military class." The 400 feet of nylon tow rope would give them the 300 feet desired altitude for a clandestine flight over 3 miles of water and 50 feet of land. Their descent would begin 1/3 mile off shore with Grav steering by pulling on the right or left rear risers. Eizzo, seated in front, would navigate with night vision goggles equipped with optical compass and reticule range finder. All of this would be done in silence using their boots to touch tap signals to one another. A special military designed HLLD canopy for high lift, low drag, was chosen to help offset the heavy weight of the two large men. The flyers' operation equipment was small and light. They had shed the helmets and life jackets in favor of light flight requirements and on the ground speed and maneuverability.

A fundamental tactic of warfare was to always try to control the high ground. That left out any attempt of entry by shore landing with a 30-foot cliff wall to ascend. A night time, silent, moonless flight would provide the stealth to get behind target Olivel for the surprise seizure.

Nep had maneuvered the catamaran to face the wind aft, its stern facing *Madre Maria*. He kept one eye on the wind meter for the 15 mph optimum velocity suitable to launch 500 pounds. The Zod had idled out in front until the tow line was completely extended and taut. The first and second officers became the launch crew holding opposite sides of the broad, "open-ready" canopy. It was constructed from woven nylon fabric coated with a silicone zero-porosity coating for low drag, silent drift in flight and descent. They waited attentively for Nep's signal to launch. The radar monitor showed a traffic free sea for a 9 nautical mile radius. The wind velocity remained steady. The "Ready" radio call came from Rap piloting the Zod, which Nep relayed with an uplink to the parasailors standing firm on the improvised flight deck. This would be the Delta team's only shot at a launch.

"Hit it!" came Nep's order to all waiting eagerly. The flyers resisted the hard pull in a tense tug-of-war to keep the tow line tight and maintain balance, followed abruptly by five calculated forward strides before the rush of liftoff. The tow boat had accelerated with a rapid surge of horsepower, the tow winch lifting the tandem parasailors off the *Sea Cat* deck skyward into the wind. Once aloft, achieving altitude would be controlled by the Zod. The *Cat*'s speakers and team member earphones picked up the background music "*I Believe I Can Fly*" by R. Kelly.

Observing his wristband altimeter, Eizzo signaled Grav to steer right at 300 feet above sea level. Rap began the Zod's 180-degree gradual turn heading toward the beach, 1,000 feet left of the target waypoint. Completing the Zod's full turn would cause the flyers to be slung with centrifugal force toward the island diagonally, their release point planned for 50 feet off shore. The roll-in-point would begin 100 feet from the drop zone, inland, a mere 100 feet west of Olivel's shelter. Angelino's intel had described the significant ground features, including an even terrain west of the convict housing cluster away from any illumination of neighboring buildings and pathways. Their daytime satellite photos had confirmed it as an ideal drop zone.

With the wind now behind them, Rap increased the boat's speed to 35 mph. Cam, remaining aboard the *Sea Cat* with Nep, stayed in constant radio contact with Rap and Eizzo reporting the one thing they needed to hear. "All *Cabo* cutters out of entry grid, current four fixes at 11, 2, 3, and 4 o'clock. Subject target in 6 o'clock shelter. Your ETA good."

Eizzo sighted their drop zone and signaled Grav to release the tow line from the harness at a decision altitude of 275 feet. He immediately began to finesse the rear risers for a 10-degree descent. Eizzo had to maintain their glide slope course while watching for any "unfriendlies," although he knew they would practically have to land on them to be seen or heard. The one friendly in their favor was the dark side of the moon. The zone was coal black and so were they in their nocturnal camouflage outfits and faces. Now over the landing zone, Eizzo began his foot-tapping countdown from ten, zero being touchdown.

The soft soil provided slight shock absorption for the stand-up impact. Once out of the quick release harness, Eizzo assumed watch while Grav reeled in the falling parasail. Eizzo opened the rear stock on his Commando II crossbow and loaded the cocking arms with a medium range bolt. He then helped Grav stuff the wadded-up parasail into his black backpack. Grav loaded his crossbow and motioned to a small cover of Juniper trees fifty feet from the sea cliff. After a sweep of the TEA with their night vision binoculars, Grav broke silence for brief radio contact with Rap idling three hundred feet off shore and with Cam reporting back on the *Cabo* boat's position, all status quo. The waypoint report on Olivel had him still in his shelter at 9:25 p.m., thirty-five minutes to lights out, and the punctual arrival of the prison guard patrol.

The *Figment* remained in the danger zone, confident they had not and would not be detected. Lori's orders were to detain the *Cabo Cruz* above the four o'clock position for as long as necessary to buy time for the landing team to complete its operation. She and Cope had more pyrotechnic tricks in their arsenal if needed.

Knowing Olivel was in his shelter, Rap slowly navigated the Zod toward the whale bones landmark. He radioed Grav for a visual update on their target area, coming back negative: *target not on the cliff.* He then quietly ran the boat ashore, shutting off and raising the outboard motors before shallow water impact. Taylor jumped into the ankle-deep surf to pull and tie down the bow of the boat above the water line. The two-man shore party walked single file to the cliff wall to the left of the gigantic skeleton and waited.

Grav and Eizzo found the ten-foot wide spread of scrub oak that Angelino had noted lying near the turn in the rear pathway. They easily identified Olivel's shelter on the end of the cluster. It was dark inside. It reminded them that the one wild card in their play deck was the Zippo lighter with the imbedded transponder. Cam reported it was active but that there was no assurance that Olivel was. Maybe he forgot to take it along on a nightly walk, or he had finished his four packs of cigarettes Angelino had given him, they wondered. If he did not appear before lights out for his seaside cigarette, they'd be forced to exercise plan B, a high risk of maelstrom they wanted to avoid. Grav radioed Rap that they were in place, ready, waiting, all clear.

Taylor had already fitted his boots with toe spikes and hands with grip spikes. He began his hand and foot ascent of the dirt wall sea cliff. Attached to his waist was his rope and pulley carabineer. When he arrived at the top, he peeked over the edge to confirm all was clear. Pulling on the down end of the rope over the pulley, Rap raised a four-foot wide, gray, rubberized canvas up to Taylor. He secured the upper edge to the removable bolts he had already secured into the wall with a Rocpec hand drill. The two corners of the fastened canvas rose higher than the center, creating a concaved middle flowing down to the bottom edge. When Rap secured the bottom into the pebble beach, they had created a slide fifty-foot long. He gave Taylor a gentle, double tug on the rope, prompting him to roll himself onto the center of the smooth, slick canvas and slide effortlessly to the beach. With a grin, Rap radioed Grav, "Ready here." His impatient response came back, "Waiting, twenty minutes to lights out!"

Less than a minute went by when the back door to Olivel's shelter opened. Both men trained their night vision optics on the standing image of a large, powerful-looking man. They had already attached special darts on the tips of the bolts. Angelino's notes aside, they required first hand confirmation of their FTM target before TA.

The subject moved forward a couple of paces and stopped. A small light flickered in front of his face then went dark.

"A lighter and cigarette," Eizzo whispered.

"Affirmative. But why won't the bastard smoke it by the cliff?" Grav grumbled.

The experienced Delta archers knew that with the target in their scope crosshairs, a short, smooth, light trigger pull would strike the subject in 1/2 of a second, the bolt traveling at 245 feet per second. It was the added seconds carrying the subdued subject to the sea cliff they wanted to avoid.

"Have eyes on target. ID on the bald head and a neck tattoo, can't read it though," Grav reported.

Nep radioed, "If he moves away from the shelter, Cam will confirm target with waypoint distance of the two tags," referring to the fixed transponder Angelino placed on the side of the building. "That can only be the Zippo. Confirmation will be your 'Go.' Copy?"

"Copy," Grav replied.

Seconds ticked away like minutes for the two covert commandos, growing more eager by the tick. Eizzo's watch showed fourteen minutes to ten.

Cam received an urgent call from Lori, "*Cabo Cruz* on the move, maneuvering 180-southbound, Copy?"

"Affirmative. Then bring it home, full throttle! Our ground clock ready to expire," Cam forewarned her.

The *Cabo Cruz* was turning around clockwise at a quick pace while Lori headed counterclockwise at a quicker pace, an abridged circumference for tactical positioning, moving ahead of the cutter by three hundred feet. "Ready?" she asked her boat mate.

"Affirmative. Reduce speed," Cope responded.

She lowered the throttle to a crawl above idle, moving the boat across the bow of the turning cutter. Cope twisted open a valve at the stern of the boat. A dark brown liquid spewed forth like water from a fire hydrant creating a four-foot wide swath of oily substance. He capped the open valve when the supply was depleted and the oil slick was eighty feet long. The *Cabo Cruz* was now 150 feet away heading straight toward the clandestine crew's surprise slick trick. Leaning over the stern, Rap ignited a white-hot flare and laid it upon the thick layer of floating goo. He was barely back in his seat when Lori lowered the throttle in a hard turn to the right, being careful the *Figment*'s rising rooster tail didn't dampen the five-foot high flames. Rap and Lori repeated the oily exercise again with an additional eighty-foot long flaming strip beyond the first. The cutter could only react one way, reduce engines and turn hard left to avoid the flaming speed bump lighting up the dark ocean and sky. They saw no other vessels illuminated by the bright blaze and two strong spotlights, only the *Cabo Cruz* and its confounded crew searching the waters and blank radar screen. The 110-foot cutter now stood still, facing east. At that moment, the full throttled *Figment* was nearing the island's southern tip, four miles distance between them. Lori had left the *Cabo* cutters wondering if their crews were now calling to their Patron Saint Michael for guidance, or rather to Saint Jude, patron saint of lost causes.

"We have movement toward the cliff," Grav whispered suddenly into his lip mic.

"We confirm movement here," Cam responded from the bridge tracking monitor.

"Copy here," Rap came back.

The Delta duo followed their target with the night vision optics, noting the occasional tiny glow of light near his face. His seeming nonchalance told them that he was relaxed, maybe even tired. It was now nine minutes to ten o'clock. Would he go all the way to the edge? they wondered. Regardless, they had to position themselves soon and swiftly, keeping the element of surprise on their side. "He who hits first, hits twice," was the tactical mantra of the Special Forces.

The attack team was in attack mode. They twisted the darts a half turn on the tips of the bolts and released the crossbows' safeties. Eizzo left the scrub oak hiding first, moving stealthily behind Olivel's forward direction toward the cliff. Grav followed Eizzo's footsteps after a ten-second count. Although their eyes had adjusted to the ebony environment, they could not let him advance further than twenty-five feet and still maintain his near invisible position. Their forward motion was in step with their target, flanking him by ten feet on both sides should he choose to run. He was now boxed in with the sea cliff and ocean in front and two of the Delta Force's most seasoned commandos behind in striking distance.

Below waited the fall team, termed by Rap "the Bag and Drag team," ready for the big drop. What they saw from below though was a tiny, hot red object flying off of the cliff directly over them. It landed at their feet, Olivel's lit cigarette butt. Rap was incensed, in his mind comparing the gravity of Olivel's multiple murders to his blatant littering of the beach, and with a cigarette butt of all things. *The bastard did deserve to die!* he ranted inwardly.

"On my three," came Grav's barely audible order over Eizzo's ear fob.

The crosshairs in the night vision scopes beamed their direct laying, red laser light dots on Olivel's back. Their two tiny red dots marked the crossbows' aim points on the shoulder blades, slightly to the left and right of the spine.

"Three, two, one," initiated the gentle trigger squeeze and instant strikes. Eizzo rushed immediately to Olivel while Grav reloaded his crossbow with a hunting bolt for backup.

The darts' intramuscular injections of 500 mL of telazol sedative was the same dosage US park rangers use on misbehaving bears, including grizzlies. That's what Eizzo believed he faced when he came up to his primal, startled subject, the same thick size as he, now turned in his direction. He was now an eyewitness to the same searing eyes that Angelino had described. In the dark, Eizzo swore he saw fire flash from Olivel's red and white orbs, now fixed fiercely on him. Olivel raised both arms behind his head as though trying to remove the two stabbing projectiles in his shoulder blades. Finding his efforts futile, he thrust his arms down hard toward Eizzo. The seasoned commando parried his strike with his massive forearms while slamming his right boot tip directly beneath his opponent's left knee cap. He then stepped aside as though allowing a lady to pass through a doorway. Olivel fell on his face like a KOed prize fighter upon the canvas with a growling groan.

"We have downed TA, evac in ten seconds," Grav radioed to his subjacent partners. He then retrieved the bolts and darts while Eizzo taped over the captive's mouth. Safeing their crossbows, they quickly dragged him to the edge of the cliff above the slide. Taylor straddled the bottom of the slide as catcher receiving the calvity headfirst, giving him a close-up ID of the perverse tattoos on the professional predator, now the fallen prey.

Rap had the Zod pushed off of the beach. Grav was next down the slide while Eizzo pulled out all of the wall hooks from above, dropping the slide to the beach. Then in deft mountaineering fashion, he slammed an easy release repelling hook into the upper cliff wall and leaped backward off of the edge with the repel rope cinched around his waist. With only a single push off of the midpoint of the wall, he landed flat-footed on the beach. A quick snap of the rope released the repel hook from the top of the cliff, causing both to fall to the ground. He gathered the slide and leaped into the boat.

Eizzo had rolled Olivel face up on the Zod's hard rubber floor with both hands bound in back. Taylor had patted the skeletal jaw of the whale in gratitude for its valuable role, covered their tracks on the beach, and then pushed the boat into deeper water before his mates pulled him in. Rap checked his watch. It was five minutes before ten. From the moment the men left the scrub oak hiding to when Taylor pushed the boat off, not a second beyond two minutes had expired.

The decision to use the outboards to launch from shore instead of silent paddles was Taylor's, reasoning that the prison ground patrol was still out of hearing range until ten o'clock. Besides, he speculated, the guards had voluntarily or under orders moved closer to all of the earlier northeastern commotion. After all, the last time they had so much Pacific island excitement was when a group of colonists had formed the prison *mariachi* band *Los Ojdidos* (The Fucked Ones).

* * *

The Zod crew, with FTM captive Olivel Morales, arrived at the *Sea Cat* to find the crew had already locked the *Figment* up into her belly. They turned their attention to uploading the Zod after the last of their FTM fugitives was laid out in his reserved cabin, still out for the count. They all smiled at the selected background music playing Ramones' "*I Wanna Be Sedated.*"

Nep called out for all to hear, "We're under way, we're staying dark. The *Cabo Cruz* is coming around at five o'clock."

Cam calculated their distance of separation at five and one half miles. They needed a minimum of nine and one half miles to be off of the *Cruz's* direct radar horizon. Nep called Taylor to the bridge.

"We still show the *Cabo Corriente* on the northwestern corner at eleven o'clock. I'm going to take the *Cat* closer to the island and around to the western side, low enough not to be picked up by her radar. If I stay on a straight westerly course now, we'll eventually come into the *Cruz's* line of radar when she comes around to the south at six o'clock. We need another five miles distance between us to be off of their horizon, out of sight. We'll take the *Cat* one mile up the western shore out of her line of radar detection, then an easy 110-degree turn to port heading northwest. Cam will monitor the *Corriente's* eleven o'clock position. I'll lock in all navigational coordinates, along with the two *Cabos'* variables into the Maptech computer. She'll steer our evasion course out of here, out of sight every nautical inch of the way."

"You're the captain," Taylor responded with his signature right facial squint, his seal of approval. It was still Taylor's mission to win or lose, and internally he could not relax until the FTM's were on US *terra firma*.

Nep's first and second mates flanked him on the bridge with Cam, four sets of eyes scrutinizing high-tech instruments to calculate the most prudent, fastest CTS away from any and all possible detection in harm's way. They were constantly mindful of the Delta Force mantra for a stealth mission: "If they didn't know they were there, then it didn't happen."

Nep unharnessed the catamaran's seven hundred horses with a full drop of the throttle and let it run. The main deck speakers blasted the music *"We Gotta Get Out of This Place"* by the Animals.

Soon safely over the ten nautical mile cutters' horizon, lights returned inside the *Sea Cat* along with celebratory smiles and high fives. Lori was the only one receiving warm, prolonged hugs. It was a Delta thing.

Mad Mary 6

McKinney had a feeling that the honeymoon of civility without Mad Mary might be over, now that ten days had passed since her imposed cooling-off period. He cautiously entered the Harbor Market Wednesday morning for his customary purchase of ice, the third such visit since receiving his last coded message. Trembling before Mary at the checkout counter was a young commercial fisherman wanting to purchase a handful of spicy beef jerky, receiving instead a lecture on how "that rot gut is nothing more than putrefied cow hide marinated in cancer-causing preservatives and spices to rid it of its stench. How many would you like?"

Still flinching from the anti-sales promotion from the anti-customer storeowner, the young man apologetically answered, "Ten for now. Sure beats smellin' nothin' but fish all day."

"Well then, you can just stuff these up your nose. And when you're dead, you won't smell nothing," she exclaimed unsympathetically, taking his money.

McKinney was reaching for the bag of ice when Mary yelled across the store. "I knew you'd fall off the wagon soon enough, McKinney. But why a sixer of *Cerveza Pacifico*, man? If you want your beer buzz back, buy Bohemia, it's got more jack-you-up juice."

He was confused by the brand and call again for a six-pack. "Did you say a six-pack of *Pacifico*, not *Corona*?" He was certain that there was a misunderstanding.

"Jesus, McKinney, there are times I think you need a six-pack of Ensure. Your caller babe said to pick up a six-pack of *Pacifico*, *comprende* now?" she asked condescendingly.

The honeymoon was definitely over, he begrudged, with her tongue wagging as before, nonstop. He was the one now wanting to toss beer bottles at her, knowing that he could well afford the fines. His mind though was more on the covert message from their enigmatic caller, not the mad in-house messenger. He needed to get out of the store and focus on the meaning of this new set of symbols. *What the hell is Taylor telling us?* he wondered as well as worried.

Ignoring eye contact with Mary, he paid for the beer while she carried on about *Pacifico* beer being no better than Budweiser because the "Bud the dud brewery" owned it. He could care less knowing he wasn't going to drink it anyway. Mad Mary's strident rant chased him from the store. "Does Mrs. McKinney know about your beer bimbo, Ms. *Corona Pacifico?*"

He sat relaxed, alone on the main deck of the *Conch II* contemplating the significance of the new symbol of *Pacifico* brand beer on the small table in front of him. He had just finished his phone calls to all five pack members inviting them to go out that morning to see "a *rare sighting of a pod of orcas,*" *alleged killer whales*, Boyer called them, their coded message for convening an urgent mission meeting.

McKinney put his analytical mind to work, determined to have an answer to the new symbolism before his associates arrived within the hour. He started with what he knew that the last coded message was a single bottle of *Corona* beer, meaning one last fugitive to capture. Then if he was captured, why not order more *Corona? Simple,* he deduced, *because there is no more to order. The covert caller can't order an empty carton of Corona. But if they have all six fugitives captured and secured for extraction from Mexico, how could they communicate that? How would they send a fresh message of their progress and make it seem significant, make it noteworthy? How?* he wondered out loud as he stared across the long teak deck of his yacht, out across the Pacific waters of his ocean backyard. A small formation of six brown pelicans skimmed the serene surface of the sea in search of a morning meal. Parallel to their flight path, a large pleasure yacht was heading northwest toward the Channel Islands. He then thought of the one thing, among many, that he didn't know: *how will the Delta team smuggle these six known fugitives across the US border?* He and his mission companions always assumed that it would be at some very secluded, secretive border crossing and at night, Delta stealth style. It was always obvious that it wouldn't be by airplane, not even private, especially with the omnipresent post-9/11 security.

He was embarrassed with himself that he had never given this any further thought over the past weeks and that once again it was so simple, so obvious now that he saw the answer before his own eyes.

The Pacific Ocean, El Pacifico, was where all six bad guys were bottled up, he surmised, *probably aboard some private boat right now heading north over international waters until they reached the latitude of Santa Barbara, and then cruise in to the coast, the US of A, on our side of the border, on our side of justice,* he posited. McKinney leaped up from his blue canvas deck chair and walked to the stern with a pair of deck binoculars to sweep the horizon with the glasses. He had no expectations of finding anything but the joy of knowing that somewhere on the ocean of his mind, justice was in motion on the beautiful blue *Pacifico.*

The close-up magnification the powerful binocular brought into view was a large white vessel with a wide red stripe running diagonally from top to bottom of the bow. McKinney's brief moment of joy dissipated with the real-world presence of the coast guard cutter *Blackfin,* Marine Protector Class, passing through the channel on its random patrol. It was the floating eyes and ears of US coastal security. McKinney purposefully lowered the binoculars so that the Blackfin would appear smaller from a distance, wishing that it would completely disappear.

20

SANTA BARBARA BOUND

Pacific Ocean West Coast

The Delta team was acutely aware that they were still far from home and their ultimate goal. Taylor had used the metaphorical equivalence of rounding the *Baja* Peninsula as rounding third base heading for home plate, Santa Barbara. Would they cross the plate standing up or go in sliding hard with cleats up? "At least we're back in known waters," Nep informed his teammates.

They watched the team congratulate one another on the Mexico phase of the mission, *A Tu Madre* being the crown jewel of the six FTM fugitives captured.

"There are a number of things you need to know as we head for the finish line. 'The terrain is to be assessed in terms of distance, difficulty or ease of travel, dimension, and safety,' *Sun Tzu*. Nep, you first," Taylor ordered, taking two steps back.

"It was only twelve miles south of *Cabo San Lucas* that *Tijuana* drug cartel kingpin Francisco Javier Arellano Felix was captured at sea by the US Coast Guard aboard the fishing yacht *Dock Holiday*. The coast guard vessel was 750 miles away from her home port of San Diego. There are two Island Class US Coast Guard boats out of San Diego that surveil the *Baja* coastal corridor, the *Edisto* and the *Long Island*, 110-footers, well-fitted and manned for their sole mission of interdiction." Nep placed his crew on alert, sixty nautical miles south of the Cape. Taylor stepped forward.

"Approximately one hundred miles north of the southern tip of the *Baja* Peninsula and *Cabo San Lucas*, the *Sea Cat* will cross the Tropic of Cancer latitudinal line, considered the beginning of "the danger zone" for nefarious northbound vessels tagged by the US Coast Guard as "Suspect" or "Vessels of Interest." We've traveled too far and for too long of time to lose the race to the finish line on the last leg. Publicly we are whale watchers tailing the grays migrating north by day, but hightailing it at night in order to maintain our schedule. The autopilot has already been programmed with our tactical Santa Barbara bound CTS," Taylor explained.

"Grays don't feed or sleep southbound because their stored blubber can sustain them," Nep continued. "Northbound they must, especially if the mother is nursing a new calf. So we won't stay with any one pair or pod of whales because of their snail pace of one to two miles per hour. But to the uneducated eye our ten knots per hour during daylight will appear legit. If we sense we're being watched by suspecting eyes, we'll slow to two per hour."

"And nighttime speed?" Rap asked.

"Twin engines at full power below a full canvas. I'd say maximum sustained speed, fifteen to sixteen knots," Nep answered.

"And if those eyes are US Coast Guard by day or night?" Grav asked.

"My only real concern will be along the US coastal waters, which is a sieve, vulnerable to drug and people trafficking as well as weapons contraband. Northbound traffic is always of special interest to our boys on the white and red boats. From the US border north, we'll likely see and be seen by the US Coast Guard Protector Class patrol boats, the *Haddock* ported in San Diego, the *Narwhal* in Corona Del Mar, the *Halibut* in Marina Del Rey, the *Blacktip* in Oxnard, and the *Blackfin* out of Santa Barbara, our only real nemesis if they choose to be. All are well wired from stem to stern with ultrasophisticated electronic surveillance, navigation, and communication equipment, thanks to our flush Homeland Security budgets," Nep concluded.

None of the crew members looked upon their brother coast guard sailors as the enemy, respecting the great responsibility they held in protecting the sea borders and the high risks they faced during countless rescue missions in perilous weather and waters. But for the sake of the mission's success, they were compelled to consider them "the opposing team," Taylor labeled them, tongue in cheek.

"We'll save the details of our Santa Barbara grid entry for when we're six hours out. For now, we'll concentrate on the *Baja* leg. Always carry a camera or binocs when on outer decks, like the whale watchers you are," Taylor stated emphatically. Campbell was ordered to prepare a special seagoing meal for the six fugitives, laced with a pharmaceutical mix that would induce a deep sleep for six hours. During that time, he would tattoo eight letters across the topside of the right wrist of each captive. Whenever handcuffed by an officer of the law, two words would speak to them, "Los Lobos," formally the benign numerical code 50807507.

The *Sea Cat* had favorable winds and high RPMs to bring her just off the tip of the *Baja* Peninsula according to her predawn schedule. Slumbering *Cabo San Lucas* was in sight with its seaside resorts, restaurants, and clubs enjoying a respite from the nocturnal revelers now passed out from the night's excesses. Locals and regular visitors to *Cabo*, if awake, would recognize the catamaran from its frequent stops there over the recent years, known as *El Gato del Mar*. Nep and his regular sea crew would also be recognized at the *Cabo Wabo Cantina*, El Squid Roe, Poncho's, Giggling Marlin, Mango Deck, and Billygen's, to name a few.

Heading due north along *Los Cabos* corridor of tourist beaches and luxury hotels, they began to see a few anchored super yachts waking up to cater to their wealthy passengers luxuriating aboard the Zein, Game On, Bad Company, Let It Ride, Chaos, and C-Bandit. The serious sports fishermen were speeding westward in thirty-foot chartered sports fishers in quest of trophy catches of black marlin, sailfish, swordfish, and shark. They had already seized onto their breakfast beer to ostensibly prevent *mal de mer*. Those less ambitious sport fishermen with an appetite for the fruit of the sea had set out in small, outboard motor *pangas* in search of red snapper, yellowtail, grouper, and mackerel.

Midmorning, the whale watching crew would cruise by the largest gathering of the gray whales along their migratory route, the lagoons of Ojo de Liebre, San Ignacio, and Bahia Magdalena. The cows that had birthed early in the warm water lagoons were now commencing their return migration north with their new calves. Nep began to track the most visible pair closest to the *Cat*. They would surface every three minutes on average for a five-second breath of air following a noisy, fifteen-foot high powerful column of water from their two top blowholes. He followed this baby-step pace routine for longer then he cared to only because his first mate had identified the white and red markings of a distant US Coast Guard patrol boat shadowing them from eight nautical miles off port. When the *Cat* slowed to two knots, the guard boat gathered on her.

"Cam, put three more crew on the port wing walk, all active," Nep ordered. He kept his eyes on the mother and calf, which were now submerged.

"Have the cow and calf surfaced off port?" Nep shouted to the crew. "I've lost them aft and starboard."

"Not here, and I know why!" Rap replied with a tone of distress.

"What's up?" Nep asked impatiently.

"Check your sonar on broad beam. Give me a count on a pod of orcas 150 feet off port, approaching at ten o'clock," Cope called back to the bridge.

The mother gray would have picked up on the high-pitched underwater sounds of the loquacious orca pod four and a half times faster than above water from miles away. Known for their deadly wolf pack approach as number 1 predator of the sea, a.k.a. killer whale, Wolves of the Sea, they cared less about stealth. They were the gray whales' arch enemy in any sea scenario. But a weak, postpartum mother with a vulnerable newborn to protect was a minor challenge for a fast, powerful, spike-toothed attack mammal, let alone an entire marauding pod.

"I count nine!" Cam called out.

"We had between seven and nine here. Where are mother and child?" Rap questioned with sincere concern.

"Still don't know. They're way overdue on their breather," he declared with equal concern.

Suddenly the catamaran mysteriously moved abruptly to the left. And then moved again equally to the right as though experiencing its first double jolt of a small earthquake.

"What the hell! Check starboard, it might be the mother," Nep commanded.

An experienced coastal seaman, he had heard stories of gray whale cows pushing their endangered calves up against a nearby boat to shield it from attacking orcas.

"No, nothing," Eizzo reported.

"Nothing port," Cope called in.

"I have an idea of what and where," Lori remarked with a tone of premature relief.

She went quickly below deck to access the ship's belly hatch centered between the two massive hulls. Moments later she reappeared with a smile of astonishment.

"Can you believe it? Mom beamed herself and baby up into our mother ship belly for safe keeping between the hulls."

"Safe if I can maneuver over into more shallow water. Orcas are too smart and agile to be blocked or locked out of an easy meal," Nep stated emphatically. "The orcas will still attack from beneath if they have any wiggle room," he added with increased urgency.

He didn't have time to relate mariners' stories of female gray whales' maternal defenses trying to push their calves onboard small fishing boats to save them from killer whale attacks, only to be savaged by the entire pod before pulling the calf off of the would-be rescue boat.

The mother was floating low in the water with the calf piggybacking atop of the dorsal fin knuckled ridge, confirming Nep's concern. From the great number of barnacles on the mother's estimated forty-five-foot, shiny long body, Lori guessed her to be an older whale, accounting for her strong and savvy maternal instincts for survival.

Taylor appeared suddenly with two crossbows and several bolts.

"Eizzo, take one. Lori, come below to be our eyes and report up to Nep. Give him the status of the whales as he moves closer to shore. Eizzo and I will be under the trap doors at both ends of the pair. If an orca approaches, we'll shoot," he ordered.

"Try for the forehead, between the eyes if you can. He'll send out a shock wave of distress sounds that will cause the pod to desist and retreat," Lori informed them.

"Where do you come up with these obscure factoids?" Taylor asked with an appreciative grin.

"Experience dating military men," she softly shot back with a reciprocating grin. "But my aim was between a different target," she chuckled.

"See why we won't give her a crossbow, Eizzo?"

"Big affirmative on that," he replied as the three hustled below deck.

Nep eased the *Sea Cat* toward shallow waters, sensing occasional hard bumps against the inner hulls. He maintained the two knots speed with assurances from Lori that the distressed hitchhikers were still safely ensconced within the boat's protective belly. The dual eighty-eight-foot long hulls had a five-foot draft, providing more of an obstacle for the orcas than an actual barrier from an attack. The battering of the hulls by the massive mammal was not a concern to Nep. He was confident in the hulls' composite resin construction with carbon fiber in the stress points being much more durable than common fiberglass boats. His worry was now the gage of the ship and getting hung up on a shoal or kelp bed.

The outer deck crew watched the approaching large, shiny black bodies with their white lower jaws momentarily rising from the water for enough air to energize the forward attack mode they were in. Wolf pack teamwork was the *modus operandi* of the killer whale, most likely students of the master *Sun Tzu*, Taylor had commented. They possessed the intelligence and speed of their slender dolphin cousins, absent the constant grin of playfulness. They were serious hunters with an appetite for six hundred pounds of food each per day. After circling the catamaran two times, the nine orcas separated. Taylor and Eizzo loaded and cocked their crossbows.

"The pod split up, four aft, five stern," Cam yelled below to Lori. He didn't need sonar to see the ominous, six-foot high black dorsal fins slicing the water's surface in different directions. Grav was stationed on the rail of the foredeck, Rap on the stern, Cope on port side, and Cam now on starboard. All were spontaneously calling in sightings of numbers, change of directions, and threatening posturing as they randomly occurred. Nep relayed the information to Lori. She conferred with Taylor and Eizzo and then shouted back to Nep, "Heave heartily! Four orcas are holding in front of the foredeck opening to force the whales out the back as the *Cat* moves ahead. Five orcas holding at the stern ready to strike once we've moved on," Lori reported up to the bridge in a single, quickened breath.

She knew that the pack's real objective was to get the mother to drop the fifteen-foot long calf off of her back from the rear, a mere appetizer for nine orcas that swallow their food whole. After a thirteen and a half months pregnancy, traveling six thousand miles from the Arctic Ocean to give birth, and lactating eighty pounds of milk each day made the exhausted mother an easy entrée as well. The orcas saw the catamaran not as a safe haven for whales, but simply as a fast food drive-through.

Nep not only stopped forward movement but put the brakes on in a deft reversal of the propellers. The *Cat* was capable of five knots speed in reverse, but for now needed only to maintain cover for its defenseless live seamates.

The moment Lori shouted, "Its working!" the male leader of the pack surged into the *Cat*'s twenty-foot wide open belly. Just as it began its dive toward the mother's underbelly, Taylor fired a titanium tip, short-range bolt at the surface of the water where it met the broad forehead of the submerging, tank-sized mammal striking it between the eyes. The orca's thirty-foot long, twelve-thousand-pound forward inertia was so great that it surfaced within four seconds from beneath the raised, twelve-foot wide fluke of the gray mother. Eizzo squeezed his bow trigger placing the bolt in near Robin Hood fashion an inch away from splitting Taylor's imbedded bolt. The orca's eyes were closed, the mouth wide open, ingesting barrels of water. The Delta archers looked from stem to stern, reloaded for the next attack but saw none. The pod was completely out of sight.

"We have a one-for-one hit," Lori reported to the bridge. "What do you show?"

"I count eight, fast-track westbound on sonar, one drifting slowly southbound," Nep replied officially. The Delta deck hands confirmed the counts and directions.

"Man, you won't see that at Sea World!" Eizzo called up to his mates.

Nep decided to sit over the cow and calf for another ten minutes, monitoring the sonar for the attack pod. There was none. Their radar showed the coast guard patrol boat nineteen nautical miles northeast on a faster track.

As though on cue, the whales emerged from their accidental den, resting tentatively on the surface in front of the *Cat* facing the open ocean. The mother's fifteen-foot high spout washed back over the foredeck. Whistles and clicks were exchanged between the parent and child, thought to be, by Lori, a maternal message of, *Welcome to the food chain, my child.*

The entire crew stood at the foredeck rail watching the whales watching them. They could look into the mother's large left eye and see themselves.

"The Alaskan Eskimos say you can see God through a whale's eyes," Eizzo shared with his silent teammates. Nep turned the dual rudders hard left to push out of the shallow water away from the stressed survivors.

Under full power and masted, fresh away on a sun setting long sea put the *Sea Cat* back on schedule. Taylor and team didn't regret the lost time for a winning cause. The next two days were uneventful, edging steadily northward along the coast. They had been sighted by all of the Pacific Coast Protector Class Guard boats on Nep's below the border watch list. Their next closest visitor was the *Halibut* near the Port of Los Angeles, coming alongside long enough to see Lori emerge from the bridge to salute them in her white bikini. After a closer official look, they proceeded searching the waters for more threatening vessels of lesser interest. The masquerade blue and white pendants atop the mast and stern poles snapped in the wind, stating their pretended purpose, the American Cetacean Society at sea.

"An honest reality pendant, reading 'FTM Captives Society,' definitely wouldn't fly," Cam said sardonically.

Standing on the bridge with Nep and Taylor, Lori reached over to the stereo system and made a selection to the accepting smiles of all on-board the top deck, "*Walk on the Ocean*" by Toad the Wet Sprocket.

One hour south of Santa Barbara, the city of Ventura, along the central coast of California, was the closest harbor to their destination. The *Sea Cat* idled south of Ventura long enough to lower the *Figment* to the sea surface with Lori, Cope, and Rap aboard. They would tie up at the harbor marina, secure and cover the speed craft before driving north to Santa Barbara. The plan was to keep the six incarcerated captives aboard the *Sea Cat* ignorant of place, time, and intent. After all, there was "no need to know," in military parlance. The captives remained healthy, albeit sedated thanks to Campbell's special ginger and pharmaceutical laced recipes.

That night would be the last night for the remaining Delta team aboard the *Sea Cat*, except for Nep and his crew. The *Cat* would anchor on the north end of San Miguel Island, the outermost of the Channel Islands in its sixty-mile long chain of four in the northern group. It formed the outer boundary for the maritime channel traffic traveling the US coastal waters, twenty-five miles from Santa Barbara. The islands themselves were highly protected members of the National Marine Sanctuary and National Parks Service. Apart from the US *Blackfin* chasing away rogue commercial fishing boats, the US park rangers were on a 24-7 watch within the island shores.

"The only anchorage allowed on San Miguel is Cuyler harbor on the windward, northeast side," Taylor stated. "Although far from ideal in winter, it will provide us with the best tactical staging area for our final covert mission launch. We will be out of sight from all channel traffic and off of the *Blackfin*'s radar. We'll first pass within one mile of the Santa Barbara harbor and the Coast Guard Safety detachment on its west side," Taylor further explained to his team before a large map. He elaborated on the coming twenty-four-hour plan in punctilious detail, including the roles Cope, Rap, and Lori would play on shore.

"I've fixed our radio onto the coast guard channel to monitor all chatter and official directives," Nep reported, as the *Sea Cat* navigated the waters beyond Ventura past Santa Barbara. Taylor had lifted his binoculars long enough to sight a familiar floating friend in the marina, the *Conch II* resting in its slip. Ten miles farther north by the town of Goleta, the innocent-looking catamaran would turn ninety degrees port, as though offing six nautical miles beyond the northwestern most tip of San Miguel to eventually be out of the line of sight from the north and southbound coastwise commercial traffic and radar from harbor vessels. Once they had hit the heavy head-sea on the western side of the island, they would double back on a dead reckoning track, slipping unseen into San Miguel's Cuyler Harbor before sunset.

It was February 4 when winter weather was historically the bane of mariners daring to circumvent San Miguel. Taylor and Nep knew this and chose it for its unpopular visitation for that time of the year. Cam joined the two men on the bridge reviewing the island's ocean map datum. Nep pointed out the narrow entry options because of heavy kelp beds and 4- to 6-foot high rocks protruding above water throughout the 1.2-mile long, ½ mile wide unwelcoming harbor.

"We'll come straight in with a south head for Judge Rock, turning fifteen degrees starboard at Bat Rock and anchoring beneath Cabrillo Overlook for protection from the strong northwesterly," Nep informed his crew.

"Holy shit, there are a ton of rocks!" Cam exclaimed as he examined the harbor map. "Gull Rock, Clover, Middle, Can, and Kid Rock. Are they joking, Kid Rock? How will I know it when I see it?" Cam questioned with amused curiosity.

"It's the tall, skinny, ugly one," Nep replied without breaking a smile.

Taylor was smiling, but his mind wandered briefly to the double irony of place and time. He recalled his North American history and the man who discovered California, Spanish sea captain and explorer Juan Rodriquez Cabrillo. Cabrillo had sailed farther than most into the sixteenth century with unsophisticated ships and primitive navigation, survived the conquest of Mexico as a crossbowman alongside leader Hernan Cortéz and anchored in 1543 in the very same spot Nep was plotting in Cuyler Harbor. Cabrillo was perhaps the harbor's first fatality, dying from an injury he received following the landing of his ship, the *San Salvador*. It is rumored that he was buried on the island, then named *Isla Capitana*, on Cabrillo Overlook where a weather-worn concrete marker designates the assumed site. Now 450 years later, Taylor wondered if the Cabrillo spirit remained.

Proceeded from the east by its sister islands of Anacapa, Santa Cruz, and Santa Rosa, San Miguel was the most dangerous to approach. A naval danger zone was officially established around the entire irregular shaped, seven-mile long, two-mile wide island.

The first thing the crew noticed about San Miguel when they sailed by was that the leeward side was treeless, covered entirely by grass, now turned green from the winter rains. Its highest point rose over eight hundred feet in the middle of the deserted island. The broken shores were bold and rocky with a few short stretches of beaches. Cuyler Harbor sheltered one of them. Nep would soon be looking for the large rock landmarks in the harbor to navigate the *Cat* and crew to a safe anchorage. Taylor's concern was for the best positioning of the catamaran for a successful departure in the darkness of early morning. If not done with precision within the narrows of the outer edge of the harbor, the morning swells and strong northwesterly would ground them with only the US *Blackfin* to rescue them.

All hands were on deck to assist Nep navigate the narrow approach. Late afternoon shadows hampered his visual judgment, relying more on instruments then deck crew. The dual hulls, rudders, and engines provided greater stability and maneuverability than a single hull ship. But the challenge remained with the "sundowner" winds picking up over the now choppy sea. A few stressful minutes and creative maneuvers later, she was hove hard, idling safely over their planned parking space beneath the Cabrillo overlook, hidden from view and radar detection behind the several large outcrop of yacht-size rocks. It was man and machine over nature, the winner of the first round. Nep quickly dropped the two stone anchors fore and aft, moored where explorer Cabrillo had anchored his *San Salvador* in 1543. The no less stressful predawn exit effort would be the final and decisive round.

With the ship and crew settled in from the successful harbor entry, Taylor called the Delta team together for their final tactical meeting. The plan for landing the FTM fugitives onto the US mainland and entering the Santa Barbara grid was reviewed and set.

"For security and safety reasons, we will go below to inform each captive individually about tomorrow's departure for the mainland. Eizzo, Grav, Cam, you'll join me in a *tour de force* visit to the six captives' cabins when Campbell brings them dinner. We'll wear top deck whites and caps with no logos and with sunglasses to neutralize personal identities. Cam, you'll bring our unloaded sniper rifle and one round in hand. Grav, you'll bring Lori's small purchase from *Puerto Vallarta*. Only I will talk—short, sweet, and to the point. The less exposure the better. Campbell will be ready in twenty minutes. Questions?" he concluded.

"No, sir," came the joint reply.

On orders from Taylor, Campbell had lightened the doses of sedatives in the food by two thirds for the FTM diners. He knew that a short night's sleep and wobbly sea legs on land would have the captives in a weakened state for hours.

The first cabin cell to be unlocked was Olivel's. It was the first time the team had laid eyes on him since the *Maria Madre* extraction. He would not recognize them from that dark, blurry night when for a split second a black-faced man dropped him like a bad habit.

Olivel rose aggressively from his cot when the door opened. He remained handcuffed in front as the other captives were. Only he and Leon Madrid spoke broken border English, mostly profanity.

"What's this, your pussy cook had to bring bodyguards to make me eat his *mierda*?" Olivel shouted with exaggerated bravado.

As stocky and rock solid as he was, Olivel shrank quickly in size and bravura when Taylor faced him toe-to-toe.

"Sit, dickhead. I talk, you listen, *comprende*?"

With Eizzo and Cam of near equal size flanking Taylor, even a stone-cold killer wasn't that brave or stupid to challenge the odds. He sat immediately.

"Tomorrow morning, you will get up very early. You'll eat all of the breakfast you're given. You'll wear the clothes handed to you. You will be taken to shore by the four of us. If you think you can jump overboard and escape, know that you will be attacked by dozens of hungry sharks with jaws like this," Taylor dramatized.

Cam reached in with the broad skeletal jaws and double rows of sharp jagged teeth of a blue shark that Lori had picked up in *Puerto Vallarta*. Olivel's unblinking obsidian eyes widened.

"On land, you'll be driven to a large building in the city. If at any time you try to run to escape, my men will aim their rifles at you," he continued in a calm monotone.

Eizzo extended his MK-13 Mod-2 Special Forces sniper rifle with mounted scope, pointing it directly at Olivel's crotch.

"Without hesitation, they will shoot this up your asshole."

Eizzo held a long, sharp pointed, .300 Winchester Magnum bullet upward for Olivel to visually examine.

"This .300 Win Mag bullet will travel at a muzzle velocity of 3,600 feet per second up your ass and out your tiny little dick, causing your balls to explode. You won't die, but you will wish you had. *Comprende?*" Taylor asked harshly.

The stunned facial expression on Olivel nodded yes. Campbell placed his dinner on a small, built-in wooden table and then was escorted out by his three bodyguards. The dinnertime show and tell was repeated the same to the five other dinner guests with the one exception of Pedro Barajas, the fugitive father of burn victim, Miguel. There, Taylor deviated from the script to inform Barajas he would be transported to a crematorium in the morning. There he would be "roasted and toasted over open flames until near death," but kept alive to suffer as his son has done. Barajas's entire body became damp from flop sweat and other bodily fluids. When they left his cabin, Cam commented that Barajas "*will definitely look forward to the sharks and bullets options.*"

"Tonight I want him to be nauseous with nightmares. In the morning, I might tell him otherwise or maybe not," Taylor reacted in a jocular tone.

Cam and Eizzo had noticed something different about Barajas's cabin cell. He was the only captive chained to his fixed bed post. The chain's reach extended to the toilet and sink in the 10×10-foot bulkhead, but out of reach from the two handmade wooden masks. They were hung opposite his bed, staring back at Barajas hauntingly, as though asking, Why? Cam and Eizzo never questioned their presence. They understood.

The only captive with an attitude during Taylor's dinner performances was Leon Madrid. He ranted on and on that he would have their heads crushed by his cartel's vice squad and their nude bodies burned in public, that his chapos were searching for him as he spoke.

Taylor silenced Madrid's *Tijuana* Spanglish with two fingers pressed hard on his windpipe. "*Eschucha me, pendejo* (Listen up, fool). You're like a room full of lesbians. You don't know dick! And your *chaparrines* aren't going to do dick because you're just one more dispensable punk *pistolero* for hire. You were replaced the day you disappeared and now already forgotten. What you have to worry about now are bullets up your *maricon* ass and sharks that eat shit, *comprende?*" He pressured Madrid down on his knees with his two digits.

Madrid sat back on his bed sulking in silence, his lip curled in a sneer, attentively listening to the rest of the dinner show and tell. Once outside of the cabin, Taylor told his performing partners, "Madrid will be okay. He just needed an attitude adjustment."

At 0400, the captives were awakened with their new clothes and special breakfast. Nep, with his first and second mates, had employed the technical genius of their navigational software to retrace their successful harbor entry track and debouched the high-risk route into the channel waters. It adjusted for present wind conditions, water depth, frequency and height of swells, and eddies. Now out safely on the open sea, it would calculate ocean currents as well. The other smart instruments would search for marine traffic and set their CTS: destination, one nautical mile off of the mainland, a distance of twenty-three nautical miles. The neap tides posed no hazards to the small draft Zod raft, which would be launched from the *Sea Cat* at that mile mark.

The crew would look and listen for the horn and light warnings coming from channel buoys and neighboring oil platforms ten miles off of the coast. The *Sea Cat* departed their hideaway island harbor with the encounter of heavy fog, bad for navigation but good news for covert cover. The entire trip would be on instruments. The only danger-alert sounding was caused by the largest creature to ever inhabit the planet, a pod of giant blue whales to the northeast of the island setting off the sonar warning when submerged and radar warning when breaching.

At 0600, the *Sea Cat* heaved, engines idled. The crew deftly lowered the Zod with Cam sitting as point navigator fore, the captives hustled on board in the middle with Taylor at the center helm alongside the *Cat*'s second mate, and Eizzo riding guard at the stern. The second mate would return the Zod to the mother ship once all of its passengers were safely ashore. This time the captives were cuffed from behind and chain linked together with a long, light, black canvas covering them for protection from the cold, damp ocean air and from visual detection. Only the Delta team wore life jackets. Nep couldn't resist playing a farewell song lowly over the main deck speakers dedicated to the departing captives by Aretha Franklin, "*Chain of Fools.*"

The Zod unceremoniously shoved off from the *Sea Cat*'s stern, headed directly to the former site of the Ellwood pier. Its historical claim to fame was that it was the only site attacked on America's mainland by the Japanese the day after they struck Pearl Harbor, a minor event by comparison soon forgotten. Hundreds of feet of destroyed thick timbers became the exposed rafters of a nearby steak house. The private pier was once owned by ARCO Oil to supply their drilling rigs on the above *mesa*, now a large vacant ocean vista park.

The landing site was chosen by Taylor for its sea and land isolation as well for easy access from shore up the eighty-foot high precipitous cliff. What ARCO did leave behind was its concrete staircase that rose in a zigzag, switchback design, making its ascent more bearable for the captives with welcomed intervals of restful landings. On the bottom landing stood Rap holding a high frequency location finder beamed out to the oncoming Zod. At the top of the aging staircase, hidden beneath the broad canopy of a ten-foot high, wind-formed woody shrub stood Cope equipped with a radio and night-all-weather binoculars.

370

Rap confirmed by radio what Cope had observed through the thick morning marine layer, "The Zod has landed." He helped Cam tug the raft's bow onto shore. Rap placed a small piece of duct tape over the mouth of each captive. Taylor and Eizzo shoved the Zod back into the tide water with the second mate now the captain of his raft until returned via a navigational laser beam to the mother ship one short mile away.

In a forced, push-pull manner, the four Delta members guided the chain gang up the high staircase, resting them momentarily at each landing. The captives' sea legs were weak and wobbly from days and weeks of confinement in their small bulkhead cells. Their newly issued wardrobe included what Grav described as American huaraches, better known as flip-flops. Taylor chose them because they were impossible to run in, yet easy to remove when strip searched.

On the ocean's edge of the Ellwood mesa, Cope greeted each captive as they stepped onto terra firma, "Welcome to the United States of America. I hope your stay here will be a long one."

Eizzo and Cam were less welcoming as they briskly told each captive, "Watch your head!" forcing them to bow down while entering the back of a long charcoal-colored panel truck. It was parked under the high canopy meadow shrub hide. The captives were commanded to sit on the rubber carpeted floor in darkness as the rear double doors were closed and locked. The team conferred with one another in front of the van while Taylor radioed Lori, strategically stationed in downtown Santa Barbara.

"We've got a 'Go'!" Taylor reported, causing the men to separate like a football team out of a huddle. He and Eizzo entered the van's cab and watched Cam and Cope board an identical truck parked fifty feet away behind a long, thick stand of eucalyptus trees. Rap walked the four-block length of the meadow grass road along the eucalyptus grove away from the ocean. Within eight minutes, he radioed, "All clear."

With the lights off, the vans quietly rolled over the old service road following the thick tree line out to a rural surface street. Rap joined Cope and Cam in the lead van. A large green road sign with white luminous letters and directional arrow pointed to the right, "Hwy. 101 South, Santa Barbara." They turned on their lights Santa Barbara bound.

21

CONFESSION MELTDOWN

Mexico City

The *Zócolo* was the everyday name used for Mexico City's large central plaza bordered by high level federal government buildings and Metropolitan Cathedral. Today, however, the first Monday in February, it would be respectfully referred to by its official name, *La Plaza de la Constitución* (Constitution Plaza). Today it would be the stage for the annual *Fiestas Patrias* (national holiday), *Día de la Constitución* (Constitution Day), commemoration of Mexico's formal ratification of their constitution of 1917, adopted after their revolution.

Government officials and employees would be the majority of the masses gathered at noon to join the president and other dignitaries to celebrate the occasion. Nationwide, the holiday was not as popular as their *Cinco de Mayo*, or their Independence Day, and therefore with less pomp at the plaza. There would be the patriotic flag waving, official bloated canned speeches and traditional shouts of "*Viva Mexico!*" Today was pure tradition, nothing out of the ordinary planned for the plaza beyond the obligatory respect to be given to the "*Como Mexico, no hay otro* (Like Mexico, there is no other)." Those in attendance and viewing on television would expect no less. More, however, never entered their collective imagination.

Mattie's youthful memories of the old Hotel Majestic were fond ones. Located on the central west corner of the *Zócolo*, her parents would bring her and brother Angelino to the seventh-floor rooftop terrace of the Majestic to view the festivities below. Her mother would play teacher to the curious siblings, explaining the importance of recognizing their country's traditions and the value of its history.

"As a citizen, you won't know where your nation's society should be if you don't know from where it came," she stressed. And today, after years of professional and personal internal observation, Mattie and Angelino knew both all too well, they regretted.

Mattie entered the hotel's rooftop terrace at precisely eight o'clock. The indoor dining area was filled with breakfast guests due to the cool outside gray morning air. The *maître d'* offered her the table of her choice. She tactically selected the outermost corner table along the terrace wall overlooking the *Zócolo* in front, the ambit of her operations, and most importantly, the Metropolitan Cathedral on the left front. Her view was unobstructed and her table private. The remaining nineteen red *Cinzano* logo umbrella tables would be fully occupied before the noontime official ceremonies began. Mattie's interest and attention meanwhile would be elsewhere long before that hour, later leaving her table to others.

Once her waiter departed with her order for coffee and a hot croissant, she dialed her cell phone and spoke briefly, "In place, in clear view," then disconnected.

She pulled a long lens camera from her deep black canvas tote bag as though she were a common tourist. Her powder-blue ski jacket, wraparound white rim sunglasses and tightly pulled ponytail hair enhanced that intended perception. She aimed the lens in the direction of the cathedral on the near north end of the *Zócolo* and set the focus on the church appended on its right side. Her position on the seventh-floor terrace provided her a complete panoramic view of the enormous stone laid plaza. Its rectangular expanse equaled three large city blocks, only exceeded in size by Red Square in Moscow and Tiananmen Square in Beijing, China, the largest.

The north-south street on the west side of the plaza running in front of the Hotel Majestic was named *5 de Febrero*, or Constitution

Avenue, in honor of the day's historical significance. The parallel street opposite the plaza along the Presidential Palace was named *Avenida Moneda* (Money Avenue). Mattie's father had joked that the presidents were allowed to choose between the two names for the palace street. On the north end of the plaza ran the *Avenida Cinco de Mayo*, and the southern end, *Avenida 16 de Septiembre*, covering all of the nation's major government holidays, the latter noting their Independence Day. Many of the city's modern streets still corresponded to the original *calzados* laid out by *Montezuma's* empire builders. Mattie and Angelino knew them all from their youthful days of exploring the inner city.

The young waiter arrived with a medium-size carafe of coffee and a fresh-from-the-oven *croissant* with a small ramekin of honey butter. She smiled with the memory of her father commenting that, "The only three redeeming features the occupying French left to Mexico were the *baguette*, the *bolillo*, and *croissant*. But Mexico had to sweeten them with her pure bee honey to make them Mexican."

Mattie's thoughts turned to the task at hand. While she was waiting for her phone to ring, she scanned the three stories, 650-foot long, red *tezontle* stone facade of the Presidential Palace across the plaza looking for any signs of her target. She would be alarmed to see him ahead of their clandestine schedule. His appearance and movements would have to be on her covert team's timeline, place, and terms for their plan to be consequent and undetected. The target's reputation for precision planning preceded him as a formidable opponent in protecting corrupt government officials as the director of the PFJ, *La Policia Federal Judicial*, Mexico's FBI and now the new all-powerful federal attorney general. Her team's reconnaissance of target Pasqual Diego Lazaro told her that he typically traveled in a chauffeured black Lincoln town car with one plainclothes bodyguard. She also knew that he would not bother to be driven the three hundred feet distance to the entrance of the cathedral, especially on a day with military vehicles, armed personnel in the plaza, and the destination being the holy sanctuary of the church.

Attorney General Lazaro knew the purpose of the proposed morning meeting and the presumed office it came from, that of

His Eminence, Cardinal Montenegro. The two would never meet publicly or privately in either's office. The subject matter was always secret, as was the meeting place. The phone invitation came from an unidentified messenger of the Cardinal's directly to the AG. It was as succinct as it was cryptic.

"Your confessional time is confirmed for the cathedral tomorrow at 8:30 a.m. by the *Cura Animarum.*"

Those last two words were the key code for the AG to accept the legitimacy of the caller and his invitation. Special appointments for use of the cathedral's confessionals for high profile individuals were not uncommon. But for such a confirmation to come with the words *Cura Animarum* (the care of souls) would never happen, the AG was told a year earlier by Cardinal Montenegro when their clandestine rendezvous began.

The parish priest officially had charge of "the care of souls" and assigned an appropriate penance to the confessor. Throughout each day, the confessional duties were assigned to several different priests in the side church, who attended to the faithful from the highly populated *Colonial Central.* Even though the cathedral was named the Metropolitan, it was not used by the masses. They were shepherded to the adjacent church, *Sagrairo Metropolitano,* on the right side of the cathedral. Its excessively ornate *Churrigueresque* style front was now the background to the focus of Mattie's attention following the sighting of a familiar priest.

Mattie instantly recognized her brother in his priest vestments through the 600-mm lens as he rounded the far corner of the church off of *Calle del Seminario.* His only disguise was large, black rimmed sunglasses. She was pleased to see a peaceful smile on his face as he intentionally looked up toward the rooftop terrace. He entered the church upon sensing a single vibration from his silent pocketed cell phone, his sister's confirmation of her sighting. He could have entered the cathedral, his destination, just one hundred feet away, but preferred the less conspicuous route among the masses. Subconsciously he harbored an aversion to the cathedral's old facade, not for aesthetic reasons with its busy Spanish baroque impression of massive volutes and pairs of twisted columns, but because he could not abide the sight of the eight-foot diameter bas-relief carved official seal of the federal government centrally located between the two high neoclassic, openwork bell towers. He saw it as a billboard on the largest and oldest cathedral in the western hemisphere advertising the union of church and state, officially married with the Mexican government's seal of approval and proxy—in his mind, partners in crime. *An alliance of church and state will corrupt both*, he recalled the wise words of Thomas Jefferson.

Once inside, Angelino bypassed the church's row of confessionals. He went directly to the left of the central altar to a broad table that supported scores of ovum candles placed by the faithful. He included his own, which was formed inside a blue glass container two inches high by two inches in diameter. Once lit, it would burn slowly in remembrance of his father. On this day, as with many others over the past five years, that memory would be the sinew of his mission.

He then proceeded to a private back passageway that led to the cathedral's lone connector door. The little known, seldom used passage would take him along the north wall of the fifty-five-foot high, barrel-vaulted ceiling cathedral behind the enormous, richly carved, exquisite gold and silver gilded high altars "To the Kings," "Assumption of Maria," to which the cathedral is dedicated and "Of Forgiveness," with their large religious marble sculptures and paintings of glory. He would secretly exit the hidden passage in the far northwestern corner of the massive building. It was softly illuminated by twenty-one votive candles lit by the laity, burning in serried ranks of twenty-one prickets supported by a tall brass stand. There, separated by five feet each were four finely carved, polished dark cedar wood confessionals pressed against the basalt stone perimeter wall. He was certain no one was aware, not even Cardinal Montenegro, of the secret of confessional number 4. It was tucked tightly into the northwest corner, different than the others, that it possessed a secret that would be revealed that morning to their target.

Mattie placed a call to their principal accomplice waiting patiently in his closed *Mi Tio's* cantina on *Calle de Guatemala* behind the cathedral.

"We have number 1 entry," she stated clearly.

"Confirmed," came *Tio Chuey's* reply, followed by their disconnect.

Minutes later, two stout men in tourist casual wear left the lobby of the modest, back street Cathedral Hotel at 94 Donceles Street behind the church. A third man remained in their seventh-floor room looking out his window with binoculars in one hand and a cell phone in the other. Soon thereafter, he received a brief call from the two stout men once *Tio Chuey* unlocked his cantina door to let them in. All three were disaffected former PJF agents loyal to deceased Agent Colima. The three had already exacted their collective revenge on their friend's captured shooter after his full confession as the *Los Lobos* hired hit man. Lazaro never knew of the revenge killing nor would suspect that one of his *lobos* would come back to bite him.

They now all awaited Mattie's last planned call.

With Mattie's terrace overhead superintendence, the plan was right on schedule. All they lacked was their planned target. Her long-range lens was again focused on the broad main open entrance of the Presidential Palace. All foot traffic was entering at that hour with the exception of a tall figure emerging halfway onto the sidewalk and stopped. He observed the scene before him from several angles. Apparently all to his satisfaction, he returned to the entrance where he stood with his back to the *Zócolo*. Seconds later, a medium-build man appeared alongside the taller one conversing. She focused tightly upon the newcomer. He had distinguished-looking curly white side-burns complementing the black wavy hair combed straight back as though facing a strong headwind. It was definitely target Pascual Diego Lazaro, she concluded. It was confirmed with the sighting of his signature single color silk tie, red being the color *de jour* matched by the silk handkerchief eloquently placed in his black custom-tailored suit coat breast pocket. She knew that the white dress shirt would be of a silk, linen blend from Hong Kong.

"*Aungue la mona se vista de seda, mona se queda* (Even though the monkey dresses in silk, it is still a monkey)," she angrily reminded herself.

That unforgettable image of his face burned into her vengeful memory now traveled like lightning to her nerve center broadcasting a sickening sensation throughout her body. She could unequivocally describe it as nothing less than odium, pure and simple.

The chilling recollection that she had once shaken his hand sickened her further. It was the executioner's hand that sent the signal for her father's torturous assassination. In her mind, it was tantamount to his having held the gun, if it were not for his cowardice. Having a homicidal proxy pull the trigger did not leave his hand clean, she and Angelino had concluded in their subjective judgment. And theirs was the only judgment that mattered that day and forever.

Mattie's covert partners, strategically sequestered in a *cantina* basement, a hotel room, and confessional were now joined by an additional pivotal partner in their plan. His brief cell phone signal to Mattie confirmed his tactical placement in the cathedral, currently kneeling as a votary visitor in a second-row pew in the pretend solemnity of prayer thirty feet from the corner confessional. She in turn called the others with the same three words, "All in place."

Pascual Diego Lazaro separated from the tall man who remained by the sidewalk palace entrance. He diligently observed the attorney general walk with an insouciant gait across the northeast corner of the Constitution Plaza toward the cathedral.

"So much for the saying, '*A donde va el violin, va la bolsa*' (Wherever the violin goes, the violin case goes too)," she murmured to herself.

Mattie kept Lazaro in her lens focus every step of the way. As he paused for the east-west traffic to pass on *Avenida 5 de Mayo* in front of the cathedral, she saw him look up between the bell towers. For a fleeting moment, she saw a broad smile on his face and wondered if it was stimulated by the government seal carved into its facade. Knowing his infamous ego, she speculated that he rationalized it as a divine affirmation of his dutiful work being for God and country, not for power and *pesos*.

Inside private confessional number 4, Father Angelino sat in obscure equanimity contemplating the church's history in Mexico. Since the arrival in Mexico of Spanish Conquistador Cortez and the Catholic Church, history had told of countless cases of corruption by such an alliance. Guilty Mexican government officials had only to ask the church for forgiveness and the church would grant it, until the next request, and the next, and the next. This perpetual process of ask and ye shall receive penance peddling had sustained both allied institutions over the centuries, Angelino reminded himself. But this time the circle of corruption would be broken, the consequences of the former PJF director's crimes made public, broadcast to every citizen in Mexico that for once there would be no penance, no forgiveness, no way out.

"Approaching," called Mattie to all team members waiting to execute their plan of weeks in the making. Lazaro had entered the cathedral's large center doorway. The tall man watched his entry from across the plaza and then returned to the entryway of the Presidential Palace.

Although Father Angelino had never been a parish priest, he was fully aware of their confessional duty. They would hear countless sordid confessions of sin, woe, and misery. They would then assign an appropriate penance and the sins would be expiated, forgiveness served up for the confessor's immediate consumption. It always reminded him of the story he was told by a cynic who claimed that *as a young boy, he constantly prayed to God for a bike. When that didn't work, he realized he had it all wrong. So he stole a bike and asked the Lord for forgiveness.*

For the faithful and hopeful, confessing made one right with God. But what about making things right with society, he had pondered, right with the son and daughter and wife of the man the confessor had assassinated? Here and now there would be no confession, no pleas, no plea bargaining he had predetermined. But things would be made right. This was not about God's forgiveness. That would have to come at a different time and place. This would be about justice among mortals, pure and simple. This priest was definitely not in charge of the *cura animarum*, the care of Lazaro's soul. Today there would be no sale on indulgences, absolution, or salvation.

The kneeling man in the far corner pew identified the target approaching the fourth confessional and whispered a call to *Tio Chuey*. Retired PJF Agent Chuey confirmed his readiness with a firmly committed, "*Adelante!* (Onward!)" Mattie was next to being advised. She immediately shifted into a sentinel posture, keeping a watchful eye out for any unusual movement of the tall man or military personnel in the direction of the cathedral. She knew that Lazaro had only to reach into his suit coat pocket to press three buttons on his cell phone to summon his bodyguard. She could only wait and watch.

Lazaro had arrived punctually at the fourth confessional tucked back in the corner of the cathedral. His slow, deliberate glance around the congregational pews viewed only three people kneeling in private prayer. He looked beyond at the surrounding fourteen subsidiary altars and saw no one. He unbuttoned the two buttons on his suit coat before opening the door. The light illumine inside only allowed him to make out the black and white vestments of a priest through the decorative wooden screen that divided them. Once seated, he identified himself and purpose with the cryptic phrase Father Angelino had ascertained from his espionage efforts, "*Amicus humani* (Friend of the human race)." Angelino's response came in a reverent tone, "*Cura animarum* (In the care of souls)."

Lazaro saw only the coupled hands of the priest raised in front of his bowed face, his elbows resting on a narrow shelf beneath the wooden screen. He noticed a large ornate ring the priest wore on his left hand, assuming it to represent one of the many priestly orders of the church.

"*A cerca se para no hablar en voz alta, por favor* (Please come closer so as not to speak in a loud voice)," the priest suggested impassively.

Lazaro complied without looking through the screen. Angelino tapped once firmly on the screen with the ring to subtly draw Lazaro's attention to it. He casually glanced over to notice the ornate ring leveled at his head, pressed against the screen, yet not seeing Angelino's thumb pressing firmly down on a side stone. Suddenly from the larger center stone, a broad, white mist projectile of fluid sprayed forth covering Lazaro's eyes and nose. His head violently recoiled against the opposite side of the confessional. Angelino knocked twice on the back side of the hardwood closet-size confessional. In an instant, the back wall on Lazaro's side sprung completely open. Lazaro rose quickly covering his burning eyes with his hands. He did not see the two stout men reaching into the secret back opening. The closest to him yanked down hard on the back collar of his suit coat, forcing it down around his arms and torso, pinning them tightly together to his side.

The kneeling man outside now stood inside the confessional alongside Lazaro, appearing as a near look-alike in all features: face, dark wavy swept back hair, curly white sideburns and stature. He wore a black suit with a white dress shirt. He only lacked a tie and pocket handkerchief. The second man in the back reached in the opening. He stuffed a white handkerchief into Lazaro's open gagging mouth while jerking the red silk one from his coat pocket. His cell phone was taken from his side pocket by the first man while the look-alike man grabbed his red silk tie like a choke collar and elevated him high upon his toes. The tie's knot was loosened, then removed over Lazaro's head and placed over his. It complemented the red silk handkerchief now fashionably stuffed into his black suit coat pocket. Lazaro's cell phone was handed to the look-alike man, who placed it on mute. The well-choreographed capture took mere fifteen seconds.

Father Angelino slid open the screen halfway with the temptation to revile his father's assassin. Instead, he drew from his pocket the silver chain and medal of Saint Michael his father had worn to his dying breath and handed it to the second man. He pulled the handkerchief from Lazaro's mouth long enough for him to take a deep, desperate breath. The medallion and chain were forced into his mouth followed by the white handkerchief. Father Angelino then sentenced his enemy with the moral ferocity and official finality of a high priest from the Spanish inquisition, intoning, "*En el nombre de mi padre, vete al infierno por eternidad!* (In the name of my father, go to hell for eternity!)"

Lazaro's horrorstricken face struggled to open its eyes, to put a face with the unknown voice. But the tearing and swelling wouldn't allow it. His attempt to speak was muffled by the handkerchief he tried to expiate from his mouth, prevented by gagging reflexes. He was pulled quickly through the back clandestine door where only a narrow beam of a flashlight directed their secret passage.

The door was closed from behind with the air-tight precision of a bank vault, appearing once more as a simple back wall panel. The look-alike man stood in the confessional facing the seated Angelino on the other side. The Father sized him up with a discerning eye, approving of his Lazaro look-alike appearance with the added red silk touches.

"Be safe," Angelino told the man with a grateful smile, then exited the confessional unseen. The look-alike man remained for a moment and then casually left for the cathedral's main entrance, stopping short of exiting completely. He called Mattie. "All is well. Awaiting your clearance."

"Stand by for my call," she replied, still starring through the long lens at the tall man standing at the edge of the Presidential Palace entrance. It would now be a waiting game. She knew the tall man would eventually grow impatient expecting to see AG Lazaro appear from the cathedral. Mattie and the look-alike man needed to buy as much time as the tall man's patience would allow.

Dividing her scoping attention between the palace and cathedral entrances, her thoughts were with the ensnared Lazaro's abductors, her covert teammates. All were willing participants in the plan to seek justice for their fallen comrade and dear friend Antonio Colima. They were former PJF agents who retired from the investigative department the same time *Tio Chuey* had for the same reasons: refusal to be a party to institutionalized government corruption. They were easily recruited for Chuey's underground operation, eager to avenge their aggrieved leader.

From her rooftop vantage point, she saw something no other visitor would see: the irony of the massive cathedral's physical inclination, its physical sinking from left to right. For Mattie and Angelino, it symbolized the church's inclination toward the government's highest office, the presidency and its declining rectitude. The added irony came with the secreting of Lazaro away into the back tunnels on the outer perimeter of the cathedral, excavated for the purpose of materially stabilizing the sinking building with broad steel, subterranean braces.

Originally built on the dry lake bed of Lake *Texcoco*, the settlement of the soft clay subsoil weakened as a bed foundation for the cathedral from century's removal of water from the soil. The greater *Zócolo* area was originally the center of *Tenochititlán*, the capital of the Aztec empire, destroyed in 1521 by the invading Spaniards. The *Cathedral Metropolitana* and surrounding government buildings were erected on the top of its ruins. The razed site of *Aztec Emperor Moctezuma II's* new palace was replaced by conqueror Hernán Cortez with the Catholic Church's principal place of worship. Their allied dominance over the people, real and symbolic, began right there, Mattie was reminded.

She had no delusions of expunging the age-old corrupt alliance with their covert operations that day. But at least its efficacy could exscind one of its principal players from the criminal coupling and expose the alliance for what it really was, a falsehood that did not represent nor serve the people of Mexico, but rather protected those who exploited them for their own private power, control, and ill-gotten gains.

Twenty-minutes had passed since Lazaro had entered the cathedral. The tall man began pacing back and forth between the palace entrance and curb along Moneda Avenue, all the while looking in the direction of the cathedral. Even he wouldn't believe his crooked boss had twenty minutes worth of sins to confess, or at best, was willing to, Mattie speculated. Noticing his increasing demonstrable curiosity, she called the look-alike man still standing in the inner shadows of the cathedral central doors.

"All clear in front. Pick your moment," she remarked with caution to the look-alike man, now peering out from the shadows.

"ETA seven minutes," came his cellular reply.

He tightened his red tie, buttoned his suit coat, and stepped out onto the top step of the gray sandstone main entrance. He looked directly across the plaza at the tall man. The official day's ceremonies were still hours away allowing the morning's normal traffic to flow evenly around the *Zócolo*. He didn't move until he was certain the tall man's attention was fixed on him. It happened within seconds. The look-alike man stood erect, raising his right hand with Lazaro's cell phone in sight. He had already scrolled the autodial screen to "*Guardia* (Guard)" and pressed the call button. He quickly descended the steps to street level, where his voice would be enveloped by a cacophony of background traffic noise.

"*Para sevirle, Señor General* (At your service Mr. General)," came the tall man's answer.

"*Me voy al Hotel Majestic. Toma un descanso. Regresare mas tarde.* (I'm going to the Hotel Majestic. Take a break. I'll return later.)" He disconnected before the guard could ask any questions. He glanced briefly upward at the hotel rooftop terrace to see Mattie's vacant corner table. Before he stepped inside the hotel's polished brass framed glass double doors, he turned to see across the plaza that the tall man had disappeared. Crossing the luxuriant grand lobby, he acknowledged the *concierge's* personal greeting before entering a waiting, empty elevator taking him to the sixth floor below the terrace restaurant. Alone in the elevator, his charade over, he removed the red tie and pocket handkerchief and folded them before placing them in the coat side pockets. Facing his reflection in the polished brass wall panels of the elevator, he parted his combed back hair to the sides, leaving a slight drop in front for casual looking bangs. The distinguished wing backed sideburns were brushed straight down. The new reflection in the shiny brass panel ceased to look like anyone he knew but the PJF agent he once was.

Mattie stood expectantly in front of the arriving elevator on the sixth floor. The powder blue ski jacket had been replaced with a well-tailored black blazer sporting a thumbnail size Mexican flag cloisonné lapel pin. Her tightly drawn ponytail was undone, her lengthy straight black hair now fashionably groomed to the sides. She held her deep black canvas tote bag filled to the top with her camera equipment and ski jacket. The no longer look-alike man exited the elevator, looked left and right before receiving the tote bag from Mattie. He in turn slipped her Lazaro's cell phone, which she adroitly transferred to her blazer side pocket. Without a word spoken, they parted after exchanging furtive smiles of satisfaction with their artifice. She entered the down elevator just as the doors were closing.

Father Angelino had returned to the adjacent church the way he came, with no witnesses. He stopped by the votum candle he had lit earlier in his father's memory. This time his silent message was not from the reverent priest son, but simply from the rectitude of a relieved son. "May you now rest in peace." The candle's short flame rose suddenly, flickering brightly with liveliness as though responding to Angelino's words. He felt compelled to respond with one final message to his beloved father. "Go with God now and forever."

Turning to leave, he saw the flame return to its normal bright-
ness alongside the scores of neighboring votum candles on the table.
He waited for a sizable group of worshippers to exit the church to
leave among them. He turned the corner he had entered the plaza
from, at last at peace with himself. He wended through the back
streets and disappeared into the city of twenty million citizens who
would soon know what he knew.

Mattie meanwhile was making her way south on *Avenida 5 de
Febrero* toward the colonial style, four-story high Supreme Court
building on the southeast corner of the *Zócolo* to the south of the
Presidential Palace. Her professional face would be familiar to only
a few who were called upon from time to time to provide or receive
official case documents at the court clerk's offices from her office of
Investigative and Judicial Liaison.

Beneath the stone-carved words *Suprema Corte de Justicia de La
Federacion National*, Mattie entered the high double brass doors. She
clipped her official ID badge of the *Policia Federal de Investicacion y
Apoyo Judicial* to her outer breast pocket for the standing guard inside
to view. The door guard matched the ID photo with the smiling face
of PFIAJ, Director Maria Teresa Colima, ignoring the name in favor
of the piquant persona for entry approval. Further down the glazed
marble floor lobby was a more serious checkpoint with magnetom-
eter arches, X-ray conveyors, and electronic baton–waving guards to
pat down visitors before they ascended the wide, legendary "hall of
last steps" staircase to the court chambers.

Because of the government holiday, there was light traffic
throughout the building. Only a dozen nonessential workers populated the lobby area. She stopped short of the checkpoint to enter the
restroom marked *Damas*. There was only a young woman entering
the first stall in a line of eight. Mattie proceeded to the eighth stall
in the row of gray metal doors. She held Lazaro's black cell phone up
close for examination, confirming it to be a custom, limited production issue with secure lines. More important to her was the knowledge that it housed a GPS tracking device. Top federal government
officials could be located anywhere in the country in moments of

an emergency. Mattie put the phone in sleep mode. She took a large wad of toilet paper and wiped it free of fingerprints.

The sound of a toilet flush followed by a metal door closure prompted Mattie to peek out her door. The restroom was empty. She would have to move fast before the next visitor entered. She hurriedly stepped out to where the nearest wastepaper basket sat by one of the sinks. She reached deep inside the basket and placed the paper-wrapped phone amid the disposed paper towels. She knew it would remain there until the nighttime, when a janitor would remove the plastic liner trash bag. It would be tossed among a ton of other trash collected from the *Zócolo's Fiesta Patria* and taken to a landfill thirty kilometers away. However, in the likelihood of a serious search for Lazaro via the GPS tracking system, a trisatellite vector of his phone tag would pinpoint the overhead location of the Supreme Court building and its multi-floor office locations above the women's lobby restroom, in itself an improbable place to search for the missing attorney general.

Reentering the lobby, she forced herself to pause a moment to view the famous staircase frescos of world renown social realist painter, Jose Orozco. Painted in large format panels flanking the staircase in a series of powerful thematic images, it was her personal favorite she wanted to appreciate more than ever on this day, titled "*Justicia–Justicia Falsa (Justice*–False Justice)." She knew that art critics kindly described the mural as "depicting the moral power of justice." But Mexican historians like her mother would say that it was Orozco's mural manifesto, a critical reflection of the government, "*hacienda critica y buria de la justicia* (criticizing and mocking justice)." The first admonitory fresco shows an avenging angel striking down corruption while opposite, its counterpart, lies slumped and asleep in a chair oblivious to the corrupters below. The sight of it made her feel that purist painter Orozco's spirit was present this day. And if so, was he likely viewing another avenging angel standing before his poignant painting?

Mattie exited the federal building unremarked, wearing over-sized sunglasses and a private smile of satisfaction knowing that she had just deposited Pasqual Diego Lazaro's virtual whereabouts in the highest court in the land. She chuckled to herself knowing that his real whereabouts was in the lowest court in the land, twenty feet beneath the northwest corner of the Metropolitan Cathedral. That impermanent court, though, was in session, dismissing the official government Constitution Day in favor of a moment of truth and consequences. The evidence against him was complete.

Lazaro's clandestine judges and jury had concluded long before that their criminal in custody would have been set free in all other Mexican courts by insular judges seated to protect their own venal brothers in crime.

"True justice can only come in our lower, underground court where truth is the only currency exchanged," *Tio Chuey* had stated to the other concurring abduction partners.

Lazaro was standing before his accusers, situated barefooted atop a ten-inch high solid block of ice, his knees wobbling. His wrists were corded tightly behind his back. A gold rope was securely tied around a steel girder above which ran the length of the fifteen by fifteen–foot earthen cavity underground. It had served as the structural engineers' tool room for subterranean support work on the sinking cathedral, now an improvised lower court. He was told the precise vertical distance of the gold ropes drop down to the base of his skull. There the rope circumvented his throbbing neck in a hangman's noose with eight coils designed to keep it tight and erect above the spinal cord. He was told the precise height of the ice block, more than the distance needed to have his body weight close the noose tightly in a choking hold, strangulating him in a matter of two to three minutes once the ice had melted. He was told of the possibility of accidentally slipping off of the ice block causing his corporal weight to snap his neck. His accusers did not discuss the third possible fatal scenario. They wanted his confession in the horrific murder of PJF Special Agent Marc Antonio Colima and of his complicity in the illegal emigration of Mexican prisoners to the United States under federal government and church sponsorship. A suicidal short jump off of the block might be satisfactory in the end, but not productive before the confessions.

For forty minutes, he had precariously balanced himself on the slippery, melting ice block that was the sole support between his numb feet and the mud floor, as though poised between this world and the next.

For forty minutes, he had been subjected to a battery of prosecutorial questions read from official investigative documents, including the confession of the shooter hired by Lazaro to assassinate Marc Antonio Colima. All of this irrefragable evidence was betokened impassively by *Tio Chuey* off camera. An overhead microphone and two studio lights helped amplify and illuminate the truth, exposing Lazaro to the digital camera six feet in front of him.

For forty minutes, the terrified Lazaro had "sung like a canary." He confessed to the crime of homicide as well as the *Los Lobos* hit men's covert plans to kill the present and future enemies of the federal government who might prevent the commission of their institutionalized corruption. Tio Chuey knew that it was a combination of factors that motivated Lozaro to confess so quickly, placing Special Agent Colima's Saint Michael's medallion, with its "sword of truth," in his mouth, describing the dark underground room as "the Devil's Confessional," and characterizing the gold rope hangman's noose as the "Rope of Truth." Lazaro had concluded his remonstrated confessions with stammering apologies, pleading for forgiveness as he felt the noose tighten with every inch of melting ice from the block. Consciously he had hoped that his finely honed courtroom attorney skills might reverse his ignominious fate. Subconsciously he knew his fate was sealed, that his personal bodyguard, the police, PFIAJ agents, nor military would come to his rescue. He tried to pretend abject humility and penitent, pleading that he was merely serving his country with orders from above. His entreaties were coolly ignored.

For forty minutes, Lazaro's tremulous, hoarse voice was recorded; his clammy pallor, imploring eyes, and grave facial expression of surrender was captured, foretelling his fate. He felt as though Dante's sign at the entrance into Hades should be before him now, *Abandon all hope, all who enter here*. His bare feet were blue and numb to the bone, causing him to now worry that he could no longer feel the ice block's declining edges. He could sense his gradual vertical decline toward the ground as the ice continued to melt. The intense studio lights heated the small, unventilated room. His dispassionate witnesses listened in an inexorable manner, heedless of his appeals.

Perspiration streamed down Lazaro's contorted face. Admissions of complicity and guilt were spewed volubly with increasing detail and sincerity, all captured on camera and voice recorder. But there was no priest to hear this confession, no penitence given, no absolution, no free pass to go back into society and repeat the same crimes with impunity, no last rites given. He was wearing down *Tio Chuey's* patience along with the ice. Chuey turned off the recorder and camera telling him to save something for his encounter with the devil. His accomplices removed the recorded discs and turned off all the battery pack lights but one. They disconnected the equipment amid the heavy breathing and begging by Lazaro to be released.

"*Ya tienen lo que quieren. No hay nada mas. Estoy jodido!* (You have what you want. There's nothing more. I'm fucked!)" he implored.

The three men turned on their flashlights to leave but not before turning off the remaining spotlight.

"*Van a mandar alquien aqui mas tarde, verdad? No pueden dejar me aqui para siembre. Yo estoy un official de la oficina Presidencial!* (You're going to send someone here later, right? You can't leave me here forever. I'm an official of the Presidential office!)" he exclaimed with righteous indignity.

"*Era* (Was)," *Tio Chuey* said with finality as he stuffed the Saint Michael medallion and chain back into Lazaro's dry mouth. He then covered it with a wide strip of duct tape that had seven large numbers written on it in black indelible ink, 50807507. It was securely placed upside down.

"Directly above you in the cathedral is the *Altar de Perdon* (Altar of Forgiveness). Pray to it because here you'll receive none," Chuey concluded peremptorily.

He joined the others headed out into the tunnel that would lead back to the temporary hole in the wall into his cantina basement. Once inside, they would pull on a thick detachable rope that would cause a rigged wooden ceiling support in the tunnel to drop, causing an enormous mound of soil and rocks to collapse in front of the *cantina's* three by three–foot wide, secret subterranean cement block entrance. No one would ever suspect that the city's most popular tequila *cantina* once had a private connection with the city's Metropolitan Cathedral. And now, like the adjoining secrets of the ancient *Aztec* temples of *Tenochititlán*, it was buried.

Back in the Hotel Cathedral a block away from *Mi Tio*'s cantina, the seventh floor, lone room guest awaited for his two accomplices to return with the audio and video recordings of Director Lazaro's pilloried confessions. There he would make multiple copies on DVD formats to be delivered by independent couriers to all of the television stations in Mexico City. Their deliveries would be timed for their eleven o'clock televised morning news one hour before the start of the official presidential-led Constitutional Day ceremonies at the Constitutional Plaza.

This was Mattie's directive: "*It takes two to speak the truth. One to speak, another to hear*," in the words of her favorite American writer, Henry David Thoreau. That put in motion the plan to go public nationwide with Lazaro's recorded confessions of murder and prisoner smuggling into the US.

The special encrypted Casper cell phone Lori had given Mattie in Las Vegas now rested in the palm of her left hand. She carefully punched the keys that would send Lori the coded signal, "I-A-H (I Am Here)." She knew Lori would take it from there.

22

LEARN JUSTICE FROM
THIS WARNING

Santa Barbara

Lori was parked on the fifth-floor open air, top level of the city parking lot overlooking the Pompeian red terra cotta tiled Spanish-Andalusia style courthouse, a prominent landmark in Santa Barbara. The first vehicles to arrive at the popular parking ramp would fill up the lower levels first at that early hour, leaving Lori undetected and free to her own devices for at least a couple of hours. Her surveillance of the general area below was interrupted with the coded text message from Mattie, "I-A-H." She pressed a key on her special ops cell phone marked with a satellite icon. Instantly the display read the GPS vector of Mattie's cell phone. She ran the locator numbers through her laptop GPS map finder; "Mexico City, *Zócolo*, Constitution Plaza, *Aveneda Moneda*" showed on her screen map. A blinking red dot put Mattie's precise location in front of a building titled *Suprema Corte de Justicia de La Federacion Nacional*.

"The Supreme Court! Mattie, you are Wonder Woman," Lori exclaimed to herself with great delight and relief. That was the cryptic confirmation she was waiting for, right on time, right on target for her Delta team's own plan. Mattie and Angelino had delivered. Looking down from the rooftop ramp, she saw the charcoal van she had been in communication with pull up near the courthouse entrance. Her team was about to deliver.

Exiting the back of the van, the enfeebled prisoners had only a few seconds to pause, standing motionless before the grand, historic Santa Barbara courthouse. It would be the stage upon which their individual crimes would be prosecuted and mittimus conveyed, their fates decided. They recognized the four-story high open clock tower, the building's defining feature, which was the platform for the high-powered sniper rifle to be aimed at any one of them who dared to attempt an escape…so their captives were told. From ground level, the fugitives could not see that it was vacant of any rifleman, or other persons for that matter since it would not be unlocked as a vista outlook for the public for one more hour.

Taylor peremptorily commanded them to move forward toward the twenty-five-foot high monumental entry arch thirty paces away. Expressions of fear appeared on their careworn faces, a fear of the unknown brought on by the harsh reality of arrival. They had all once lived in Santa Barbara and all knew that this building was the local landmark of the law, a final destination they never contemplated as theirs. The Mexican border was all they ever considered when committing their respective crimes of murder. They never knew that a straight line of escape to the supposed safe haven of Mexico could ever come full circle like a boomerang back Santa Barbara, the scene of their homicides.

The high vaulted open archway was the main entrance to the courthouse on the right and the house of records on the left. But it also served as the fifty-foot long passageway to the popular sunken gardens beyond, which were now in view. Taylor and Eizzo appreciated this significant moment in time and place, passing beneath the Roman style triumphal arch. They had finally arrived, triumphant in the proud Delta team's long, indefatigable odyssey to bring in the bad guys. Now it was up to the United States judicial system to right six wrongs.

As they took that Rubicon step out from the arch of triumph onto the lush green esplanade, they also took their first deep breaths of denouement, of a Delta mission accomplished. The self-appointed devoir of the so called Six-Pack sponsors was completed, their *raison d'être* realized. For them, the mission was a tool for the purpose of regenerating a legally binding treaty with Mexico allowing for the unconditional extradition of all felony homicide fugitives from US criminal justice. They would soon celebrate upon hearing the media's first public broadcast and later publication of the news: "Six Fled to Mexico Fugitives from US Justice Captured. Found wandering freely on the Santa Barbara Courthouse grounds."

Referred to as a garden, the enormous expanse of terraced lawn bracketed by towering pines and palms, pepper trees, flowering bushes, and exotic plants was actually a popular city park cradled in the L-shaped configuration of the three quarters of a city block–sized courthouse. Its Mediterranean landscape design of subtropical and coastal plants created a verdant park that invited the public's daily use for picnics, lounging, strolling, or festivals and civic events.

The early morning hour allowed these unexpected visitors to enter the grounds undetected by the local law enforcement officers and news media gathered in front of the police station just one block away. Lori's earlier recon revealed no external security cameras. The dispirited prisoners stared vacantly with mute curiosity at the pacific scene before them, not realizing it would be their last direct contact with the natural green earth. With a fluttering whistle, six taupe mourning doves glided from their high redwood perches to a new vista atop an outcrop of wisteria a few yards from the terraced steps, as though wishing to be personal witnesses to the unfolding events.

Pausing momentarily to receive a radio message of "All clear" in his ear fob, Taylor joined Eizzo in scanning the panoramic view of the open, empty garden. They were alone. Taylor spoke into his hidden mic, "We're moving, ETA thirty seconds." Eizzo silently guided the disoriented group down the shallow series of eight sandstone-terraced steps into the middle of the lowest level, broad rectangular lawn, the size of two full tennis courts.

Taylor stopped, turned, and motioned upward toward the top of the clock tower, feigning an official signal to an imaginary sentry. The ruse would serve as a final warning to the prisoners that any escape attempt would be answered with the rifleman's .300 Win Mag bullet. That also served as Eizzo's orders to cut off the plastic restraints from the prisoners' wrists, which sported the Los Lobos tattoos. Again,

Taylor spoke into his mic, "Code SBPD, code SBPD." At that precise moment, an anonymous phone call was made by the radio recipient at a remote location to the Santa Barbara Police Department contact. "The six fugitives are waiting unarmed in the courthouse sunken garden, all wearing street clothes and flip-flops. They have no restraints. Their names are sown inside their shirt collars. Homicide Detective Tom Richards can ID them. *Book'em, Dano!"* concluded the monotone female caller with no traceable number.

Taylor took a quick moment to observe for the last time the craven countenances of the soon-to-be condemned men. The fear on their faces lay in their doomed eyes. The once defiant attitudes had disappeared. They all averted his eyes, especially Barajas, whose normally evil eyes looked haunted, off in a place he was not familiar with. What he did realize at this moment was that his life was over. What Taylor saw was a dead man condemned to hell. At last a smile formed effortlessly across Taylor's warrior face.

"*Oiga, escucha bien* (Listen, listen up)," Taylor ordered. "Santa Barbara lawmen are all around this park. They are coming to arrest you. Do not move or they will shoot you in *los huevos*! They will escort you into jail, then into court. There is one last thing to know." Taylor paused to recall correctly the exact Mexican refrain in Spanish. "*De la suerte y de la muerte, no hay quien se escape* (Of fate and death, there is no escaping),' he quoted with his best facial squint for effect.

With those parting words, he hurried to join Eizzo's quick pace up the stone steps and through the archway where two parked black Ducati 1098 motorcycles were waiting curbside, deposited minutes earlier by two riders who then left in a charcoal van.

In no more than thirty seconds, no less than twenty-two officers of the city and county police and sheriff's department converged on the sunken garden and stunned fugitives with guns drawn. The first responders on the scene handcuffed their new prisoners, their Los Lobos tattoos duly noted while reciting the Miranda rights in Spanish. Complying with the international Vienna Convention treaty, the Mexican consulate in Los Angeles would be immediately notified that six of their citizens were in US custody as felony fugitives from outstanding warrants for capital one murder.

Each prisoner had two armed SBPD escorts. Their promenade to the south side of the courthouse on a stone walkway along Santa Barbara Street led to the old court jail with its evocative grand main entrance. The languid fugitives were met by an unwelcoming, gigantic, heavy, dark wood grilled double door that rose twenty-eight feet in height.

Carved into the wedge-shaped stone arch above the jail entry-way was a Latin quote that would best caption the scene of the six captured fugitives who fled to Mexico, only to be returned to face justice in the United States. The beige stone read in large Roman letters, "*Dies Cite Justinian Monition* (Learn Justice from this Warning)."

The publicity component of the mission plan immediately kicked into motion with anonymous calls going to the local media, all on standby at the SBPD station. They had made certain that news reporters from Envision and Televise Mexican television networks and *La Opinion* newspaper were present, promising them, "*Noticias sensacionales*! (Sensational news!)" They were told to follow the police for the preferred photo op and background information at the police station. Detective Richards would fill in the blanks from his files of *prima facie* evidence of capital felony killings and field case investigations. The standby press corps was told that they were soon to become witnesses to the US justice system being put into play for six Mexican national fugitives who dared to get away with murder simply by stepping one foot across a border. The truth would be told that there was no evidence to indicate, let alone prove that the FTMs were captured and transported back to the US. They were also reminded that the FTM fugitives were fortunate to be tried in a country with the presumption of innocence on their side as opposed to Mexico's Napoleonic judicial code of presumed guilty until proven innocent and with no open oral trial or jury.

They had anticipated the Mexican consulate in Los Angeles to protest all the way to the US Department of State. But with no proof of transborder kidnapping or involvement by court-sworn federal or local law enforcement authorities in this unprecedented event, their diplomatic complaints would go nowhere. The US government at all levels would appreciate the honest, plausible cover of total deniability. Their hands were clean, their collective conscience clear.

This they would swear to under oath in a court of law repeatedly and effectively. The Mexican consulate would then be asked to look internally at the evidence their government had regarding the illegal dumping of their criminals into the US.

Detective Richards received a downloaded digital copy of Mexico's Attorney General Lazaro's full taped confession of his government's surreptitious dumping of current and former prisoners into the United States. It described in detail the recently uncovered *Los Lobos* underground immigration prisoner scandal. It was supported by the unabridged criminal records of all six convicts e-mailed directly from the Federal Judicial Police Division, office of Investigative and Judicial Liaison, Deputy Director Maria Teresa Colima. Her official prisoner incarceration documents corroborated the illegal, organized transfer of known, matriculated Mexican criminals out of the country.

"If six fugitives from justice suddenly and mysteriously appear one morning walking about freely in Santa Barbara, no international laws or treaties are broken if they should be recognized and subsequently apprehended by local law enforcement," would be the repeated response to all official Mexican protests and inquiries. The fugitives had no evidence to the contrary and certainly no credibility when relating their individual incredulous, creative stories of capture, "all fictive tales of desperate convicts pleading their innocence," would be the District Attorney's stated opinion. After all, who would believe that a fugitive was extracted from a heavily guarded island prison in the Pacific Ocean surrounded by patrol boats and marines, or trapped and transported in a porta toilet in the middle of the world's most populace city with no one noticing, or snatched from inside a popular whorehouse frequented by scores of Mexico's most murderous narco cartel *sicarios* in the most notorious drug cartel killing fields in the world, or discovered in a remote forest while caging wild birds, or lifted off of the daytime street inside the heavily patrolled Mexican border with no witnesses, or pulled from a secluded, cloistered, fortress monastery in the mountains of southwest Mexico? Who would honestly believe such stories of incredible, daring, and panache, the stuff of fiction writers? After all, *if nobody knew that the Delta team was there, then it didn't happen, did it?*

Book's Bird List

Heermann's Gull
White-Crowned Sparrow
Brewer Sparrow
Vesper Sparrow
Chipping Sparrow
Savannah Sparrow
Bald Eagle
Red Tail Hawk
Red Shoulder Hawk
Loggerhead Shrike
Cactus Wren
Resplendent Quatzsecual
Mayan Macaws
White Heron
Crested Caracara
Golden Eagle
Laughing Falcon
White-Faced Ibis
Lesser Yellowlegs
Whimbrels
Double-Crested Cormorant
Cattle Egrets
Willets
Long-Billed Curlews
Spotted Sandpipers
Ruddy Ducks
Bufflehead Ducks
Mourning Doves
Inca Doves
White Winged Dove
Hilota Dove
Black Banta
Northern Pintails
Gadwalls

Shovelers
Redheaded Duck
Scaups
White Heron
Snowy Egret
Cormorant
Anhingas
Lily-Walkers
Lilac-Crown Parrot
Red-Crown Parrot
Painted Bunting
Grass Land Yellow Finches
Red Warblers
Barred Parakeets
Tufted Magpie
Black Throated Magpie
Tamaulipas Pygmy Owl
Socorro Mockingbird
Gray-Breasted Woodpecker
Mexican Chachalacas
Black-Throated Sparrows
Green Jays
Blue Grosbeaks
Cassin Kingbird
Guatemalan Screech Owl
Rufous Hummingbird
Sparrow Hawk

Also visit:

www.zazzle.com/birders
www.birders4birds.org
www.fledtomexico.com

CPSIA information can be obtained
at www.ICGtesting.com
Printed in the USA
BVHW071402091120
592841BV00005B/938

9 781648 951954